TIME
of the
BROKEN EAGLE

DAVID HAZARD

TIME *of the* BROKEN EAGLE

For permission to quote or reproduce, contact:
info@lostlakeseries.com

Follow David Hazard and LostLake:
LostLakeSeries | AscentPublishing

ISBN 978-1-7356825-0-1

This is a work of fiction. Any resemblance to persons
living or deceased is purely coincidental.

Artist: Mark Ivan Cole. Find Mark online at:
markivancole.wordpress.com
Facebook: MarkIvanColeArtist / Instagram: @markivancole

Permissions:

For images of the people,
places and wildlife of Lost Lake
visit:

LostLakeSeries.com/sketchbook

LOST LAKE

THE SOLITUDES WILDERNESS

MOHAWK CAVES

LOST MOUNTAIN

MOHAWK CAVES

FLOWLANDS

EAGLE ROCK
MOUNTAIN

THUNDER
FALLS

ARROWS

ARROWS

THE BOW

ARROWS

GARNET RIVER

PEREGRINE
MOUNTAIN

TRINITY
MOUNTAIN

LAKE
PLACID

CAMP ROAD

LOST LAKE
ESTATE

Prologue

LOSAR / ASH WEDNESDAY
February
28TH

Sahmdup Yangzen—12:06 a.m. EST,
Adirondack Mountains, northern New York State

Something was wrong with the dream.

A moment before, Sahm was in a deep sleep when a voice out of the cool blackness inside his log cabin had startled him, as if someone had seized his shoulder and shaken him.

"Cetan!" the voice had called—but was it within his hazy mind or sounding on the dark, cold air of his room?

He had blinked awake in the moonlight falling silently through the curtain at his bedroom window, listening intently. All was quiet except for small sputters and pops coming from the woodstove out in the small, cedar cabin's main room, followed by the skittering of ashes falling into the orange-glowing bed of coals. Behind these homely sounds, though, this particular silence felt deeper than night. Within that depth something or someone was waiting.

Holding his breath in the stillness now—whether awake or still asleep, he wasn't sure—he stared up at the split-log ceiling and stretched his arms out from under the heavy, red wool blanket into the chill.

If this is a dream, why do these covers feel so heavy and rough?

Then it occurred to him that this was the first night of Losar, Tibetan New Year, a night when the veil of time and space thins and auspicious events occur. Some said, even magic.

But, he thought, *auspicious signs can sometimes arise from malign powers as well as benevolent ones.*

"Cetan! Where does your fear come from? Have you forgotten my voice so soon?"

The second call unnerved him, and he sat bolt upright. The voice was next to him, the tone urgent. He knew that voice, but how could it be? Only one person called him by that nickname rather than his given name, Sahmdup, or what everyone else called him—Sahm.

He slipped out of bed half-wary.

The pine-plank floor was cold beneath his feet. Real enough. But how could the voice be real and not imagined? He was here in the United States, in the Adirondack Mountain wilderness of northern New York, and not back at home in Tibet, twelve thousand miles away. He was living in a cabin on the vast estate of a benefactress. She had generously brought him to this wild retreat surrounded by deep forests, and housed him in a cabin down the shoreline from her lodge beside her private lake. Yes, hearing *that* voice here was impossible.

This is a dream, he assured himself. *Nothing more.*

As if to confirm the thought, the night and the moonlight falling through his bedroom windows had a strange quality that gave everything a vivid, crystalline edge.

He brushed his fingers over the surfaces in his room and was undecided again. The rush-bottom chair, the painting of a moose, and the wooden wall peg where he had hung his Nike sweatshirt and pants all felt solid and very real. Out in the cabin's open room, moonlight poured in through lakefront windows, revealing that the sitting area with its blue Persian carpet, overstuffed chair near the fireplace, the small, glowing woodstove, and the long pine table—all of it looked very solid. Again he felt confused.

If not a dream, then, was homesickness tricking his mind? No one was here; no one had called to him. Kate, who had found and brought him here, was far away in Washington, DC, and would return tomorrow. Except for the caretaker, asleep in his own cottage over by the river bridge, he was all by himself tonight on this secluded property in the vast, winter forests.

He turned to recross the cold carpet and bury himself back under the soft, thick covers in bed. A dream bed or a real one, he didn't care, he was sleepy.

"*Cetan.*" Tibetan for *eagle*. The tone was mildly scolding.

This time when the voice called, the room shimmered slightly, as if it were only a reflection in water, an illusion, and the voice a pebble dropped in to ripple its surface.

"*Are you so sure that what you see and touch is the only reality? Do you remember nothing I taught you?*"

No. No. No, Sahm thought, frozen in place. *Impossible.* The one whose voice kept calling was all the way around the world in a mountainside hermitage in the Himalayas.

Behind him, the cedar front door's heavy wrought-iron latch clicked. He spun around to see it gliding open and allowing a tide of freezing February night air to flood inside.

"*Come. We need to talk.*"

Outside, he plunged down the cabin's three front steps and strode out from under the surrounding tall, white pines. Here he stood, barefoot and shivering beneath the open, moonlit heavens beside the frozen lake that sprawled before him. Back in summer when he had arrived here, the lake at night was obsidian glass, reflecting a thousand stars and the constellations. Tonight, under white moonlight, Lost Lake was a blue-shadowed wasteland of ice chunks and swirled snowdrifts.

Look and listen, he told himself. *If there are portents in this night, they will be shown.*

The sub-zero air had engulfed him in a great current that poured down from the Arctic tundra through Canada, not very many miles to the north. His whole body was cooling rapidly. Standing here in only a tee-shirt and gym shorts—he'd been too enthralled to slip on his boots—he felt his cheeks, hands, and feet start to sting and burn. Would the voice he knew so well speak again?

All he could hear was the sound of Thunder Falls, pouring down from Lost Mountain behind him to the northwest.

All around him otherwise, stillness hung over the frozen lake and every mountain peak. Moonlight reflected on the snow mantle, turning it blue where hardwood tracts stood winter-bare and charcoal where the evergreen groves and deep ravines lay in shadow. Stars shimmered blue on the black sky.

No, he argued. *This* must *be a dream.* Nothing like this had happened to him before. This had the qualities of a lucid dream, strange and yet intensely real.

As he sharpened his attention, though, a strong sense grew—that the whole world and sky was just a thin veil, a scroll that could roll back any second to reveal something hidden behind it. Just a dream then, or a different reality?

He decided to end this tug-of-war in his mind. He would offer a challenge.

What do you want, Grandfather, if this is you? Is there something you wish to show me—he added,—*quickly, before my feet freeze?*

"An important time has come. Step in, and fly to me."

"Step into what?" Sahm startled, speaking out loud to the air.

"The Bardo, of course."

How is that possible? he balked. He had never achieved the kind of mastery required to enter that great passage behind the world of solid form. Only the greatest yogis and those passing between lifetimes travelled those invisible corridors.

"Tonight, it is allowed for you to come to me. Let go of all doubt." This time, the voice was nearly shouting, clear as the voice of Thunder Falls and so close he felt a warm breath against his ear.

He whipped his head around, peering in all directions. There was no one anywhere near, but now the sight of Lost Lake's panoramic setting startled him—so much that he staggered backwards and struck one ankle bone painfully against the cabin steps.

The forms of things had begun to ruck and shift.

To his left in the east, Eagle Rock Mountain, and the three ridges known as The Arrows still rose into the starry sky, but now the top edges of their dark hulks shivered with a blue-green aura. In front of him across the lake, Trinity Mountain stood outlined against the night by a faint light emanating from the small town far beyond it, but now its glowing ridge-line wavered snake-like.

His hand went up to his mouth in surprise, and he saw that even his fingers were shifting shapes and shimmering. His body felt like air, water, fire, and an energy deep as his bones prickled like needles within his veins, muscles, and skin.

All the mountains and trees began to waver and change.

He looked right, toward the estate's western edge and Peregrine Mountain and the Flow Lands. Every outline of every tree, boulder, and ridge was starting to leap in a bluish flame that grew stronger. In another moment it began to engulf the world—and him. He felt as if his skin was dissolving and his spirit was releasing into the air.

"Am I dying or am I dreaming?" he tried to shout, but his voice was thin and high, like the shriek of a great bird.

"When you ran from me, did you forget everything about who you are and all your first teachings? Your path is not finished, it is now beginning. That is why you must come."

A roiling energy that started at the crown of Sahm's head now circled down like a whirlwind through his throat, chest, gut, and groin. Surges of inner heat shot up and out from his gut through every nerve-channel, until his whole body hummed with the roar of *lung*—the life-force. His hands fanned out into wings of fire, his fingers into feathers of flame. His feet blazed, dissolving the ice and snow into hot puddles. Lines of sweat turned to sparks leaping from his temples.

Charged with lightning bolts of energy, Sahm saw the night sky rolling back and the *Bardo* opening wide before him, as if a highway were opening in the cosmos over Lost Lake.

"Do not cling to your physical form. We have only this night while the Bardo stands wide open, and much to talk about. Enter in, and take to the air."

Alright, Grandfather. But you must help me, because I do not know how.

As soon as the words left his mind, he shot up and out, circling low over the blue, ice-cobbled surface of the lake. Then he was speeding like a winged creature just feet above the snowdrifts, toward its eastern shores, where groves of hemlock stood silvery and shadowed in the moonlight. Wind rushed in his ears, and he felt his body collapse and saw himself change into a stream of yellow, red, green, blue, and white lights.

At the far shoreline, he shot upward over the flickering stands of hemlocks that roared like fire, clearing the tops of the winter-bare hardwoods and the burning-blue-snowed slopes of Trinity Mountain. . . continuing like a shooting star, higher and higher over the flaming mountain crags and high snow-filled passes, until they looked like a bolt of dark, wrinkled cloth dissolving into a red-gold conflagration of pure energy surging far below him.

Lost Lake rapidly sank away behind him into the flickering darkness. A thought passed through his mind—dimly, as if memory was the dream and what he was experiencing now was the hard reality—that he had lived in this small valley for more than a year, splitting wood and cleaning cages in an animal clinic on the property.

"You are in this world to do much more than clean up animal filth, Cetan. That is why you must come. To be shown."

He let this waking dream-state lift him. Spiraling higher up the black slopes of the night, with mountains, lakes, and rivers growing smaller and smaller below, Sahm turned himself directly eastward. Then the night sky rolled open completely, and he shot out swift and brilliant as a diamond-point of light.

Dhani Singh Jones—12:39 a.m. EST, Washington, DC
He stood with his back pressed tightly against the wall, and quieted his breath. Hard to do with his chest pounding. When the door opened, would he be concealed well enough in the narrow space made by the door and the wall, or would they find him? The faint glow of a distant streetlight seeped in through the window of his room here in juvenile detention.

Please, please, please, he begged the silent, threatening darkness.

No sound came from the hallway, and yet he knew—something always told him—when they were coming. The nights he had ignored this knowing, he had paid severely for it, and no one in the detention center seemed to give a damn what the other boys did to him.

Tonight the knowing had come from a tapping on his foot under the blankets. Half-groggy, he had listened to taps, though *listening* was a messed up way to think of it. But then, he always felt messed up. That had to be the reason craziness like this scrambled his mind.

Get up, a voice in his head seemed to hiss. *Hide. They're coming again.*

The realization of what was happening out in the hallway struck at the same moment he felt something tapping on his foot beneath the covers. Throwing the blanket back, he saw a huge roach scurry off the cot, leaving him confused. Was this stupid crap happening to his mind again actually real—the thought that a creature was speaking to him? Or had the whispers coming down the hall towards his room alerted him?

Now, behind the door, a stab of anxiety shot through him at the faint scrape of the metal doorknob turning. That, he definitely heard, and pressed himself tighter against the wall. He sensed the three other guys who shared this dorm room were awake but pretending not to be. It didn't matter. They wouldn't help him anyway.

In the dark, quiet footsteps moved toward his bed, where he'd left the covers thrown back. The sooner they decided he was not there the better.

Someone whispered and swore.

More horse-whispers. How many of them had come to torture him this time? It sounded like three.

"See if he's under any of the beds."

"Not in the closet."

"Let's go check the can."

"Or the shower. He always takes his showers in the middle of the night. He doesn't want anybody to see him."

"Or he's afraid of dropping the soap."

"Maybe he's in the kitchen, getting a knife to slit your throat."

"Yeah, he's psycho enough."

"We gotta get rid of that kid before he offs us in our sleep. I hate him."

He had felt that hatred. The duct tape around his face and mouth. Pillow cases tied around his neck and wrists. His head shoved in dirty toilets. Punches to the ribs and gut. Punches to both thighs, to Charlie-horse him. Knees to the groin, till he nearly puked. Hair pulled out of his head while ripping off the tape. And humiliation next morning at breakfast.

"Rough night, psycho?"

"Probably dreaming about matches and a can of lighter fluid."

"Nice hair style. Wha'd you cut it with, a lawn mower?"

The footsteps moved back toward him, out the door—one, two, three, he counted them this time—but the door remained wide open. Strange, because they always closed it when they left him doubled-up on the floor in pain and fighting back tears.

He was about to step out from his hiding spot and slip into the hallway, where hopefully he could make it to the night attendant's office before his tormentors caught him. When he placed his hand on the door's edge, something stopped him. From under his bed came the tiny, hissing voice—the roach again?

One of them is still here. Standing in the dark. Listening.

There was no sound. No breathing. Nothing.

Just another faint message, sounding in his mind. *Don't move. Don't breathe.*

"You're in here, psycho," said a whisper in the dark. "I know you are. Everyone else wants to have a little fun with you. I want to wreck your face. I'm gonna find you."

His throat choked with fear and his mouth went dry. He knew the voice. It belonged to Leo, a kid in M-13, arrested for beating an old man unconscious for the twenty stinking dollars in his wallet.

With a *click*, dim light from the small bedside lamp flooded the room, making Dhani's stomach wrench. Every muscle froze, and he waited for the door to fling back and Leo to dig strong fingers into his neck.

But there were other sounds—first, the bedclothes being flung onto the floor as his tormentor searched under the bed, then the closet door being pulled open and clothes being shoved aside.

Leo swore. Then there was silence for a moment before he spoke in a low voice. "I know exactly where you are, psycho."

Nearing panic, Dhani almost shouted.

The light went off.

In the dark again, Dhani heard Leo's footsteps approach the door. For a split-second, he thought of slamming it outward as hard as he could, using it like a heavy battering ram to smash Leo in the face. He could be out the door running before Leo recovered enough to grab him by the throat and punch his face to pulp. His muscles were water, though, and he was shaking too hard to move.

And then Leo's footfalls were past the door and out into the hallway. Maybe to search for Dhani in the kitchen or the TV room.

For a long time, he remained behind the door, pulse racing. If he didn't find a way out of this place, they would mess him up and leave him scarred and in pain for life. Or maybe he would lose his mind totally and wind up in a padded cell, playing hide-n-seek with talking animals.

Steve Tanner—also 12:39 a.m. EST, Loudoun County, Virginia

Waking in the moonlit dark, he rolled on his back and stared up at the small crack that ran jaggedly across the bedroom ceiling. Out in the rolling, night fields of the northern Virginia countryside, a fox was moving along the farm stream, barking.

So many nights he had stared at the ceiling in this tenant house, thinking the crack was like the dividing line between now and the time when he'd had a life. The time when he had slept in his own bed and not one offered in charity or pity, with someone warm and beautiful at his side, tangling their legs, half-waking and reaching for each other to make love, then gently sliding back into sleepy bliss in each other's arms.

At that thought—the terrible, haunting, sweet thought of Olivia, which was never far from his mind—he felt the torturous ache inside his ribcage. An attempt had been made to patch the ceiling crack, poorly and heavily painted over. The jagged tear in his soul would never be patched. How could it be, when his life had exploded and ripped him open to the core?

Rolling onto his side, he looked at the pale green numerals on the clock face—*12:43*—and it occurred to him what day it was: February, Ash Wednesday.

Exactly a year ago at this time, she was still with me.

Images of the moment life stopped tried to come back, from the time before he took refuge here on a friend's farm, trying to find even a little relief from the pain.

What a fool's venture.

He pressed his eyes shut, wanting sleep to take him back. There was no point in pulling the blanket over his head, hoping the dream that woke him would not return again. He'd had fragments of it before, but never as vivid or prolonged as it had been tonight. . . .

Olivia had come to find him as he was readying his climbing gear.

"I think you love mountain climbing more than you love me, Steve Tanner."

"Not more. Only as *much,"* he had said in the dream, teasing the way he had before the gulf between them tore open.

Tonight, as always, she had begun to turn away. He was compelled to watch, unable to take his eyes off the smooth, tan skin and slender curves of her body, the dark hair, the high cheek bones and tapering arch of her eyebrows. More than her physical being, he could see the brightness that was Olivia. Every inch of her was as he remembered, and his skin pulsed with want and he reached to touch her—her cheek or hand or the smooth curve of her back. Just one touch.

She was so close, but he understood that, *no,* he was not allowed to touch her. Was she still angry? As he reached out in the dream, she continued to back away, the dark brown warmth and depth of her eyes meeting and holding his, saying without words,

I have to show you, my love—something you need to see.

No, not angry. She was smiling. Beaming. But hiding some mystery.

The dream had shifted, and they were standing apart from each other in a field of nodding blossoms on the side of a mountain. They

19

had been here before, but again, this time it was far more brilliant and vivid, as if painted by lasers. Over them, a shocking blue sky reached up to forever and all around them a meadow filled with yellow, perfectly petalled sunflowers dramatically fell away, plunging endlessly down and down into a blue-shadowed gorge. Ahead, at the far end of the meadow, rose a thick forest of tall pines.

For a moment he had felt some great *sense*. A half-born realization. But then it was gone.

Why do I feel like I should know this place? Where is this?

Olivia smiled again, turned away from him, and began walking then running from him through the field of perfect flowers, brushing her hands over the yellow blossoms as she moved, looking over her shoulder, willing him to follow.

He obeyed, but his legs were heavy, unable to run, frustrating him. A small lightning of pain jabbed at his heart and jolted through his body, as if he knew what was coming.

No!

Olivia had moved further ahead of him, her gleaming smile a beacon. Beyond her, at the far side of the meadow, the front edge of a pine forest stretched away up the mountain and down into the gorge, forming a wall. As she moved toward it, an arched opening appeared among the thick branches of the pines. She kept glancing back at him, drawing him after her with her eyes.

Still his legs had been unable to do what he needed, and the distance between them kept opening and opening. He had the sense that if he could get to her before she reached the edge of the field, the opening into the trees, she would give him the secret he needed to know. His legs were leaden, though, and his heart banged inside his chest.

What is it? Wait for me. Show me. Please.

Olivia reached the place where the flowers and grasses ended and the tall pines began. She moved swiftly under the opening formed by arched boughs, slipping into the shadows inside the deep forest darkness. Then her image and every trace of her disappeared under the trees, like a light gone out.

At the end of the field, Steve's legs had failed, and he came to a standstill. A helpless, powerless, horrible feeling overtook him. All he could do was stare at the front edge of the forest, knowing that even if he could enter it he would not find her.

Something she knew remained hidden from him, right there at the edge of knowing, but beyond his reach.

A cold fire had run over his skin, up his neck and face, burned along his scalp.

Why did she come back if she was only going to be taken from him again?

Taken. No, that wasn't right. He gave her up. He should have been with her, but he had stubbornly turned away at the wrong moment. What happened was his fault. He could have stopped it. If only he had, she might be here to show him what he needed to know, the secret of the light that was in her.

All this he knew, as the dream dissolved. . . .

Steve was on his back staring up at the crack in the ceiling, a thin stream of tears running down the sides of his head onto the pillow. Sleeping or waking? The dream had been so powerful tonight he wasn't entirely sure. Sometimes he thought Olivia really was actually right beside him, trying to reach through a veil that divided them. Tonight she had wanted to tell him something. Why couldn't she?

He rolled on his side again, his face hot with anger. He felt ripped from soul to body by the ragged fault-line inside him, the one that had torn open exactly one year ago on this day. And now he was condemned to remember, every night forever. His chest ached so much he had to think to breathe.

Burying his face in the pillow, he begged, "What do you want me to see? Please. Come back and show me. I'm sorry. I'm so sorry. Help me, Olivia."

Dhani Singh Jones—1:17 a.m. EST

"JONES."

The boy startled at the loud voice in his ear, and dropped the stale dinner roll.

Wheeling around, he was eye to eye with a juvenile detention officer—the one who seemed to like to nail him. The guy had come up so close behind Dhani that even over the reek of bleach used to clean the kitchen floor and metal surfaces he could smell the cheap cigarettes on the officer's clothes and breath.

"Why did you have to yell like that?"

The officer grinned. "What are you doing out of bed? The kitchen is off-limits outside of mealtimes. That's the rule, and you know it."

He didn't mention the near attack, and how he had waited until the halls were silent again. Hunger pains had kept him awake.

"I'm starving. I missed dinner. And I had a bad dream that woke me up."

"If there's a schedule, you always make sure you ignore it, don'cha?"

"I just don't hear the announcements sometimes. And look—they're gonna put out food anyway."

The guy lost his grin. "You 'just don't hear' a lot. What are you, deaf? Or do you just like giving people a hard time?"

Dhani bent down and picked up the roll. "Can I just have it? Please. I'm really hungry. My stomach's burning."

The officer stuck out his hand. "Breakfast is in a few hours. You won't die. Now I gotta write you up. Again. And I hate paperwork. Ya know what I think about people who make me do more paperwork?"

So many rules that didn't make any sense.

"You don't *have to* write me up, do you?" A simple, honest question. It was just a dinner roll, stale, left out in a basket on a counter for the very reason that someone might be hungry in the middle of the night. He hadn't gone in the pantry or the refrigerator.

The officer poked Dhani hard in the chest with his stubby finger-tips. "Give it or I'll take it from you. You know I can. You know I will. There's a reason we all live by rules, son. And you're in here because you broke a really big one."

You don't have a clue what I really did.

Dhani put the roll in his hand, bullied into obedience once again. He had seen this officer get physical with other kids, twisting one guy's arm until he screamed, taking pleasure in inflicting pain. He had to find a way to get out of this system and the mess he was caught in, whatever it took. All he wanted was to get out of here and help his mom move far away from the man they both called "the Monster." If he could just find her.

He slumped back down the hallway toward his room. If only he could stop thinking about her the way he had last seen her, with black-ened eyes and a swollen face. Now she was in hiding, and that made his anxiety about her worse. If she would just contact him, tell him she still loved him despite what happened.

He felt like his whole life was on hold until he knew she was okay. And now he was also trapped in this system by what he had done to save his mother, with no way to get to her.

I hate this place. I hate my life.

In the dark, he flopped down on his bunk and hoped the horrible dream would not come, with the screams of the man in flames.

Sahm—1:36 a.m. EST (1:36 p.m. Tibet)

He slipped like quicksilver flame over the black night ocean, face-for-ward into the pink glow of a rising sun that swiftly rose into the eastern sky before him. Islands, then deserts, then broad tundras passed far below. Wind and rain and sunlight poured around and through him in a mixed torrent. A range of ermine-white snow peaks jutted up from a flat plain cut by rivers. India and the Himalayas.

He'd had dreams of flying, but, if this was another, the sensations and sights were sharper than any before.

He arrowed over mountain peaks that spired below him, dazzling under a noontime sun. To the north, he recognized the white-capped flash of Mount Kailash—Tibet's holy, crystal mountain—surrounded by white threads of smoke rising from the fires of a thousand pilgrim encampments. Even in the harshest weather, the faithful had come to circumambulate the holy mountain. Still he streamed onward.

"When you ran from me. . . ."

The gentle admonishment he'd heard back at Lost Lake still stung. He had fled from Tibet, after all, because of the threat of capture. And yes, from something else, too—a path he was not ready to settle his life onto. At this moment, however, the thrill of jetting through free space overrode his anxiety about the encounter about to take place.

In an eye-blink, his destination came rushing at him. Mount Chenrezig, one of the most sacred peaks of his religion, Bön, arched high in the azure sky, rising above and behind the tree and boulder-strewn shoreline of Five-Color Lake. The spires of sixty-meter-tall deodar cedar trees draped in gangly mosses reflected like thin, silver saw teeth in the lake's blue-green mirror as it glinted in noonday sunlight. He passed over a small village of stone houses straight toward one of the surrounding massive and craggy peaks.

One ledge, halfway up the treacherously steep slope, rushed at him faster. . . closer and closer. . . . The rocky shelf hung between a sheer rock face and a narrow trail right beside a cascading waterfall, and on it was a small, yak hide shelter painted with symbols. From the fire beside rose the sweet smell of wood smoke and juniper.

Then his feet planted on the rock ledge, where he had lived for a long time. He felt his body tingling to life, as if his whole being were a limb that had been slept on and was now reawakening.

All this is impossible, he thought. *It cannot be real.*

In front of the shelter, seated on a twisted cedar log beside a fire of branches and dung chips, was a familiar form. He was wearing a black, skin coat that fell from shoulders to ankles, and sat watching Sahm's arrival. From beneath the beaked and misshapen leather cap trimmed with fur, the old, lined, pleasant face with black shining eyes beamed at him, clearly pleased.

"*Sangye*—Enlightened One," said the old man. He bowed from the waist, his hands pressed palm to palm before his chest in a gesture of respect. He started to drop to his knees and reached out to touch Sahm's feet. A gesture of highest reverence.

Sahm reached down and took his grandfather by the arm. "No," he said. "Please do not do that." He sat the old man gently on the cedar log.

A cold draft came up the cliff, and Sahm stepped up to the stone fire circle, stooped to pick up a spruce limb and lay it quickly onto the guttering flames.

The shining eyes, set in a face creased with years and laughter, followed his every motion, as one riveted on the movements of a master. "So now you have experienced the *siddhi* of flight. It was the most fitting way to draw you back, *Cetan*—don't you think so?" The old man smiled, speaking in an ancient form of Mongolian, a dialect his Bönpo ancestors had spoken from before the dawn of Tibet, when much of this high, isolated plateau was called the kingdom of Zhang Zhung.

Sahm's heart warmed at the tone. *Always only love and compassion. Never anger.* He answered in the same, ancient tongue. "Grandfather, is it really you?"

This brought a short, soft laugh. "Who else did you want to see? Some pretty girl?"

"No, Grandfather. I mean, is this really happening or are we meeting together in a dream?"

The old man's eyes shone, and he made a quick, sweeping gesture with his right hand—indicating the mountain's sheer rock face and the plunging cliffs that dropped away from the broad ledge into a steep gorge, which ended in the lake a thousand feet below. His grandfather had secluded himself up here so that he could, like other hermit yogis of the Bön religion, listen to the voices that spoke from all things, even animals, rocks, water, fire, air.

Reaching into the fire with a heavily calloused hand, the old man lifted a brass kettle that had been sitting and sputtering in the red embers. Reaching with his other hand into one of two goatskin bags at his feet—the black one—he lifted out a leather mug and poured from the brass kettle a stream of steaming, dark-gold tea. This he handed carefully to Sahm, who stepped closer and accepted it from his hand.

"Real. . .or a dream. What do you think?"

Sahm lifted the leather cup to his lips, smelling fresh, golden oolong and cardamom scents he had not enjoyed for a full year, and sipped. His lips were cold, so the liquid felt good going down and sent comfort into his whole being. In a moment, these familiar tastes helped his wild and electrified body-energies return to normal.

"I think I am happy to be home, Grandfather. And if I am really here, it is because your wisdom and power brought me back." He did not want to break the dream, if that's what this was, by calling it that.

Despite the vividness of this place, doubt remained. Could he really have entered the *Bardo* and come back to this remote dwelling, where he had spent years training with this beloved man who possessed such rare wisdom and gifts? He was still a novice really, not practiced in the higher yogic arts yet. He had heard about *siddhis* like mind-communication and yogic flight since he came to this hermitage at seven years old—but only by his grandfather's powers could he have come here. In comparison, he had mastered so little.

His grandfather touched the log beside him with one hand. "Sit, *Cetan*." He rose and shambled over to the shelter. The tent's yak-skin flap parted, and in a moment he returned with a heavy, brown blanket of woven wool.

Sahm allowed his grandfather to wrap him in the blanket, stooping to tuck the lower part of it around Sahm's legs. Then the old man sat down at Sahm's right side and reached for a crooked stick to stir the embers. The scent of many wood fires, wild herbs, and roasted game emanated from his skin coat.

"Grandfather—master—it is I who should serve you."

With a gruff noise and a strong wave of one hand, the old man dismissed this, and continued stirring the fire.

"No, it's true. You raised me from a boy and taught me all I know. You were teaching me my path."

"Why have you left it?" his grandfather asked gently, staring steadily into the flames.

Sahm had sat on this very log and been pressed for answers by his grandfather many times. He knew exactly what was happening now. The older man had summoned him here, to ask questions and listen deeply to his every word, weighing his meanings—searching for any secrets Sahm might be hiding behind those words—staring deeply into the flames and embers to scry for signs that might appear this day.

For all his joy at seeing his Grandfather, this was an encounter he now dreaded. He was here to be examined.

The old man now handed the juniper stick he had used to stir the fire to Sahm. He had seen his grandfather charge this very same stick with energy, making many prayers and offerings to the spirits of mountains, trees, and the cascading waterfall.

"When you hold this, all the Great Ones around us listen and witness."

They were now holding court, and no words could conceal anything.

Next, his grandfather reached down into a second goatskin bag—the white one encrypted with symbols. Sahm knew the fire had been prepared with tree resins from that bag—red and white sandalwoods, eucalyptus, and spruce. The old man threw in another handful, which sent a heady blend of fragrances rising on tendrils of white smoke.

"This is to purify."

He also pulled out his *phurba*, and used the ornate, ceremonial dagger to make seven magical cuts at the air.

"This is to cut away all illusions."

Sahm knew what this meant, that he must speak with a pure motive and not to try to obscure the truth. Which now made him feel uneasy. If he said the whole truth plainly about why he had left, would it hurt this beloved old man? He had no wish to do that, and would have to make his way carefully through whatever came next.

His grandfather lapsed into a barely audible chant, preparing himself to see into his grandson's soul. Not like an inquisitor, Sahm knew, but like a soul physician, looking for that special human malady—self-deception. The ritual fire was summoning a thousand Buddhas and ascended bodhisattvas, along with the mountain spirits, as witnesses to their conversation. Soul retrieval—the art of looking deeply into the layers of another's being—was one of the skills the old man had just begun teaching Sahm before he had slipped away from here by moonlight one night.

"Why did you leave and abandon your training and your path?"

So this was it, the point of the dream or summons, whichever reality had taken hold.

Sahm chose his words cautiously. "Grandfather, for years you opened and cleared my mind to understand my calling. You taught me faithfully in the sutras and in the first principles of the higher yogic arts. I am grateful.

"And one of the things you taught me," he tried to steer the conversation, "is that nothing in the changing world of form is fixed. And that the workings of our *karma* are not fixed. We have come into this world to complete our course and fulfill our role, but *how* we live out our calling on that path"—he paused, picking his next words with care—"how we do that is still open to our own choosing."

There was a subtle change all around and within Sahm, as if the air pressure had shifted. He felt as if he had slipped up with his response, and began to sweat.

"Have you chosen this new path seeking only your own peace and happiness?" The old man peered intently into the fiery coals, but Sahm could sense his grandfather's spirit searching deeper into his own, gentle as the hands of a doctor, exercising one of his perfected *siddhis*—the ability to feel another's spiritual energy like a pulse. It was of critical importance to answer the old man's questions with complete honesty, no matter what the cost.

"You know why I escaped to India."

"Yes, the government has arrested others who are known to possess powerful *siddhis* and then set impostors in their place. That is true. Their penetration into our land and our ways is profound. They are now forbidding our children to be taught in our own language. But they cannot capture our spirit."

"And there was word that government officers were in the villages, asking my whereabouts," Sahm interjected.

"You were driven away by fear, *Cetan*? Or by indifference to the needs of others?"

Sahm felt his grandfather's mind reaching deeper into his, and hesitated. Had he acted only out of self-interest? That could set in motion a dark wave in the ocean of *karma*. Before speaking, he searched within himself for the truth.

"There was no word from the Teachers or Guides, directing you to leave," his grandfather pursued. "You are young, and your actions seemed very impulsive. What did you think you would accomplish by leaving your place and role here, which is to help end suffering among the Bönpos?" Again, no anger; a question, to sift his soul and help shed light on his truest motives.

Sahm had warmed comfortably under the heavy blanket. The mountain air was chill. He opened the right side of the blanket and wrapped it around his grandfather's shoulders. The old man, accepting the offer, slid closer to him. Assured by the old man's closeness, he felt ready to answer.

"Would I have been able to guide and serve our people from prison?—supposing the government had allowed me to live. No one has heard from or seen the Oracles and most learned and gifted yogis who were kidnapped. You know they are most likely dead."

"We are part of a greater pattern, and we have to live out our own *dharma* within it. The powers that try to control us now will someday fall."

"I know why you have called me back—," Sahm said, getting to the point, "—to be sure my mind and spirit are clear and unclouded. It was not because of fear. But if I had not left then, I might have been taken, as well. As it was, I was pursued west to Ngari Prefecture and only barely escaped south over the border into the high ridges of Himachal Pradesh."

He turned his head and was going to say more about all the hardships of the trek, but was stopped by a sight that sent a pang through his heart.

Eyes shining with the hint of tears greeted him. His grandfather had leaned his face close to Sahm's.

"I raised the energies that brought you here now for two reasons, *Cetan.* First, so you could tell me the truth about why you left, because I made a vow to guide you on your path and you were only at its beginning. But I also brought you back because I am your grandfather." The eyes now filled with tears.

This was not the cold, condemning examination Sahm had dreaded. He felt as if a warm hand were holding his heart.

"Sahmdup, my young eagle," you did not even give me the chance to say goodbye."

Looking at the *phurba* lying in his grandfather's lap, Sahm felt a sharp pain in his gut, and thought, *The worst cuts are the ones made by love.*

Steve—4:53 a.m. EST

Over and over, still awake, he whispered at the faded dream, "Help me."

Why would she want to help him? Why would anyone? He'd been an ass, and he didn't even know why he'd been so angry and on-edge that morning. Every word of that conversation replayed itself. . . .

"Can't these kids get their own ride?"

"They're in juvenile detention and foster care. Not likely."

"Great. I did combat duty in Afghanistan and can't find a good job, and punks in juvie are getting free healthcare, free rides. Perfect."

"They need to be seen at the free clinic in Southeast. And you just called my guys *punks*?"

"Yeah. Punks. There, I said it again."

"Steve, these are kids who are falling through the cracks. They're like my kids. There's a chance to help redirect them away from dead-end lives."

"Oh my god, Olivia—'falling through the cracks'? Why are they in juvie? You don't land there by being Kid of the Year."

"Stop calling it 'juvie.' And you don't know these young men and women. There's always more to a story. And why are you so angry and aggressive this morning? No, not just this morning. I've felt it ever since you got out of the Marine Corps."

"Maybe because I worked hard all through school, then went to serve my country and witnessed friends get shot up." He paused and wouldn't look at her, as if there was something he wasn't saying. "I pushed myself to earn rank in a deadly war zone—then stuck around when the U.S. pulled out, to train mountain forces and run secret ops against the Taliban. Do you know what it was like to live in the cold in a dug-out trench or snowbank on high alert for days before they finally yanked us, too?"

"No. Because you shut me out and won't talk about it."

"It messes with your mind and body. Then I come home to no job and liberals giving the country away in handouts like free healthcare and a wife who wastes our gas giving rides to kids who have—"

Olivia's eyes flashed. "Who have *what*? You don't know anything about these kids. Not a thing. Steve, I have an idea what you went through to serve our country. You did crazy-good things.

"But my hard work is here, and it goes on and on. And we're losing thousands of young people, because so many safety nets are gone or failing. And as for 'free healthcare,' with all the budget cuts they're lucky to get band-aids and aspirins. Last week the clinic was out of sanitary wipes, and the staff brought them in. You don't know how hard this job is becoming or, frankly, what you're talking about when it comes to any of my young people."

"Right. And their mommies didn't love them. And they grew up in bad neighborhoods. What's to know? See, I can talk bleeding-heart-liberal talk."

Olivia took a step back, stunned and angry. "*That's* what I am—a 'bleeding-heart liberal'? This is my life work you're trashing. This is *me* you're trashing. I went to grad school for my degree in public health for this. *This is who I am.*"

"I'm sorry I'm fresh out of compassion. Because right here in good old America I now can't find the kind of job that'll pay me what I want."

"I know that. But you're not talking like the man I married."

"Hey, if you don't want to be married to me anymore, then—." The sentence trailed off.

Tears rushed to Olivia's eyes, but anger kept them from spilling. Her hands were shaking. "What?—then I can *leave*? Is that what you were going to say to me? Who *are* you?"

He did not flinch. "I'm a guy who worked my butt off to make platoon leader in the Marine Corps. I trained hard every single day to keep men alive in severe mountain conditions with the Taliban all around us. I busted it out every day. Nobody handed me anything. That's who *I* am."

"Why did you leave the Marines if you're so unhappy here. . . and with *me*?"

"You know the military cut back on troop deployment. I thought I'd take the out so we could start our life together. I love you."

Olivia was silent. The angry look had not passed from her face. She turned from him toward the door. "You love me. That's a sweet thing to say after venting all over me, Steve. What a perfect morning to hear all this."

"Why—what's different this morning?"

"*Nothing.* None of your damn business." She picked up her satchel of case files, and stepped out into the hallway.

A little wave of remorse rose. "Olivia, wait. I want you to meet me later."

"Meet you where?—and you must be joking."

"There's this big event going on at National Cathedral. Father Tom wants us to meet him there. He's going to introduce me to a high-ranking senator who might have an opening on his security staff soon. He's had email threats from antifa bastards."

"Seriously. You just got through griping that you can't find a job, and there might be one waiting for you on silver platter? You're unbelievable."

She was right. He should apologize. Why could he never find the words to do that?

"It's this big Ash Wednesday service. That Palestinian priest who just won the Nobel Peace Prize is going to speak about the suffering people of the world. That's kind of right up your alley, right? Meet me, and then I'll take you for lunch. We can talk."

"Well, there's three problems with your offer. One—I'm feeling kind of sick right now, so the thought of eating has no appeal. Second—'this is right up *your* alley' just made things a whole lot worse. I'm the queen of 'suffering people', is that it? And third—the last time I was around you and Tom and his Washington big-shot friends, I stood there twiddling my thumbs, while you traded war stories and completely ignored me. Even if I did show up, you'd most likely leave me standing there all by myself."

Fire flashed up his face. "You snob. Tom is a spiritual director to those men. You're so much for the down-and-outers. There are up-and-outers, too, you know."

"Oh, *please*. They're the most powerful men on earth. They start the wars your friends get killed in."

He clenched his jaw. "Maybe you're right. Maybe you should stay as far away from me today as possible."

"No problem. I have an appointment I need to keep anyway."

Sahm—5:26 a.m. EST (5:26 p.m. Tibet)

"Tell me about this woman. When you met her, what could you see in her?"

Sahm had finished the stew of goat meat, *droma* gourd root, and butter. High above them, circling on strong updrafts coming up the gorge, two broad-winged Himalayan eagles, the gold and black *lammergeyers*, were passing in and out of the rising smoke, drawn by the scent of roasted flesh. He was thankful to know that villagers below still made the dangerous climb up to this mountain fastness to bring gifts like raisins, tangy yogurt and honey,—a clay bowl of which was now placed in his hands—to support the aged yogi here in his isolated, spiritual practice. Nothing had tasted as good or felt as satisfying in the whole year past as this meal with his grandfather.

Touched by his grandfather's heart, he was glad now that he had been brought here to submit to all these questions. The man who was listening so carefully to his every word knew him better than anyone and was concerned only for his soul's progress.

The old man seemed satisfied, though Sahm detected there was more he was not saying.

Still, the sun was about to slide into the massive V created by two mountains off to the west, and he would have to go very soon. Back at Lost Lake, he would be needed and looked for. Yet he wanted his grandfather's heart to be fully at ease, to have his blessing, and his agreement that, in fact, he had taken the correct path to fulfill his *dharma*.

"Her name is Kate Holman. I met her in Dharamsala," he said finally, beginning the story. Again, he knew it was crucial to give an accurate account, while still choosing his words carefully, and tried to recall the meeting exactly. . . .

Morning light had poured down the green foothills of the lower Himalayas. He had risen at daybreak and left his hidden encampment on the steep slopes of the Himachal Pradesh to join the morning *kora* walk around Dharamsala's main shrine. With ease, he had slid in among other circumambulating pilgrims whose low chanting and prayers formed a current of comforting sounds.

It wasn't that the woman's garb made her stand out. Among the red-, yellow-, and saffron-robed monks circling the temple, there were many westerners in blue jeans, hiking boots, knitted caps and down jackets. Many Tibetans, Nepalese, and Indians were dressed like that, as well. It was the finger of invisible light that suddenly fell on her and singled her out, shining white with her at its center and radiating out into a halo of rainbow colors. And it was the look on her face, when she turned for no particular reason and stared straight at him—completely unaware of who she really was or her own greatness or the energies and white light emanating from within her person.

What was it about this woman? What wisdom and what answers was she here seeking? Sahm had been surprised to sense some doorway deep in his mind swing wide, and witness light and words pouring in. Perhaps the few *siddhis* his grandfather had transmitted were starting to work.

As he passed by her, he said without forethought, "You must open the school. That is why the property was left in your hands."

The woman stopped stock-still. Her right hand quit working the string of amber mala beads. Her mouth fell open, and she stared at him with a disbelieving look. Then she pushed the yellow pashmina head covering back onto the shoulders of her gray coat, as if to hear him better.

The light in and around her shone brighter.

"What did you say?"

Sahm repeated the message.

"Why did you tell me that? I mean, how did you know I came here hoping for an answer to that specific question? No one, not even the friends who came with me, know what I'm thinking about doing."

As he had ever since leaving his grandfather's hermitage hundreds of kilometers behind him, Sahm concealed his true, full identity from her. You could not know when the person right next to you might turn informant for money, and even in India he might be found and dragged away. That—and how would she even understand or believe him if he told her everything about himself?

So he had given her the simplest, truthful answer. He had been a skilled mountain guide to foreign tourists in eastern Tibet before the area where he lived became highly restricted. Tourists rarely got into his region now, and he had left to find work. So much truth, and so much left out. He also told her—saying it for the first time out loud—"I am feeling constricted by my culture and the old traditions, and by what is expected of me back in Tibet. It is like a coat that has become too tight. I want to get away from all that for now."

"But how did you know?" She had started to press him again about his uncanny insight, but then held back. It was not the first time he had encountered westerners who felt it rude to pry. Perhaps she simply resolved that she had accidentally crossed paths with a Sherpa who had strayed from home for some very private reason. He also detected a kind of deep knowing about her, the sense that she was an old soul able to rest in the presence of great mysteries. He was glad she had not pressed him further.

It was in that moment, in a blaze of unexpected revelation, he had realized he needed to help her in her work and that his skills would be important someday, even if he had fled Tibet and the great role for which he had been trained there. . . .

"We met early every morning for almost two weeks, to perform *kora*. In the end, she asked me to come work with her in America. She is starting a school in the mountains where she lives, to help young men and women who have lost their way. If anyone can help teach students about living in the mountains it is me—don't you agree, Grandfather?"

He had left out the part about concealing his true identity. His statement about the approaching men from the government and fleeing from their harmful intent, that was true enough.

"She is compassionate, that is not in question," his grandfather responded. "You are posing as if you are a Sherpa, and that is not who you were born to be in this lifetime. Carrying bundles is not what I was training you to do."

Sahm remained silent, and the old man stooped and slid his hand into the white goatskin bag again. Sahm expected him to pull out his brown, yak bone dice and perform *Mo* to divine what the powers would say about him accepting Kate's invitation and work at her school. Instead, the wrinkled hand withdrew from the bag another herb.

Sahm sat up, recognizing the plant—one with great powers.

What is he doing now?

Steve—6:07 a.m. EST

Steve rose and took a hot shower. Clearing a circle of steam from the bathroom window of the tenant house where he had been hiding from the world for too long—a full year now—he stared across the frosty farm field at Father Tom's house, a hundred yards up the hill. No new snow had fallen, and the faintly-pinking morning sky looked clear. At least he could drive more fence-posts today and keep himself busy, exhausting himself completely before falling back into bed again.

Like that's *working.*

He turned to the bathroom mirror, wiping the fogged glass so he could shave. He had to see Tom again this morning. He would hike up the hill as soon as the lights were on, because he couldn't stand to be here any longer. The small, healing community Tom had assembled after stepping away from active parish work in DC was no help. Yes, there were other men and women with losses, like children killed in car accidents, spouses lost to cancer. But—he lifted the razor to the lathered reflection, fixing his eyes firmly on the line of his chin—how many of them could no longer look themselves full in the face? How many of them were haunted by their own hostile words and terrible actions?

In the white porcelain sink basin, a thread of red came off the razor blade and curled into the stream of water circling down the drain. A thin line of blood appeared under his chin.

Perfect. Just what I needed to see today.

Memory flooded in. . . .

. . .Where the hell was Olivia? He looked back through the huge sanctuary. The National Cathedral had filled to capacity, every seat occupied by a special guest or dignitary, except the seat next to him, which he had wrangled for her. Maybe she would punish him by not showing.

No. That's not her style. She would forgive him. Easily. It was in her compassionate nature. She would ask what was really behind his agitation and anger, and he would not be able to tell her. She would come if she could. If she'd finished hauling juveniles and keeping her appointment. He would text her and say where he had left her ticket— outside, with Thi.

"Steve, you scored a guest pass! Good for you," Thi Martin had called to him as he had climbed the front steps. A cameraman and a producer from Thi's TV network-affiliate station were jammed beside her, along with the rest of the media pack in the roped-off area. Thi, whose grandparents were Vietnamese refugees, had interviewed Olivia about her English as a Second Language program in Southeast DC on Thi's morning talk show, and after that the three of them had met for drinks and become friends. Her being here was perfect.

"Passes are hard to come by," Thi said, sounding impressed. "Only high-ranking people get inside. There have been so many threats on this guy's life, security is crazy-tight."

Steve handed her a pass. "I had to beg a second one. Give this to Olivia, please. If she shows up."

Thi shot him a curious look. "Why wouldn't she show up?"

The Senator's entourage swept him along inside. Seated many rows in, he craned his neck, looking back over his shoulder from halfway up the cathedral's packed nave at the entryway doors, trying to see through the forest of bodies. *Why wouldn't she? Oh, because I made her angry, almost made her cry, and for about a jillion other reasons.*

His watch had flicked closer to noon. The suited security officers standing beside each row of chairs cupped their hands over the tiny lapel mics to be heard over the murmur of the crowd.

Two minutes to show time.

He had felt surges of agitation. He had done everything but shine the Senator's shoes to secure that pass for Olivia, and then sent her a text and left a voice message. On the other hand, he knew it would be a monument to forgiveness if she did show up, considering the brutal way he'd spoken to her. His wrestling match was not over, though. He felt his anger was justified, because he hated the way freeloaders were given a helping hand when so many veterans he knew could not get good healthcare or work. But why did he unload his anger at *her* of all people? He loved how much she cared about people. Most of the time. Even if her parting words still rankled.

"Tell your Senator to stop handing over trillions to the military and billions in corporate welfare. It makes me sick that they cut the few million that was helping pull my young people up out of dead-end lives," she'd goaded him before banging the apartment door shut.

The suits hand-signaled each other. A pipe-organ volley began. If Olivia didn't arrive in the next few seconds. . . . From two seats away, the Senator was still prattling on about "how terribly hard" it was to find campaign funding. Seated at Steve's right side, Father Tom, the old family friend who had made the connection, kept nodding and looking deadly bored. The Senator loved to hear himself talk; no response was needed. Yeah, this guy was probably a power-grabber and definitely a sack of hot air. So what? *A security job with him has to pay well.*

If only he could take back the words that rang inside his skull.

"You say you're feeling sick this morning? Well so am I, Olivia. Liberal-speak does it to me every time."

Then the crowd rose, falling silent, as up front a door behind the high altar opened and two robed figures emerged—the Bishop and the Dean of the cathedral—followed by a shorter, gray-bearded man in a black suit and white collar. The Nobel Laureate.

Turning one last time, Steve spotted Olivia at that moment, at the back showing her pass to the head usher—who shook his head. Her shoulders slumped at the indication it was too late to be escorted up the center aisle to the empty seat at Steve's side.

Why had she been late today of all days? His irritation returned. What was the big deal appointment she could not skip or change?

"Blessed are the peacemakers," the speaker began.

Oh God, direct hit, he chastised himself. *Man up, and apologize.*

Twenty minutes later, when the Laureate's speech ended, Steve jumped to his feet and tried to slip out into the aisle, but was blocked by a guard. "Don't move until your row is released."

The front three rows were being allowed to move slowly in single-file to an open floor in front of the altar, where the Bishop, Dean, and speaker stood waiting to shake hands with a few high-level guests. The security guards formed a tight line at the back of the cathedral. The row Steve was stuck in wasn't moving any time soon.

"My wife's waiting for me in the back."

The officer had placed one hand to his earpiece, listening, and ignoring him. Steve moved his head side to side, hoping to catch sight of Olivia.

A hand grabbed his jacket sleeve. "Not that way. Come with me." The Senator was tugging him backwards, away from the central aisle and toward one side of the cathedral. "There's a reception downtown at a private club for a select group of VIPs. You're going to be in a rarefied atmosphere, my boy, and get to shake hands with power and with a Nobel Laureate. Let's beat the rabble out of here."

For half a second, he thought of excusing himself, explaining he had someone important to see and that it could not wait. Then images of himself in the Senator's security entourage changed his mind.

Leaning close to Tom, he said, "Can you try to get to Olivia for me? Call her or something? Tell her I had to go if I want a job."

The Senator was still pulling his sleeve, and he started to move away, looking back one more time. For a moment, the crowd parted and he caught sight of Olivia, who was looking straight at him.

Seeing him moving away, leaving her there, her jaw fell open and she shook her head—then mouthed something to him.

Even at this distance, he could make out her words and the question she was asking. The very same one she had asked this morning as she left him.

Wheeling, she walked away quickly, out through the cathedral's front doors toward the street.

Dammit. It would take a lot, but he vowed he would make it up to her later.

Sahm—6:29 a.m. EST (6:29 p.m. in Tibet)

For a long time after, the old man was silent, staring into the flames. Sahm suspected that he was reading the curling plumes of white smoke, and knew not to disturb him. He sipped the tea that had gone cold in the leather cup, the yak butter clumping in tiny, pale beads.

After another long stretch, his grandfather let his eyes drift from the fire. It was safe to speak.

"Why did you use the *myrobalan* herb in the fire before, Grandfather? Are you ill? If so, why did you not tell me?"

His grandfather made a scoffing sound, turned and looked straight into his grandson's eyes. "No, I am quite well, better than ever before, but it may take a long time for us to find each other again. What I do now, I do because I am not settled in my mind about you. I am not completely certain that you are on the right path. You are concealing something from me."

"You taught me and trained me in so many things, Grandfather, and I can be of benefit spreading our teachings in the west."

"It is your personal *dharma* that concerns me. It is a piece of a much greater *karmic* pattern. Are you so sure you are ready to do what will be needed of you, when the time comes? And beyond that, the west where you have fled is in a very dark age—asleep in the material realm. Will they allow you to teach them even the most basic things?"

"They are awakening, Grandfather. Women like Kate and some of the men I have met are the proof of it. But you did not tell me—why use such a strong, cleansing herb?"

"To hear what the fire has to tell us about your life. And to open and purify your way back."

The fire was snapping, popping, sizzling, and gesturing vigorously, and Sahm knew his Grandfather was listening carefully, knowing its language and movements.

"You are not going to try to persuade me to stay?"

"I was hoping your role would be here, to clear away the forces that have engulfed our own land. But now you have chosen a different way and made promises to others to help them. A portentous alliance has been set in place between you and this woman, also between you and her young people whom you promised to teach, and these purposes must be worked out."

"*. . .a portentous alliance.*" What did that mean?

Before he could ask, Sahm felt his body becoming lighter again. Saw his hands becoming transparent. Felt himself slipping half into a dream state.

All of this was *just a dream. A portent, telling me that I made the right choice to help Kate.* That was it. He would wake from this lucid imagining, and find himself under his thick wool blanket in his bed back in one of Kate's guest cabins. Of course he had not flown here; he had never been instructed in that secret skill.

"That is correct, *Cetan.* You do not have the full power to accomplish such feats yet," his grandfather said, reading his thoughts. "If you practice the *Dharma*, that may come in time, when you need it. And I will call on another—the Great One of our lineage—to help you, now that you have gone from my tutelage."

"What did the fire say to you, Grandfather?"

"Though you did not know it, you were led from here out into the world for some greater purpose—perhaps for all people. And that one day great *siddhis* will be yours."

The old man stared harder into the fire, his expression suddenly turning wary.

"What else do you see, Grandfather? You look startled."

"I do not know for sure. Something hidden on the distant horizon, over there in the west where you have gone."

"Why do you look so concerned?"

"Continue to prepare yourself, Sahm, and awaken others," the old man said, his eyes flashing, his voice serious now and forceful. "Remain alert."

Sahm had now become weightless, and in another moment his feet left the ground. He rose again into the air, moving out over the gorge rising higher with the updrafts. Above him, one lone *lammergeyer* was circling, calling as he spiraled upward, and for a second his consciousness flipped and he saw himself as if he, too, were a winged creature. He tried to call down to his grandfather, but his voice had become like a high-pitched wind whistling among reeds.

Suddenly, he was moving forward again, speeding toward the western horizon. Even with the wind shrilling in his ears, he could hear the words his grandfather called after him, urgent and close.

"The Great One who began our ancient lineage will rise to guide and protect you, my Cetan!"

With all his might, Sahm willed himself to go back, wanting to ask, "Protect me from what?" But he could not stop his body from rising as he rushed past the huge bird as it called out to him.

The bird's cry distracted him from something that had just caught his eye, a pinpoint of blue light that shone from within the *Bardo* like a signal beacon—and yet he had the impression, before the shriek, that maybe this was not just a light but the radiance of some great being, watching from a distance.

His grandfather's shout further distracted him from the light. The old man was growing smaller and smaller below him, calling out, "Time is counting down."

"Counting down to what?"—he tried to say, but his words came out only as the shriek his voice had become.

"This will keep you on your path, and keep your mind clear about who you really are."

From high above, Sahm saw the old man draw back his right arm, and launch with a powerful throw some small, glinting object.

As Sahm sped westward in a stream of light, he looked over his shoulder and saw the object his grandfather had flung, shooting after him, flashing brilliant and sparking like a small bolt of lightning. Above him the pinpoint of blue light shone brighter.

In the dwindling distance, his grandfather's skin tent lay sagging, gray, long abandoned, and all but destroyed by the mountain winds. He turned his face westward.

Such a strange, strange dream.

Steve—6:45 a.m. EST

He dressed and stepped out onto the porch.

The first thin edge of winter sun had now risen red in a cold blue sky, and now it was spilling light down the surrounding ridges of Father Tom's farmland. Its early rays cast long, gray shadows from the stretches of four-board fence he had repaired in the last two weeks. Staying occupied, exhausting himself until he collapsed in bed at night, was no longer cutting it.

Why did she have to leave him that day, before he could tell her he had gotten the message her lips had formed silently, and that he would try harder?

Up the hill, a light shone in the window of Tom's study. There was also a blue Mercedes in the gravel drive beside Tom's old, red Ford pickup. It was early for a visitor.

Damn.

Steve turned up the collar of his parka, and rubbed his hands together. He would wait until the guest left before trudging his way uphill to the farmhouse. There was no real refuge for him here. Or maybe anywhere. It irritated him that Tom steadfastly refused to tell him what to do with his life now, because he sure as hell had no clear direction. He hoped whoever it was would leave soon so he didn't have to stay alone here with these memories that continued to fly at him even now while he was wide awake, more vivid and urgent than ever. . . .

. . .Even with guards opening a way through the pressing bodies, it had taken a few minutes for the Senator's entourage to escape the huge sanctuary. Junior Senators, businessmen and lawyers had crowded around, wanting to grab the Senator's hand and ear. They had finally exited the cathedral from a side door across a broad driveway from the Bishop's Garden. The Senator's driver was standing on the pavement, holding open for them the back door of a black Humvee.

It was then he had heard the unmistakable sound coming from the street out in front of the cathedral—like steel balloons popping, four times, then once—followed by shouts and screaming.

In that second, his world broke into spinning pieces.

In one half of it, at some distant place in the back of his mind, his mind was clear and he knew. *Gun shots. Out on Wisconsin.*

And in the other half, his mind was going dull and his body was an unmoving glacier, his legs unable to obey his impulse to be, not here with these strangers, but *there.*

He could never forget dodging the car that squealed out from behind the Humvee to escape the threat of gunfire. Or sprinting past the dashing reporters and camera crews, the crowds dropping to the ground, outdistancing them all to cross the cathedral's broad front lawn to reach the sidewalk along Wisconsin Ave, where the fallen figure lay.

What met him had imprinted on his mind like a scene in a nightmare. The slender body crumpled on the pavement. . .the fleeing form all in black, now a full block away and turning to disappear between two buildings. . . the dark eyes looking up at him, pleading, with a flickering light. One of her fists clenched, as if squeezing something. Blood was escaping underneath her in pools and red lines over the cement, from too many point-blank wounds to the chest to stanch.

He had dropped to his knees, and cupped her face in his hands. His voice fraying as he shouted her name.

And then they were swallowed in a maelstrom of bodies, pushing, shouting.

"*Paramedics. . . move, move MOVE!*"

The eyes fluttered and closed.

Numbness flooded his body, and his soul was crushing.

Thi Martin had pushed through the wall of EMTs and fallen to her knees beside him, seizing the clenched hand, which slowly relaxed open into hers.

From that moment on, Thi's voice would always be screaming in his head the words that stabbed him over and over—"*Save her, please! She's my friend. Ohmygod, save her!*"

. . .Steve's strength left him, and he turned back inside. Even if Tom tried to change his mind and get him to stay here, he had to escape this torment. Sure, Tom had been strong, kind, and caring, even fatherly. But all Tom's care had not helped, not even yesterday when he had asked—no, *begged*—Tom to tell him what to do with his life now, in the aftermath of such pain and personal failure. He was only really good at being one thing, a warrior, maybe someone's security guard, but he had not been there to protect his own wife from random violence. So how would it work, with his head in this pit of aching memories, every time he protected some stranger for a paycheck?

The terrible moment of Olivia's death would always replay, he was convinced. And nothing he could ever do and no place he could ever go could help him escape his guilt or pain.

He would keep the appointment with Tom, later when the Mercedes was gone—or maybe tomorrow or the next day, if he felt up to it.

Given the night he'd just had, the thought of dealing with what to do with his life suddenly made him weak with exhaustion.

All he knew was that he was so, so lost, with no clear idea how to find his way.

Dhani—7:21 a.m. EST

Two women had opened the sliding window from the kitchen and were placing trays of sweet rolls on the counter.

His hunger pains were eating him alive.

Someone pulled the tray away as he reached for it.

The same detention officer was grinning at him. "Sorry, buddy. Looks like no breakfast after all."

"What? You can't deny me food."

"Your case worker just called and said she's coming to meet with you in fifteen minutes. She said it's real, real important and I'm supposed to make sure you're ready."

"Can I get a sweet roll?"

"Breakfast is in—," he checked his watch, "—twenty minutes, and you gotta go wash up. I told your case worker I'd be sure you got a quick shower and shaved. You always stink, Jones. That hoody always stinks. Don't you even care about keeping yourself clean?"

Dhani ignored the insult. No way was he going to tell this guy or anyone why he avoided the gang showers—just one more on his long list of secrets. No one would ever understand why he did what he had to do.

The officer picked up a sweet roll, took a big bite, and grinned, chewing. "Damn, that's tasty. Now get out of here, Jones."

Dhani dropped his head, defeated. In the months he had been here, no one, not even one person, had given him a break. And at least three years of abuse lay ahead of him.

When the officer turned to walk away, Dhani made hand gestures at his back.

Sahm—7:56 a.m. EST

The sound of something striking the wooden floor boards startled him. His skin was ice-cold.

It made the other person who had entered his cabin jump at the same time.

Sahm was standing in front of the armchair across from the woodstove, with a clear, early sunlight streaming in the windows—and with Jo staring at him, her eyes wide with shock.

She had been squatting down, not eight feet from him, sliding sticks of split red oak into his woodstove. Her leather gloves lay on the floor beside the stove, and leaping up had made one loose braid of her dark blonde hair fall from under her red knitted cap and down the front of her blue sweater.

"Wait—no, no, *no*—that's not possible. You weren't standing there thirty seconds ago when I opened the door and called your name. How on earth. . .?"

Sahm searched his mind quickly for an explanation. He must have fallen asleep in the armchair. There was, after all, the wild dream about his grandfather in Tibet, in which he had flown. "I was. . . outside maybe."

"Sahm," Jo replied, wiping her hands on khaki coveralls. "It's freezing outside. You're in a tee-shirt and shorts. And there's no way you came in after me. But besides that, you almost let your fire go out. Very bad idea."

"Thank you for filling the woodstove, Jo," he said, sounding like he was just awakening.

"Look, never mind that. I came because I need your help. Fast. I was driving my Jeep up the camp road to the barns, watching this young eagle circling above Kate's lodge. It was so weird. Out of the blue, something knocked it out of the sky. I've watched a peregrine taking down an eagle when its territory is breached. But there was nothing. No other territorial birds. No gunshots."

49

Jo turned and followed her own footprints of melting snow back to the cabin door. "I got as close as I could, and it looks like it may have suffered a broken wing when it came down. But I'll need help to tranquilize and examine it."

She nodded at Sahm's dark green parka, which hung on a peg near the door. "Dress warm. We have to scoop this bird up off the camp road before it freezes or a predator finds it, and then get it to a cage in one of the barns where it's warm." Then, as she stepped outside onto the porch—"Hurry. Please."

When she closed the door behind her, he looked down, at the floor beside the armchair. Something had struck the floor sharply there, just as he was coming awake.

Stuck by its tip, in one pine plank beside his left foot, was his grandfather's *phurba*—the treasured, magic dagger the venerable yogi had used as long as Sahm could remember.

He stooped and pulled it out of the floorboard. There was no mistaking the quartz crystal finial or the silver triangular blade clasped in the forged-bronze dragon's head that formed its handle. So many times Sahm had witnessed his grandfather call up the Elemental energies of the world—earth, air, fire, water, and the all-surrounding ether. At the end of each ritual, he had thrust the dagger into the ground beside the person his magic was intended to bless and protect, calling down the powers with a final plea. . . a prayer. . . a powerful intention.

Words arose in Sahm's mind, from the foggy tail-end of his dream or whatever it was that had taken place in the night. As his grandfather hurled the *phurba* after him, he called out.

"*What is concealed in great darkness must be brought to light. What is broken must be made whole.*"

He sensed that the wheel of some great event was already in motion, though he could not guess what it might be. And now his grandfather had bound him by a strong intention to play his part in whatever might come. The old man's very last words rang in his mind.

"I did not ask you to stay, because it no longer matters where you are in this world. What is coming upon us all, you cannot escape. No one can. Wherever you believe you can hide, it will find you. There is no more hiding. Everyone who cares about life on this earth is needed now."

Sahm held the *phurba* up to the light pouring in through the front windows, wondering what was so dire about this particular time.

"Sahm!" Jo thrust her head in the door, impatient. "The eagle. *Now.*"

I will return to my path, Grandfather. No matter what lies ahead for me.

With so little training completed, he hoped he could do whatever was needed of him.

Washington, DC / Georgetown—8:07 a.m. EST

A young couple approached arm in arm on the walk alongside the canal, and it was prudent to wait before continuing the cellphone call.

Then—"A whole year has gone by, and you're telling me you're still unable to gain access to the room again?"

"Security has become super tight," said the voice on the other end. "And don't try to turn this on me. It was one of yours who went rogue."

"We took care of that. What about scrapping the first plan for a new one?"

"Access to every place worth penetrating is impossible for the fore-seeable future."

Silence. "So you can't come up with anything else?"

"Locate the missing piece. That's your job."

"Why can't we order a new one?"

"It was a signature piece, made to do both the functions we need. It can only be duplicated and coded by the maker."

"And you were going to find him and get a replacement."

"He disappeared overseas again. You need to stop pushing me about what *I* should do. Your people made the big mistakes."

A cyclist passed. "The transgressor has paid for his crime against our righteous cause."

"The husband has to have it."

"She had it on her at the cathedral, but you said it wasn't on the body or with her effects. So I agree—he has to have it. But he totally dropped from sight. The lease ran out on their apartment, and he hasn't used a credit card or his phone. His truck tags are dead. Either he's a master of evasion or someone's doing a great job of sheltering him."

"It's possible he learned what she had in her possession."

Morning joggers shuffled by. "Very doubtful. Even if he found it, he wouldn't have a clue what it's for. The guy will surface. Like you said, they always do."

"And if he doesn't?"

"My gut says he will. We just have to find him, since you can't get us into the room again."

Hesitation. "All right. We're stuck. I don't know why, but I'm sticking with you guys. I should ditch you and let the backers deal with you."

"Let's speak plainly. We know too much about each other to break our alliance."

Throat clearing. "We stay with the original plan and hope for a break. But from now on these conversations have to stay under two minutes. Someone could pick us up on their scan. Throw away that phone. In a week, another burner will be waiting for you. Same location.

"And remember, we stay as low-tech as possible. Whatever kind of grunt work it takes, we have to keep all the high-tech surveillance from picking us up."

1

MARCH

2ND

"Dhani Singh Jones."

The young man in the black hoody and jeans did not turn his head to look at Judge Sewell. Instead he kept his eyes fixed out the window at the dome of the U.S. Capitol building eight blocks away. The early March streets of Southeast Washington were still gray with late-winter grit.

He had not heard from his mom. Where was she?

"Are you paying attention to me, son. What I'm talking to you about could mean the difference in your whole future. It could possibly keep you from doing prison time.—*Son*. Are you listening?"

Dhani turned his head. "I try to. What are you going to do with me?"

Judge Sewell pushed back the laptop in which he'd been scanning through the young man's sealed file and leaned back in his office chair.

"Yesterday, your case worker told me you expressed an interest in hearing what I had to say. If I was your age and in as much potentially serious trouble as you are, I'd listen up when the juvenile justice system made me a great offer."

Dhani stared at him, as if uncomprehending. "What offer?"

The older man stared across the stacks of manila file folders and white forms that had landed on his desk early that morning, even before these first appointments. His tie was askew, his white shirt looked slept-in, and he chewed on one black plastic bow of his glasses.

"Son, I truly don't get it. There is a new program opening and I want to recommend you for it. At least I think I do. But the woman who has started it is a long-time friend of mine with a great idea, and I only want to send her young adults who I think will succeed. Young people who care about their future. Do you?—because you don't seem to."

He kept his eyes fixed on Dhani's.

Dhani felt him pressing for a response, and felt himself withdraw. Another adult male intruding in his life, trying to push him around. He considered the few details of the program he had picked up. Outdoor survival training. A school curriculum. Wildlife rehabilitation—he sort of understood what that meant. And eleven other people from the juvenile system.

"How long would I have to stay in it?"

"It's a three-year program. If you do well, you stay in, and this record—," Judge Sewell glanced at the laptop again, eyebrows raised— "gets expunged. Wiped clean. If not, if you act out badly again, especially like this or anything remotely like it, you cycle right back into the system and when you're eighteen you can be prosecuted. This is a very serious offense, son, and I have the discretion to recommend you for this chance to start over clean today. Or not. You do realize that, correct?"

Dhani noticed a look enter the judge's eyes. The piercing stare had changed into something like. . . kindness. Almost a plea.

Why would he give a crap about me?

"I'm waiting, son. There's a line of young people I have to decide on coming through this office today. Maybe this will make it easier. You now have sixty seconds to make up your mind. Your high IQ qualifies you, but I'm not recommending anyone who isn't willing to try—and I mean try hard."

Again, the pressure. "So where is this place—like, over in Maryland or something? Will I be able to see my mom? Have you guys found her yet?"

"No, we haven't. The program is in the mountains of upstate New York, about five hundred miles from here, give or take." He looked at his watch. "It's nine fifty-nine, son, and I have to interview another candidate in one minute. You now have thirty seconds."

He didn't want to go back to the juvenile facility. Word of what he'd done had leaked out, and the taunting and bullying was miserable. Still. . . .

Five hundred miles away is so far. But his mother was clearly still in hiding from the Monster, like she'd said the last time they spoke five months ago. Probably still trying to protect him by not bringing him back into her life. The Monster terrorized them both. It was too freakin' bad the bastard had survived.

"Why so far away?"

The judge was pushing back his chair. "The idea is to get you out of the bad environment you've been in, teach you some very important life skills, and keep you from falling through the cracks. My friend who's starting the program has a thing about rescuing human equity—investing in people. Young people especially.

"Look, the system's budget is tight and getting tighter, and we don't have enough good services to help you guys. We're losing a lot of you, and my friend—her name's Kate—is trying something new to see if we can make a small dent in that problem. She's an exceptional woman. A rare person. Good lord, you'll even get a little spending money. But I'm afraid your time is up—." He stood.

"Okay. Yes. Please, your honor. I'd like to go."

Judge Sewell drew in a long deep breath and let it out slowly. "You don't know what a relief it is to hear you say that. You're making the right choice, young man. Referring to me as 'your honor' is a good sign. Showing that you *care*, and showing *respect* is going to count for a lot. And one last thing."

Dhani shifted uneasily. Three years at a wilderness training school. What had he just agreed to?

Judge Sewell's assistant opened the office door to usher in the next person. He held up one hand to hold them off.

"There is something unusual about you, young man." He slipped off his glasses, and leaned across his desk toward Dhani. "For one thing, the horrendous police report that's in this file doesn't match at all with the guy I've been talking to over these last months. You haven't given anyone a bit of trouble at the detention center, despite these stupid little 'violations' that one officer keeps reporting. I've learned to trust my instincts in the twenty-plus years I've been doing this, and there's a kind of brightness about you that makes me believe in you.

"On the *other* hand," he continued, picking up a pen and making a note, "you act like you don't care what anyone's saying to you. I think you can be successful in this program. . . *if* you don't let your impulses take over. Apparently that's what got you in such serious trouble."

You don't know anything about me and my 'impulses.' You just think you do.

The judge had moved to the office door and opened it. "Good luck, son. I want you to succeed. I believe you can. I'll be monitoring both your grades and your actions. And pay attention. Show us all that you're listening and you care about this program—and that you care about *yourself.* No one can care more about your life than you do. If you remember nothing else, please remember that."

He signaled the assistant to usher in the next appointment.

From a worn armchair in the waiting area, a girl with dark hair looked in through the open door. Her eyes met Dhani's. Every feature of her face was perfect—the arched brows, the cheekbones, the full lips. But her expression was flat, kind of sad-eyed and depressive looking.

Her body was perfect. She looked nineteen, but she had to be younger, around his age, if she was being considered for this program.

Freakin' hot. If she's in, maybe this won't be too crappy.

He felt a hand on his shoulder and turned.

"Son, you're not listening again. What's with you? I said the summer part of the program starts in June. I'm going to need the next two months to clear all the paperwork. That's one small reason this system is broken, in my opinion. Too much paperwork. In the meantime, you need to stay out of trouble. Totally. One slip-up of any kind and I can yank you out. Then you'll sit in a cinder block building for three more years—and maybe be prosecuted after that. Got it?"

Dhani shook the judge's offered hand. "Yes. Sir. Got it." That's what older men who had power over him always wanted, to control him totally, force him to obey. "I'll do my best."

His case worker rushed in, slopping coffee from a partly crushed paper cup onto the carpet and herself. She was his third one in less than a year.

"Damn.—Sorry, your honor. I know you don't like swearing in front of the kids. But this is a new skirt and god knows I can't afford to buy new clothes on my salary." She turned to Dhani. "Now I got to get you back, then see eight more clients today. *Eight.* And my car is acting up—again. C'mon, Denny."

He didn't bother correcting her. She would probably be gone soon anyway, just like the other exhausted caseworkers that came and went. He was trying to catch the eye of the amazing looking person as she passed him entering the judge's office and clearly avoiding eye contact with him. She looked too well put-together to be in the system.

So what's your story, hot girl?

Father Tom Baden stared out between the frost fingers on the window of his study, his gaze roaming over the winter-burned grass on the hill out at the western edge of his farm.

He had been awake since before dawn, deeply troubled about the young Marine veteran who had been staying in one of his tenant houses for that last year. He had seen the lights come on down there two days ago just after 4 a.m. but Steve never showed up for the meeting he had requested. Not surprising. It was the one-year anniversary of his wife's death, Tom reminded himself, and all the horrible, painful trauma of that day.

He should not have waited for Steve to come see him, he chided himself. He should have reached out on the anniversary of Olivia's death. Now, he sat waiting again for Steve to show up—it was after 9:30 and he had to be awake—eager to tell him about the amazing offer that had come with a timing that was too good to be true and too obvious to be ignored.

Would Steve answer the invitation left for him last evening in a note taped to his door, though? It was their only way of communicating when Steve wanted to isolate, since he didn't even have a cell phone anymore. Even if he did show this morning, Tom expected resistance. A whole year of solitude had intensified one of Steve's worst traits, his pig-headed insistence on doing absolutely everything his own way. Even when it was clearly detrimental.

Tom felt a passing doubt about his own judgement.

Should he have allowed Steve to cut himself off completely from everyone? On the other hand, caring for Steve here at the farm was the only way of preventing him from disappearing entirely. Stealth and evasion had been part of his military training and he excelled at it, making it possible to survive dangerous missions. Bringing him here was the only thing that prevented him from dropping off-the-grid entirely and living holed up somewhere else totally like a hermit, without any human contact. Like so many people after a deep wounding, Steve had withdrawn from life entirely. It seemed to Tom that, far from the last year being a time of healing, Steve's self-imposed isolation had only intensified his suffering.

Given what had happened two days ago, however, on Ash Wednesday, he felt sure that something great was now in the making. Or it would be, if Steve would just make the right call.

Now it was 9:47, and the sun was about to clear the top of the magnolia tree in the boxwood garden outside Tom's study. Would Steve come in response to the urgent note?

Absently, he noticed Clayton, his tenant farmer, driving his battered, blue Chevy pickup through the gate that opened to the far hillside, then hopping out to close it behind him. Most likely, he was out checking for any newborn Angus calves that had slipped miraculously into the world during the night. Clayton was a bright soul, who loved his young wife, Lissa, and their brand new son, and loved working the farm. Tom counted them as a small miracle in his life. Lord knew, he could not think of many. His own personal life had taken hard turns. . .but that was another matter. Life could catapult you from all you wanted it to be face-first into a living nightmare. That he knew only too well.

Tom found himself hoping at least one man's nightmare would come to an end—Steve's. His future was hanging in the balance. A week ago, nearing the anniversary of Olivia's death, he announced he was unsure about staying here on the farm under Tom's care. . . .

"Where will you go? What will you do?" Tom had asked, careful not to sound too intrusive. Dealing with Steve was tricky.

"I don't know. Colorado maybe. Find a crap job, and earn enough to get by. Ski. Do some climbing. Get it together, hopefully. I can't just stay here fixing fences, hauling cattle, and soaking my head every night in memories. And I can't stay anywhere near DC. I'm too close to where my life went to hell.

"Look, I don't mean to be ungrateful, Tom. You've done more than a family friend should do. Given me a place to hide from the world. Taken on a messed up guy during your break from the Episcopal Church. Practically carried me through really bad days and nights. With my parents both gone, my sister dead, too, I had no one else to turn to. But I've been crushing time here for a whole year. I've gotta move on. Do whatever."

Tom decided to challenge this poor substitute for a plan. "Do you think that if you go to Colorado the memories will stay behind you back here?"

Steve's eyes flashed with anger. "Then you tell me what to do. You're the God guy. There's nothing behind me, and I can't see anything ahead. The only decent-paying jobs I'm good at are on security staffs, and there's no way I can deal with that. I wasn't even there to save my own wife."

Steve was trapped in the darkness of his soul. Tom had not been able, even with months of constant support and gentle counsel, to help him resolve any of his guilt or find a next step.

"Giving spiritual direction doesn't work that way. No one can tell someone else what to do."

"Well, I'm asking you or God or whoever to tell me. Or I'm just re-upping the tags on my truck and driving, and I don't give a crap where I wind up." . . . .

Tom focused on the tenant house again, hoping Steve would answer his invitation. Sunlight touched the window of his study, and Tom reached up to place the fingertips of one hand on the icy glass, greeting its rays. He smiled, feeling that maybe a greater light was rising after all—that maybe something truly great was about to happen.

On the very anniversary date of Olivia's murder, two days ago, an old friend had paid a surprise visit, and afterwards he had walked her out to her car. As she began to pull out of the gravel drive, she had braked her Mercedes and called to Tom with an afterthought. "I'm glad you're in, Tom. But by any wild chance do you know someone who can train young people to—"

What she urgently needed for her new program had stunned him.

Maybe I do know someone, he had thought. *If only Steve will recognize the incredible thing that's happening here.*

What came next would all depend on Steve's decision. Given his present state of mind, there was no guarantee it would be a good one.

During his morning meditation, Sahm felt a surge of concern—for whom?

Yesterday, after a year of ignoring his practice, he had set up a meditation altar on a small table next to the woodstove. He had neglected this important duty when he first came to Lost Lake, to block from his mind the things that were expected of him. He was tired of other people's expectations. The events of *Losar* had shaken him and changed his mind. Now, the small table held a little *thangka* with a painted image of fierce Vajrapani, also a single white stone, and a clay dish for burning herbs and incense. At the center was a small, blue Buddha-like figure carved from stone, and beside that lay his grandfather's *phurba.*

He tried to ignore the nagging sense of concern, but it kept returning until he paid attention.

Since his journey through the *Bardo,* it seemed to him that there were movements and voices just beyond the veil of sight and hearing. They came and went from his mind. He remembered what his grandfather had told him many times. "Within you lies a great ocean of abilities, *Cetan,* gathered within your soul from many lifetimes. But they must be reawakened and developed."

He stared at the *phurba.* His grandfather had wanted to get his attention, shock him into returning to his path, awakening powers he had ignored. Plunging this dagger into a pine floor plank from twelve-thousand miles away right at his feet had done it.

He knew what to do now. Letting his mind empty, in a moment it sharpened into focus with the image of someone.

Kate.

She looked pleasant, smiling as always. No reason for concern. At the center of the image, though, within her there was a small, dark cut.

What did it mean—danger? An illness?

He got up and retrieved his small goatskin bag, and took from it a *myrobalan* leaf. Beginning a healing prayer, he placed it in the offering dish, struck a match, and held the little feather of flame to it. The plant's sweet scent rose on a silver thread of smoke. By this action, perhaps he could dissipate whatever energy was troubling Kate.

An even stronger sensation came, like a small pressure within him.

Kate needs you. Go to her.

A voice deeper than his own had spoken, and it startled him. Except for the night of *Losar*, he had not experienced such a force since meeting Kate in Dharamsala.

He threw on his coat and boots.

"Come, Vajra," he said to the huge, charcoal gray half-wolf Jo had entrusted to him.

The sun was falling through broken clouds that had dropped six inches of snow overnight. On the path behind the guest cabins along the ridge to Kate's lodge, Sahm encountered the head groundskeeper, shoveling the walkway. Grady, young and robust and pitching the powdery snow far back over his shoulder, was bundled in a heavy coat and knitted hat. He did not see Sahm coming until Vajra charged up and sniffed at his hand.

"*Whoa!—daggone!*" Grady jumped and yelled in surprise. "This big guy scares the heck out of me when I don't see him coming."

The animal stepped back, silent and noble looking, watching Grady with penetrating, gold eyes.

Leaning on his shovel, Grady's breath came out in puffs. "If you're headed to the lodge to find Kate, don't bother. Ivy's working in the kitchen, and when I asked where Kate is she had no idea. Maybe she went into town."

Not so—the words came to mind forcefully.

"If she's driving, I hope she's careful. Since she got back from DC last evening, it sleeted and the road to town's iced over. But you know Kate. Nothing's going to stop her once her mind's made up."

She is at Thunder Falls.

"Perhaps she climbed the trail," Sahm said, nodding at the clouded slopes of Lost Mountain on the estate's northwest corner.

"No way. The trails are snowed-in."

Find her—the push was stronger.

It occurred to Sahm that what happened to him during *Losar* was not a singular event. He thought of the fire ritual his grandfather performed. Was it what his people, the Bönpos, called a *transmission*?—the awakening of a latent skill within a novice by an adept? That could explain the way his occasional knowings were clearer and more insistent today.

Beyond Kate's sprawling lodge, Sahm and Vajra crossed the camp road and passed beyond the first barn she had turned over to Jo. It housed her wildlife veterinary clinic, along with cages for small animals on one side and larger mammals on the other. He should be in there cleaning cages.

They crossed a small, wooden bridge over the Garnet River, where a second barn stood. Inside it, Jo was building a huge water tank for injured aquatic creatures. Also wall racks full of aquariums for lizards, frogs, turtles, and other denizens of streams and ponds she would rescue and study. On the other side was an aviary for injured birds. This was where they'd taken the fallen eagle the morning it was found.

He pictured the magnificent creature, hunkered on the lowest branches of its enclosure. Whatever was wrong with it was a great mystery. There had been a moment, though, when his eye and the eagle's had met in a split-second flash something like recognition. That was all, then nothing. The young bird just could not, or for some unknown reason, would not fly.

Just beyond this second barn, he turned north along the path to Lost Mountain. Now, he was facing into a current of icy air that flowed over the Garnet River's frozen surface and could hear water murmuring under the ice. Pulling his wool scarf up over his nose and mouth against the bitter cold, he heard the voice again.

Yes. This way.

For a quarter-mile, the path hugged the river, then turned into the snow-drifted forest and rose steeply up the eastern slope of Lost Mountain. As he struggled up it, ice-coated rocks under the snow tripped him more than once. The trail was treacherous today and the cliff over Thunder Falls would be covered in ice, making it more dangerous than usual. Clearly, she had taken this path, though. The snow's crust was broken by footprints and marks left by hiking poles. Why would she make this treacherous climb today, especially after a very long drive home just yesterday? His concern for Kate grew.

Vajra ignored the path, zig-zagging his way through the surrounding trees, alerting to noises in the winter-bare forest. The half-wolf had been a constant companion for more than a year. The magnificent creature's senses were always on high-alert, and he was fiercely loyal, protective. When a branch cracked beneath a heavy sleeve of ice, he let out a warning wolf-cry that echoed off granite faces in the brittle cold mountain air.

In a half-hour, they reached the first fork in the trail. One arm of it veered left, to the northwest, and continued upwards toward the peak of Lost Mountain. One veered right, and Sahm took that, following Kate's footprints. In thirty yards, it emerged above Thunder Falls onto a ledge some eight feet across.

When Sahm walked out on the ledge, the sound of falling water rang across the slopes. He was several hundred feet above the now distant lake, which looked like a white puzzle piece amid the stands of iced evergreens and winter-gray hardwoods. Wind had swept the ledge clear of snow, leaving only ice on the rock surface. Kate's tracks had vanished. She was here, or somewhere very near. He could sense her presence like a pulse.

But where was she? To the east rose Eagle Rock Mountain. In the southern sky, far off, he could see the dark stain of more snow clouds moving in. It would be dangerous to stay up here long.

Cautiously, he stepped close to the edge, *shoo*-ing Vajra back to prevent him from slipping. One misstep and either one of them could slide into the roaring current and plunge over the falls. Icy spray stinging his face, he scanned the view below, where the water landed in a deep, roiling pool.

There was only a slim chance a fall would land you between the circle of broken boulders that surrounded this first pool. The water churned there, black and foaming, before roaring over a second waterfall that dropped into a lower pool, then flowed south as the Garnet River. Kate had told him that before she and Jim bought this tract twenty years ago, an occasional hiker would attempt the leap—unsuccessfully. Rescue workers would find their broken body caught on rocks or branches in the shallower current down-river near where Kate's barns now stood.

Behind him, Vajra howled and pawed at the base of Thunder Rock, the massive stone that created a back wall for the ledge.

"Sahm!"

Kate was calling and waving down at him from above.

"Step back!" he called. *"Ice."*

"I wouldn't take foolish chances," she said, after he had followed a short, winding path through a stand of cedars to join her. "See, I wore my crampons."

The broad, flat top of Thunder Rock was clear except for a few, lacy traces of snow. Kate had seated herself on a small green throw, to buffer from the cold. She was smiling, but now Sahm felt a strong, deep, unsettled energy pulsing from her.

"Why did you climb up here in such conditions?" He pointed at the darkening sky. "Another storm may be coming."

Vajra was beside her, and she stroked his head. "Hello, boy, you're panting. I'll pour you some water. You could use a few swigs, too, Sahm. Though—look at you—you're hardly sweating."

"Why did you not come to talk to me," he persisted, "if something is troubling you?"

She stopped pouring water into a metal cup, and studied him. Her bright, easy expression had changed to one of intense interest. "You knew something was bothering me. Is that why you followed me? Someday you'll have to tell me how you know these things. I can't imagine every Sherpa in Tibet has your unusual abilities."

Sahm ignored the remark about his being a Sherpa, by which westerners usually meant you were a human pack mule for their expeditions.

"Let us say we are trained to pick up signs and signals," he dodged, knowing if he said the truth, she might not believe him or it would require a long explanation. "Signs like the cloud behind your eyes now. Please tell me why you've come up to this dangerous place alone."

Kate stared at the estate buildings far below, where they spread in an arc along the north shore of Lost Lake.

"I think more clearly when I'm away from *all that*.—Oh, who am I kidding? Sahm, I was feeling strong and so sure about the program we're creating, then an old memory came back. I thought I could escape it up here, but it followed me."

Sahm squatted beside her. "What is following you?" Even as he spoke those words, an image formed in his mind's eye—a small, dark trace at the center of Kate's spirit. Something was buried there.

"Three years ago, just before Jim died, I told him I wanted to start a program to help young people who need a big boost to redirect their lives. He laughed at me. 'What do you know about kids?' That was cruel in itself, because he had denied me what I always wanted, which was to have children.

"I told him I wanted to invest in human capital. The world needs every one of us working for its good. He scoffed at me even more. 'People are a waste of time,' he said. 'Money is the only capital worth investing in.'"

Sahm thought, but did not say, *Such a poor view of other human beings. And of the world.*

"Jim said, 'You're a fool to believe do-gooder intentions will help anyone. Especially young people today. They're all self-centered. All the goodness in the world won't change people if they're flawed. It's genetic in some people—especially in other races.'"

Kate winced. "He actually said that, Sahm. I felt sick."

The farm road looked forlorn, or maybe that was just how Tom saw it now. Clayton had finished in the fields. Steve still had not emerged from his white, clapboard tenant house.

Strangely, as the golden light of morning strengthened toward noon, Tom felt a darkness around him. It unsettled him. Only once before had he felt it this strongly, and that was many years ago.

During his campus ministry days at Georgetown, where he had first met Kate, a very troubled looking young man had asked to meet. The morning was bright, and they met on a bench at the university's boat center on the Potomac River. . . .

"The road just ran out," the young man had said, staring with gray eyes at the river. "It's over."

"What do you mean?" Tom questioned.

"I just flunked out of med school. It's all over for me. My father and grandfather are doctors. No other schools are going to accept me. There's no road ahead for me now."

"Failures are like signposts," he had smiled and told the distraught

young man, "pointing in a new direction. What you need to do is stop feeling sorry for yourself, stay open, and find that new path."

The conversation took turns Tom had missed. The young man pulled deeper into himself, his eyes blank, his body slumped. He stopped talking, but Tom kept pouring on a babble of cheerful encouragement. "It's not that bad. Shake it off and move on.". . . .

Tom snapped his mind out of the memory, but not before seeing the picture that was scarred into his brain. He had missed important signals. And a Washington *Post* photographer was there when the young man's body was pulled from the river.

Now he stared through the broad light of noon, in a haze of inner darkness left by that image. No sign of Steve. Was this war for another young man's future a fight that could be won? Did he himself have any better sense now of how to help someone than he did back then? His beliefs told him he had to try. He stared down the farm road, wishing he had some kind of ability that let you see inside another person's soul and know what was really going on there.

Snow had now begun to fall again over Lost Mountain and over the lake below. Big, soft flakes, falling from gray clouds coming together overhead. Sahm remained quiet, listening to Kate. The pulse of her soul had changed in a way that pained him. It felt jagged now, and in his mind's eye the dark trace in her soul had grown into a gash.

What was he to look for, in this search within her being? What would he do if he found the root of her trouble?

"I've got some great people to staff the program now," Kate was saying, "but I keep hearing Jim's voice in my head. I couldn't believe I was hearing such toxic thoughts from a man I'd known all those years. Before that, I thought that the relentless pursuit of money was what had changed Jim. I'd watched him become more greedy and distrustful the more money he stuffed in the bank. But when he said those racist things, I realized his prejudice had been there all along. My wanting to spend some of our huge fortune helping people only brought it out."

"So," Sahm said, fishing for the deeper matter, "you opened your heart and told him your deepest dreams."

"I did. I told him I wanted to help vulnerable young people who've had a rough start and fallen down in life. I said I want to see them trained in life skills, survival, and how to care for other living creatures. The things that are the spirit and backbone of this program. When I told Jim I wanted to turn two of our barns into wildlife rehab facilities—exactly the way Jo has set them up—he said, 'Oh good, a petting zoo for young criminals.'"

"Those are very bitter words."

"They stung, but not as much as when he said, 'You're not going to use my money for that kind of nonsense.'" Her voice choked. "I realized he didn't think of it as our money, certainly not mine. Everything I thought *we* had built together was *his*. In his heart, I had no real share in any of it."

The pain Kate had been concealing now emerged in a look of deep anguish.

"That last part was the most devastating. And now I wonder. Maybe I am what he called me. Just a well-intentioned 'do-gooder' who has a lot of money that someone else made. Maybe I'm being an 'idiot'—that's the word he used—and no one ever changes. Am I just an idiot, spending someone else's money, Sahm?"

How, he wondered, could such a generous, open, great soul have married such a tight, closed, shrunken one?

"*No*," Sahm countered, shaking his head forcefully. Now he knew what the dark gash within her was—a deep soul wound. "In Tibet, we say such words are a 'poison arrow.' Why would your husband say such things to you?"

Kate let out a long breath and let it dissipate in a plume on the icy air. "Maybe he was trying to protect me from myself? I am an idealist, it's true. I always look for the good in people, or at least the potential for good. In this world, that might be foolish. Maybe even dangerous."

"It is dangerous *not* to look for goodness in other people," Sahm responded, his voice forceful. "It *is* dangerous to be fearful of people, rather than compassionate. Fear causes blindness and unfavorable actions. Very bad *karma*."

Kate reached out and squeezed his arm. "Let's hope you're right, Sahm. Jim liked to tell me over and over, 'Well-meaning people can do a lot more harm than good' and 'Just throwing money at a problem doesn't fix it. People have to want to change enough to work for it, and most people are lazy and don't want to work.'"

From the forest beyond the waterfall, another tree limb broke under its burden of ice. Vajra, who had curled at Sahm's feet, bristled and barked, then settled again.

"Some of the young people coming here have had terrible things happen to them," Kate continued, stroking the half-wolf's ears. "Others have done very harmful things. I want to offer them a new perspective on life and a new start. Maybe I'm tampering with the lives of people who are already on a bad course, and that can't be changed. Scars from the past don't go away overnight. Some never do."

"Compassion is a strong medicine, Kate. But it will take time to do its work. Give them that time."

The look of pain left, and her smile slowly returned. "I hope I can be strong enough to follow my own heart for this whole, three-year trial program. I hope that's enough time for these young people to grow. The effects of poor upbringing and the rough worlds they grew up in will be very hard to change. I don't doubt that."

"Much compassion, Kate. That is what it will require."

The snow was falling heavier, and the sky was darkening fast. A long silence fell between them—on Sahm's part, a focused, listening silence. Above them, two red-tailed hawks circled. One plunged into the trees on the far side of the falls, probably after an unwary mouse or squirrel.

They needed to go back, but Sahm sensed strongly that his purpose here was not done. Words of wisdom his grandfather had said came back, words he had only half listened to before.

"We cannot know the outcome of every action. We cannot know from the beginning who our actions and words will awaken. We can only do what we believe is right, and in that way we start a new pattern in the movements of *karma*. It is up to other people to see that new pattern and move along with it. Then it can be said we have brought about change."

Kate said, sounding wistful, "Some of these young people will move against the new way of thinking and being, won't they? Or they won't see the new possibilities at all."

"That is not in our power to determine." How many times had his grandfather warned him not to predict the outcome of any action—to speak and do only what was good and right in the present moment? He felt as if the old man were right there with him, suddenly speaking into his mind right now.

"To be enlightened," he repeated, "is to understand that our whole *karma* can be lived in a single moment. If that moment is filled with compassion, we will see miracles."

Kate responded with renewed strength in her voice, "I can't imagine what I would do if we had not met in India. You're here to save me from myself, Sahm."

The great message to him during *Losar* had now become clear. Lost Lake was not a place of escape. His skills were needed, even demanded, by whatever powers had led him here and wanted to work through him.

A fleeting break in the clouds brightened the sky for a moment, and a silver light surrounded them.

"A new pattern," Kate said with conviction. "That *is* what we're creating for these young people. A new way to be. Training them how to take responsibility and care for themselves in a tough setting. And there's Jo's part of the program, giving them the responsibility to care for injured creatures. I hope these things will influence them in a new direction. That's really all we can do, isn't it?"

The pained energy radiating from Kate had eased considerably— and yet a small trace remained. Sahm wanted to say they should go before the trail down closed in with the new-falling snow. Instead he stroked the thick fur on Vajra's neck and shoulders, forcing himself to wait. Like the dark clouds and coming storm, something else felt as if it was about to arise.

"I just can't seem to get over. . . ." Kate choked up again. "Jim wanted to turn Lost Lake into an exclusive retreat for wealthy business executives. He wanted to do it for tax purposes. That plan was spelled out in a letter he left me along with his will, and I was expected to carry it out. Sahm, he never once asked about my wishes— *not once*—knowing how much I love this place. My soul is here in this wilderness. He just. . .didn't care. His total disregard for me was devastating."

So that was the tip of the arrow, then. Jim's heartless disregard for her. This was what the sense of urgency had driven him here to find—Kate, her deep heart-wound opened and the poison that needed to be countered.

"Jim is no longer here and Lost Lake has come into your hands," he said. "That is a result of past *karma*, as well. His and yours. All this was given to you."

"Two thousand acres," she said, scanning the panorama below. "Hard to believe."

She relaxed completely now, and the light fully returned to her eyes.

"It *has* all come into my hands, and Jim's letter obligated me to nothing. And this *is* the right thing to do. Keep reminding me, Sahm.

Your words are good medicine. I listen to you and it pushes back the fears and doubts. I have to follow *my* conviction, I know that. This place wasn't placed in my hands so that wealthy executives could have yet another luxury getaway. I can't *not* do this.

"And anyway," she concluded, "it's all set in motion. As I was driving home from Washington and Virginia yesterday, I heard from my friend Judge Sewell. He's deciding today on the first twelve young people for the Lost Lake Program. He believes he has the right ones for us to start out with. He'll make final choices, and they'll begin having their health checkups in a week or so. There's just one more piece to fall in place."

"What is that piece?"

"We still don't have a really qualified, wilderness survival instructor, though we may by the end of today. Fingers crossed, Sahm."

He looked at her uncomprehending.

"'Fingers crossed' means I'm making a wish, for good luck. We need to find that instructor very soon or I don't know what I'll do."

"There is no luck, Kate." The words came out of him without forethought. "Only choices."

13TH

Steve was coming up the farm road. Finally. After two weeks of avoiding contact.

Tom had held off Kate's anxious, almost daily inquiries as long as he could. From his kitchen window now, Tom could see by Steve's face that his mood this morning was dark. A bad sign. He went to the back door in the kitchen to greet him, and pour them both cups of strong, black coffee.

"I've been hoping you'd come to see me," Tom said, when they were seated in the armchairs next to the study window. "It's been too long,"

Steve slumped down, staring with vacant eyes into his steaming mug. He had not shaved and maybe not even showered.

"I have an offer for you."

The younger man did not stir.

"A couple of weeks ago when we last talked," Tom said, "I told you spiritual direction doesn't involve telling people what they should do. I'm going to go against that rule today."

Steve looked up.

"Right after we last met and you said you were leaving for Colorado, Kate Holman, phoned very early one morning. She's a long-time friend, and she insisted on meeting with me right away. She was already driving out to the farm from DC, and sounded very determined. That's Kate, a very strong and passionate woman.

"She's starting a program for young adults who are falling through the cracks in our society. These are people who our system has no other way to deal with than to place them in juvenile detention. Some are in trouble, some are warehoused there because there aren't enough foster homes or else foster care hasn't worked for them. She hopes to give them a way to start over in life, and here's the thing.

"She's got twelve of them coming to the pilot program on a property she owns up near the Canadian border in northern New York. It starts soon, and she has a couple of problems."

Steve frowned. "And?"

"The woman she hired as a liaison between the juvenile justice system and the program became pregnant and decided she wants to be at home for a year or more. Kate needs to replace her."

"If you think I'm interested in that, I'm not."

"No. I said *I* would do that. I'll be going north soon to help her administer the program."

Steve sat up a little. "You're going to take a position way up in New York? What about the farm?"

"I'll be away a lot, yes. But also transporting the students back and forth to DC for important appointments and personal business. As for the farm, Clayton manages the property and Lissa manages my books. The place will be fine, and I'll stop in occasionally when I'm back in the area."

"What about the people around here who come to you for help and support?"

"That's always been informal, and I have a very strong feeling this is what I'm supposed to do. I'll see that the people here are taken care of. But, what I have to say next isn't about me."

Steve looked wary.

"Kate's property is in a wilderness area, and the guy who was going to head the mountain and winter survival part of her program announced he's taking a job with a climbing outfitter at a resort in St. Moritz, Switzerland. Too lucrative and glamorous an offer to pass up, I guess. She's desperate to find someone with the kind of leadership and great survival-training skills this guy had. She needs that new person right now."

"And you're telling me this because I trained mountain forces in Afghanistan?" Steve replied. His expression was flat.

"You were highly commended for exceptional leadership skills under extreme conditions. You taught your men how to survive in brutal, mountain terrain in all seasons, including the dead of winter.

Yes, that's why I'm telling you. And—," Tom rushed on, because Steve was already shaking his head, "—and what exactly are the chances Kate would show up on my doorstep with an offer like this right after you told me—no, you *challenged* me—to tell you what your next move should be?"

Steve rubbed the stubble on his chin with one hand, and blew at the steam rising from his coffee.

"I don't even like punk kids. They're total bums and slackers, and they get handouts they don't deserve."

"You don't know these young people are punks or bums or slackers. You've got a harsh judge inside you, Steve. Everyone deserves help, especially when they haven't had a fair chance in the first place. I believe these young people deserve one."

"The thing is, I don't believe that, though. That's why Olivia and I had our huge disagreement. You know that's what we fought about that morning."

Where the next words came from, Tom did not know. "What if you're being given another chance?"

"For what?"

"To understand Olivia's heart."

Steve's face went red and he sat bolt upright. "You sonofa—. How could you say that to me?" He stood, slammed his cup down on Tom's desk, its contents splashing, and started toward the study door.

Tom leapt to his feet and stepped in front of him. "Running away? That's not what a Marine does."

Steve tried to push by him. "What you just said is manipulative as hell."

Tom met him chest to chest, his face in Steve's face. "*Is it?* You said yourself you have to move on. That doesn't mean just dragging your body from one place to another. It sure as hell doesn't mean running away. That's what you're doing, and it doesn't work."

Steve tried to push by, slamming into Tom with his shoulder. "I don't need this."

Tom blocked him again. "Where are you running to, Steve? You need to find a way to move on. *Really* move on inside. Hiding from life somewhere else won't do it."

Steve's eyes met Tom's, which were flashing anger. "I can plan my own life."

"*You have no plan*," Tom challenged. "You've got a Marine buddy in Colorado, who offered you a sofa to sleep on."

"Move, Tom. Or I'll move you."

Tom clenched his jaw. "You haven't resolved anything about that horrible fight you had with Olivia that morning. If you don't, you can run anywhere you want, and you'll get exactly *nowhere*."

Steve's fists were clenching.

"What if your way forward is to see what Olivia was trying to tell you?" Tom pressed. "What do you think she keeps trying to show you in all those dreams you tell me about—the ones where you say she's trying to lead you somewhere? Do you think those are just to torture you? Do you enjoy torturing yourself with all your self-condemnation? It's terrible to watch. It must be terrible to live with. Is that how you want your future to be?"

Steve was caught off-guard. Where he was right now, totally stuck in his life, was a terrible way to live. It wasn't living. And he didn't have a single, damn clue where he was going or what he would do. Tom was right that his plan to go to Colorado and bum around was no plan at all, and he had always thrived with goals and direction.

Tom's pulse pounded in his neck. "So, what are you going to do?"

"Stop pushing me, and let me think."

Tom stepped back. For no reason, or maybe to let the tension of the moment dissipate, he randomly reached out and straightened a small picture on the study wall. Then adjusted it more.

"That thing's always crooked, you know." Steve's voice had calmed a little.

Tom relaxed—and in a moment grinned at Steve, whose steam had gone out. "I did push you. It just came over me. I'm not sorry, though. Someone's got to challenge all those walls of resistance in you."

Steve let himself smile faintly for the first time in days, maybe weeks or months. How often did a man find a friend this loyal? Tom had stuck by him relentlessly through the seven horrible levels of hell this last year. Sat with him through some very long and bad nights. No soldier he'd ever met had a tougher warrior spirit. Before, he'd dismissed priests as falsely nice guys in dresses. Then he met Tom Baden, and nice was not the word he would use. Loyal and in-your-face to a fault said it.

He let another full minute pass before saying, "Well, *I'm* sorry, Tom. You put up with a lot of crap from me. I don't know why I go snap-o like that. I know I can have a flash-fire temper. So are you going to tell me the details? Or did you already forge my signature on a contract?"

Tom moved back to his desk. "You're a pain, Tanner. Sit down. Kate emailed information about the program and a job description you can read."

"I owe you the courtesy of reading it, I guess."

"You don't owe me anything."

"I said I'll read it, and then I need a couple days to think."

Tom flinched a little. Kate needed an answer. *Now* would be good.

Tom found himself on an uncomfortable edge—not for the first time in his life—the one where all his efforts ended and, if a plan was right, powers beyond his own would have to come into play. He wanted to say, "You've had a year to think, Steve," but pressed his lips together, forcing himself to say nothing. It seemed they were both poised on the edge of something momentous he couldn't name.

"If luck is on your side," Steve said, "maybe I'll like what I read."

"There is no luck," Tom pushed back. "Only choices."

CHAPTER ONE

14TH

Dhani crawled out from the rear seat of the sixteen-passenger van,
following the girl who couldn't stop talking the whole way here to the
clinic. If she sat near to him on the way back, he decided, he would pull
his hood around his face and pretend he was sleeping.

The narrow streets of Southeast DC were crowded with Friday
morning commuter traffic, and it occurred to Dhani as he and the
others jostled around inside the speeding van that this trip was like
a nightmare ride to Hell. Even though this exhaust-leaking vehicle
from Social Services had picked him up early—6:00 a.m.—it was taking
freaking forever to get to the free clinic. They had wound all over the
city in the tangle of rush hour to pick up a girl from the young women's
detention center. Every time the van hit a pothole, Dhani's head hit the
van's ceiling. The only good thing about any of this was the driver's
swearing, slapping the steering wheel, and shouting at the other drivers.

"Was your mama on crack when she had you?" "You are either
dumb, stupid, or ignorant." "Oh you do *not* want to cut me off, *muthuh*."
Strings of profanity decorated the air.

"Are you supposed to be swearing like that in front of us?" Dhani
asked her.

"None of your damned business what I do."

The driver was lost, circling around a block, making it worse. "I
know K Street. But how am I supposed to know the difference between
Third *Street* and K. . . and Third *Place* and K? DC streets are so damn
confusing."

At the Third Place and K Street Clinic, she barked. "Everyone's
butt *out*."

Thankfully, at least there was no doctor on duty at the free clinic
this morning, because Dhani been had told to expect a thorough, full
physical. That had made him crack his knuckles anxiously. Instead, a
young woman who said she was a nurse took him into an office to take
his temperature and fill in his answers on a medical form.

79

"Any heart problems."

"Nope."

"Asthma."

"Nope."

Really, his mind was elsewhere. The same pretty, dark-haired girl with the blank expression, the one he had seen at the judge's office, she was here for a checkup, too. He had seen her come in the front door as he entered the exam room. Maybe he would luck out and she would have to ride in the same van back, and maybe he could get up the nerve to talk to her. At the moment, he hated his shyness around girls.

The young case worker gave him a five-second look-over from head to toe without even asking him to unzip his hoody. "A doctor should really be doing this. But you look pretty healthy. Where did you get those little round scars on the back of your wrist? It looks like you scratched off chicken pox."

He pulled the sleeve of his hoody down over the three white spots that were exposed. "Yeah. That's what they're from."

"Roll up that sleeve. I should take your blood pressure."

"I don't want you to."

Back out in the waiting area, he slumped in a wobbly plastic chair, as other kids were called away to the examining room one by one. The place was almost full now, with only one or two open seats left. One of the other case workers was trying to explain to an intern why the couple in front of them, who had four small, wide-eyed children in-tow, were staring and looking fearful.

"They're Bhutanese refugees from a camp in Nepal. If you looked in their file you would have seen they just arrived here in DC a month ago and don't speak any English. Not a word. Talking slower and louder to them won't help. Call the translator service, and see if it's possible to get someone over here."

Two of the kids who had come on the van were seated across from Dhani in the waiting area. The wiry, wise-ass kid, Garrett, was trying to read a dog-eared copy of *Sports Illustrated* and the talky-talky, red-haired girl, Emmalyn, was acting fidgety.

She snapped her gum. "I hate waiting. It makes me nervous."

Garrett dropped the magazine and looked around to see if anyone could hear him. "Wanna slide outside for a cigarette? We'll tell 'em we're feeling a little sick from the van ride and need some air."

"We'll smell like cigarettes when we come back in."

"We'll say the driver was smoking."

So Garrett was *that* kid. He had to know, as they all did, that smoking was strictly forbidden if you were underage—and both he and Emmalyn looked to be about fifteen, just like Dhani. Like him, too, they probably also knew you had to grab any chance to slip around the rules, because there were a whole bunch that made no sense.

"Hey, scary quiet kid." Garrett looked over at him, placing two fingers up to his lips, sucking in. "Wanna smoke? All I got on me right now is legal stuff, though."

Emmalyn laughed—a goofy laugh. "Oh god. Are you sure you're going to pass the pee test?"

"I drank three liters of water this morning."

"You could die from doing that," Dhani said.

"I was joking, doofus. If I drank three liters of water, I would have pissed my pants in the van on the way here."

Emmalyn laughed again. "Stop it. Be nice to him."

"What are you, a goody-girl?"

"No, but my mama says we should treat everybody nice. That's in the Bible."

Garrett swore.

Dhani slid down in his chair and stopped listening. He studied the pretty, dark-haired girl, hoping she didn't catch him staring at her.

"CLAIRE CHAMBERLAYNE-PIERCE," the receptionist called out. "Are you here?"

"I just go by Claire," she replied, her expression flat.

The older woman looked at the ledger, her voice tinged with annoyance. "Oh, excuse me. Is that your legal name now—*Just* Claire?"

"It's what I prefer," Claire replied, maintaining her cool. She was looking at a picture of a pretty, dark-haired woman that was hanging on the wall behind the reception desk, the frame swagged with black cloth. "Did someone you worked with just die?"

"A little over a year ago. She was a beautiful person. Everyone's favorite case worker. Shot to death up in Northwest in broad daylight, and she had just been here that morning. We still miss her."

"That's horrible. I'm sorry."

"Well, *Just* Claire, you're on the list right after—," the receptionist looked up and noticed Dhani, who was watching Claire, "—*that* guy. And he's done now. So you can go right into the examining room."

"Oh goody," she replied, staring back at Dhani, with a look that said, *"Why are you watching me?"*

In that moment, Dhani thought he saw something else behind the flash of irritation. Maybe, like him, she was wary and keeping certain things to herself. Besides the fact that she was mesmerizing, that made him want to know her all the more. Yeah, if she was in the program, too, he would definitely have to figure her out.

The intern had led the Bhutanese family to a corner, where the parents sat ignoring the four children who were chasing each other in a circle, screaming.

Shortly, Claire emerged from the examining room, followed by the clinic helper.

"GARRETT OBER."

Garrett stood, and smiled at Claire. "Hey, there's an empty seat right over here by me. Why don't you grab it? I'll be back in couple minutes."

Emmalyn folded her arms and looked wounded. "Uhh. Really?— Such a flirt."

"Hey, it's not like we're out on a date here. Just chill."

Claire remained expressionless and looked around the room. There was an empty chair next to Dhani, and when she looked his way their eyes met.

Dhani opened his mouth, and what came out was, "They didn't make you do a pee-test, did they? They didn't make me."

Garrett, who was entering the exam room, snorted over his shoulder. "Holy crap. You *are* a doofus. Who asks a hot girl if she just took a pee test?"

Dhani sank low in his chair.

Claire walked directly up to him. "Was anyone sitting here?"

He sat up a little. "No. Um. You can if you want to. I'm not sure why you would, though."

Grateful and relieved, he smiled as she slid onto the chair and her arm brushed his.

"And the answer is *no*," Claire continued, sitting beside him. "They didn't make me do one of those tests. Which is surprising, considering all the other embarrassing and intrusive things that happen to you in this system. I hate that everyone else has the power to make decisions about my life. It's like they've got invisible handcuffs on us all the time. We're always having to out-think them."

. . .*invisible handcuffs*. . . . Dhani liked how she spoke and that she thought about out-thinking people.

"So—," he began and faltered.

"So—*what?*"

"What did you do to wind up in the system?"

"Well, aren't you little Mr. Investigator."

He wanted to retreat, but grinned and took a chance. "Am I being *intrusive?*"

She didn't smile.

"Sorry. You don't have to tell me anything."

"No, I'll tell you. I figure since we're going to be in the same program, pretty soon we're going to be sitting around a campfire singing 'Kum Ba Yah' and being pressured to tell everyone stuff we don't want to talk about. In case you haven't figure it out yet, that's the best way to get brownie points. You let them think you're being 'open' and 'honest' and 'vulnerable.' Crying a little works, too."

Her eyes looked hard, which surprised him. Then the look he thought he had seen behind her flat expression—one of sadness—flashed for a second and was gone.

"I didn't do anything to get into the system. My parents are a couple of spoiled brat rich kids who got caught dealing cocaine. They're in prison for twenty years."

"Twenty years? Musta been a lot of cocaine. But it doesn't make sense that you're here. You didn't do anything wrong."

"No, but my grandparents on both sides are FFV."

Dhani had a blank look.

"First Family of Virginia. They're what's known as 'old money', and they have big-deal, 'blue-blood pedigrees.' My parents weren't married when my mom got pregnant with me. They were in college and doing a lot of drugs. The first time they got busted for cocaine use, they were cut off from all the money. By both sides. That was their excuse when they started dealing drugs hardcore. They were angry about being disinherited."

Dhani was following along, most of it anyway. "When your mom and dad went to jail, wasn't there anyone else to take care of you?"

The flat look came back. "My so-called grandparents said that since my mom was on drugs I might have been 'damaged' during her pregnancy. I wasn't their 'problem.' That's what I've been since then. Someone's problem. And that's why I hate having both their last names."

"Wow. Sorry. That really sucks."

"What also really sucks is that people in this system act like they know you, when they only know you as a case number. They put on this pretense of caring about you by using your first name at the start of every sentence."

She crossed her legs, clasped her hands around her knees, and leaned toward Dhani with an exaggerated look of concern.

"'So, *Claire*, how are you feeling today—are you angry, sad, scared?' 'Tell me, Claire, why did you punch your foster sister in the face and chip her teeth?' 'You're always so quiet, Claire, tell me what's going on in that bright mind of yours.'—Oh, and flattery. They love to use flattery to make you think you can trust them and open up. But you can't."

"Can't what?"

"Trust them *or* open up. Are you even listening?"

Someone interrupted. "Why *did* you punch your foster sister in the face and chip her teeth?"

Dhani and Claire looked across the room. Emmalyn had obviously been eavesdropping, and was wide-eyed.

"You try living with everyone dumping on you because you're 'the poor little rich girl.' What would you do if your foster sister stole your makeup, your jewelry, and your clothes because 'your parents will just buy you more. . . *when they get out of prison, ha ha ha.*'"

"Is that how you landed in juvenile detention?" Emmalyn pursued.

"No. I was running illegal bitcoin transactions on the dark web. What do you think?"

Emmalyn blinked. "What is bitcoin? What's a dark web?"

"Oh my god, read a newspaper."

Dhani was thinking that behind Claire's expression were so many of the intense feelings he had, but never dared to let out. "Did you knock her out at least?"

Claire looked at him uncomprehending.

"When you punched your foster sister. Did you knock her out? Because if she stole your stuff she totally deserved it."

She grinned, then laughed. "You're too funny. Actually I didn't hit her, I pushed her away when I caught her stealing from my purse one more time and she hit her face on the dresser. I don't hit people. She screamed and said I assaulted her for no reason, and because of that they said I was a troubled, high-risk kid, and sent me to detention nine months ago. Ridiculously unfair. But you know, it's not like we have any adults who really stick up for us, do we?"

"What if you told them the truth?"

She laughed again. "If you give them any information it always works against you. It doesn't get you out of their control, and they send you for counseling with some poor slob who's already overloaded with social services kids. Total waste of time. And boring. 'Why did you hit her, if you knew that would get you in trouble?' 'Do you understand what antisocial behavior is?' And then you wind up having to tell them, again, every stupid detail about your rich, drug-dealer mother and father and the wealthy grandparents who pretend you don't even exist."

Garrett came out of the exam room then, and paused. "What's up? Everyone looks so serious. Who died?"

"EMMALYN HATFIELD," the case worker called.

Emmalyn rose, staring at Claire, now with a solemn look. "So how do you handle all the anger you hafta have?"

"Oh, Lord. You sound like a shrink," Claire shot back.

"Don't use the Lord's name."

"The Lord's name isn't 'Lord'," Claire responded.

"I'm serious," Emmalyn said. "If I was you, I would be really angry."

"Thank you. But I'm not. I'm over it all."

Garrett smirked. "You look like you don't give a crap about anything. But you sure sound angry."

18TH

Sahm finished stacking the cord of firewood under the shed roof on the sheltered east side of his cabin, facing the forest. Grady's crew had dumped it there for him. The protective evergreens and the little shed roof attached to the cabin would keep snow off the woodpile.

This last stack would keep the woodstove burning through the end of winter.

The sense of urgency that had driven him to find Kate had not fully left him.

Something is coming.

Now his muscles were burning. Walking a few paces toward the forest that sloped up Eagle Rock Mountain, he leaned against a huge boulder at the woodland's edge. A glacier had dropped the seven-foot tall, granite giant here millenia ago. It now rested beneath the gangly limbs of a four-story, white pine thirty feet from his cabin. He would rest up here in the late winter sunshine that was reflecting off the lake, then go clean cages over in Jo's barns.

Pressing his back against the rock, he felt a slight movement made through his heavy coat, as if an electric feather was tracing across his shoulder blades. Surprised, he saw the world start to shimmer again, just as he had seen it the night of Tibetan New Year. The trees and snowdrifts in the woods wavered, then became solid again.

His grandfather had called on great powers of the earth to help Sahm. At odd moments, with no pattern or trigger he could detect, the energies that seemed to have awakened in him came and went. He thought of Kate and how she seemed so much lighter—actually, physically brighter—after their encounter up on Thunder Rock. That day, he had felt like a shaman's magical bone flute, lifted and played through by invisible forces and set aside again.

He was turning these things over in his mind, when a voice came from behind.

"Ever see what's on the far side of that big boy?"

Randy Wolfmoon, the climbing instructor who lived in one of the eight cabins down the lake, was walking toward him. The morning had warmed a little, and Randy's parka was unzipped, revealing his thin, muscular build. "Almost no one knows it's there, because it's well hidden."

Randy walked past him, around the boulder and the white pine, and pushed through a thick stand of rhododendrons. He stopped on the far side of the stone giant among last year's broken, brown ferns poking up through melting snow. "Take a look. Surprised you didn't find this already. You'll like it a lot."

Sahm followed, pushing branches aside and looking where Randy pointed.

The whole side of the boulder that was concealed by the under-growth was covered in rusty stripes made by the stone's iron oxide, also in gray-green shields of lichen. At chest-height, chiseled into the stone, was the image of a bird with its wings spread wide. It was maybe two feet across and distinct enough but eroding. Wind, water, and ice had dimmed the ancient artist's rust-colored totem.

"Petroglyph. Probably carved by my people, the Mohawk," Randy stated. He ran his hand over the rock, but not the image. "It's an eagle. A messenger from the spirit world. The elders I know say this boulder marks a very sacred place. Which is why Kate hasn't told anyone we found this glyph. She doesn't want someone harassing her to haul it off to a museum. She believes this spot is sacred and the stone needs to stay here."

Did that explain what had just happened? Sahm laid his hand on the boulder just above the eagle image. Sunlight filtering through the wind-stirred branches of the white pine made the image appear to be moving. He felt again for a sign from the stone, but nothing came. The rock was rough, cold, and still. Perhaps he had only imagined what he had felt.

"Some say it's a wisdom stone," said Randy. "But, you know, the old ones believed in a lot of things that are just myths and legends."

That this stone was known to connect to the old powers made Sahm smile. He knew what all Bönpos know—that everything, even a so-called inanimate object, has its own type of energy and consciousness.

"Do you not believe in the old ways anymore?" he asked.

"I didn't for a long time," Randy replied. "I thought that what my ancestors believed was backward. I thought their old ways were to blame for them losing out to the Europeans. But then I started to lose something of myself in science and western culture. And I began to think that maybe the old ones knew what they were talking about when it comes to our connection to everything. Now—well, let's say I'm opening myself to the old ways again."

"To be open is good," Sahm nodded. He thought about how he, like Randy, had also tried to pull away from the ancient paths.

Running one hand over the boulder's rough gray and rust-colored surface again, Sahm startled, thinking he caught the sound of faint whispers just out of hearing.

20TH

By the eighth ring, Steve wondered if anyone was home at the other end of the line.

Tom had left a note on the tenant house door. "Urgent. Call 303—"

Now, seated in Tom's study, he could see Tom outside with Clayton, probably planning how to manage the farm while he was away. He knew he had kept Tom waiting for days for an answer, and to Tom's credit he'd backed off and hadn't pressed.

The whole thing about teaching punk kids, though—well, it was a barrier he could not get past.

The phone was ringing at the other end. Judging by the tone of the note, he guessed his buddy in Colorado had found a job for him. That would make it much easier to escape there. It would be hard to tell Tom he was turning down Kate Holman's offer, but it was what it was.

"Hello?" a woman's voice answered.

"Hey, it's Steve Tanner. Returning Karl's call."

"Karl didn't leave the message, I did. I'm Sheri, his wife." Her voice sounded strained. "I wanted to let you know Karl is in treatment."

Steve fast-rifled through the possibilities—*cancer, kidneys. . . .*

"What's the diagnosis?"

"Diagnosis?—Alcohol and opioid addiction. He also got into fentanyl, and he overdosed."

"Whoa, sorry. I had no idea."

"No idea? You guys were such close buddies in Afghanistan and you didn't know he was an addict even while he was there?" She backed off. "I'm sorry. That was unfair. I'm sure most of you guys weren't using. It's just—," she sounded like she might break into tears, "—it's been really hard getting him to admit he has a serious problem. I have a bunch of bad bruises to show for it. This is a very, very bad time for you to come out here."

Steve was still focused on Karl. "How long will he be in treatment?"

"Months, I don't know. I love him, but I want them to keep him for as long as it takes. I'm not letting him in this house again the way he was, losing it, punching holes in walls. I don't think my father and brothers will let him come near me again."

He flipped through his memories of Karl. Fun. Loud. Ballsy. The mental image of him shooting up, hitting his wife, jammed Steve's circuits. "Is he going to be okay? Are you okay?"

"I don't know. I'm a total mess right now and so is he. What I do know is, I don't want him to become one of the twenty-two combat vets who off themselves every day. I know the V.A. is a mess, but there are other ways to deal with your problems. Why don't you guys face your issues before they ruin your lives?"

"What if you are being given another chance to understand Olivia's heart?" Tom's words landed like a kick in the gut.

"Sorry, Sheri. Really. Tell him if there's anything I can do. . . ."

After the call, he stared out the window a long time, until Tom came back into the study.

"Steve?"

He stared out the window.

"Come back from wherever you are, Steve. You do know how to disappear when you want to."

Go. . . no go, Steve thought. *This is it.* "Tell me more about this wilderness survival program. And about this Kate Holman. What are you guys expecting—the real wilderness survival deal or nicey-nicey stuff? 'Cause I definitely won't do that."

An hour later, standing outside the back kitchen door, Steve looked only a little less undecided. "Tell me you really think this is a good idea."

Tom shook his head. "Up to you now, Steve. Am I calling Kate or not?"

Five minutes later, after waiting on a knife-edge, Tom watched the younger man's back recede down the farm road.

Be grateful, he thought, *for first small steps.*

Steve's verdict—"Sure, whatever"—was not the enthusiastic reply he was hoping for. Yet Tom felt more buoyant right now than he had since the tragedy that took Olivia's life and invaded the young man's mind and soul. And his own. But what a difference a chance offer could make. Or was it more than chance? Given all he had gone through in his own life and in the institutional church, the truth was he had lost a lot of ground in his own faith. Maybe there was also a chance that could be turned around.

Kate answered on the first ring and sounded happy he was calling.

"You told me when you visited that morning," said Tom, "'Maybe Lost Lake will be a place where we can see miracles happen.' Well, I believe I have the first one for you. Or at least maybe the rough beginnings of one."

27TH

The impression was stronger the closer he got to the first barn. The sense that some energy was building had returned.

Sahm entered the clinic, knowing that Jo would not be there—she was away for three weeks at conferences—and as he quietly slid open the big door that led into the aviary he remembered yesterday's encounter with Jo and her vet tech, Ron Cambric.

"All the tests are done and the experts have weighed-in," Jo had told him.

He had smelled the usual scents of medicines coming from the various enclosures, and also the more pungent smell of straw dirtied with animal waste that he would need to sweep up. The door of the eagle's enclosure was closed tight, and Jo and Ron stepped back from the one-way glass they'd been observing the creature through.

"What's happening with this bird just isn't normal. No injuries. No disease. It's so weird."

This morning, alone, Sahm stared into the eagle's private enclosure, his senses burning like nerve endings coming awake.

The eagle was a mystery.

"Who are you? Why have you come?—Are you even real or are you a spirit?"

The eagle's eyes opened slowly, peering at him with intensity.

Sahm felt the gaze searching within him, as if trying to awaken old, old memories. . . .

. . . *of circling on the wind, high in an icy blue sky.* . . .

Then the eyes closed and the eagle ducked its head again.

Behind the twitter of smaller birds convalescing here in the aviary, a deep silence hung in the air like a thick veil.

2

APRIL

4TH

Dhani's hands slid down the rough climbing rope, searing burn-stripes into his palms. The teetering rope bridge, the hand-over-hand rope across the mud pit, and single-rope swing across the stream had raised blisters on both palms. On his right hand, a small red stripe appeared where the skin had torn through and the raw, red flesh stung.

With the fresh cuts, he flexed his hands and winced.

"Usually it's the fat kids that can't climb the ropes," one of his gym coaches had jeered, humiliating him in front of the fifty or so other guys in class by grabbing Dhani's upper arm and digging his fingers into the thin bicep. "You should lift some weights, dude. You're weak."

Others were passing him now, scrambling up the twelve-foot wall of boards—even the hot girl Claire, who leaned back until her body was almost parallel with the ground and was hand-over-handing it up the rope right beside him.

He flexed his stinging hands again, and watched her, dejected. In the mild, April afternoon air, she was hardly sweating. He was soaked.

Dhani fought back embarrassment and the intense desire to quit. Eric Trovert, one of the psychologists running the Lost Lake program, had set up this day, with a ropes course and a picnic at a church camp out in the Virginia countryside—*why?*

"So we can start to get acquainted—all you guys and us," Trovert had said, with a wide, hey-I'm-your-new-friend grin. He looked to be in his early thirties, fit, and his teeth were so white Dhani wondered if they were real.

Right. Everyone was going to get acquainted with the fact that he had very little upper body strength. *Good call, Trovert. So how come you're not out here running the course?*

"Hey, hoody man," a voice called from above.

Rocco, the muscly guy, was hanging on at the top of the wall by one arm, reaching down with the other. Dhani had watched him scale the wall like it wasn't there and disappear down the other side, and now he had swung himself back over to this side. "They said you're having trouble. Try it again and grab my hand. I'll pull you up."

Dhani looked at Claire, who was almost to the top. Accepting help meant further humiliation.

"C'mon."

Dhani's face brightened redder and hotter than exertion had made it already.

Rocco had taken off his t-shirt and even if he hadn't, anyone could see he was solid muscle and didn't look like most other guys their age. He had a swarthy complexion, the shadow of a beard, and now, shirtless, you could see the five-star tattoo beneath the hair on his left pec. He was still reaching down, offering to help, the thick muscles in his thighs and calves flexing.

Right. You're posing up there so everyone can see you're hot.

Compared to Rocco, Dhani felt like an idiot. A mouse. *"Everyone"* meant the ten other kids at this stupid, get-to-know-each-other event.

Why didn't Trovert plan a day that was more chill, like just a bonfire with barbecue, hotdogs, burgers, cold ones, and excellent music pumping on some wireless bluetooth speakers?

He shook his head at Rocco and glared at the wall. He could just walk around it.

"Don't do it, dude," Rocco insisted. "Don't give up. Just get up high enough to give me your hand. I'll help a little and you can use your legs—see, like she's doing."

Now Carter, the really athletic-looking girl with the cold blue eyes, had run up from behind, grabbed the swaying rope Claire had abandoned, and was scaling the wall. At the top, she heaved herself up onto the highest board, then disappeared down the other side.

Dhani felt miserable. *Yeah—like the girls are doing and I can't. Perfect.*

The reason he couldn't climb, he wanted to shout, was that someone had once twisted his arm till an elbow ligament tore. That remained behind pressed lips.

Rocco was still reaching down to him. "Let me help you."

Gritting his teeth, Dhani threw himself up the wooden wall. Grabbing the rope as high as he could, he pulled his body up with all his strength, banging his knees against the boards, bruising his kneecaps and ignoring the burning pain in his hands. Hanging on with his left arm, he shot his right, weaker arm up further and grabbed the rope higher above him, flailing his legs until he'd hoisted himself another two feet. His feet scrambled and slipped against the boards below.

A huge hand thumped him between the shoulder blades, grabbed a fistful of his hoody, and he felt himself yanked upward. Legs kicking and feet sliding, Dhani pushed as best he could.

"Geez, you're sweating like crazy, dude. It's hot out here. Why don't you lose the hoody?"

With a huge heave on Dhani's part and Rocco's, Dhani was at the top of the wall and threw one leg over so that he was straddling the top board.

"No offense, but that thing kinda smells." Rocco wiped the hand he had grabbed Dhani's hoody with on his red gym shorts. "Like I said, you're soaked. Didn't they tell you we were doing a ropes course today?"

There was actual concern in this guy's voice, Dhani thought. But he did not look Rocco in the face. He looked at the ground below him on the other side of the wall.

"How do I get down?"

"See the pegs in the wall? Put one foot on the second or third peg down, swing your other leg over, and slide yourself down a little till you can grab the first one. They're staggered—left, right, left, right—all the way." Rocco slid over the back side of the wall, and took two steps down—then back up. "Like that."

Dhani hesitated. His hands were shaking.

"I don't like heights either," Rocco admitted. "My hands get sweaty and shaky."

Another one of the girls had arrived at the wall—Tia Leesha, who seemed scared of everything, even the ladybugs out here in the country. Also another of the guys—the short, thin, blond kid with the Arab-sounding name, Jalil Malik. He had taken off the black knit Kid-robot cap he had shown up in and it was stuffed into the waistband of his shorts, and now he stood at the bottom of the wall eyeing it.

"Oh, no way." Tia Leesha closed her arms around herself, grabbing her elbows. "We city kids. Why they making us do this course?"

Jalil clasped his hands together and bent down, offering her a step up.

"I can't climb no rope."

"I'll push your butt," Jalil smiled.

"You don't touch my butt."

"Okay then, you're on your own." Jalil turned to the wall, and grabbed one of the ropes. "Hey, can you give me a hand?" he called up.

Rocco ignored him and shouted down to Tia Leesha. "Come on, girl. Just get up high enough so I can grab you."

"Hey, you helped that other kid," Jalil said, huffing, struggling up the rope.

Rocco continued to ignore him.

As if she had noticed Rocco peering down at her for the first time, Tia Leesha's face broke into a grin. "Oh well, if *you're* gonna grab me." She stepped toward the wall.

"Just your hand."

She began grunting her way up the rope. "I... accept...."

Dhani had enough of girls showing him up, and he needed to make room.

He slid his second leg over the top board, looking down carefully between the wall and his body, until his right foot met the third peg down. Then he lowered himself a little, and grabbed the top peg with his left hand.

"Come on, girl. You got this," Rocco was saying from his straddle position. "You don't even need my help."

Dhani had made it to the ground, and didn't hear the muffled reply.

Breaking into a jog, he set out again on the wooded path that led back to the picnic and recreation area. At least he wouldn't be the last one to reach the end of the course.

From behind, he heard Rocco call after him.

"*Hey, you're welcome.*"

They were two hours south of New York City, heading north on the interstate. When they had packed the truck before daybreak this morning, Tom said, "You look a little brighter today."

With his decision, Steve felt in control again, the way he had as a platoon leader in the Marines. "Yeah it's a relief to be in motion. The more I've thought about it, the more I like the idea of heading to the mountains. I like the wilderness. Always have. I like the way it challenges you. I'm much better there than in cities and suburbs."

As the sun rose and miles blew by, banter with Tom ranged from hockey—their team, the Capitals, was headed to the playoffs—to Tom's role at Lost Lake. Steve was especially aware today that Tom rarely mentioned his wife. "What does Germaine think about you taking on this job instead of going back into church work?"

Tom gripped the steering wheel and shifted a little in his seat. "Not a clue."

"Did you email and tell her?" A few details came back to Steve's mind. Germaine was an art restoration expert, specializing in ancient architecture and artwork. She had been in Europe for some vague amount of time. Steve had never seen her once during his year at the farm.

"Yes, I did," Tom said. And no more.

Steve had not asked Tom about Germaine's long absence and he decided not to press him now. It was none of his business, really. He needed to focus on the survival program that was shaping up in his mind.

Just north of New York City, Steve looked up and noticed someone standing on an overpass above the interstate. As the truck passed under it, the figure of a young boy looked down on them, staring.

For a second, Steve's eyes locked with the boy's, and he felt his pulse pick up. Kids even younger than this one planted I.E.D.s in Afghanistan.

". . .Steve?" Tom repeated. "I said what do you think about the Caps trading their goalie to Colorado? He's the best in the NHL."

"Oh, uh—bad decision." The image of the boy staring down would not leave his mind. For some reason, his neck and shoulders had become tense.

In three more hours and two hundred miles, they were into the mountains of upstate New York. As soon as the truck angled off the highway onto a narrow back road, the world was transformed.

Steve stared out the side window, rubbing his neck, trying to ease a dull headache. A late-season snow had blanketed the forest-covered mountain peaks and river valleys with a thin coating of white. The pine trees looked like brushes dipped in silver ice. He felt shaky.

"Kate says this time of year is called 'Mud Season,'" Tom said. "When all this snow thaws, everything turns into a sloppy mess."

Steve was barely listening. His heartrate picked up as the mountains surrounded and closed in on them. He was scanning the thick clusters of trees hanging over the road, a habit that had stayed with him after his return from combat.

What are you looking for—snipers? he mocked himself. *You're not in a war zone anymore.*

In another hour, Tom slowed his truck to a crawl as the entered the east side of Lake Placid village, a postcard town with a small lake bright as a mirror at its center and ringed by tall, jagged mountains. "There's the Olympic Center, where the 'miracle on ice' took place. No one expected our U.S. hockey team to crush the Russians."

Steve studied faces along the street. Tourists flooded the sidewalks, dipping into shops or wandering into the streets, generally oblivious of moving cars and trucks. He was carefully searching faces and studying hands in coat pockets. Every micro-expression and every small gesture could mean something.

All the Corps' training is still there. Like it's hardwired into me.

He rubbed the tight neck muscle that was now giving him a splitting headache and forced himself to look away.

Tom looked over at him. "What's up?" Then winked. "You maintaining radio silence?"

"Too long in the truck, that's all," he lied. From all around, he sensed the potential for danger.

Two miles west of the village, Tom turned up a heavily wooded mountain road that became steeper, narrower, and more rugged as they bumped along. An old, blue van wheeled too fast around a curve, and as Tom swung right to avoid it, a branch slapped at the side view mirror.

"Not a good place to run off the road," Tom said, staring into the steep, rocky ravine and roaring stream beneath the narrow bridge they were passing over. The twisting road kept rising up a heavily forested slope, and they passed sudden openings in the trees that revealed dramatic, snow-covered mountain vistas to the east.

"Sure is beautiful," Tom said. "But man, these mountains look like they can be real hostile. There's six million acres of mostly raw wilderness surrounding all these high peaks and river gorges."

Once again, Steve was no longer listening. He was fighting to maintain control.

Kamdesh.

That was the last place and time he had felt hemmed-in and trapped by high mountains and an ominous silence. One that concealed ambushers who watched through the scopes of rifles and mortars. Every one of them waiting for a moment when his squad's guard was down.

He had not let his guard down. Even when he wanted to. He had not even slept fully, deeply, for months, amped-up by the pills the Corps had issued. When he did, there were dreams. Faces of those lost.

"By the way," Tom asked, "have you been thinking through your survival program?"

That had been forgotten a couple hundred miles ago. "Yeah. I have."

In five more jolting miles, Tom hit the brakes outside a gate that closed off a dirt road. Beyond the *No Trespassing* signs, the twisting track disappeared into deep, winter woods.

Steve rolled down his window. The scent of pine, cedar, and balsam flooded the truck. Out among the trees were boulders the size of Tom's pickup, where anything could be concealed. Behind the small, rhythmic clicks of the old truck's engine, Steve felt the disquieting silence of the wilderness.

"Kate calls this her 'camp road'," Tom said, jumping back into the truck after opening the gate.

Steve's palms were damp. "I thought Lost Lake was an estate? This looks like the road to nowhere."

"That's the idea. Keeps people from driving back in to her place. We've still got two miles to go. Hang on."

Steve's hand clenched the door handle. *Hang on. That's what I'm doing.*

Sahm knew he must act quickly, if the imperative that had just come to him was correct. It was now or never.

After the morning he was guided to Kate, he had been largely distracted by work in the clinic. But at odd moments, he continued to sense voices and movements flowing around him. One moment, he would be scraping out enclosures in the aviary. The next moment, an *almost*-heard voice in the back of his mind tried to tell him something. It was like listening to a radio signal coming in and out—mostly out—of range.

I must make my mind clearer, he had chided himself.

This morning, he had climbed on top of the boulder beside his cabin and cleared his thoughts, when an inner directive rushed at him with force.

His mind focused on the female northern goshawk that had been delivered into Jo's care by State conservation officers. The poor, battered creature had made a poorly-timed *swoop* in front of a logging truck, probably fixated on a small rodent, and collided with its windshield.

"Unlikely she'll recover," Jo had said before leaving on her break.

"Are we putting her down?" Ron Cambric, her vet tech, had asked, shaking his head sadly.

"Not yet. She's really struggling, but I want to give her a fighting chance."

After exhaustive medical intervention by both Jo and a local avian vet, though, the goshawk had failed to thrive. The treatments were dictated by the injuries. Styptic powder to stop blood-loss from three broken long-feathers. But the bird had first shrieked in pain, then grown listless, showing no interest in food or water. Her weight dropped by ounces a day, and she clung, eyes shut and tilting to one side on a low branch in her enclosure.

Ron had said yesterday, shaking his head. "She's not responding. It takes a lot for Jo to want to put an animal down, but tomorrow's probably it for this poor girl."

In his mind as he rushed, Sahm heard again the bird's shrieks of pain. The thought was back, more like a faint voice.

Take the phurba. You know what you must do.

He made his way down the lakeshore, the dagger resting in his pocket. What he had to do would be swift and merciful. It was Saturday, still early, and he knew that in Jo's extended absence, Ron would not rush to show up to complete his rounds. If he hurried, he would beat Ron to the goshawk's cage.

The closer he got to the clinic, the stronger and clearer the voice grew.

Free her from suffering.

Inside the aviary, Sahm watched the goshawk through the bars of her enclosure, admiring her. A mask of blue-gray bridged the yellow beak and surrounded her golden eyes. Dark-blue-gray feathers formed a mantle over her shoulders, and a white-and-black band of feathers wrapped her breast. She was emaciated and tilting at more of an angle than yesterday, her breastbone sharp as a keel, and looked nearly dead. How she still clung to her perch, Sahm did not know.

Slipping his coat off quickly, Sahm prepared himself. He would be quick about it. Taking the *phurba* from his coat pocket, he held it out in front of him—then he made three, swift, strong, horizontal slices in the air, and began uttering a prayer.

To his surprise, a tingling began under the arch of his ribcage. It shot up to his shoulder, down his arm and into the fingers of his right hand, in which he held the *phurba* pointed at the goshawk.

The bird lifted her head and stared straight at him, its dark pupils widening then narrowing to points as it focused on Sahm's face. Eye to eye they held each other's gaze.

From the depths of memory, Sahm recalled his grandfather performing this ritual for a dying horse owned by a widow.

Noble and beautiful one of the skies, Sahm chanted, moving toward the goshawk, *the ancient forces of the Earth have sent me to end your pain and struggle.*

The *phurba* felt hot, as if a current was flowing from his hand out through the blade.

May you, and I, and all sentient beings be free from suffering—

"Sahm! *Stop!*"

Ron was striding through the door, looking angry. "What are you *doing?*"

"I came to free this poor creature from pain."

"By stabbing her? Oh my god, when we put them down, we don't do it that way. We use a drug. A kind of medicine to stop the heart."

Confused, Sahm let the hand holding the *phurba* sink to his side. "You use a medicine to kill?"

Ron approached the cage, carrying a small, tan leather satchel. "Only when we have to, yes. It's kinder than letting her starve to death. She still hasn't eaten. Jo told me this morning not to prolong her suffering, and to give her a shot of pentobarbitol. It acts in seconds."

"Healing her is kinder still."

"Hey, come on, man. It's hard enough for me every time I have to do this. And what exactly were you doing?"

"I was offering a prayer for her release from suffering."

Ron looked skeptical. "So wait—you were trying to heal her, not kill her? Then why are you holding that dagger looking thing?"

"It is part of a very old ritual I am trying to recall. In our way of thinking, the *phurba* makes the prayer more powerful by cutting away bad *karma* from previous lifetimes. It can also heal her by imparting life energy."

"You think this bird was alive in other lifetimes. As what—another animal? A person?"

"That, I do not know. But yes, every living thing moves along a spiral of many lifetimes. Up. Or down. Will you give her just a little more time? A prayer for healing has gone out to her. She is resting, and does not appear to be in pain."

Ron looked inside the enclosure at the goshawk, tilting on her low perch. She appeared to be sleeping.

"She's such a beautiful girl. And you're right. She is peaceful. Jo may be really ticked at me, but I'll ask if we can give her one more day."

Sahm slid the *phurba* into his coat pocket again.

"Before you go—," Ron nodded toward the freezer against the far wall, where road-killed rodents were stored, then at one of the large enclosures, "—the eagle can use another rabbit."

Then he added as an after-thought, "Don't do this again, Sahm. If Jo had caught you, she would have tossed you out of here on your head. You've been here long enough to know that the rule is minimal contact. You feed and keep them clean. That's all."

"Chamberlayne-Pierce," Emmalyn asked. "What kinda name is that?"

Claire was walking just ahead of her, with Dhani trailing after, on the gravel path from the picnic pavilion to the parking lot.

"You did great on the course, guys," Eric Trovert had said, clapping his hands. "You helped each other a lot. Now you seven—Rocco, Claire, Carter, Garrett, Emmalyn, Makayla, and Dhani—get the coolers and supplies from my SUV. The rest of you set up the tables. Work as teams, and let's keep the great connections going."

Claire sounded annoyed at Emmalyn. "It's just a name. I wish Trovert hadn't announced it to the whole world."

"It's a great name," said Makayla.

"Well, I hate it, so there's that. And I get teased about it a lot."

Dhani thought Makayla was one of the sweetest and thinnest girls he had ever met. Her collar bones showed beneath her tee-shirt, and her cheekbones weren't high so much as protruding above slightly sunken cheeks. How had she made it through the ropes and obstacle courses, when she looked like she could break? But she had been genuinely nice, and smiled shyly at him all day.

"It's still kinda cool," Makayla finished, and let it go.

Carter snickered.

Garrett, the wise-ass guy they had met at the clinic, butted in. "It's a rich-girl-sounding name."

Claire muttered something at him.

Rocco was already at the SUV when they got there, along with the girl named Carter Madison. He had opened the back end, and inside were three very large white coolers. "Hey, Garrett—that's your name, right? How about you and me grab the big heavy one."

"Nah. How about *me* and Carter work as a team. You can have this guy instead." Garrett slapped Dhani on the chest, and looked at Carter. "How about it there, Ponytail? You wanna be with me?"

Carter turned to him, cold blue eyes void of any expression.

Dhani had been thinking all day there was something about this girl that made him uneasy. She was pretty and athletic, but she seemed to be looking through everyone, coldly, as if they weren't even there. She reminded him of a shark.

Carter ignored Garrett, took hold of one handle of a cooler, and looked at Claire. "You. *Cham-ber-layne-Pierce*." She said each syllable distinctly. "Take the other side."

Claire grabbed the handle and avoided looking at her.

Garrett stepped up to the big cooler Rocco had his hand on. "Guess it's you and me, muscles."

Dhani was left to haul the third cooler with Emmalyn, while Makayala—obviously too thin to carry such a load—reached for the bags filled with paper plates and cups. He wondered if his time in this program was going to be like every gym class he'd ever been in, where he was picked last or paired with someone else no one wanted on their team.

The two of them stepped up to the back bumper of the SUV, and took opposite handles on the cooler Rocco had already lifted out and set on the ground.

"*Whoa!*" Garrett yelled, staggering backwards and scraping his sneaker down the side of Dhani's ankle. He dropped his end of the cooler. The lid popped up, and ice and soft drink cans clattered out on the ground.

"That's ridiculously heavy."

"It's not that bad," Rocco responded. "Come on. Pick up the cans, man. Let's go."

Instead, Garrett looked over at Carter who had a faint smirk on her face. Pink crept up his neck, and he glared at Rocco. "You did that on purpose. You gave me the heavy end."

Rocco covered his mouth with one hand to hide a grin. "The heavy end? Dude, if you couldn't handle it, you shoulda said so. It's all right. This isn't a contest."

"You saying I'm weak?" Garrett glanced at Carter then back at Rocco, his face flushed red. "I can handle it."

"Like I said. It's okay if you can't."

Without warning, Carter dropped her end of the cooler that she and Claire had lifted. Claire staggered, and nearly fell over the top of it. "What the hell—"

"Yeah. We saw how you handled it," Carter said, pushing past Garrett. Squatting, she tossed the scattered soft drinks back in the cooler. Then she took the handle, stood, and looked at Rocco. "You got your end?—Lift."

When Rocco and Carter were twenty yards down the path toward the pavilion, Garrett kicked hard at the gravel parking lot. Claire, who had regained her footing, rolled her eyes. Emmalyn stared after Rocco. "God, he's strong."

Dhani was staring absently at Garrett, who noticed.

"Shut up."

"I didn't say anything."

"Well, I did. I said shut up."

"Tell me again what Judge Sewell told you," Kate said. "Exactly."

Bay Trovert pulled a small piece of paper from her coat pocket. "I'll read it to you. But you haven't told me where we're headed."

They were walking at a good pace down the dirt road from Kate's lodge toward two large, wooden outbuildings.

"Grady wants me to check something he thinks he found. I wish I'd been here to take the call instead of meeting with the Sheriff. It's the third time he's asked for assurance that the young people coming here won't cause trouble in town."

Bay unfolded the paper with her notes. "Let's see. Sewell says he's still 'one-hundred percent behind the program we're creating here, of course'. But he's run into a problem with someone connected to the juvenile justice system in DC—a woman who is, apparently, a real stickler for details. He used the words 'power trip.' She needs to see the wilderness survival curriculum before she signs off."

"If he's talking about the woman from Child Protective Services, she received one. I sent it certified."

"Sewell told her you hired in a new trainer, someone you thought was even better qualified. She wants to know all about him and whether or not that part of the program has changed." She added, "To be honest, Eric and I also feel a bit unprepared, since we don't know anything about this guy Tanner, either."

Kate ignored that. "I hope this woman can get out of her own bureaucratic way. Why make it hard for us to help young people create a better future?"

They had arrived at the first outbuilding, a wooden-framed structure. Kate examined the doorknob and the wood immediately around it.

"If these are the small scratch marks Grady's worried about, for all I know they could have been here a while. Black bears try to get into buildings and even cars, if they smell even a whiff of food."

"Do you keep food out here?"

"Grady stores dried foods in case we're stranded by a blizzard. He thinks someone was trying to get in. But who would come all the way out here to break into a storage building for boxes of pasta, bags of rice, and canned beans? Grady seems to be on-edge lately, like everyone else around here, at the thought of juvenile offenders coming."

Bay studied her. "What are you holding back, Kate?"

"What makes you ask that?"

"You usually give direct answers unless you're uncomfortable about something. I asked you about Tanner and you totally ignored my question."

Kate stopped tracing the scratch marks with her finger. "You're amazingly perceptive. One reason I'm glad I hired you and Eric."

She faced Bay directly. "Steve Tanner lost his wife just over a year ago. It was a terrible tragedy. Tom Baden, my new administrator, hand-picked him, though. He says he has every reason to believe Tanner will be a great addition to the Lost Lake program. In fact, he has an unusually high degree of faith that Tanner should be here."

"But. . .?"

"Tanner wants to start over with a 'clean slate'. He doesn't want everyone knowing and talking about his loss. He doesn't want to sense that people are feeling sorry for him. Tom says he would hate that. So unless he brings it up with you, that information needs to stay between us."

Bay started to object.

"Leaving the past behind is foundational to this program, Bay. You and Eric insisted on that as an important principle. We're staking everything on the belief that pulling people out of their old environment into a new one will help them change. As far as Tom and I are concerned, Tanner is the perfect man to be part of us."

Bay did not sound convinced. "Eric and I have a lot riding on this program."

"So do I. And right now, I just want to know that you believe change and moving ahead is possible for everyone. Including Steve Tanner."

Bay was not ready to let it go. "I know you've been under pressure to fill the position. All I'm trying to say is that keeping secrets and siloing information can set us up for problems."

"The fact is, it's already part of our written agreement with Tanner." Kate pushed back, adamant now. "With everything else I have to do to prepare, and with Grady going overboard about watching the property, I have to know. Are you with me on this?"

Bay threw her hands up in surrender. "Alright. I can accept this as a matter of respecting someone's privacy."

Kate was quiet for a long moment and looked back at the small scratches around the doorknob, then the half-mile back down the dirt road at her lodge. "If someone wanted to break in, they'd just kick the door down. Doubtful anyone would hear it from all the way out here. Grady needs to calm down. The Sheriff, too. And—." She stopped.

"And me?" Bay smiled at her.

Kate returned the smile. "Have you heard from Eric how things are going down in Virginia with the get-acquainted day?"

"He sent a text just before I drove out here. They were about to prep for the picnic." Bay tucked the paper in her coat pocket and pulled out her phone.

"*Ropes course a success. Everyone is helping each other. Excellent day. Couldn't be going better.*"

"Hey Hoody, he's talking to you."

Garrett, who was seated in the front row of benches, had turned around and slapped Dhani's knee, hard. "Pay attention," he said, adding under his breath, "doofus."

Dugan, who was sitting next to Garrett, laughed. "Hoody. That's a good one."

Dhani felt dismal. Garrett was a flirt, a big-mouth weakling, and already proved he could be mean. He couldn't care less what Garrett said, but he'd thought Dugan might be cool. Not just because of his look—a fade haircut and retro glasses that reminded Dhani of a black activist from the 1960s whose name he couldn't remember—but because he had let Dhani step ahead of him in the line for burgers. He had seemed like he had some class and kindness. Now, however, Dugan appeared to be on Garrett's side, mocking him.

"Dhani?" Eric Trovert repeated. "Do you want to answer that question?"

Dhani stared. From the corner of the back row, where he had tried to hide, it was really hard to hear. Trovert had asked, "What did you do that got you into trouble?"—or at least Dhani was pretty sure that was the question.

"Oh. Um. My mother's boyfriend was asleep in bed, and I dumped lighter fluid on him and set him on fire."

Heads jerked around.

Carter laughed.

Someone swore.

Dhani felt every eye drilling into him.

Emmalyn smiled, then her expression changed. "Good Lord Jesus, you're not joking, are you?"

Jalil gave her a disbelieving look. "Who jokes about something like that?"

"Did he die?" Emmalyn pressed. "Even if he didn't, you're like a psycho killer."

Eric cleared his throat, and attempted to shift the atmosphere. "Yeah. Um. Well, one of the rules about today—one for us all to remember—is that we're here to meet each other for who we are right now and who we want to become in the future."

The others were whispering to each other, some smirking, some with shocked or disbelieving expressions.

"So, Dhani," Eric moved on quickly, "What I asked was—what do you want to get out of being in this program?"

I'm an idiot.

Everyone was still looking—but now, in a very different, backed-off way than they had looked at him all day. Like they had just found a severed limb lying on the ground.

The truth about what he hoped for by being in the program, he had sworn never to tell. So he offered instead—"To, um, be a better kid. And not do bad things."

Garrett looked around the group. "D'ya think?"

"You're kidding me," Steve said, as Tom made the final turn on the camp road, onto a small, granite bridge beside a gatekeeper's stone cottage. Beneath them flowed a silver ribbon of a shallow river. On the far side was a sweeping gravel drive, and the mountain valley in which Kate's estate lay now sprawled in full view. At its heart lay a pristine lake, surrounded on all sides by wooded slopes. A hundred yards up the hill to their left was a huge, two-story, rustic lodge.

"Where did these people get this kind of money? Their place looks like a luxury inn."

"Kate's husband was in information technology. He and a partner built some kind of system to process huge amounts of data extremely fast, patented it, then built a successful business and sold it to an even bigger, multinational corporation."

"What's he do now?"

"He's gone. Massive heart attack a few years ago. He left Kate with quite a lot of money. This is just one of her homes. The others are near D.C., Switzerland, England—oh, and one down in the islands, too."

They passed two immaculate, cedar-sided barns—"They house the animal rehab part of the program," Tom said—and rolled up in front of the lodge's massive front entrance. From this high point, they looked down on two rows of log guest cabins that curved around the north shore of the lake.

"There's a waterfall, and miles of hiking. Also a protected wetlands."

"How many acres is this place?" Steve's earlier stress was waning, and he was suddenly eager to be out on rugged trails again.

"Not sure, but it takes in around three square miles of lake, wilderness, and mountains. I think that's what she said. Kate stocks the lake. You fish, as I recall."

"I did."

"Maybe you can get into it again. I'm sure there are poles and boats."

Wilderness. Fishing alone on a lake. Very few people. Steve grinned. This could be good after all. Stepping out into the fresh, crisp, clean mountain air, his pulse was no longer racing. The edgy sense that he was being viewed through a gun scope had almost left him.

Kate greeted them at the front door, and her manner put him even more at ease. She was simply a beautiful, fit woman in her middle years, easy, kind, and welcoming. Knowing what he now knew about her loss, it was the look in her eyes—one of understanding and compassion—that made him almost relax completely.

"Steve Tanner, welcome to your home away from home." She took his hand in greeting, and their eyes connected. Something in them told him she knew he needed a home.

She definitely knows about losing someone.

"You're exactly what we need here," Kate said moments later, as she served filets and wine by a roaring fire in the lodge's great room. Outside, shadows of the mountains had fallen across the icy lake and the wood was vanishing into night. "In fact, I count you as a godsend."

Tom raised a glass to him, with a proud, triumphant smile.

Steve forced himself to smile back.

Before you ramp up your hopes and expectations, let me meet your little darlings and see if they can handle what I throw at their sorry butts. I'm sure there's at least one or two fakes or freeloaders I can eliminate for you.

7TH

"You don't know where she is?"

Since the crappy, get-acquainted day, Dhani had been chewing his knuckles, hiding them in the sleeves of his hoody so no one would see how raw and red they were. After he had opened his big, stupid mouth, no one had spoken to him the rest of the day. And now, with departure date nearing, he still had not heard a word from his mother.

The other end of the call was silent for a long moment.

"How did you get this phone number?" his grandmother finally asked, sounding tired or angry, he couldn't tell.

"It was in a file." He did not say it was on a sheet of paper in a legal file, which he had slipped off Judge Sewell's desk when an interruption pulled the judge out of the room for ten minutes. He didn't say he was calling from an office in the detention center, because he knew what she would say automatically—exactly what she had said before.

"Who knows, Dhani. Maybe she's on one of her extended 'vacations' again. Vegas. The Keys. You know she likes to travel and party, party, party. I assume if she wanted you to find her, she'd get in touch. If you can find a friend's family to stay with, you're in much better hands, let's face it." Here it was. "And before you ask, *no* you cannot come live here with me and Howard. We can barely pay our bills as it is."

He had known better than to ask if she would take him in, since a doctor had once pressed the system to find somewhere for him to go and there had been no takers. Clearly, his grandmother preferred to fantasize a scenario in which he was someone else's responsibility. Telling her he was now in lockup would probably sever ties completely.

"She hasn't contacted me. I just wondered if you knew why."

"I don't know a thing, and I don't want to know. Long as she doesn't come around here asking for money again."

He didn't want to hang up, but he didn't know what else to say or even why he was holding onto this conversation. For a moment, he thought of the woman on the other end of the line—his "nana," who had let him stay with her one weekend and made him pancakes.

"Dhani. I'm sorry your mother is a bad seed. But it's not my fault. I did right by her. And I can't clean up her messes."

There it was again, the automatic response from his own grand-mother. He was just one of his mother's messes.

"Listen to me," she finished. "Stop looking. Considering the men she chooses, she could even be in a morgue somewhere. And anyway, it's my bedtime."

The phone went dead.

11TH

The night attendant slipped out a back door, like he always did around 11:30 p.m. and again at 2:30 a.m. These clockwork breaks had allowed Dhani to slip into the office and make his phone call four nights ago.

Now he had another mission.

He had heard the office door three rooms down from his bang open many times, which was how he knew the schedule and slipped down the hallway to see what the guy was doing outside even on the coldest nights. Mostly, he just paced along the back of the building, having a smoke and spitting in the grass. Sometimes he talked on his cell phone—which, here in this section where everyone was considered high risk, he was forbidden to have. Dhani guessed he was calling his wife or girlfriend. Sometimes they argued. Sometimes it got ugly.

Tonight, he was trying to keep his voice down, but sounded like he was nearly strangling on rage.

He pulled the phone away from his head. Stared at it. Then slammed it up against his ear again. "*I. Don't. Have. Any. More. Money. To give you.* What don't you *get?*"

He continued pacing down along the back wall of the detention center, pulling his hair with one hand, then stopped, facing the chain-link and razor-wire fence at the left side of the building and stood with his back to Dhani.

Dhani chewed his knuckles. Could he really pull this off?

"*You stupid—!* . . .Yeah, I said *STUPID,*" the guard shouted, between agitated puffs on his cigarette. "Why do you give your brother money every damn month, when I give it to you for *our* bills? He's not even looking for a job, and we're not getting any of that money back. *Ever.* . . . Yeah, yeah, I don't *care* what he promised."

Even in the dark, Dhani could see him doubling his free hand into a fist and striking himself on the forehead over and over.

Now was his chance.

His steps made no noise as he moved carefully, swiftly across the exercise yard, past the basketball court and behind the three tall, thick yews in the corner. He found the opening in the eight-foot fence right where someone had told him. The chain-link barrier had been cut, pulled closed again, the escape hole held together with four short twists of steel wire. There were security cameras, but with this attendant outside and the others watching Netflix as usual, very likely no one was at the monitors.

He untwisted the steel-wire loops till they came free and hung them carefully on the fence so he could find them when he returned. Then he slid one leg out through the narrow opening.

As he tried to slip his body through, the chain-link squeaked. He stopped, heart beating faster, listening.

From back across the yard, he heard—"I gotta go. *I GOTTA GO!*"

The attendant had lost his cool and apparently forgotten he was trying to be outside undetected.

Dhani squeezed the rest of the way through the opening.

For more than an hour, he half-jogged, half-walked the dark sidewalks from the Virginia suburb where the detention center was located to the bridge that crossed the Potomac River into DC. Every car that passed and caught him in the crosshairs of its headlights posed a threat. If the attendant had actually done his job, which included a bed check—unlikely but possible—he would have found Dhani's not too convincing pile of blankets and bunched-up pillow and notified the police. At any moment, a cruiser could pull up. As he passed from the night's concealing darkness into the halo of one streetlight and then another, however, none of the cars passing him even slowed.

He was paying careful attention now to street signs. He didn't know exactly the way he should go. . .and yet somehow he did know.

Crossing the bridge into Georgetown, he continued trudging east, his feet starting to hurt, to the Foggy Bottom Metro station near 24th Street. He had been walking for two-and-a-half hours and felt the burn and pinch of blisters on his toes, but that was the last thing on his mind.

I hope she's home. She better be home. Or someone better be able to tell me where she is, or. . . .

Or what?—was his next thought. No one was helping him and he was powerless to do anything about it. His stomach tightened in a knot of frustration.

When he arrived at the first metro stop, the station was empty of commuters and no trains were running. It was now almost six a.m.

"Saturday, son," the homeless man on the bench outside told him, barely raising his head from inside the dirty blue Superman blanket he was wrapped in. "Trains start running at five on weekdays, but not till seven on weekends."

By seven they would know he was gone and that would be bad. He had grossly miscalculated how much time he needed to find his mother and get back undetected.

But then, he realized, he had not thought this through the whole way. He had no plan for getting back before they roused everyone for breakfast. When he had made his run for it, he felt confident and excited. Now, footsore and exhausted, he felt anxious and miserable.

He was too far in to go back, though. In his head, he tried to map his way from here to where he needed to go—up New Hampshire Avenue, pick up Rhode Island, beat feet further uptown to LeDroit Park. Since it was Saturday, he would almost certainly find someone who knew where she was, if not in the projects, then maybe at the small grocery store on the corner, where they had been allowed to get food on credit when their stamps ran out.

But in his mind, the street map of DC became confused. There was a kind of grid to the numbered north-south, east-west streets. The problem was there were circles and parks and also streets that radiated at angles across that grid. How far up Rhode Island Avenue did he go? All the way, or did he take a turn somewhere?

A morning bird on a wire above him let out a long *twirrr* of musical notes. Strange, he thought, how he always believed they were trying to tell him something. A little boy's fantasy.

Relax, the thought came, as the bird twittered. *Just go. You'll find your way.*

It was true. He had found, from the time he was a little boy, that if he followed some kind of instinct it would lead him. Now, it was almost as if a voice was speaking inside his mind, the way he thought he had heard the roach.

You always do find your way.

He wished his mother had the same instinct, instead of the one that led her unerringly in the direction of bad men. Hopefully, she would be just waking up and happy to see him.

But the woman in the office of the public housing apartments only stared at him over the stacks of files and empty paper cups on her desk. It was now 8 a.m., and she looked nice enough, but tired and like she really did not want to be here on a Saturday.

"Hon, I can't give out that kind of information about a former resident. Who are you again? Why you looking for her?"

"I'm her son. I need to find her. In our old apartment—some other lady answered the door, then she slammed it in my face."

The woman smiled sweetly. "Of course she did, son. What you expect, banging on people's door so early on Saturday?"

"Wait—did you say *former* resident?"

"Your mama is no longer here. She left in a big hurry. Left stuff behind. You live with your dad or someone else who might want to retrieve it? We only store it for a hunnert-an-twenny days, then it goes to Goodwill. That's policy, and I'm sure it's been here longer than that already."

"She didn't just move to another apartment in this building?"

Somehow he had it in his head that she'd just secretly slipped into another unit in order to hide.

"She's gone, dear."

She's not here. She's NOT HERE, his mind shouted. Why hadn't his inner sense of guidance told him that?

Because you really, really wanted her to be here. You love her, and nothing anyone said would have stopped you.

121

The fact that he had blocked out anything but what he wanted to hear did not escape him. But that was not important at the moment. Why wouldn't his mother tell him how to find her? The Monster must have returned. Whenever they had run, he had threatened to find them, and did.

He's threatening her again, or she wouldn't be hiding.

"Pleasepleasepleaseplease-*please*, do you have any information at all about my mom in your files? I have to find her."

The woman looked skeptical. "How do I know you're not from some bill collector? I could maybe lose my job."

"Do bill collectors send young guys like me to collect?"

She relaxed again and smiled. "Oh, they'll do anything to get an address. But. . .you're smart. And you're not going away until I look, are you?"

She pushed her chair back and turned to one of the beat-up, gray metal file cabinets behind her. Some of the handles were missing. She reached toward one that looked like someone had punched or kicked the drawer fronts.

"I may have a note in here, come to think of it. Can't recall for sure what it's about. I told you, she got out of here fast, in the middle of night"—then she balked, looked past Dhani, and nodded toward the office's entry door. "Is this somebody lookin' for *you*?"

Two police officers had stepped inside and were moving swiftly toward Dhani, until there was one standing on each side.

Crap.

One held up a small photo beside Dhani's face, and nodded.

"Dhani Singh Jones, right?"

He let out a deep breath and his shoulders sank.

"We got a call to pick you up. The detention center was pretty sure where we'd find you."

"Not very smart, son."

He looked at them, then at the woman. "I just came here to get some information I really need."

"You *need* to come with us. Now."

The woman had turned back to her desk. No smile on her face now. "Sorry, son. You best go."

He glanced toward the door. *I've got to find her before* he *does.*

Both officers grabbed him by the upper arms and dug their fingers into his thin biceps.

"Don't even think about it."

"*Oww.* You're hurting me."

In another moment, plastic zip-ties were cutting into his wrists, and he was shoved into the back of a police cruiser.

18TH

As they entered the entryway door of Kate's lodge, Steve knew he would have to force himself to keep his head in the game this morning. Tom's news, that he would have to submit his plans to two psychologists, ticked him off.

"This place could be a luxury resort," Steve said, trying not to sound irritable, "and she's opening it to delinquents." That thought worked against the rising excitement he had felt upon first arrival.

"It was modeled after the Adirondack great camps built by the super-rich robber barons in the eighteen-hundreds," Tom replied.

They had approached from their cabins down along the lakefront, giving Steve a chance to fully take in the massive, sprawling cedar-log structure. Rustic columns made from huge tree trunks supported the broad roof-spans of the entryway, which faced south toward the lake. Two-story wings spread out to the west and east, and there were a lot of chimneys to be seen.

Lah-dee-freakin'-dah.

Inside now, none of the other instructors had arrived yet, and the great room was quiet except for a blaze burning in the massive stone fireplace. Today, Steve would meet the wildlife veterinarian, who specialized in animal rehab and would run that part of the training.

Somebody Rondeau, he recalled. *Better man than I am—handling angry, injured bears and little, scratching, biting animals.*

He had put on his game face because he had not done what Kate asked of him. His part of the training program was scattered in fragments in his head.

"This is really strange," said Tom. "It's 9:05, and it's not unusual for the others to be a little late, but Kate's always on-time. She's a stickler. Let's find her."

In the huge kitchen at the rear of the lodge, the cook, Ivy, pointed a wooden spoon at the rear stairway.

"Kate ran up there for her radio phone. Very upset look on her face. She said for you to go upstairs and do a walk-through on your own—see the classrooms and study areas—and she'll meet you soon as she can."

"Something's up," Tom murmured. "Ivy had a worried look."

From an open hallway upstairs, they looked down on the great room. To their left and right, long second-story corridors ran in two directions, where they passed by eight guest suites, each with a large parlor and a fireplace. Windows framed spectacular mountain views from every room.

"Classrooms," Tom commented. "Chairs and writing tables are coming in next week."

Steve was distracted by the original paintings and sculptures scattered throughout the rooms. One small painting was an original, signed by Picasso.

"This third wing," Tom said, pointing down yet another corridor, "is Kate's private domain."

Down the back stairs, they arrived again at the kitchen.

"She's not up there," Tom said to Ivy.

"Don't know how you missed her. She's in there now." Ivy waved a paring knife at the back hallway toward the office suite at the far end.

"She flew down the stairs, talking on a radio phone. Something big is definitely going on. I'd wait till she calls you in."

They could see down the long corridor into Kate's office. She was standing at her desk, holding the receiver from a desk phone up to one ear, talking, and holding in her other hand the radio phone. Her back was towards them.

"Two calls at once," Tom said, eyebrows raised. "I'll stay here. Maybe you should wait outside."

From a stone terrace out behind the lodge, Steve had a view of Kate's horse paddock next to the larger of the two animal-clinic barns. Beyond it, the Garnet River ran through stands of pines and hemlocks. To the west and northwest, he could see the peaks of Peregrine and Lost Mountains.

Steve was only too happy to stay out of whatever was going down. He sat on a low wall next to an outdoor fire pit, and counted chimneys.

Ten. . . . This place is a palace. Kids from juvie don't deserve to come to a place like this. Some little art thief is gonna rob this poor woman blind.

In fifteen minutes, he tired of glancing at his watch, and stood to go back inside.

"HEY!"

A lean, young, dark-haired guy approached the terrace at a sprint and made a perfect scissor-kick leap over the low wall. "Where's Kate?"

"She's on an important call."

The guy was built like a marathoner and had on a tee-shirt that said, *Keene Valley Running Club.* "Did she get ahold of her helicopter pilot?"

"Kate owns a helicopter?" *Of course she does.*

"I can't wait. You come with me. I may need you for the rescue."

"Who's in trouble?"

"Rondeau, probably. I got a call and half a message before my cell service dropped us. Truck's out front. Let's go."

"Ron Cambric," he said, sticking out his right hand, as they bounced over the rutted camp road. "I'm Rondeau's vet tech."

"Steve Tanner. Outdoor survival guy."

"The Marine. Mountain forces. Afghanistan."

"That's me." Kate better have honored their agreement, he thought, and not told any more about him.

"Did you train for cold water rescue—treating hypothermia?"

"Yeah. What's up?"

"Rondeau got a call from a hiker. Someone's dog was trapped out on the ice on a pond behind Big Burn Mountain. They phoned the rescue squad, who told them to call Rondeau, who called me on a radio phone to come help. The last thing I heard was, 'Crap, the ice is breaking. I'm going out.'"

"If the ice is breaking, why would anyone go out on it?"

Ron shot him a look. "You don't know Rondeau, when it comes to rescuing animals."

Every joint in Steve's body felt jarred by the time Ron had blasted down Kate's muddy camp road, sped over the winter-heaved back road toward town—then made a sharp, sudden right turn onto two ruts leading up a heavily-wooded incline.

His head hit the side window. "Is this even drive-able?"

"Old fire road."

Trailing beside a stream for one long, tortuous mile, Ron finally slammed the truck to a halt.

"Rondeau had a rope. That's all. I've got a couple thermal body suits in the back. Grab 'em, and let's move."

Steve sprinted the trail, following Ron through the ankle deep, soft snow. From under the thinning snow cover came the sound of running melt water, and the warmth of pale sunlight coming through the trees cut through the cool air. As they jogged, Steve began to sweat inside his coat.

The ice on this pond has to be really weak.

There were other tracks just beside the trail, made by snowshoes. From up ahead, Steve could hear barking—a strange bark that had terror in it. After a final turn in the trail, they came out at the edge of what Ron had called a pond.

This is their idea of a pond?

The body of water was as big as several football fields, its shoreline rugged and zig-zagged, angling around boulders and fallen trees that had toppled from the surrounding wilderness into the lake, which, Steve guessed, was probably two hundred yards across. Beyond it, above the trees on the far shore, rocky cliffs rose up to a mountain ridge.

Out near the center, maybe seventy-five yards from shore, a black lab was trying to claw its way out of the dark water up onto the surface of the ice. It was soaked, shaking, and panicked looking.

A man in a red thermal coat and gray knitted hat, his bear paw footgear discarded, was at the lake's edge, bracing one leg against a boulder. With both hands, he gripped a yellow rope, which was lashed to the trunk of a hardwood tree behind him.

The guy began to spew loud and anxious words. "I knew the dog was in trouble when I saw it limping around out on the ice and heard the surface start to crack. So many underground springs feed these ponds, the warmer water coming up from below makes the ice thinner in places—places you don't know about, until the ice breaks and you fall in. Poor dog got out there, then froze in fear when the surface started breaking up. That's when I called for help. I wasn't going out there after him. I love animals and all, but *that—*," he pointed with one glove, "—is purely foolhardy."

Some fifty yards out from the shoreline, a figure in a khaki jumpsuit, black ski mask, gloves and boots was crawling, foot by slow foot, commando-style over the rutted surface of the ice.

Ron had slid his way twenty feet out on the frozen lake. He had grabbed onto the yellow rope, which was spooling over the ice as the figure moved further and further out closer to the open circle of black water where the dog was thrashing.

The dog's barking had turned to pitiful yelps, sounding almost like human screams.

The hair stood up on Steve's neck.

"*Geez, Rondeau,*" Ron called out over the noise, "I'm gonna yank you back in. This is stupid. You shoulda waited. I called Kate, and she's calling for copter support."

The lab's front claws were slipping, losing their frantic grip on the ice.

The crawling figure violently waved Ron off.

That dog probably won't make it anyway, Steve thought. *Ron should just yank Rondeau back to shore. He's being stupid.*

"I don't even know if that rope got tied really good onto that carabiner," said the hiker.

Steve looked at him, questioning.

"The carabiner clipped to the belt of that jumpsuit. Everything happened so fast. I'm standing here, calling the dog. The dog starts trembling and shaking. The ice falls through. I phone for help. Next thing I know, somebody's running up the trail, throws a rope at me and says, 'Tie one end on my belt, and the other end on that tree. I'm going out.' I did my best, but it was all so rushed."

The pieces fell together in Steve's head. Kate gets an emergency call. Tries to phone her helicopter pilot for help. Ron finds him waiting, enlists him to rescue the impulsive rescuer. But why wasn't Ron dragging Rondeau back to shore?

"Some of these glacial ponds are deep—maybe thirty, forty feet," said the hiker. "That ice gives way, divers will have to hunt for the bodies."

A loud crack, like a gunshot, rang in the cold, clear air.

Steve flinched and dropped to a crouch.

"Ice is busting up." The hiker shook his head, pointing. "Get ready to haul in one body or two."

An echo of the *crack* came back from the mountain ridge.

Agitated, Steve grabbed the rope and pushed the guy aside. "Give me that."

"Stop—*NOW!*" Ron was yelling. "The whole surface is breaking up."

The figure far out on the ice was maybe six feet from the lab now, still crawling forward.

The dog stopped barking. It was panting heavily, its head barely above dark water, just one paw clinging to the jagged edge of the ice hole.

The figure ignored Ron, and inched closer, one arm held out in front, beckoning the dog.

A crack opened suddenly under Ron's feet, and he nearly fell. Slipping and retreating backwards to the shore, he swore.

"*Ron?*"

"*Steve?*"

Two voices came from the trail behind them—Kate's and Tom's.

"*Over here!*" Steve called back.

In the next second, the ice beneath the rescuer dropped away, and Steve saw Rondeau disappear under dark water. . . .

. . .and come up sputtering and slapping for a handhold on the ice. The weight of the now- soaked gloves and jumpsuit dragged him down into the water. No sign of the dog.

"*Pull. Pull. PULL!*" Ron shouted.

Steve was already instinctively pulling back on the yellow rescue rope.

For a second, the soaked figure came up out of the water a little— then fell back as the rope slipped loose from the carabiner on Rondeau's jumpsuit.

Steve and Ron crashed backwards onto the rocks and snow.

"*Ohmygod, ohmygod. . .!*" the hiker was shouting. "I knew that was a stupid thing to do."

"*Shut. Up!*" Ron yelled at him.

Steve had bounded to his feet and was ripping off his gloves and jacket, kicking off his boots.

"What are you doing?" Ron's eyes were wide.

This is not going down this way.

Steve started out onto the ice, which instantly cracked under his first step. He dropped to his stomach. . .

. . .just as the sound of a helicopter broke over the high ridge at the lake's far side.

Kate and Tom were there now, Kate wildly waving both arms to signal the pilot.

"*He sees us!*" Tom called, over the roar of the blade as the helicopter rapidly descended. Then he shouted to Steve, who had crawled back to shore. "*Were you* really *going out there?*"

"*Calculated risk,*" he shouted back.

The helicopter's dramatic, sudden drop, brought it to a hover just feet above the black water. They could see the figure fighting to keep from sinking, as the wind of the copter's blades blew clouds of loose snow and dead gray leaves in all directions. The co-pilot had opened a side door and was lying on his belly reaching one arm down. The figure in the water was barely able to reach up.

Ron clenched his fists. "Suit and boots gotta weigh a ton."

Two hands reached, and clasped each other by the wrist.

The helicopter raised up a little, the rescuer started to come up out of the water with the black dog barely held under one arm—and the two hands slipped apart.

Both of the soaking wet figures dropped, plunging back down into the hole, disappearing under the icy dark water.

One head popped up—the rescuer's.

"*Forget the dog! Too heavy!*" Kate shouted, her voice drowned out by the helicopter's noise.

Far out on the pond, Rondeau's head vanished under the water again.

"I can't watch this," said the hiker, ducking his face.

The helicopter dropped dangerously low, the co-pilot leaning further out so that just his hips and legs anchored him in the aircraft.

"He leans out any more, he's gonna fall in, too!" the hiker shouted.

The head emerged from the hole and one arm stretched up again, but only a little. Clearly, Rondeau was losing strength.

The two hands met again. This time the co-pilot grabbed with his other hand, turned his head and called back over his shoulder.

When Rondeau lifted up out of the lake, water pouring from the jumpsuit, one arm was wrapped tightly around the limp body of the black lab. The co-pilot yanked them inside the copter.

"They'll go straight to the hospital in Saranac," Kate said, her voice full of relief.

"But I brought the hypothermia suits."

"Good call, but the rescue squad gave them to the pilot, too."

As they jogged the trail back to the fire road, Kate's radio phone sounded.

"What?—Speak louder, I can't hear you," she shouted into it. *"Where?—Alright, we'll meet you."*

From up ahead, Steve called back to her. "They're going to the hospital—in Saranac, right?"

"No, we're not going to the hospital."

"Bad decision," Steve shot back. "I think—"

"Only one of us is making the calls here," Kate preempted, "and at the moment it isn't you."

Steve's eyebrows went up.

"Don't be offended," Kate said, jogging up the slushy path. "It isn't me either."

In fifteen minutes, they were back at the estate and the helicopter was settling down in the northern meadow behind Kate's lodge.

"I'm sure Rondeau insisted we come here to the clinic," said Ron, "to save the dog."

A figure jumped down from the open side door of the craft, wrapped in blankets.

Steve's jaw dropped. *"That's Rondeau?"*

Ron glanced at him. "Yeah, why?"

"Joe"—the person he had pictured in his mind, when Tom first mentioned the name—was not Joe, but *Jo*.

The wind from the helicopter's slowing blades kept moving the blanket aside.

And Jo was a very nice looking woman, at that. Bedraggled, blond hair hanging around her face, lips blue, shaking with cold—even so, she was one of the most beautiful women he had laid eyes on in more than a year. Maybe ever.

"Jo, you get inside." Kate was pushing her toward the house. "Why didn't you put the hypothermia suit on?"

"Didn't need it."

"Your whole body is shaking. We'll get you clothes and coffee. You guys—," Kate ordered, pointing at the barns, "—carry the dog into the clinic."

Ron elbowed Steve, as the co-pilot hefted the limp, lifeless-looking lab out the copter door. "Give me a hand."

Jo Rondeau was passing Steve now. He could not take his eyes off her face, her long, smooth arms and athletic body, which appeared for another second as she tried to keep the blanket from slipping again. She saw him watching her.

"Ron, give him a shot of adrenaline," she ordered, ignoring Steve. "His pulse is extremely weak. Get him into a cool water bath and slowly bring his temperature up."

"You gotta go bring yours up, Jo."

"I'm fine. Get going. I'll dress and be there in five minutes."

With a quick glance at Steve, she said, "Don't stand there—help him."

19TH

Time in the frigid water had done considerable damage to the lab, who clearly was in bad shape before he fell in. Even after hours of Jo's life-saving ministrations the day before, the dog's vital signs were still erratic this morning.

Steve had returned to the clinic to check on the animal's progress—and to learn something more about this Dr. Rondeau. Standing a few feet back from the stainless steel examining table where the dog lay, watching quietly, he was fascinated by her movements. She was poetry in motion, with hypodermics and disinfectants.

The dog, a young male, was emaciated, its bones and hips like tent poles under the sagging skin and patchy black fur. Everything indicated he had been starving for some time before plunging into the icy lake and was even more weakened now by the ordeal.

"His pulse was weak but steady this morning," Ron reported. He was beside Jo, recording notes on an iPad. "Now it's erratic again."

Jo focused on the lab's left front paw, which was continuing to turn darker shades of blue-gray. "I hate to say it, but this may have to come off."

"Would you take it at the wrist joint, or take the whole leg?" Ron asked.

Jo noticed Steve but ignored him. "Let's see what happens in the next hour. I've gotta get his temp up." Her tone changed. "That IV bag is empty, Ron. Start a new one. Pay attention."

"What will you do with him after? If he makes it?" Steve asked, stepping up to the table where the dog lay unmoving.

"That's premature, but—," she reached out, signaling to Ron for stainless steel probe, "—I'll rehab him as much as possible. Find a good home."

"Better than the one he had, I hope. Apparently, his owner didn't give a damn about him." Steve ran a hand gently over the angular ridges of the dog's ribs. *Nice animal. Too bad.*

"He's numbed up," Jo said, carefully working the thin probe into the dog's right front paw. For several minutes, she gingerly pushed open the wound, gently cleansing it with a reddish-orange solution. When she finished her examination, she swabbed-in a thick, clear salve.

"This could turn gangrenous. Looks like it was injured and infected for some time. We have to let him stabilize before I do more, though."

The paw looked like it had been sliced by something, then chewed on, probably by the dog himself. The small bits of flesh she had carefully cut away and dropped into a stainless steel dish were a sickly gray and yellow, and there was a rotting smell.

"There's necrotic tissue up to the radiocarpal articulation, with pus inside it."

Ron made a note.

Steve glanced at her, curious.

"Dead flesh up to the wrist joint."

So that was the source of the smell.

"The freezing water shut down circulation here even more than it apparently was already. It's a wonder this guy could walk at all. Shows he's got spirit."

Steve rubbed one of the dog's ears gently between two fingers.

It rolled its head and looked up at him, with a half-dazed, half-pleading look. And something else, like recognition.

Oh god. Don't do the sad dog eyes. "Poor fella, you almost starved to death. Who'd you run away from—some deadbeat?"

The lab's head dropped back heavily onto the table.

"How are you awake," Ron said, sounding incredulous, one hand on the dog's foreleg, "with all the sedatives I'm pumping into you?"

"Be really careful, Ron, his vitals are incredibly weak. We don't want to stop his heart, just keep him under enough so I can work on him. And please take your hand off his leg." She looked fiercely at Steve. "You need to get back, too. Neither of you have gloves on. We're fighting a very serious infection here—down to the bone. I don't need your germs getting involved."

"I scrubbed," Ron protested. "You know I always scrub."

She shot Ron a severe look. "This is touch and go. Don't give me crap."

He removed his hand. "Alright, alright. I'll get gloves. I was just trying to comfort the poor guy."

Steve had stepped back a pace, out of the line of fire. Had the look in the dog's eyes sent some kind of message?—He wasn't sure.

"Most people here in the Adirondacks work really hard just to get by, Tanner." Jo focused on the paw again, her statement clearly directed at his remark about irresponsible pet owners. "They work multiple jobs in the summer, and when the tourist season is over it can be subsistence living. The economy is really tough if we don't have much snow and the skiers and snowmobilers don't come. A lot of people barely get by."

Steve focused on her again. "Maybe people like that shouldn't keep pets, especially if they're on the dole," he tossed back.

The lab whimpered and dazedly tried to pull its paw away.

"*Ron.*"

"Sorry, Jo. I don't want the anesthesia to kill him."

Jo turned to Steve, with a look like the one she had just given Ron, her voice bristling. "Listen. I'm nobody's judge. Maybe you shouldn't be either.

"Maybe someone *was* cruel to this dog or neglected him. Or maybe he was a pet someone really loved. Dogs are great companions for people who live alone through long, hard winters up here. Also for men who are out doing handyman work at remote camps. Maybe this guy wandered away from a young mom, who is right now struggling to feed her family. Or from an older person who relied on him as a best friend. And then this dog followed that hiker into the woods hoping for a handout."

Steve kept his mouth shut. *Spare me the lecture. If you can't take care of a dog, don't own one.*

After a few quiet and intense minutes, she looked at him again, but differently. "In case I can't locate the owner—how about you? Maybe you can keep him."

Surprised after the tongue lashing, Steve shook his head. "What would *I* do with a dog?"

"Learn how to love and take care of him."

Because I do such a great job loving anyone.

"Or maybe I'll keep him here at the clinic." She focused on a small scrape on the dog's nose. "If he survives, he'll make a great mascot."

"Tell you what," Steve said. "If he lives, maybe I'll take him."

"Even if the paw comes off?"

"Do you think it will?"

"If there's a necrotizing agent involved, like a severe bacterial infection, then yeah. His defenses are really low, though. He may not even make it through an amputation."

Steve felt a twinge. He had seen dogs in the military that stayed beside their handlers who had been wounded or killed. He hadn't had a dog since he was a small boy.

Jo reached for a gauze pad, the faintest smile playing on her lips. "What will you name him?—if he lives."

"Oh, already he's my dog."

"I believe animals can sense whether someone cares about them or not. I saw how he looked at you. And you seem to care. I'd only let him go to a person who cares about him."

One of those—a bleeding heart animal lover. Say no.

At the same time, a different voice in his head said, *What if he showed up here for you?*

That was spiritual sounding garbage. It sounded like what Tom had said to manipulate him to come here. He would resist that voice.

"He's a strong fella," Jo continued. "Even when he was going down, he was still fighting to get back to the surface. If he pulls through, he deserves a chance at a good life."

These people and their idea that everyone 'deserves' something.

He felt her pushing and backpedaled fast. He didn't need to play nursemaid to a needy dog, who, if he lived, would likely be minus a leg. "I'll think about it. Maybe."

Right now, there was a more important issue he had to deal with. Immediately.

20TH

Judge Sewell kept running one hand through his thinning hair. On the desk in front of him, he flipped through the two reports, one from the detention center, the other one from the apprehending officers.

"What were you thinking, son? I offered you a great chance to start over in an excellent, new program, and you do this."

Dhani had slumped down in the hardwood chair.

"Sit up, young man."

He pushed his feet against the floor and straightened himself.

Did he even want to be in the program or leave DC? He had seriously blown it the day of the ropes course, causing the other kids to shun him the rest of the day. In the van on the way back to the detention center that afternoon, he had tried to slide into a bench seat with Dugan, who pointed to another seat. "Not here." Jalil also shook his head. "Sit over there." From the back, someone had whispered, "Freak."

"Why won't anyone tell me where my mom is?"

"I told you, son, we don't exactly know right now. From what we can tell, she seems to be moving around a lot."

That, together with what the woman at the projects office told him—"She ran,"—raised his anxiety.

She needs me. She's hiding from him.

It was as if Judge Sewell had read his thoughts. "What your mother needs—what *you* need—is to be in this program. I wouldn't have pushed you during our first interview if I didn't believe this is a great thing for you. I thought I had a hunch about you. But I'm rethinking it now. Look at this."

He picked up a small stack of files. "I've got four good candidates— maybe better ones—right here, and I can replace you with one of them. A lot is on the line, son—and you've almost cashed-in your whole future in one moment's bad decision."

Dhani stared and said nothing.

"You're highly intelligent, according to your test scores. But give me one good reason why I shouldn't send you back to detention right now and give your spot away to someone else. Because it seems to me I should."

Kate blew on the hot liquid in her cup, and looked across her desk at Tom. "This should be something stronger than tea. Well, here's the news. One of the young men, Dhani Jones, ran away from the detention center a week ago. He didn't get far before he was picked up by the police. Sewell has been trying to sort out the situation before telling me, which he did early this morning."

"What was the boy doing?"

"He went back to his old neighborhood, the projects. He claims he was trying to find his mother."

"Hardly a crime."

"That was his story anyway."

"Does Sewell think he's lying? Was he up to something else?"

"John's been trying to decide. The boy's mother is nowhere to be found and he's understandably upset."

"The court doesn't know where she is?"

"They think they do. But she has a history of hooking up with violent men, then having to get away from them. She picks up and runs a lot. This young man has been in and out of eight schools."

"That's a lot of instability. So—if this young man is out of the program, has the judge picked a replacement?"

"He's still looking through his files for another likely candidate. As I said, he's still making up his mind about this boy."

Tom wanted to tell her how difficult it is, in his experience, for people who are damaged to truly change. And that the last thing she needed if this program was to be a stellar success in its first year—one of the judge's stated conditions—was a boy who posed a flight risk. She herself should take the lead and reject him as a student.

He started to say, *What's to decide?* but held back. Kate's whole point in creating this program was, as she put it, to help "rescue human equity" and put the lives of troubled and difficult young people on a better track. Was this boy going to be a danger to others, though, and to the program?

Kate took a sip of tea, and took the conversation in a new direction. "I need to talk with you about Steve Tanner."

"You were pretty brusque with him after the rescue."

"I wasn't brusque, I was rude. I was upset with Jo at the moment. She was foolhardy. But that's no excuse. I'll smooth it with Steve. He was a Marine, and I'm sure he won't melt if I bark at him once in a while, but I'll save that for when it's necessary."

Tom nodded, pleased to see both the assertive side of Kate and the diplomatic one.

"There's something else we need to discuss about this man, however. I think you know what it is."

23RD

The note on the wire barrier said: *Clean out and disinfect the enclosure.*

The goshawk was gone.

"Her body's in the freezer," Ron told Sahm, when he walked from the aviary back to the clinic. "Jo wants to autopsy her to see what she can learn."

"I don't understand," Sahm replied, upset. "Only two days ago you said she was getting stronger."

"We thought she was. She suddenly gained a few ounces, even though she'd almost completely stopped eating and drinking. And she got feisty for a day or two. It doesn't make any sense. We're not sure how she lived as long as she did. Something gave her an unusual burst of strength there at the end."

Sahm wanted to say, *You should have let me complete the healing ritual*—but with Ron's harsh warning still sounding in his head, he thought better of it. Also, there was remorse for the fact that he had not completed his training in Tibet. What had he left out of the half-remembered ritual?

Moreover, now that he knew he had been brought to Lost Lake to resume his secret yogic path, how would he learn those ancient healing arts now—not to mention the most secret arts?

3
MAY
10TH

Dhani threw himself down in a seat halfway back on the coach. It smelled acrid, like cleaning fluids, and he hoped that wouldn't give him a sore throat. Through the tinted window, he could see the other kids outside in the glaring, humid, mid-May morning, stowing daypacks and duffel bags in the compartment underneath. One or two at a time, they climbed the steps and shuffled down the aisle, sliding into window or aisle seats.

Judge Sewell's last words played in his head. *"I'm still going to take a chance on you, and I'm not even sure why. No screw ups. Clear? Not. Even. One."*

No screw ups. That was the goal ever since he was sent to detention.

"And," Sewell had finished, *"because your file says you're an 'extreme loner', I want you to show me you're really going to make an effort by reaching out and making a friend. One friend. And let me know who that person is."*

He just hoped he could go without any weird incidents. No cockroach or bird voices in his head. People had recoiled from him, the few times he had even joked about it.

Dugan bounded up the steps, sweating. "Man—hot out there. Nice and air conditioned up in here."

Two of the girls moved toward the seat right in front of him now—the blonde girl named Makayla, with the narrow, pretty face and cool haircut that slanted across one eye, and the girl named Imani, who looked like she was possibly African American and maybe Hispanic. Imani in particular looked like she could be a high-fashion model, with her perfectly styled hair and the edge of her left ear lined with exotic silver studs. She did not look to Dhani like she had just come out of detention. When they saw him they looked away.

Make a friend. Sure thing. "There he is. The bizarro world kid."

He didn't want anyone near him anyway. He turned his body toward the window, pulled deeper into himself, and stared outside at the sidewalk. The Troverts were talking with the bus driver. He liked Eric, though he asked more questions than any of the psychologists the system had forced him to see. Even so, he was an easy-going and athletic but not competitive-meathead kinda guy. Also not the paid-friend kind of counselor, but someone who seemed really interested in you. And anyway, being vague and dodging him would be easy. Bay, on the other hand, with her piercing blue eyes, was the one who put him off. He didn't like the uncomfortable feeling that she could see right into him.

"You're hesitant to leave DC, aren't you?" she had said, when he was stowing his duffel bag under the bus. "I see it in your eyes."

He would have to remember to not make eye-contact. No one could be allowed to guess the full truth about him.

Makayla and Imani had slipped into seats together three rows ahead, clearly staying away from him.

He pulled his hood up, yanked at the drawstrings, and closed his eyes. He'd just sit here and rot the whole ten- or eleven-hour drive to this Lost Lake place.

In a minute, he felt his seat shake, and sat up.

Claire was placing a blue, canvas daypack in the overhead rack. Then she stooped to slide her purse beneath the aisle seat next to him and slid into it, her elbow bumping his.

Dhani smiled. "Hi. Yeah. You can sit here."

Her face was blank. "Thanks for the permission."

He stared, and fumbled for what to say next. What drew him today were her eyes. The dark brows were arched, and she needed no makeup to be pretty. He imagined she would not look so standoffish if she ever smiled.

She reached down into her purse and pulled out a small pad and a pencil.

From the corner of his eye, he kept glancing to see what she was doing. Writing notes to herself?

Using her left hand, she shielded the paper from him. "You're watching me. That creeps me out."

"I didn't think anybody would want to sit by me, and I was just interested in what you're doing. Being friendly. That's all. If I walk up to anyone in this group, they walk away. They act like I'm psycho or something. Sorry I invaded your privacy."

The others were boarding the coach now, most moving past them toward the back. Two or three nodded at Claire and said, "Hey." No one looked at him.

"Maybe it was that thing you said about setting someone on fire. No one wants to be near you."

"Then why are you sitting here?"

"Because if I'm near you, no one will bother me."

That stung.

"You're sitting by me because that will keep everyone else *away*?" He slumped back in his seat. *Thanks for sharing.*

She stared down at her hands. "Sorry. That was mean sounding."

"Not mean *sounding*. It was just mean."

Her jaw dropped. "Wow. Tell me exactly what you're thinking, why don't you?"

It's okay if you say rude things, but it's not okay if I'm honest? I see how it is.

Claire was quiet.

Outside, the loading had finished, and the others boarded the coach and found seats.

Claire's look had softened a little. "Are you okay with me sitting here, or do you want to be alone? There's plenty of room. I can move to another row."

"No. I mean yeah, you can sit here. I don't really care." He looked around at all the empty rows of seats, and hoped she didn't move.

Israel Aubrey, who called himself Ray-Ray, was seated across the aisle. He had picked up on their friction and was half-watching them but pretending not to. When he saw Dhani look up at him, he flashed a bright grin, the kind that made his whole face light up, and shrugged.

Dhani nodded. *Girls—right?*

"Are you sure?" Claire pressed him. "I was rude. And you seem to like being alone."

"Not really. But I guess everyone thinks I'm a freak. So I just deal with it."

"I don't."

"What do you think? You heard what Emmalyn said about me."

Claire's voice dropped. "That you're like 'a psycho killer'? First of all, Emmalyn is sweet, but she's way too chatty and not real bright. I can sort of tolerate her."

"So. . .?"

"So, I think you are. . . ."

He waited, and watched her expressions shift as she considered. "You think I'm what?"

"I think I'm not sure about you yet. Some of these other people are cool. Like Makayla and Imani up there. They're awesome, actually. Pretty, but not pretentious. Just good girls. But some are big talkers, who try to impress everyone. I hate it when people do that."

"I thought you would be scared of me."

"Because you set your mother's boyfriend on fire? Why did you do that?"

"I don't know."

She scrutinized him. "Did that really happen? Or are you pathetically trying to impress us all that you're a badass who did some horrible crime?"

What could he say that would not lose the first, tiny foothold he had just gained with this girl he really, really liked and was scared of driving away? She seemed to dislike guys who said stuff just to impress. And a lot more than this new friendship was at stake.

So he lied.

A pale sun shone through sheets of a soft gray mist over Lost Lake, and the morning air was cooler than Steve expected. He stepped out of his cabin for a run down the estate road, and rubbed his hands to warm them. The porch thermometer read *38*. It was May, and he could see his breath.

Across the lake, he could see that the snow cap had melted off the surrounding peaks. Two of Grady's guys were mowing the swath of grass, which was just starting to grow, between the camp road and the strip of sand along the waterfront. The fact that this was a very long, cold spring and the ice had only just disappeared from the lake was the least of his troubles.

Maybe a morning run would rid him of the jumpiness he had been unable to shake. Maybe it was there because two weeks ago, when he and Kate discussed the gear he was ordering, she had surprised him at point-blank range. . . .

"Are you really ready for this? I mean ready for these young people. They're not your average 'nice, clean-cut kids'. We don't know exactly what it will mean to live and work with them, but I'm hopeful. From the day you arrived, I've sensed that you're a bit on-edge. And to be perfectly honest, I've heard you can be judgmental."

Rondeau. So he was being watched and reported on. Good to know.

"These are not servicemen and women you can bark orders to. Are you certain you're ready to do this job?"

He had looked her straight in the face, and not said the whole truth. "I always give one hundred percent."

Kate had not missed the dodge. "One hundred percent of *what* is the thing that I'm asking you about. Steve, I really thank you for accepting this challenge, and I think it will be one for all of us. And I'll give you my full support, but we all have to be committed to the same goal—which is giving these young people the skills they need to change their lives and futures. Attitude is so important." . . .

Geese calling as they flew north over Lost Mountain brought him back to the present moment. He pushed his arms back, stretching tight chest muscles, squatting to work his tense quads. He felt fatigued. Since arriving here, he had still not slept well. No dreams, so at least that was a relief.

The truth was his head was not in this game yet. Coming here to the mountains had done it. He kept reliving frigid spring mornings crawling out of a tent in the high ranges of Afghanistan. Not all the memories were welcome.

At least, so far, there was relief from the punishing night visions of following Oliva only to see her leave him again and again.

Drawing three deep lungfuls of cold air, he set out jogging along the waterfront path, passing the other guest cabins, nodding at Grady's workmen, then angling across the new-mown grass onto the camp road.

A four- or five-mile run would start to clear his head.

Beyond Kate's lodge, the road descended, and his muscles were warming up. When he crossed the stone bridge by Grady's cottage, a cold draft slicing down the river from Lost Mountain cut through his sweatshirt, hitting him like an icy slap in the body.

His skin tingled, his mind cleared, and he felt exhilarated. *Hit me, baby, one more time.*

Now he could think and address his immediate problem.

His cabin mates, Mike Yazzie and Randy Wolfman were both easy-going. That was not the issue.

"We've both got Native American blood," Randy had smiled, the evening of Steve's arrival.

"Both of you?" he had questioned, looking at Mike Yazzie.

"What—you never saw a Black man who's half Indian?" Yazzie replied, grinning. "Lots of inter-marrying. There's a who-o-o-le bunch of us."

And there was no BS.

"Kate's sweet and all, but she bit off a lot bringing kids here out of juvie," said Yazzie. "Bad habits die hard."

"You should know," Randy razzed him.

"Aw come on now, man, you can't talk," Yazzie grinned at Randy, then looked at Steve. "Ol' Wolfmoon here and I both went through a little bit of rehab some years ago. We're both clean as a whistle. Not even a drop. You don't drink, do you? You better not here on the estate. Kate's rules. Anyway, Randy and I both know what we're up against here. And like I said, Kate's a great person for starting this program. She's just—"

"—inexperienced," Randy finished for him. "We don't think she really knows what she's in for. Which is why we've all got to have her back. She could easily get conned."

So, no namby-pamby, "please go easy on the poor babies" garbage from these guys.

On the other hand, sharing a cabin and living in close quarters was not going to work. After his year of solitude on the farm, every little sound—clicking pens, a dry cough, scraping a spoon in a pot—was like fingernails clawing at a blackboard.

Most irritating were the questions about him and his past.

"Ever been married?" "Got a girl?" "Maybe one had him." "Maybe more than one." It was light-hearted guy stuff, but it made him uncomfortable.

Some questions got under his skin.

"Where did you serve?" "What kind of action did you see?"

He pushed himself to jog faster. He sure as hell didn't need anyone dislodging memories he had buried and left behind.

Following the zig-zagging wooded road, he tried hard to take in the deep quietude and natural calm all around him. In among the gray hardwoods, pale green fiddlehead ferns pushed up through rust-colored leaf litter. For a half-mile, the river rushed along on his left, its voice a calming sound. Then the road took a hard right, and he was alone with the light rustle of wind and the sound of water trickling in some hidden rivulet nearby in the woods.

He took in deep breaths, rich with all the scents of the wilderness. His mind would not settle down. If he was chasing peace, it eluded him. The trees growing tight to the road and forming a canopy over it closed in, the way all those questions pressured him to remember.

Yazzie's voice was loud in his mind. "My uncle served in Iraq and he saw some bad things go down."

The voice of a platoon buddy came back now. *"Tanner, did you hear. . .?"*

Randy had ramped up the pressure. "Looks like you were pretty lucky—no injuries."

"Did I hear what?"

"About what happened to those poor guys at—"

His breathing was shallow and his feet fell like lead hammers on the road. He didn't want to think of the name of the place. Inside the circle of dark green fir trees he was passing, a thread of fog rose from the damp forest floor, catching a pale shaft of early sunlight—ghostly.

"Eight dead. More wounded.—Tanner, did you hear me?"

A mild shock passed through his body, like another cold jolt of wind.

He needed quiet and open space. Not being closed in anywhere, with voices that wouldn't shut the hell up. He was grateful Mike and Randy had gone to DC with the Troverts to chaperone the students on their bus trip north. The shared cabin thing was not working at all, they were returning tonight, and he knew he had to be out of there when they arrived.

"Tom said it, Steve. You can't keep running."

That voice stopped him dead in his tracks, as if someone had actually spoken out loud and not in his head. His pulse was suddenly racing. *No, no, no, no, no.* Turning in a circle, he stared down the road in both directions and into the woods, listening, looking. It was like she was right here. Damn those guys and their questions that had started unearthing the past again.

Olivia?

This was more than remembering her voice, as he had before. It was a strong sense of her near presence. She was here with him, in his heart and soul forever, of course—but could she also be *here* here?

No. He didn't believe in such things.

I'm not running, he argued back—if only with the voice of accusation coming from his own mind. He had come here and made a commitment to Tom and Kate to teach survival skills, and a Marine always lived up to his word. Without that, he would have no pride left at all.

If he was going to make this job work, though, dealing with kids he didn't like or trust, he needed space, distance from everyone, and quiet. Maybe there was a room in one of the barns.

No, he was not leaving. But he needed to make an evasive move, and make it now.

"Hey, my man up there," Dugan called from the rear section of the bus, "—Ray-Ray, correct? You had your head in that book since we left DC."

Dhani had dozed for a couple of hours, all through New Jersey, where, from the coach window, he had seen only gray, cement barriers and, around Hoboken, a mountain of old tires burning. Apparently, they had passed New York City now and—road signs indicated—they were still headed due north. Here, the cityscapes fell away, replaced by green, rolling hills.

He stretched and looked across to Claire, still occupied with her pad, at Ray-Ray, who turned his head to look back at Dugan.

"Read us somethin'," Dugan called out.

Ray-Ray flipped a few pages in the small book resting in his lap, and stopped. "'Perhaps there has been, at some point in history, some great power whose elevation was exempt from the violent exploitation of other human bodies. If there has been, I have yet to discover it.

"'But this banality of violence can never excuse America, because America believes itself exceptional, the greatest and noblest nation ever to exist, and one cannot, at once, claim to be superhuman and then plead mortal error. I propose to take our countrymen's claims of American exceptionalism seriously, which is to say I propose subjecting our country to an exceptional moral standard.'"

"That's Ta-Nehisi Coates," Dugan responded. *"Between the World and Me.* That what you readin'?"

"Second time. I guess you read it, too."

"Right after I read James Balwin. He tells it like it is. 'You can only be destroyed by believing that you really are what the white world calls a *nigger.* I tell you this because I love you, and please don't ever forget it.' He was writing to his nephew, like Coates is writing to his son."

"That's from *The Fire Next Time*," Ray-Ray responded. "My father got mad when he caught me reading that book. He said—*my* dad, a Black preacher—that Baldwin was promoting racism."

"What? He was one of the most important voices of the Civil Rights Movement."

"My dad's all about holiness and surrendering your life to God and getting into heaven. Not so much about demanding rights."

Emmalyn was staring horrified at Dugan. "You used the *n*-word."

"Girl, I was quoting Baldwin. When you use a word other people have used to put you down, you take back power over that word."

"But how is it fair that you can say it and we can't? I don't get it."

Dugan shook his head. "You don't get it. That's a fact."

Twenty miles down the road, Jalil called out, "Guys, we need to lighten the mood in here."

The coach was now moving along between the rock palisades on either side of the Hudson River.

"Anybody want to play a fun game? I call it, *Whudjoo Dooo?"*

The chaperones were seated far upfront, talking among themselves or resting.

Dhani looked over the back of his seat.

In the rear of the coach, where the other four guys and a few of the girls sat scattered around, some alone, some in pairs, Jalil was standing on a seat. He was wearing a black beanie with the name of the rapper GUNNA across the front.

Dhani looked past Claire, whose eyes were now closed, and across at Ray-Ray, who shook his head.

Yeah. Someone needs attention. The wannabe kid.

No one had responded to the challenge.

"Come on," Jalil pushed. "You can either tell us what you did to get your butt tossed in the system. Or we can all guess. How about you," he called, "pretty lady up there, with all the hot ear piercings. Imani—right?"

Imani turned in her seat to look back. Dhani had not really noticed the day of the ropes course, but did now with the sun slanting through the coach windows, that her eyes were a pretty shade of hazel. He wondered how soon guys were going to be fighting over her.

"Why don't you go first, *Hat Boy*." Then she turned back to her conversation with Makayla.

"Hey, hey," Garrett, the wise-guy kid who had lost it at Rocco during the picnic jumped in. "I'm the one who gives out the nicknames. That's my thing."

Jalil ignored him. "Hat Boy. I'm good with that. Okay, I'll go first. I got caught putting white powder up my nose. Oh yeah, and selling."

Imani turned again, and glared at him. "This is your idea of lightening up the mood?"

Claire stirred a little, and muttered, "Lovely. A coke head."

"Musta been selling a lot of stuff, Hat Boy, if they put you in detention," said Dugan. "So—you still using? You sure jumpy. Can't stop slapping on things."

"Hey, I'm a drummer. That's what I do."

Emmalyn, who was standing, halfway hanging over the back of Rocco's seat, looked at Jalil wide-eyed. "You said you play the guitar, too, right? Wow. Guitar *and* drums."

Garrett and Dugan looked at each other, smirking.

"Keyboards, also. Amiright?" Garrett said, winking at Dugan.

Jalil grinned. "Yeah. Pickin' that up, too."

"Thought so." Garrett and Dugan broke up laughing.

Jalil focused on Rocco. "Hey, big guy. Yoked Man with the abs. Tell us what you did."

Rocco shook his head. "Not playing."

"Come on, *Tats*," Garrett prodded. "I'm gonna guess—*teenage escort for rich guys, rich women—both?*"

"My name is Rocco, not Tats. But you—," he hesitated for effect, "—can call me Rocco. Or *sir*."

Emmalyn snorted and laughed.

"Okay then, how 'bout I call you Gangbang."

"I'm not in a gang."

Dugan leaned forward. "What about those five little stars on your left pec and right hand? That's *La Stidda*. I looked it up. If you didn't want us to know, you shouldn'a showed your body off during the ropes course."

Emmalyn leaned further over the seat back, and stared at Rocco's right hand. "What's *La Stidda*?"

"Name of an Italian gang," Dugan replied. "He definitely a banger."

"Sicilian," Rocco responded, sitting up. His left leg was twitching. "The ink's in honor of my grandparents. They came from the old country and built a successful business here. That's all. Someone made me get it."

"Right, right. Someone *forced* you to get a tat? Hey, no worries, man. Your family can be in whatever *business* you wanna be in. And you're not the only one here declaring their posse."

Rocco did not reply. He reached up and moved Emmalyn's arm, which she had allowed to slip down and rest on his shoulder.

"Hey, what's wrong?" she protested. "I'm just being friendly. You wanna see my tattoos?"

"Pass."

She leaned down over him. "Don't know what you're missing."

"I'm sure."

Dugan nodded toward the front of the coach. "Speakin' of tats. There's beautiful *Imani* up there." He raised his voice to get her attention again. "She bangin' with some *reeeal* evil guys."

Imani turned around sharply. Her voice was cool, her tone smooth. "Really. What do you think you know about me?"

"I know you got a *B*, a *G* and a *F* tattoo on your inner thigh. Saw that on the ropes course, too."

She stared him straight in the face, not blinking. "You don't want to be looking at my thigh. Seriously. My guy won't like it when I tell him. He may want to meet up with you."

Emmalyn's face shone with excitement. "What's BGF for?"

"Black Guerilla Family," Dugan replied. "Whole bunch of 'em in DC and Baltimore. Maybe one right here on this bus. Bad. People. You don't wanna know. Back in the day, one of 'em even snuffed my hero Huey Newton, who co-founded the Panthers."

"Well, Mr. Malcom X Glasses, you're not as smart as you think you are. Smart men don't walk on streets where they're not welcome. You should redirect your attention now."

Garrett laughed loud. "Well, Mr. Malcolm X. Glasses. Good one."

Dugan pushed his glasses to the bridge of his nose with one index finger. His grin was gone. "I'm gonna call *you* out, Sir Mocks-a-lot."

Garrett stood up. "Let's leave Tats and Miss BGF alone. How about you, Cold Eyes?" He was looking at Carter.

Across the aisle from Rocco, Carter was flipping through a magazine. She lifted her head and turned it very slowly until she was staring at him. Her brows came together a little, as if she were considering a strange bug, deciding whether to crush it or let it live—but her eyes themselves were an empty blue and her stare blank. Then she turned slowly back to her magazine.

154

"Okay. That just made my point. Thanks for playing."

Carter casually flipped a page. "My boyfriend shot someone in the head during a robbery."

"So."

"I was driving the car."

"Yikes, so I guess your boyfriend is in prison for a while."

"The guy's dead. So yeah, he's in for a while. I got less, because he swore I was waiting in the car and didn't know he shot someone."

"But did you know?"

The look she gave him was still blank, mostly, but with the faintest hint of malice.

"So that's dark." He backed off and redirected to Emmalyn. "How about you, Southern Comfort. What did you do—feed somebody grits with codeine? Underage, with truck drivers back in them hollers?"

Emmalyn was open-mouthed, her sweet expression gone. She looked like she could cry.

Makayla whipped around and stood, her eyes flashing. "Why are you being so horrible? Do you think you're funny? Because you're not. Why are we doing this game anyway? We're supposed to be in this program to get away from our past and try to start over."

Garrett gave her his wise-guy smile, with one corner of his mouth pulled up. "*Try* is the operative word. How many of us do you think are gonna make it through this program for three years—or even *one* year?"

Jalil made a bid to regain the attention. "Hey, Tia Leesha. You seem like a really sweet person. How'd someone nice as you wind up in juvenile detention."

Tia Leesha was sitting in the row in front of Rocco, looking out the coach window, resting her forehead on the cool glass. When she lifted it and turned, her face was gray and the dark brown cloud of her tight curly hair was damp. Her stomach started to heave and her hand flew to her mouth.

"*Oh no, no, no, no, no!*" Dugan shouted, lurching back. "Nobody's pukin' on *this* bus."

"Well, she is."

"*Get her a bucket.*"

"From *where* get her a bucket?"

"Hat Boy, give her your hat. Quick."

"Uh, that would be a *NO*."

Claire leapt up, startling Dhani, who had recoiled deeper in his seat to avoid the conflict. She grabbed her small leather purse from under her seat, and dumped its contents on the cushion.

Moving quickly back to Tia Leesha's side, she held the purse up to the pale girl's face. "Go ahead. Throw up in here if you have to."

Emmalyn gaped. "That's Michael Kors. You're gonna let her puke in a Michael Kors handbag?"

"She's sick." Claire put her hand on Tia Leesha's shoulder. "And anyway it's just a knock-off."

Still flipping through her magazine, Carter said in a loud voice, "Big surprise."

Claire ignored that and—now that the sick girl was leaning forward, stomach wrenching mightily—gently rubbed her back.

In a moment, the stomach heaving subsided, and Tia Leesha sat back, beads of sweat running down the sides of her face. "I didn't do it. I didn't throw up after all. I just feel road sick."

"Motion sick," Emmalyn corrected. "And holy crap, you really were gonna let her barf in your purse. That's the kind of stuff the Bible teaches."

Garrett laughed. "The Bible teaches you to let people puke in your belongings?"

Dugan burst out laughing, clearly back on Garrett's side.

"Not exactly, but it says—"

Claire interrupted, flashing a look at Emmalyn. "I just believe in being good to people. That's all." She turned back to Tia Leesha. "Let me help you walk up front. I bet they have some Dramamine. Or maybe we can pull over at a rest stop to get you some fresh air."

She helped the girl to her feet, and as they passed the row where Dhani was, Claire dropped the purse, in which Tia Leesha had not heaved after all, on the cushion of her seat.

"That was sweet, girl," Makayla said, as the two moved past her toward the front of the coach.

Imani nodded. "You are golden."

Dhani stared at the purse and the contents that Claire had dumped out. A skinny black pencil, two long things in green paper wrappers, a wad of tissues, and a wallet. Beneath the pile of purse stuff was the pad of paper she had been occupied with. With one finger, he carefully moved things aside.

The top sheet was covered with small, pencil sketches—a stream with stones and rapids, Ray-Ray's face, and also Mike Yazzie's profile. Each image carefully rendered. And good. Turning to the next sheet of paper, he had a strange, dizzying moment. . . .

He was inside Claire's mind, glancing in a mirror, watching the black lines spool out from the pencil in her hand, drawing a portrait of herself, disliking the picture that was appearing on the paper. . . .

Then he was back in his own head, confused. Where did the dislike for the picture come from? The image was pretty, like her—and like her, expressionless.

Imani was right, Dhani thought. Behind the mask and distance, Claire was golden. A nice person, and talented. Watching her lead the still-gray, sweating Tia Leesha upfront to the care of the Troverts, he felt confused by her, but liked her even more than before. He wanted to put everything back in the purse as a kind gesture.

Or maybe she'll hate me touching her stuff. As always, he felt unsure and undecided.

Yazzie came down the aisle, stopping midway. "Everything okay back here?"

"Perfect."

"Exceptional."

Emmalyn smiled at Yazzie, whose athletic build was very apparent under the white, *Lake Placid* tee-shirt. "Very fine."

He nodded. "Stopping in five minutes. Nearly twelve-thirty. We'll take an hour break."

Emmalyn smiled as Yazzie returned to his seat. "That is one fine looking Black man."

Dugan, Ray-Ray, and Imani said together, "Oh. My. God." Dugan added, "Racist much?"

When the coach pulled into the rest area, the things on Claire's seat remained untouched.

Steve pulled the small power boat up to the narrow wooden dock on the little island's southern, less windy side, then raised its 18-horse motor to keep the blades from churning into the sand. The lake was shallower here, and the early afternoon sunlight reflecting off the sandy lake bottom made the water look khaki-gold.

Tom, who had come with him, jumped out onto the dock and threaded the boat's front rope through a metal ring in one of the wooden pilings. "Checking out good fishing spots today, I see. I'll bet Grady can tell you some great ones."

"Not if he fishes for them," Steve forced a smiled. He felt a little guilty not telling Tom the real reason for checking out the island. It would have brought more probing questions he would need to evade.

After the run this morning, his chest had been tight with a low-level anxiety. When he had found Kate, privately, he had simply stated he preferred the solitary life. She suggested he check out Osprey Island, this small hump of land out on the eastern side of Lost Lake. "I understand your need to be alone. I love solitude myself. There's a small cabin. A U.S. Congressman friend of mine stayed out there once, when he came with his staff doing some sort of environmental study—he wouldn't say what. Use the boat—you'll like the view from the middle of the lake—and go take a look."

The island was small, with a narrow footpath around its irregular shoreline. Circling west from the dock, the path dipped close to the water and became boggy and crowded with blueberry bushes. Then it rose until, on the western edge, it passed the carcass of an old cedar that weather had stripped down to a gray skeleton and wind tilted over until it almost touched the lake. The water was deeper here, sunlight vanishing into its darkness.

"Kate stocked the lake," Tom reminded, looking down into the water. "Trout, perch, bass. Some pike."

The tightness in Steve's chest was still there. "So you told me."

"I'll bet they hide out here. This is a good place to hide."

He ignored that.

"A nickel for your thoughts," Tom prompted. "A dollar if you're honest."

"My thoughts are, it's a sweet little island. Kate thought I should see it." Ambiguity was a great evasive tactic.

He looked out across the expanse of water they had just crossed, at the western side of the lake with its lodge and cabins. All the demands on him would happen over *there*.

Rounding the northern shoreline, which was strewn with lichen-covered rocks, they came to the east side of the island. A narrow, wooden footbridge on cement pilings connected it to the eastern lakeshore. Small riffles of water slapped lightly at the wooden slats. Beyond the bridge, along the shore, a footpath passed by, heading around the whole lake.

Anyone could wander out here to the island. That did not ease his agitation.

"What about your training plan?" Tom asked, sounding like someone trying to be nonchalant.

"Yep."

"Yep, what? Can I see it?"

"When I'm done with it." He had not put pen to paper once or been able to.

Nearing the dock again, they picked up a trail through undergrowth, which led to the center of the island. All around them were short fir trees and a few red pines, also clusters of white-blooming bushes and twisted rhododendrons, whose roots miraculously anchored them to a thin layer of mossy soil. All of this crowded the path, and every footstep snapped a windfallen twig or branch.

Better. He could hear an approach.

On the island's highest point, there was a small cabin. Kate had called it "rustic, but warm and friendly". He just needed a roof over his head.

The cabin did look rustic from the outside, with rough-cut cedar siding. The roof was steep, tin, painted dark green, the gutters full of rusty pine needles. It occurred to him that someone wanted to conceal this hideaway even more here among the trees. A plus. Next to the small front porch was one of the large boulders that were everywhere here in the north, guarding the entryway. That gave it a fortress feel he liked.

Stepping around the huge stone, Steve mounted the two steps with a single stride.

The interior was exactly the opposite of what he expected. The open, main room was bright, owing to large windows facing east, south and west. It was paneled, from planked floor to vaulted ceiling, in light-toned wood. Two skylights let in even more brightness from the south. It was, as Kate had said, warm and friendly.

In the middle of the southern wall was a fireplace, with glass doors on either side, leading out to a screened porch, furnished with a wooden rocking chair and a low, knocked-together, wood table. Simple. Rustic. Through the rear screens, he looked out into a shady clearing. In its center was a huge red pine, the biggest tree on the island, with a trunk so thick it would take two people stretching to reach around it. Its boughs reached out over the porch, but still allowed filtered light to flood in.

Whoever designed this place loves light. Kate, of course.

His chest expanded and, finally, he relaxed fully. Maybe this place would help him to escape the shadows that pursued him. For the first time in months, he felt brighter. Even a little buoyant.

Tom was watching him closely. He could see the change.

The rest of the exploration was quick. A small bedroom with a rustic, wooden bed and dresser, a narrow bathroom with a chemical toilet and a shower fed by rain-collection barrels outside. Switching on lights in the kitchen, he realized the whole place—including the stove, refrigerator, and water tank—was solar powered. This one modern amenity kept the water pipes from exploding in the deep freeze of winter.

Tom ran one hand over the rough mantle piece. "If I needed a place to escape from everyone, I'd come here."

Back on the dock, Steve continued to breathe deeply, relaxing, taking in the scent of fresh lake water.

Quiet. Solitude. . . .Light. An island refuge could make this gig work.

"So, are you staying?" Tom asked, loosening the boat's mooring rope.

"Out here? Did Kate tell you she offered it to me?—Why not? It's a great place, right?"

Tom faced him squarely. "I mean, are you staying with the program? Because if you're second-guessing, you need to make up your mind. Right now."

"What are you, a mind reader? Yeah, it crossed my mind."

"Crossed your mind? You've been retreating into yourself since you got here. You've made it known you don't like people who are 'on the dole'. . ."

Rondeau again. He would have to be careful around her.

". . .and you haven't given us your training plan. If you're not staying we'll need to scramble to find someone to take your place. The outdoor training starts in just three weeks."

"This—," Steve indicated the island, "—puts me in really good headspace."

Tom got quiet, smiling a little. "You might become a monk out here."

"Not unless monks swear a lot."

"I was going to bring that up."

"I know, I know. I have to rein it in."

"What I'm asking is, can you really handle being here?"

Steve bristled and almost said, "Can you?" but lobbed back a lesser challenge. "Will you stay if I don't?"

"Of course. Remember—we both made a commitment."

Good old Father Tom. Direct as a right-hook to the jaw.

Steve relaxed again, and laughed. "Yeah, I can handle it. And yeah, I know I made a commitment. Okay?"

"Good. Because a bus with twelve students who need solid, steady, adult leadership is arriving in a few hours. And we need to be there for them from day-one. *All* of us. *All in.*"

One more, small, evasive move. "I'm as in as I can be—for one year. Remember, that's all I promised. Kids like these are not my forte, but you can be sure I'll teach them some discipline."

Tom hesitated, but did not pursue that.

In two minutes, the boat was cutting through the chop and spray kicked up by a northern breeze coming down Lost Mountain back toward the lake's western shore.

Tom gripped the throttle, feeling not as sure about things as when they had arrived here. It wasn't because of Steve's shifting moods or the boat's tilting motion as it pounded and tilted across the rough water. He had read the records of the young people who were about to arrive, and felt unsettled by the knowledge of what a few of them had done—not just Dhani Jones. He wavered now between belief and doubt.

Was having Steve here—still struggling, half-hearted at best—the right thing after all? Had he too quickly overlooked Steve's true dislike for "kids like these"? Was it a big mistake to see the meeting of Steve's lostness and Kate's urgent need as a sign from on-high?

Maybe the guilt of his own past failings had become a drive to make Steve's life work out, whatever that took.

Under the sound of the motor's roar, Tom whispered a prayer.

"How do you say your middle name?"

In the rest stop cafeteria, Claire had come up beside Dhani. The building was crowded, loud, and smelled strongly of grease from the fryers. She had to raise her voice to ask her question.

He answered loudly. "It's Singh, a last name—like *sing* a song. How did you know I have two last names, like you?"

"When you got money out of your backpack, I saw the name tag."

Garrett had come up behind them. "*Sing?*—Should be *Singe*." He smelled like nicotine. They were not allowed to use tobacco or alcohol or any other substance during the program, so obviously he had ducked somewhere outside or into a restroom to sneak a smoke. He laughed at his own joke. "Yeah—that's what I'm gonna call you. *Singe*. Because you burn stuff."

Dugan was beside him, also smelling of cigarette. "He only burns people, is what I heard."

Claire stepped between them and Dhani. "Why don't you guys leave him alone and go buy your lunch. Oh, look—they have footlongs." Her voice became even louder. "You can take a whole footlong in your mouth, is what *I* heard."

Dhani smiled for the first time that day.

Dugan laughed. "Oh, zing. You're a funny girl. I like you." He offered her his fist to bump.

Claire ignored him.

Garrett was not laughing. "Be careful around Singe, Rich Girl. You won't look good as a big lump of charcoal."

Her eyes narrowed. "I'm not a *rich girl*."

"Oooo, you gettin' under her skin," Dugan laughed. "Come on, dog. We can't afford to make the pretty ones mad."

"You're right. We're gonna be out in the woods. She may be all we have for a long time."

"Let me make it clear," Claire said, thrusting her face close to Garrett's. "Neither one of you are going to *have* me. Ever." She stepped back and smiled. "I'm looking for something higher up the food chain than you two."

"*Ohhh!*" Dugan laughed, and slapped one hand on his chest like he had been stabbed—and as Garrett started to reply, he grabbed his buddy by the arm. "Come on. We need to move along before this girl guts you like a deer. I'm gonna do what she say, and get me a footlong. Nom, nom, nom. And some cheesy fries. Bus is gonna be pulling out in thirty minutes. Why isn't this line moving? Let's go upfront and cut in." He winked at Claire. "You're *very* good."

When they were gone, Dhani said to Claire, "Thanks. But people have always made fun of my name."

"Singh. Is that Indian? You kind of look like you could be from India."

"It comes from my real father, I think."

"He's from India?"

"Maybe."

"You don't know?"

"I never met him, and my mom doesn't talk about him."

"Why not?"

"I don't think she knows if the Indian guy she was with back then is really my father or not."

"Oh."

There was an awkward silence, which Dhani broke in a moment. "You left the pad on your seat and I saw your sketches. They're really good."

Her face hardened. "They're crap."

"No," he objected. "They're really, *really* good."

"I wish. But here's the thing. I left my pad covered up on my seat, so please don't paw through my stuff again."

The rest stop stretched into ninety minutes, with the Troverts keeping Tia Leesha outside recovering on a bench. Everyone from the bus was through the cafeteria line, and had come out to the grassy lawn next to the blacktopped parking lot. Other travelers were pouring out the door.

Dhani nudged Claire, and nodded toward a woman in leathers who was straddling a motorcycle. "When I saw that woman inside, I thought she was a guy. Didn't you?" He thought she would relax and laugh about it with him.

"No. I didn't think that." She remained serious. "Does it bother you she looks kind of man-ish?"

"I was just saying."

"People are the way they are. You aren't their judge."

Thinking he was building a connection, he had misstepped.

"SONOFA—"

Rocco was standing near them in the parking lot, his pullover drenched with a huge splash of dark liquid running down the back of it and dripping onto the blacktop. He glared at Garrett, who was three feet from him holding an empty soft drink cup.

"Why'd you do that? What's wrong with you?"

Garrett held up both hands in a gesture of innocence. "Accident, man. I tripped and lost my balance." He pulled a crushed napkin out of his jeans pocket. "You want this? Too bad about your shirt. Looks like it's stained."

Emmalyn appeared to be shadowing Rocco. "It sorta looked like you tripped. But it also sorta looked like you flipped your drink at him."

Rocco reached out to accept the napkin from Garrett. Stepping forward, he caught the toe of one tennis shoe on the pavement, stumbled, and dumped the soft drink he was holding on Garrett's jeans.

"Jerk!" Garrett's face turned red with rage.

The half-full cup of soda had landed square on Garrett's fly and was running in dark streaks down both legs of his jeans.

"Ohmygod," Emmalyn snorted. "Looks like you peed."

"Hey, I tripped," Rocco defended. "You saw me. I had an accident. Just like you had an accident."

"I could—"

"Could what? You mean you and your home boy could do something *together*, right? Because you, alone against me? I don't think so."

In the back of the coach, Garrett slid his legs into the dry jeans he'd retrieved from his duffel bag.

"I don't think he's a bad dude," Dugan said. "You been provoking him. Callin' him Tats. Tossing your drink on him." He kicked back in Garrett's seat. "We gonna spend a lot of time with these people. Maybe he got you back, maybe it was just an accident. Like when he stepped on your foot at the picnic, and you were so sure he did it to humiliate you in front of Carter.—Why you like that chick anyway? She got those scary, shark eyes.—Man, you really need to chill."

Garrett buttoned the jeans and pulled up the zipper. He started to say something, then his angry expression relaxed into a grin. "Not a bad dude? You wanna know what he just said? '. . .you and your *Black boy* can try to take me together.' He just punked you."

Dugan sat up, his jaw clenched. "He called me *boy*?"

"*Black boy*. Pure, unadulterated racism."

"Oh, no way. Nobody calls me *boy*."

Garrett shrugged, dropped into the aisle seat in the row with Dugan and slapped his leg. "You can take that from him if you want to. I mean, if you want to let him disrespect you."

It was past sunset when the coach eased carefully across the stone bridge entering the estate. Up the hill, all the lights were on at Kate's place, giving the lodge a golden glow in the deepening blue of evening. A thin sliver of moon reflected in the lake.

As they rolled onto a lantern-lit, stone-paved courtyard behind the great house, there were shouts.

"WHOA, this place is ridiculous!"

"Check me in!"

The coach came to halt.

"Coming up the hill, you couldn't even see the whole back part. This place goes on forever."

"It looks like that wing over there with all the glass has an indoor pool."

"*One* person lives here?"

"I thought we were gonna be sleeping in little tents or tree bark huts or something."

Eric Trovert had risen and taken the coach's microphone in hand. "This is where most of your classes will be held." He pointed out the left side windows of the coach. "Over in those barns is where you'll be trained to care for animals in rehab."

"Nicest barns I ever saw."

"They look better than my house."

"Let's introduce you guys to Kate Holman," Bay announced. "She's the founder of the program, and she's your host. I believe her cook, Ivy, has a hot meal waiting. First, let's unload, and I'll assign your cabins. Three in each one."

The driver had hopped out and was unloading their duffel bags.

Makayla stepped off the last step, rubbing her bare arms and sounding unsure. "It's a lot colder up here than in DC. A lot."

"We're a few hundred miles north. Not far from Canada," Bay said.

"Five hundred, seventy-one point three miles exactly," the driver pitched in, slinging the last bags from the storage compartment onto the stone pavers.

Tia Leesha wrapped her arms around herself, squinting into the surrounding forest. "It's so *dark* here. No street lights. And what lives in these thick woods? They got wolves up here? I'm scared of this place already."

Night was rapidly descending. The empty sound of a cool wind whispered among the pines.

"Less scary than DC by about a million times," said Jalil. He was drumming his hands excitedly on his thighs. "Can't believe we lucked out, getting to come to *this* place."

"I hope this means that whole, stupid, '*Lord of the Flies*' thing we did on the way here is over," said Imani, slinging the strap of her bag over one shoulder.

"What's '*Lord of the Flies*'?" asked Emmalyn.

Garrett smirked. "Read a book much?"

Makayla pointed a finger at him. "Don't ruin this. It could be really good."

"Why would I ruin it?"

"Just because you probably can."

Claire hoisted her duffel bag to one shoulder, and turned to the rear entrance of the lodge. The courtyard was next to a broad, stone terrace that led to two large, French doors. They were wide open, and a warm, welcoming light streamed out into the evening dark. She felt like royalty, and started toward the lodge.

A figure stepped directly in her path, blocking the light.

Carter. Staring at Claire.

Unfazed, Claire walked toward her, until they were a foot apart and face to face. "Excuse me. You're in my way." She side-stepped.

Carter stepped in the way again, staring, with a vague half-smile. "Does this look like the finishing school your parents were going to send you to before you got busted?"

Dhani came up, stumbling under the weight of his duffel, seeing Claire harassed. Here was his chance to earn points—and to make a friend, like Judge Sewell had ordered. "Hey," he said to Carter, sounding anxious, "why are you bothering her?"

"I don't need help handling bullies. That would be you," Claire responded, otherwise ignoring him. She pushed past Carter, bumping her shoulder.

Stay away from me, creep-o.

16TH

The black lab remained in a kind of limbo, not improving and not getting worse.

In the early morning dark, Sahm rose with the poor creature on his mind, feeling frustrated about the dog—and other things.

First, it was pouring rain outside, and low gray clouds hid the mountain peaks. He would have to stay inside for his meditation practice. Also, Jo had heard from Ron about his prayer for the goshawk, and had forbidden him from using healing practices with the animals. He had backed off.

How could he obey this order, though? Since he had reconnected with the old earth energies through the boulder beside his cabin, whatever was awakening in him was gradually growing stronger.

Brewing himself a strong tea made with wild herbs, his mind was on events of the past few days.

In his meditation practice, it had suddenly become easier to shift his mind away from its normal focus on the sounds, smells, and images of the outer world. With little effort, he could enter a state of mind that was wide open and clear as sky. A huge leap forward he had never achieved in Tibet, when his mind was occupied with escaping.

Then there was the sign.

Three mornings in a row this week, he had stopped randomly at different spots along the lakefront to let his mind rise up the surrounding mountains to the sky. Immediately, two golden perch had swum up and spun before him in the shallows, exulting in the freedom of the water. They resembled one of the eight auspicious signs of Tibetan Buddhism—two golden fish, circling in delirious freedom from struggle in this lower world of form.

On the third day, one of them said, in his mind, *"He is coming."*

"He is here," said the other.

He did not see them any morning after that.

Who is here? he wondered now, confused, adding more wild herbs to the red clay teapot.

And then there was another thing to deal with.

He had become aware at odd moments, not just of whispered directives but also pulses of life-energy racing through his whole body. He thought of Tagore, the famous Hindu poet, who had called this sensation "the life-throb of ages dancing in my blood." He felt it randomly, spontaneously, coming from things all around him. From Vajra, when he ran his hand over the half-wolf's rough fur. From the tender, new, spring plants when he searched for them with the program's naturalist, Laurel Wysocki, to make teas and medicines.

When this sensation came, it streamed up his spine, across his shoulders, down his arms, and out through his hands. Sometimes it came with thoughts that guided him.

Vajra has a small thorn in his front paw. Look.

Cut and dry this herb. It will clear the lungs.

Before the herb tea had finished steeping, he felt the energy rise.

"Open yourself. Now. Go deeper."

This last voice did not seem to come from within his head, though.

Abandoning the kettle, he went to the cabin's front room. Before his meditation altar, he bowed with his face to the floor, then sat cross-legged. In a moment, his mind became clear as air. . .

. . .*where a young eagle passed across Lost Lake from one horizon to the other. . .then back again. . . horizon to horizon.*

The one was joined by another. . . then another, and another. . . until there were dozens, hundreds, and more, covering the sky. . .their thousand thousand cries shaking the mountainsides.

Sahm's eyes came open. He was sitting in a pool of warm light. Through the front windows, he could see sparkling drops of water dripping from the eaves. The clouds and rain had moved on, and the lake shone with sunsparks.

How long had he been in deep meditation? Where had he been?

His thoughts came back to the young eagle, not the one in his meditation but the enigmatic one in a safe enclosure in Jo's aviary. They had rescued it from where it had fallen on the camp road twelve weeks ago. It appeared to be perfectly healthy, without injury to its bones, wings, or internal organs. Yet it would not fly. It sat in its enclosure, behind a one-way glass in the sliding door, protecting the bird from

172

over-exposure to humans and becoming used to their presence. That was hardly necessary. It ignored everyone.

Sahm glanced at the small statue he had placed in the center of his meditation altar. The blue lapis figure was no bigger than his thumb. A Great One—an ancient who came thousands of years before Siddhartha, who became the beloved Shakyamuni Buddha. This was the One his grandfather and the Bön yogis of their lineage revered, whose name was not to be spoken except with other adepts.

It occurred to Sahm to wonder if the bright blue light he had witnessed while passing through the *Bardo* at *Losar* had something to do with this Great One. Was he present with Sahm in this lifetime's journey? On the other hand, why would such an exalted One involve himself in such mundane affairs as those Sahm had joined himself to here at Lost Lake?

He shook his head and dismissed those musings.

Before the small figure, Sahm had set the *phurba* to strengthen its power. There was also a small, white divining stone passed on by his grandfather and a small, painted *tsakli*—a rough picture on a square of canvas of the fierce protector Buddha, Vajrapani, with its blue visage, fangs like a tiger, and yellow-orange halo of fire.

Each was only a meditational tool, a stepping stone to a higher level of awareness. Something besides the objects themselves held his attention, though.

All the pieces, especially the central blue figure to whom the altar was dedicated, were awakening in him subtle vibrations that Sahm could feel on the air, in his bones, and especially in his hands.

He began a prayer, one that had to be said silently to keep secret the name of this powerful Enlightened being, who was emanating from the small, blue lapis statue, his light filling the space in front of Sahm. This Great One's name had been entrusted to only a few Bön yogis, like his grandfather, down through the millenia via secret and rigorous training.

Were there any left to honor this beautiful, powerful, compassionate being? Sahm wondered. To do the kind of work he sent adepts to do—the care and preservation of the natural world?

Words came to his mind, but not *from* his mind. This time they were clear and distinct.

"Yes, there are others. They are being awakened and collected together from everywhere, like drops of water filling a beautiful mountain lake."

He startled, staring at the lapis figure of the One who had spoken into his mind. A shaft of sunlight through the cabin's front windows had ignited it bright as a blue flame, and from it emanated a brilliant aura in a halo of all colors.

"It is beginning."

Are there truly any others? Sahm asked, letting his doubt speak. There was no point in hiding it. *Any who have not been kidnapped and killed? Any who are awakened and skilled enough?*

"The work does not require many. Only a few with true belief and desire."

How will I find them? Where should I look?

Laughter. "There is no need to look. As the danger becomes clearer, I am the thought in their minds that awakens them and the vital energy in their bodies that brings them together."

How will I know them?

"They will come to you."

It occurred to Sahm that this was the transcendent One, who cared for all creatures and the earth itself, and he thought of the young eagle. *Please—if you know—why does he lack the power to fly?*

"Tahgs" was the response, a Tibetan word meaning *a sign.*

The sudden shafts of sunlight fell through Dhani's bedroom window. He had fallen asleep looking out at a black night sky filled with stars, hours later half-awakening to an early rain drumming on the cabin roof. Now, a flood of clear light crept across the green blanket, falling full on his face. Blinking, he tried to open his eyes, and imagined he was lying under a waterfall of light.

There was a new feeling inside him on this first morning here. As if a bird had awakened inside the cage of his ribs. It was a feeling he had not experienced since he was a little boy.

Dressed, stepping outside, he closed the cabin door quietly behind him. It was very early, just after 6, and he wanted to be alone. He crunched his way through the leaf litter and fallen pine cones, out from under the tree line and down to the lakeshore.

The surface of Lost Lake spread before him, smooth as a mirror, silver in some places and blue as the cloudless morning sky in others. Only far out in the middle was the surface lightly wrinkled by streams of moving air. Sharp rays of sunlight were angling down, striking the plumes of fog rising from the water, igniting them into what looked like burning wisps.

The feeling he'd had upon waking—one of *exaltation*—filled him even more now. It made him remember the one birthday party his mother had given for him, when he was maybe four. Before the men started moving in. Yeah, four. He remembered the number candle. They were happy back then, never very sad and not terrified.

He walked to where the lake met the sand, and stopped when the soles of his sneakers touched the water line. Currents of cool air moved down from the peaks all around. He blew on his fingers and pulled them inside his sleeves.

Out on the lake, something flashed, and the great feeling inside him began to soar. Sunlight was in his veins; he was air. He imagined he could keep walking right out on the surface of the lake as an energy trapped within his skin pushed to break free.

Down the shoreline a hundred feet or so was a turned-over green canoe with tan wood trim. He broke into a jog, then a sprint, kicking up beach sand with his heels.

Beside the canoe were two paddles, lying in the sand. Flipping the craft, he looked out at the sun striking the silver-blue lake, Osprey Island beyond, and rising in the east above that, the three ridges of The Arrows. He felt an urge to shove the canoe out, jump in, and glide across the smooth surface, powering his way with all this racing energy around the island, exploring the far shoreline from the water.

He pushed the canoe's front end into the water. Gripping a paddle in one hand, he stepped in, immediately lost balance—flipping the canoe sideways, pitching him down on one elbow and hip in a line of stones and pebbles at the water's edge.

"*Ouch.* That had to hurt."

Embarrassed, he whipped his head around. Walking towards him from the direction of their cabin was Ray-Ray, holding a paper coffee cup.

Dhani jumped up, rubbing his elbow.

"You okay?"

Claire was also approaching, coming from one of the other eight small cabins, the one closest to Kate's place.

Great. He nodded.

When she reached him, Claire carefully brushed the sand off his sleeve. "That was a bad fall. Let's see your elbow."

"It's okay."

"You landed in the stones. It might be cut." She started to pull his sleeve up and expose his forearm.

Dhani pulled back. "No. I'm good. Really."

She raised her hands in surrender. "Okay. Calm down."

"I was just going out for a canoe ride."

"I saw. Do you know how to canoe?"

It occurred to Dhani that he didn't. "Sort of." His wild elation was fizzling out.

"I'd like to go out," Ray-Ray said, looking at the lake. "That language tutor and martial arts guy—Yazzie—he said the water in these lakes is crystal clear because it's so cold most of the year. He said, in a lot of places you can see all the way to the bottom, and watch fish swimming around. I really wanna see that."

Claire looked from one to the other. "Do either of you guys know how to paddle a canoe?" When they didn't respond, she took charge. "I can teach you. Dhani, you're in front because you look lighter. Ray-Ray, you're in back. Each of you take a paddle."

Ray-Ray smiled and set down his cup in the sand. "And you... just get to ride along in the middle?"

"That's the plan. We have two hours till breakfast—are we standing here, or canoeing?"

The only thing Dhani didn't like about the morning paddle was that Claire was behind him, and he wanted to see her, maybe even have a conversation. He didn't know how to start one, though, so it didn't matter. The canoe slid over the silky blue water, leaving a wide V spreading out behind them and, with Claire's direction, he almost got the hang of paddling.

"Dhani, you need to dig your paddle deeper into the water," Claire instructed. "Make smoother strokes, like I told you."

"Sorry." He felt like an idiot.

"Sometimes you have to look hard at a person, and realize he's doing the best that he can," Ray-Ray said, in a bold voice.

Claire turned her head to stare at him. "I know. But he's splashing me."

"I wasn't ragging on you," Ray-Ray replied. "It's a line from 'On Golden Pond.' Kathryn Hepburn says it about her pain-in-the-butt husband, Norman. I've been thinking about that movie since we got here. I mean, look around you. This is Golden Pond on steroids."

Claire smiled a little. "'Norman, you old poop.' One of my foster moms watched that film on Amazon a million times. That's my favorite line. . . . So, Ray, you read serious books and you like films. You're interesting. What else do you do?"

"Gourmet cooking. Especially French and Cajun."

Dhani dug his paddle deep into the water, feeling even more stupid.

They were passing the south end of Osprey Island now, twenty feet out from the thick trees and brush of its shoreline. The sun had climbed, and its light penetrated deep into the lake, turning the water golden. Ray-Ray was keeping up a constant patter about truffles and saffron, one Dhani had no way to break into. Ray-Ray seemed so relaxed around girls, during the ropes course, on the coach ride, and now with Claire.

He decided he wanted to ask Claire what was bothering her this morning. He had seen it in her eyes, more than just a concern about him flipping on his butt.

"I like some hip-hop, too," Ray-Ray was saying, "but I like the blues fusion coming out of north and west Africa even more. You ever hear of Vieux Farka Toure? Amazing guitarist, and—*oh my god*," he whispered suddenly, lifting his paddle. *"Look. Down."*

Dhani pulled his paddle from the water, laid it on his knees, the drops falling from it sending concentric rings opening out on the lake surface like silver blooms. He started to lean over the side of the canoe.

Claire quickly put her hand on his back. "Slow. Not too far. You'll flip us."

Given that she'd been ignoring him, the correction stung a little, like a rebuke. She confused him, first making him feel as if she liked him, then making him feel like he was a child to be watched over. He wanted her just to like him.

"What the H is that?" Ray-Ray whispered, peering and pointing down into the water between them and the island.

"What the '*H*'?" Claire repeated. "Do you mean 'hell'?"

"My father is a preacher. He never let us swear.—*Look*. What *is* that thing?"

Leaning—carefully—Dhani could see, down along the sandy bottom in the clear water, a huge fish, almost a yard long. Its thick body was swaying side to side, propelling it forward as it kept pace with the canoe's slowing glide. Even at this depth, maybe ten feet, he could make out its features—light, bar-like splotches along the body, fins reddish with dark spots, its face long and pointed like a beak.

And then the great fish angled its body upward, and swam straight at the canoe, surfacing just in front of Dhani. With a flap of its tail, it splashed at him—and as he recoiled, it flipped its body and one eye caught the sunlight. It almost looked as if it had winked at him in a welcome greeting.

At that instant, whether in his mind or in the open air, he heard the sharp clanging of cymbals and the sound of deep horns blowing. The sound flared so suddenly and loud he cupped his hands over his ears and turned to Claire and Ray-Ray, who did not seem to notice.

"*You are a strange one, Dhani.*" His mother's voice sounded in his head. "*Always making up that you see things and hear animals talking. People avoid people who are like that.*"

He dropped his hands, and all he could hear was water lapping against the canoe.

The fish had swum to the bottom again, where it angled lazily into shallower water. It passed within a cluster of swaying reeds beneath the shadow of a bent cedar that tilted out over the lake. There it waited, almost hidden, tail barely moving, inches above the sand and rocks.

"Did you see that?" Ray-Ray said, amazed. "So freakin' *weird*. It like, came right up to greet you."

Clare sounded unsettled. "More like an attack."

"That thing was huge."

179

"Two-and-a-half or three feet," Claire added.

"Were those teeth?" Dhani asked.

Ray-Ray was excited now. "Man, let's make spears and come back here and see if we can catch it."

"You want to provoke it?" said Dhani. "No way I'm ever swimming in this lake."

"It's just a fish, not the Loch Ness monster," said Claire, dismissing it all. "It lives way out here away from the swimming area, so I'm sure we're all safe."

Dhani had turned enough in the canoe that he could see Claire now—and in the subdued moments that followed the fish encounter he erased from his mind what he had seen and heard. And made his move.

"What's wrong with you today?" he asked her.

Her eyes clouded. "Excuse me?"

"Back where we found the canoe, I mean. You looked like something was bothering you."

"Well aren't you perceptive."

"So. . . ."

She sat back against the strut. "That girl—Carter."

Ray-Ray snorted. "The girl with the scary shark eyes. What's up with her?"

"I think she hates me for some reason."

"What did she say?"

"Nothing. She just stares at me, with that cold, empty look. Thank god, at least we're not in the same cabin."

"She looks like that horrible girl from that movie 'The Ring'," said Ray-Ray. Lifting his arms, he dangled his fingers down over his face. "Does she stare at you through her hair—like this? And crawl at you on all fours?"

Claire relaxed and laughed.

"Hey," Ray-Ray continued, "you got us. Me and Dhani here. We'll protect you from the demon spawn. Right?"

Dhani brightened a little. He was supposed to make friends; Sewell's orders. But it seemed so hard. "Yeah. You got us."

An angry shout came at them over the water. Way back on the lakefront where they had set out, a man in a red flannel shirt waved his arms wildly, signaling.

"Uh-oh," said Ray-Ray, "I think we might be in trouble."

Claire rolled her eyes. "First morning. Off to a great start."

A knock at the front door jarred him awake.

I thought this place was going to be private.

Steve rolled out of bed—*7:03.* He had slept well the first few weeks out here, but now he was jolting awake in the dark hours, sensing there was something he should remember—though what it was stayed just out of reach, along with whatever he'd been dreaming. He rolled out of bed in his boxers.

Eric Trovert was out on the little front porch. "Hey, sorry. Looks like you're just getting up."

Steve scratched his ribs and yawned. "Looks that way. What is it?"

"Everything okay?"

"Why wouldn't it be?"

"I usually see you out jogging by now, so I thought it was safe to come by."

Steve stretched, and released some of the night's tension from his shoulders. "Um, you want coffee?" He hoped Trovert would say no.

"I'm good. I came to ask if you want to do some rappelling this morning. Tom said you're trained, and he and Kate are orienting the students all day. Today's a freebie before the program kicks into high-gear."

Now that Steve was waking up, a vague uneasiness was rising. He needed to be outside and moving. "You got ropes, carabiners, harnesses?"

"I do. Turn right at the end of the footbridge and the trailhead up The Arrows is about a quarter-mile down the shoreline. There's a big cut-out curve in the cliff there, called The Bow. We're gonna drop down into there. How about, say, nine?"

"Got it."

Eric paused on the steps. "You sure everything's alright?"

Go the hell away. "Right as rain."

When Eric was gone, Steve filled the coffee pot at the kitchen tap, and suddenly his stomach felt tight. A jolt of memory—the forgotten dream—kicked him in the *solar plexus.* . . .

Olivia lay on the sidewalk.

Thi, her friend, was grasping her hand, shouting, "Hang on. My god, hang on."

Her eyes were locked on his, and he was willing her not to leave him.

Olivia's hand relaxed into Thi's, and let go. . . .

He drank the coffee scalding hot. Why had he agreed to go rappelling, when all he really wanted to do was curl up into a ball under the covers? Also, on first meeting, the Troverts made him feel vaguely like he was on a glass slide under a high-powered microscope. Or maybe just the fact that they were shrinks made him uneasy.

He made his breathing settle. *Ignore Trovert. He's just a paid kid-friend, who thinks he's a mind reader.*

He had come out to this place to deep-six the past. Everything. The dreams were only flickers in the night, the voices only occasional whispers. The mental and physical challenge of rappelling a steep rock face was probably exactly what he needed.

He showered the last, fading images away under water as cold as he could bear.

Grady, the groundskeeper, was waiting for Dhani, Claire, and Ray-Ray on the shore. They could not see his eyes behind the blue-flash sunglasses, but he was clearly disgusted. He slammed his fishing pole and tackle box down on the sand, and grabbed the paddle Dhani was holding.

"What do you guys think you're doing? This is my canoe."

"We didn't know. It was just lying here."

"First day, and you broke two rules. One, you never go out in a canoe without life jackets. Two, you don't take someone else's property without asking. Maybe the way you were raised. . . ." He stopped himself, then repeated. "Don't take things without asking. Most people know that."

Ray-Ray and Dhani stared at the ground.

Claire looked like she was thinking. "Are you going to report us?"

"Have to."

"We made a mistake. It won't happen again."

"Doesn't matter."

She looked at a pole and tackle box in the sand beside him. "Looks like you're going fishing."

"That's why I hauled my canoe out here last evening. Now I'm late getting out on the water. After they stop rising, they lie on the bottom all day."

She nodded. "What do you fish for in this lake?"

Grady paused, eyeing her. "Lake trout, perch. If you're lucky, northerns."

"We saw a really big fish. It was—what do you think guys, *this* long?" She opened her arms wide.

They nodded. "Easy." "Maybe bigger."

"Seriously. What did it look like?"

Claire described it. "And we saw where it hides."

"Are you sure its back fin was down near its tail?"

"Positive. It swam right up to the surface, like it was going to jump out of the water at Dhani."

"Game fish don't swim *at* you, they swim *away* from you. They're wily. I think this is bull."

"Suit yourself," Claire shrugged. "Your loss."

Grady let down his guard. "If you're not making this up, that's a northern pike. Kate stocked this lake with some, but I've never seen even one. I just assumed the eagles and hawks got 'em." He was thoughtful now. "You use a steel leader for those, and even if you do they can still snap your line. They're intense fighters. Where'd you see it?"

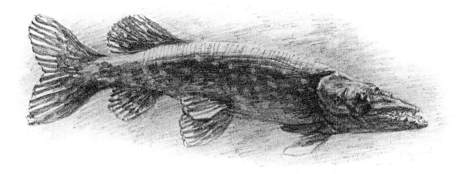

"If I tell you, will you not report us?"

Grady gave her a wry smile. "Is that how you get by in life, cutting deals?"

"Do you want to know where your big fish is?"

He shook his head. "Kate has no idea what she got herself into. Where is it?"

Claire was unflinching. "Deal?"

"Because I'm a good guy. Next time, though, you ask. And use life vests. This lake is small compared to other Adirondack lakes, but there's a ninety-foot drop halfway between here and that island. You fall in and go down, they may not find a body to ship home to your parents."

Claire's voice was cool. "I don't have a home. Or parents."

Grady's hard edge vanished. "Oh. Sorry."

"Don't be. And we won't touch your canoe again. Do you want to know where your fish is or not?"

Steve stood at the edge of the cliff, a low wind blowing up the rock face. The drop from this highest ridge of The Arrows was sheer, with broken boulders at the bottom. He guessed the fall from here was eighty or ninety feet.

Randy Wolfmoon had joined them at the top, while Mike Yazzie waited below for the rope to drop.

"These guys are the safety squad," said Eric.

Looking down, Steve felt adrenalin kicking-in. His body tingled, and he realized how much he craved that after feeling nearly dead for so many months. The idea of "a safety squad" was a downer. So Trovert was *that* guy.

Ten feet back from the cliff, Eric cinched the rope around a red pine that looked beaten and twisted by a hundred storms. Leaning back, he pulled with all his might on the rope. "This guy's roots are anchored in the ridge. Rope's brand new and a hundred feet long. Did you find the helmet and figure-eight?"

Steve tightened the nylon harness around his waist and hips, then hooked a carabiner through the steel loop. "This was in my bag, with my climbing shoes—a fast descender."

Eric and Randy studied the device as Steve worked the rope through it. "You can pretty much free-fall, and brake just before you hit bottom."

185

"Figure-eight gives you a slower, smoother descent," said Eric.

"I can use the rush."

"You haven't done this descent yet, though. Maybe you want to take it easy the first time. Figure out how the cliff works."

Eric was about to say more—but Steve quickly tossed the coil of rope off the cliff and backed up until his heels were off the edge. More cool air rushed up at him from inside the great, rocky curve of The Bow.

"You got it down there?" he shouted down to Mike Yazzie, who was untangling the rope from between two sharp boulders where it had snagged.

In a moment, Yazzie's *"All clear!"* sounded from below.

Steve stepped back, planted his feet on the rock rim, then leaned back into the open air until his upper body and legs made a forty-five degree angle.

"Hey, your helmet," Randy said, reaching it out to him.

Steve grinned and pushed out hard with his legs—plunging out of sight down the rock face.

Eric and Randy dropped to their stomachs at the edge, and stared down the cliff after him.

"Are you going to talk to him, or do you want me to since I'm the climbing instructor?" said Randy.

"I'll do it," Eric replied.

In an hour, Randy traded places with Yazzie, who was ready for a turn on the rope.

Steve made a third descent, pushing himself way out from the cliff, dropping and swinging into the broken rock face—narrowly missing a jagged outcrop. Pushing off again at an angle, he swung in wide arcs back and forth across the sheer rock face. On his next thrust, he launched out too close to a sharp granite seam and scraped his leg.

An explosion of swearing echoed around inside The Bow.

"Can you say *death wish*?" Mike said to Eric. "Who vetted this guy?"

"Tom Baden."

"And you say Kate really trusts him? Turns out he's a hot-shot and doesn't listen to anyone. Hell, he doesn't even want to be around anyone. Why's he here?"

Steve refused an alcohol wipe from Randy's first-aid kit to clean the shallow slice along his thigh. "Hey, it only hurts when I stand or walk," he joked.

When they finished rappelling, Randy and Mike walked ahead of Steve and Eric on the shoreline trail.

"I guess you know you'll need to rein-in the whole wild man thing when the students are around, right?" Eric said.

Steve was still enjoying the rush of the adrenalin high, and the remark grated. "Hey, I was hired to be a wilderness survival trainer, not a Sunday school teacher. I want some fun while I'm here, too."

"Understood. Like it or not, though, we're the ones these kids will be watching. We set the good example."

When they reached the footbridge to the island, Steve headed across without looking back. "Have a nice afternoon—doc."

"Hang on. Everything okay?"

"You asked me that this morning. And yep, I'm still fine."

Alone in his cabin, he got a cold IPA from the refrigerator and slammed the door. Kate had a policy that there was to be no alcohol anywhere on the property.

He popped the cap and saluted her. *Save your policies for the delinquents.*

21ST

Every day, when Sahm cleaned Jo's animal enclosures and refilled water troughs and bottles, he looked in on the black lab especially.

It was four weeks since the dog had been rescued, and last evening Sahm had overheard Jo telling Ron, "He's still barely holding on. I keep waiting against my better judgment to do the amputation, hoping he'll regain enough strength."

"What about the chance of gangrene setting in?" Ron had asked.

"It hasn't. Not yet. But all the antibiotics aren't knocking the infection out of that foot either. I don't want to risk finishing him off by putting him under for a major procedure."

Before stepping into Jo's operating area, where the lab was lying listless in a holding cage, Sahm recalled a distinct message that had come. This morning during his meditation, words were spoken into his mind.

"Rescue the rescuer."

Jo was the rescuer of animals. What did the message mean?

Who is the rescuer? he had asked.

"Palden."—which meant, *the Glorious One.*

Palden was a title given to great, spiritual teachers and adepts. Despite her many gifts, that was not Jo.

The dog. Maybe he is one of the great masters moving between lifetimes. Maybe he is one who is to be gathered here and that is why he does not depart.

Sahm felt a surge of conviction, coming from behind that invisible veil all around him. This was an important being. He felt a sudden strong urge to set aside Jo's prohibition against him touching any of the animals in her clinic. And yet—he had not been able to help the goshawk.

For a split-second, he had the sense of who might be speaking to him. *I ask for your help. . . .*

Opening the steel-barred door to the dog's holding cage, he leaned in over the lab. The smell of disinfectants, medicine, betadine, and animal filled his nostrils in the enclosed space. He wished he could clear these unnatural scents by burning one of the juniper wands he had cut and dried—but then Jo would know what he had been up to.

Surely, simple healing prayers would not harm the dog in any way.

He began to chant the traditional Medicine Buddha recitation—that, he remembered. Mostly.

I prostrate myself at the feet of the Excellent Ones, who, enlightened for countless eons, manifest through wisdom and compassion in limitless emanation bodies, curing sickness. . . .

As the words slipped from his lips, smooth as healing waters, a vague image came to mind—a figure seated cross-legged, blue and radiant as a jewel. But instead of the begging bowl in its lap or the wand of the healing, myrobalan plant, this figure had a golden light glowing from its heart center. Not knowing what else to do, Sahm continued the Medicine Buddha prayer.

I praise you, Who radiates the light of compassion that surrounds and embraces all sentient beings—you, Who dispels suffering here in the lower realms and cures sickness and disease, begin to heal this Glorious One.

He had leaned down close to the unmoving dog, and could smell the disinfectant used to clean his gashed paw. The dog's sides were rising and falling, just a little, with the weak effort his life-force managed to give to inhaling and exhaling. Sahm broke the prayer, to call silently,

Palden—if your work in this place were finished, you would know it and be free to move on. Yet you linger between this life and the next. I beg you to stay if you have been drawn here—

He heard the clinic's outer door opening, and in a moment Jo entered the examining room.

She found Sahm arranging supplies in the walk-in storage closet.

25TH

The afternoon orientation hike around Kate's property was wrapping up.

"Do you have kids?" Imani asked her randomly.

"I wish I did. But no."

"So you live out here all alone?" said Ray-Ray.

"Not now. I've got all of you here to share this great place with me. Think of it as your home away from home."

"Wow. This *whole place*?"

After a tour around her estate, Kate had led them out behind her lodge, along the curving dirt road that brought them back to her greenhouse and garden and two large, storage buildings. Out behind those buildings, they could see a huge meadow that lay in a valley between Lost Mountain to the northwest and Eagle Rock Mountain to the northeast.

Heads were turning in every direction.

Tia Leesha looked uneasy. "So, what lives around here?—in all these dark woods, I mean."

"A lot of beautiful, wild creatures," Kate smiled. "But I have to warn you—some of them are dangerous. You don't want to go near the deer. You'll see a lot of them in this meadow, and they're beautiful. But do not go near or try to feed them. Their hooves are razor sharp, and if they get upset they can rear up and slash you. There are coyotes, too, and even some evidence of mountain lions."

"What kind of evidence?" asked Dugan.

"First, there was just scat, some claw marks on trees, urine scent. Now there've been a few sightings."

"Oh-god-oh-god-oh-god," said Tia, flailing both her hands.

"That's why, for safety's sake, we've created a 'wander line' around the property. It's a perimeter to stay within. Besides the possibility of encountering wild animals, the Thunder Falls overlook has a sheer drop-off, and the first pool right below it is filled with sharp rocks. So is the lower pool. A fall from the top could be deadly."

"What happens if you go outside the line?" asked Jalil.

Kate nodded at Bay, who'd come with them, along with Tom. "Bay will give you each a map and take you on a walk around to show where the markers are. And of course you respect other people's privacy. That means getting together only in communal spaces in your cabins—not bedrooms—and outside. You can enjoy the great room in my place, too. I'd love for you to use it during the daytime."

"But what if you accidentally 'wander' outside the line?" Garrett pressed. He looked at Carter to see if she caught his little joke.

"No sirens will go off, if that's what you mean. But the map and markers are very clear. It won't be difficult to learn the boundaries."

"Can we ever go outside this 'wander line' thing?" Garrett asked again. "Like can we just hike out on our own or go into town if we get bored?"

"In time, when we know you can handle the trails, we'll extend the short-hike limits a bit. For now, you'll need to have an adult with you. And as far as town goes, we'll schedule group trips. Everything you need is here."

Bay stepped in. "You really need to understand that people get lost in this wilderness every year. Some are never seen again, and they starve to death. Sometimes their remains are found months or years later. Sometimes there's no trace."

There was a sober silence.

"But," Bay lightened the mood, "we've got a great outdoor program planned. You'll learn all about survival, wild edible plants, maybe some cave exploration. You just have to follow our guidance."

Imani still looked uncomfortable. "*Cave* exploration?"

"What?" Rocco teased her. "You didn't read the travel brochure? Sounds amazing to me. And hey, I got your back."

"You'll also be working with Doctor Jo Rondeau," Tom added now, "doing wild animal rescue and rehab. In the fall, you'll work with tutors and art and sports instructors. You won't have time to be bored."

"I'm just saying *if* we're bored," Garrett pushed.

Dugan leaned close and elbowed him. "Give it a rest, man. This place is like a mountain paradise."

When the group broke up, Tom walked Kate back to her office. "I think we've got maybe a couple weeks, three at the outside," he said.

"Until what?"

"Until they start testing the boundaries."

Kate waved this off. Her talk with Sahm had lifted her spirits and boosted her confidence about the program again. "There are so many great things for them to do here, Tom. The Troverts and Jo and Steve are putting together an exciting, fascinating program. Everyone will be too involved to get into trouble."

From the meadow, the group of students had split, most heading back to the cabins or the lakefront.

Garrett walked slowly along the road, letting everyone get ahead. Except Dugan, who he grabbed by the sleeve.

"C'mon, man."

"Where are we going?"

Garrett did not answer, but led him toward the bridge that crossed the Garnet River.

"Dude, I'm not your puppet. Where are we going?"

"Just follow me."

Beyond the bridge, they passed around and behind the second animal rehab barn, and found the trail Kate had pointed out earlier, leading up Lost Mountain to Thunder Falls.

"What was that all about back there?" Dugan asked. "I think you were pissing off the head guys, talking about getting bored."

"I wasn't buying the big sales job about this 'great program'. I'm not really the eat nuts and tree bark, sleep on the ground kinda guy."

"Oh yeah? What kind of guy are you?"

Garrett did not answer.

The trail wound for a hundred yards, with the river on their right and a sloping ridge of trees and tumbled rocks on their left. Shortly, they came to a spot where the path angled left and north and began to climb. A tree on each side of the trail was marked with a bright yellow blaze two feet tall and four inches wide. A five-foot yellow pole had been driven into the ground beside the trail.

Garrett laughed. "Here's the stupid 'wander line.' Talk about overkill."

He kept walking past the yellow blazes into the woods.

Dugan halted. "What you doing, dog?"

"You asked what kind of guy I am." Garrett was thirty feet up the trail into the woods already. He turned around, his arms outspread, smiling. "I'm *this* kind of guy."

"We just got here. I don't want to get labelled a trouble maker already."

"I've got a cousin downstate. Already talked to him."

"You planning to ghost?"

"No. But let's just say I have other plans. I didn't come here to learn how to rub two sticks together to start campfires and put band-aids on Bambi. If you're chill, I'll let you in on it later."

Dugan looked uneasy.

"You want to let them own you? Go ahead."

"No, no, no, no, no, man. Don't do this. I gotta do this clean. I got a record to clear up. So do you."

"*Shee*-it, why don't you go back and have a *nice* dinner. Listen to Emmalyn say stupid crap, and pat scared little Tia Leesha's hand." Garrett's smile flashed. "Or you can watch as Rocco owns your woman, Imani. I'm gonna check out—," his voice went spooky sounding, "—*the forbidden waterfall*. You coming or not?"

Dugan turned, and started back along the river trail.

"Just remember," Garrett called after him, "girls like bad boys better than scared little rabbits in cages. Bad boys always win."

Dugan slowed.

"Hippity-hop back to your cage, little bunny. Nibble nibble on your carrot."

Dugan turned and came back. "I hate you, man."

"No you don't. Because I'm going help you get through this program with your nads intact instead of in a jar. Tanner can't help you survive the same way I can."

"Hey, I liked Tanner."

"We met him for like five minutes the first night."

"He's a Marine. He's the *dude*."

"Forget him. He sucks. Let's check out the falls."

28TH

He couldn't fish.

He couldn't sit still long enough.

He leaned the pole against the gray trunk of the dead cedar, and when it slid and fell to the ground he left it there.

Some part of Steve's mind knew that Eric confronting him the day they rappelled together was not unreasonable. Why did it set him off? The great rush of pleasure he had felt back on the cliff had morphed back into agitation.

He was glad there was no meeting today, no reason to run into Trovert. In every encounter now, Eric's presence ground on his nerves a little more. He needed to stop this agitation ruining the good buzz he got from being out on this island.

In the cabin, he went to the refrigerator, took out a beer and forcefully popped the cap, throwing the bottle opener on the counter. Then paced around inside the rear sun porch, gripping the long-necked bottle tightly and downing the brew in long pulls. The place felt too confining, and he walked down the back steps into the clearing.

Late afternoon sunlight slanted down through the red pine's branches, and a low spring wind moved the boughs.

He liked Eric at one level. That was confusing. He liked Bay. Randy and Mike, too. Kate was a gem, really.

Jo?—he didn't want to think about her at all right now.

A distant part of his mind told him he was being a jackass and that it was more than reasonable for the program leaders to expect him to be a role model. He had been one to his men in the Corps. Why was he behaving like an angry kid now?

He didn't care.

Hoisting the empty bottle in the air, he saluted. "Here's to you, Trovert—and all the rest of you perfect people. Good for you, for being icons of virtue."

Draining the bottle, he drew back his arm and hurled it hard as he could at the red pine—where it smashed.

4

JUNE

1ST

Even at half-full, the moon was bright enough to wake Kate. But then, she hadn't been sleeping soundly.

Once she was awake, her thoughts took over, jumping from one issue with the program to another—then started the list over again. The Troverts had concerns about Steve's reclusiveness. They were also concerned about one of the girls, Makayla, who was throwing away most of her food at every meal. Steve and Jo seemed to be in tension about something. She could sense it in their coolness toward each other during staff meetings. And late yesterday—the troubling call from John Sewell.

After tossing, flipping, churning, and twisting the bedclothes, she slipped out of the large four-poster. A cup of the wild mint tea Sahm had gathered would help her ease back into sleep, or at least distract from her troubled thoughts. She did not turn on a light but rose quietly—and stopped in the dark, halfway to the door.

Through one bedroom window, down the slope near the lakefront, she thought she noticed movement. Was it just the pale moonlight sending a cloud shadow sliding over the grass? Or had she seen some-one walking behind the first cabin, where three of the girls were lodged.

There was no rule against being outside at night. She did not want Lost Lake to feel like a prison. Trustworthiness was highly important. She wanted that emphasized, wanted the students to understand and act trustworthy.

More moving shadows. This time, she thought she saw a figure standing just two feet from the cabin's back wall. A boy, trying to see inside a girl's bedroom?

If someone was out walking the grounds, it could be Grady check-ing on things. One of the staff, like herself, unable to sleep. Or one of the young people out for a smoke. She hoped not. In warm, dry weather, forest fire was a danger and there was no smoking anywhere on the property. Would they honor that?—another anxious thought.

The moon was out from behind the clouds and the shadows ceased. No one was out there.

Down in the kitchen, her thoughts were back on the program, and she paced, circling the central island twice. *No, no, no. Don't go over your list of concerns.* She would go back to her suite, and see if one of Sahm's meditations could calm her anxious mind. Clearly, it was caus-ing her to see problems where there were none.

Before climbing the stairs, she remembered a book she'd been reading, by a Buddhist teacher, which she'd left in her office. Mainly, it taught that in the normal course of life things fall apart, and come together again, and fall apart again. Learning to live with that state of reality was the way to personal peace.

Was one of the young people outside tonight, creeping around, already pushing the boundaries of her program? Would this all come apart?

She found the book on her desk, open, pages-down.

"Spiritual awakening," she read, *"is frequently described as a journey*

to the top of a mountain. . . . At the peak, we have transcended all pain. The only problem with this metaphor is that we leave all others behind. Their suffering continues, unrelieved by our personal escape."

Friends had asked, with shocked faces, "Why would you open up your beautiful estate to *those* kids? They've been in trouble, because they're nothing *but* trouble."

Her answer was: the thought of young people who didn't have a chance from the start deeply disturbed her, and she couldn't ignore that.

"On the journey of the warrior-bodhisattva, the path goes down not up, as if the mountain pointed toward the earth. . . . we move toward turbulence and doubt, however we can. We explore the reality and unpredictability of insecurity and pain, and we try not to push it away. . . ."

Something fierce rose up when she thought about the young people now here at Lost Lake. She would fight for them to have better lives. Every step she took into their turbulence—knowing some would push the boundaries—made her more confident, not less, that this was the right thing. Hadn't Sahm told her that when they met in Dharmsala? She was determined not to leave these young people failing at life, but to walk them through the messes they had made and help them repair their lives.

The tea and the book relaxed her. She thought of her pillow.

Crossing through the back hall from the office to the kitchen, she passed the French doors leading outside. The moon was disappearing behind clouds again—and a quick movement caught her eye.

Just beyond the doors, a large shadow passed swiftly.

Her mug struck the slate floor and shattered.

2ND

Rocco had kept his distance from Garrett. Tough, since they shared a cabin, along with Jalil. When he opened his bedroom door to the knock before breakfast, he was immediately wary.

Garrett stood in the hall, his right hand extended. "I wanna make things right between us. I've kinda been a jerk."

Rocco shook his hand. "No hard feelings."

Garrett was grinning.

"What's funny?"

"I have an idea. You hear the shower running?"

"*Jalil!—get out of the shower, man. Now!*" Garrett banged on the shower stall's glass door.

"What do you want? I gotta rinse off. You can wait till—"

"*The cabin is on fire. You gotta move, move, move. Now.*"

Jalil pulled open the door, eyes wide. "You serious?"

"Yeah. *Move.*"

"Where's my pants?"

"No time. Take this towel. *Run.*"

Jalil grabbed the towel and threw it around his waist. Dripping and soap covered, he slid past Garrett to escape the bathroom. "What happened?"

"Don't know. Get outside *now.*"

Jalil sprinted down the hall to the front room ahead of Garrett, charging toward the front door. "You or Rocco smoking or something?"

"Just go. *Just go,*" Rocco shouted. He was pulling open the front door to let him pass.

As Jalil charged through the open doorway, Garrett grabbed the back of his towel and yanked it.

Jalil lunged outside onto the front porch, soaking wet and naked.

"*What the—?*" he yelled, wheeling back around to the door which had slammed behind him. "What did you do that for?" He hammered his fists on the door. "*You guys? I'm gonna—*"

Sounds from the lakefront path cut him off.

Imani and Makayla were staring at him, hands over their mouths, laughing.

Jalil covered himself with his hands, and swore. Then turned and began yanking on the locked door handle and banging.

"LET ME IN!"

Through the door, he heard a faint, "Ask nicely."

The girls were still laughing, but they called out in support.

"Let the poor boy in. His face is bright red."

"So are those cheeks."

"LET ME IN!"

At breakfast, Jalil avoided the end of the long table where Garrett was seated with Dugan, and the table where Rocco was talking with Imani. He approached Makayla at the buffet.

"Did you guys set that up with them?"

"No. We were just out for a jog." With a spoon, she poked at the bowl of fresh fruit like it was a dangerous thing. "They said they saw us coming down the path, and just timed it right."

"I'm gonna get them back."

"I wouldn't. Rocco's twice as big as you and Garrett's weasily and mean."

Jalil picked up a plate, eyes dark and pouting, and forked four pancakes.

"It *was* funny. Admit it," Makayla coaxed him.

He faced her directly. "Were you laughing because you thought it was funny. . . or were you laughing at, like, like. . . ." He ran out of words.

"Do you mean was I laughing at *you* or at. . . ." She glanced down.

"Yeah."

"That's stupid. Why would you ask me that?" She turned away, toward the table.

Jalil called after her. "Hey, if you're a guy it matters."

She kept walking.

"Two little spoonfuls of scrambled eggs and some fruit?" he called after her. "That's all you're eating?"

"You couldn't tell who it was then? Not a clue?" Tom asked. "And no, I don't think I'm overreacting."

In the gray light of the clouded morning, walking the lawn, Kate had confessed she felt foolish for screaming. "If it was a person, they had on dark clothes and a dark hat. I told you I'm not sure what I saw."

"The boy, Jalil. He always wears dark clothes and knitted hats."

Tom stopped, staring down at a stretch of damp dirt beside the road—then looking back at Kate's lodge. "Look at this. Footprints heading toward your back terrace. They look like they were just made."

"Well, Jalil is very slim and average height. This person had to be much bigger. One of Grady's men could have made them. These are big boot prints."

"Hold on," Tom said, his voice louder. "These boot prints just suddenly stop. Like the person who left them suddenly stepped sideways out of the dirt onto the grass. Maybe they realized they were leaving tracks."

"Tom, stop. You're getting carried away. I said I don't know if I saw anything. It was late and I was sleep deprived."

"What about security cameras and lights?"

"Jim was all about security. He had armed guards all over this place—not just in the cottage by the bridge, actually walking the property all day and night. He was terrified we'd be robbed or one of us would be kidnapped and held for ransom. So much for thinking eight hundred million can buy you peace and security."

Tom looked up from the tracks, startled, but said nothing. The amount of Kate's fortune stunned him. So did the fact that she could be doing anything with her life, or lying on a beach on the French Riviera, and yet here she was concerning herself with the welfare of troubled young people. The generosity of her spirit overwhelmed him again.

They had crossed the road down to the lake front, and Kate was scanning for footprints, but there were none on the narrow strip of sand.

"I haven't seen any cameras or lights," Tom said again. "And it doesn't seem likely Grady can protect this place—unless you're counting on him to run someone down with his Kubota tractor."

Kate smiled. "The lights were just a bad idea. They came on every single time a deer or raccoon or a bear triggered them. And that's all he ever caught on camera. It was a total waste, paying the security company to review the footage and see Bambi and his mother three or four nights a week."

"This place is so remote, though. We're two miles in from a paved road—and from there it's seven miles into town. You're not even a little concerned?"

"Actually—no. All I had to do is scream, and if there was someone out there it scared us both."

Tom was not ready to dismiss the incident. "Maybe we should make the grounds immediately around your place off-limits. No one has any reason to be looking in your back door. You do lock up at night—right?"

Kate abruptly changed the subject. "John Sewell phoned yesterday. He got word that a prosecutor in Virginia is trying to locate one of the students in the program."

"Who?"

"You have all the information I have. John's looking into it and will get back to us."

"I don't understand how some of these kids ever wound up in juvenile detention."

"Terrible flaws in the system, Tom. That's how. There is always so much more to people than meets the eye—either good or bad."

As the words came out, she remembered something Jim had said many times, late in the marriage, after his fight for success and money had altered him. *"People never change for the better. They only get worse in time."*

What if he was right, and none of these young people would change? It was the tip of Jim's poison arrow still stuck in her.

They came to where the shoreline curved toward the northern bay of the lake.

Tom was watching her closely. "You just went off into your head somewhere. What are you thinking about?"

"Nothing," she dodged. "—Look, it's a merganser."

Floating on the glassy water was a bird that looked much like a duck, but with a ruddy breast, a long, thin orange bill, and red eyes.

"I'm onto you," Tom laughed. "You're a master at changing the subject."

She smiled. "You rarely see mergansers on land. Their legs are so far back it's hard for them to walk."

"Back to the safety issue. We should at least consider having them sign-in to their cabins by, say, 10 p.m."

She hesitated. "I want them to know we trust them. But you're right. Their safety is at issue. We'll discuss your idea with the Troverts."

"And we should talk about security for your lodge."

She held up one hand. "Let that go, Tom. I won't live my life in fear. And now I need to meet the Troverts, before they hold their last orientation meeting and pass the students on to Jo this week.

Dugan stared at Garrett, as they headed to the Trovert's morning session at the fire circle by the lake. "You pulled that prank on Jalil with Rocco, just to make Rocco think you want to be friends now?"

Garrett smiled. "Like they say, 'Keep your friends close, and your enemies closer.'"

"You're diabolical."

"True dat. I *am* the devil you never saw coming."

"Where did you go last night?"

"So you were the one following me."

"Naw, I just saw you out my window. But I didn't follow you anywhere."

5TH

The smallest vibration began in Sahm's hands, much like what he'd felt when performing the healing ritual for the goshawk. The feeling started in the center of his chest, ran up his torso and out his arm, palm, radiated out his fingertips, until he felt as if they were filled with tingling heat and miniature lightnings.

The sense that he must heal the black lab had grown stronger in the two weeks since Jo had nearly caught him praying over the comatose dog. Feeling compelled, he slipped into the clinic early, leaned into the lab's enclosure, and returned to the prayer he had been chanting.

I purify the negative karma. . . .

It felt as if his words were falling on the dog like drops of healing ointment. The energy in his fingers grew into a pulse pouring out of him. *Who is guiding me to do this?* He was beginning to get an idea.

At that moment, he also felt himself passing into the dreamlike state he now associated with these occurences, and a flamelike glow had appeared at the very center of the dim gray light outlining the dog. The flame was very small, flickering from white to orange, to red, like an ember fluttering between rising and going out. He entered into the sickly gray aura and bent down lower—his breath pouring over the limp figure an ancient prayer like a medicine.

Palden—Glorius One! I have heard, I have heard that you must not leave us. Perhaps you were not able to save the one you were with, yet you are here among others now.

Without thinking, he gently lifted the injured paw in both hands, and felt a circuit of energy flow from the lab into him and back into the dog—and with it, stabs of pain. His mind's eye opened and, for just a moment, he saw visions. . . .

An older man, face lined with deep grief, sat slumped in a chair holding a bottle.

His wife has died, Sahm understood, as if voices were whispering the account. *He is alone and lonely and terrified of the empty future.*

He looks at the kitchen table, where bills and letters are heaped in a pile. He sees the dog, hears it whimper for food, yet he cannot get up from his chair, where he sits... and sleeps... and drinks liquor. One day, he opens the house door and strokes the dog's head before driving him away. "You were hers, not mine. You were a good companion to her—better than me because I couldn't go near her at the end. I'm sorry I'm such a lousy excuse for a human being, but I can't even take care of myself right now." The man stroked the lab's head and back....

Sahm could feel jolts of pain and anguish pass from the man into the dog. His chanting continued, along with the flow of energy.

Let us together purify the negative karma. I beg you, Glorious One, to remain until the end of this present dark age, with its chaos and strife. Let go of this anguish and suffering. Remain with us here and continue to help us.

Instantly, Sahm felt a great jolt like electricity race back out from the dog's paw, scalding his hands, leaping up his arms, and exploding under his breastbone—so powerful that it stopped his breathing. Then he began to cough, violently, as if he were choking.

Then just as quickly, the fit was over. The pain was released. In his mind's eye he saw black specks appear and burst and slide down the air before him like oily webs.

Sahm took a moment to recover, then finished.

May you, and I, and all other beings live long and happy lives... and may we see the faces of other Buddhas arise....

"What are you doing?"

Startled, he dropped the lab's paw.

Jo had come up quietly behind him. "I told you—I *know* I've told you a number of times—not to have direct contact with the really wounded or sick animals. This one in particular is fighting a life-threatening infection, and there you are holding his wounded paw. Do you not respect my authority here?"

Sahm stepped back from the cage as Jo stepped up and closed it.

"I was not trying to harm this dog in any way, Jo. I was—"

"I don't need to know what you were trying to do. Look, Kate wants you involved in this part of the program. She insisted I have you help out here in the clinic, to give you something to do between the wilderness hikes and survival campouts. But you have to do exactly what I tell you. You clean cages and enclosures, Sahm. You stock the supply closet when shipments come in. That's it."

He started to explain more, but she cut him off.

Dhani rubbed the weird ache in his ribs. Was it imagination, or was he starting to feel the pain of these wounded creatures? "Here's the thing. Ron told me he found you doing some strange ritual over the goshawk. Now I'm going to tell you plainly. We use science, not superstition or magic or whatever you're doing. Do you really and truly understand what I'm saying?—Do you?"

This was Jo's realm. And of course he understood.

"Yes, Jo."

"I really like you, Sahm. You're pleasant and kind. Ron likes you, too. But I will only give you one more chance—*one*, that's it. If you mess up again, I'll inform Kate that you're completely out of the animal rehab part of the program. You'll be banned from being anywhere near the animals or this clinic."

6TH

Jo stood behind the stainless steel table surrounded by the students. It was just after breakfast, and there were yawns all around.

Dhani had slunk to the back of the group, trying to keep his eyes off the poor creature lying on the examining table.

"We'll start your animal rehab orientation here in the clinic. This sedated guy here is a coyote. He was struck last evening, crossing a mountain road four miles from here. The x-rays just showed me he has a broken pelvis and needs surgery. This is a pretty common case."

Dhani wished that Jo would hurry this part of the orientation. He wanted to see the rest of this barn, which she and Kate had transformed from a horse barn into a surgical and rehab clinic. Hurt animals, like this coyote, made him sad. . . .

He was loping across a mountain road on the way to his den, when a car slammed into him. He felt ribs shatter and acute pain. . . .

Jo said the other barn housed birds. He imagined all kinds, flying from tree limb to tree limb within large enclosures, the way he'd seen sleek hawks and rare, golden parrots at the National Zoo in Washington. Watching these creatures gracefully gliding and maneuvering on thin air filled him with elation. A rare feeling for him, and one he wished for now.

"Speaking of cases, we found a young eagle downed on the property a few months ago," Jo told them. "Now *that* is a really unusual one. There is no visible reason why he just sits on a low branch, never flies, and barely interacts. He's in the aviary in the barn across the river."

He had to get away from the animal pain in this room and see this strange eagle.

Jalil took a step forward from the group surrounding the examining table, and reached out to touch the animal's fur. "Do we really get to work with animals like this guy?"

"Whoa—don't touch him." Jo's assistant, Ron, was checking a clear plastic fluid line that ran from an IV bag hung on a metal pole down to the coyote's left front leg. He grabbed Jalil's arm. "His rabies test hasn't come back yet. He doesn't look active, but there's always a chance he's a carrier."

"Yes," Jo replied to Jalil. "You'll be divided into four teams of three, and trained under very careful supervision, yes. This barn houses the large mammal enclosures on one side, this clinic in the middle, and the other side houses small mammals. There's even a large tank for water mammals. Very cool," she smiled. "Wait till you see it."

"Why are we learning how to take care of wounded animals?" Imani asked. "Nobody really explained that to me."

"You'll learn a lot of important life skills by learning to care for other living things. And a lot about yourself. I may require your team to sit up all night sometime, to monitor a sick or injured animal. In adult life, you have to set aside your own needs and wants to care for someone else. Big lesson. Also, working here with Ron and me will help you learn how to carefully follow directions."

Ron winked at them. "Heads up. Jo's a stickler."

Tia Leesha didn't appear to be listening. "What was that howling outside last night—was it wolves lookin' for this guy?" She shuddered. "It was like a scary-bad movie out there."

"That was a local coyote pack. Maybe they were calling for him. There haven't been any wolves in these mountains for a long time," said Jo, "except for Sahm's half-wolf, Vajra."

In a corner of the clinic, a strong-looking, dark-haired man was shelving bags of feed in an open storage closet. At the mention of Vajra, he looked over at the group and nodded.

"You'll get to know Sahm on your treks. He's a Sherpa from Tibet, and he works here in the rehab area. Out in the mountains, he'll help you with set-up and take-down."

Rocco whistled. "That guy's built like a wrestler. Must be tough. He owns a wolf?"

"A half-wolf and half-Shepherd mix. Some college kid bought the dog as a pup, then learned the hard way you can't keep an animal with wild blood in an apartment. He made that clear by destroying the place to the tune of a couple thousand dollars damage. Animal control called me after they seized him. He took to Sahm right away, so that's who he lives with now."

She looked over at Sahm who was hard at work again. "Sahm has some sort of attraction to wild and injured creatures. Anyway, Vajra's dark gray and looks like a wolf, but he's harmless—unless something attacks Sahm, then watch out. A squirrel can't come near Sahm without Vajra getting all ferocious. Wolves are pack animals, and fiercely protect their own."

Dhani's mind had wandered out of Jo's intro and was already with the eagle and its mysterious inability to fly. He felt sad for it.

"Follow me," Jo shifted. "I might as well show you the indoor- outdoor run behind the barn here, where this guy'll recuperate until he's transitioned back to the wild. That's always our goal."

When the group trailed outside after Jo, Dhani hung back and made his move.

Across the small wooden bridge, he slipped into the second barn and into the half that housed the aviary.

Inside that open space were rows of tall, built-in enclosures down each side of a central aisle. They looked to be ten or twelve feet wide and just as deep. From inside one, a small brown owl focused its gaze on him, and clacked its beak. In another, a huge, black bird—either a big crow or a raven, he didn't know how to tell—pounced from branch to branch, lifted its wings, and shot a gray-yellow mess on the floor. The rest of the cages were empty.

One enclosure was blocked from view by a wooden panel hung on a metal track with rollers. That one, he guessed, housed the eagle. With a little push, he slid the panel easily and quietly along its track, revealing a wire barrier right in front of him. Inside the huge cage was a small forest of narrow trunks, limbs, criss-crossed branches. Perched on a low branch at the back, no more than six inches from the floor, was a ruffled creature that did not look much like the eagle he had seen at the Washington zoo.

The bird was facing into a corner, like a child being punished, with its talons hooked around the branch. Jo had said this was a young male, about a year old. It was mostly brown with a dull-colored beak, not the white-headed, yellow-beaked creature he expected, and it looked pathetically small and plain engulfed by the big enclosure. Not very impressive. One wing was lifted and its head was tucked underneath it. Everything about it—its drab color, lowered head, and the hunch of its posture made the young eagle seem sad. That was the only word for it.

In spite of that, Dhani found the curved, sleek lines of the eagle's body strong and beautiful. He imagined how aerodynamically perfect this creature must be, what a master of the air.

You should be flying. Not stuck in here.

As Dhani thought this, the eagle suddenly alerted, lifted and swiveled its head, until it was staring straight over its own back. Its golden and black eyes narrowed, focusing sharply on Dhani.

Surprised, he stared back.

You seem okay to me. Why can't you just. . .take off?

As if in response, the eagle shrieked—a sharp cry that split the barn's quiet air. At the sound, the small owl shrieked back and the black bird began a loud, throaty croaking.

Dhani pulled his fingers from the wire barrier, and nearly stumbled backwards. His blood raced, and he was acutely aware he should not have come in here alone. "Jo's a stickler," Ron had just said. Reaching for the sliding panel, he started to glide it back over the front of the eagle's enclosure.

Swiftly, the eagle turned on its branch, leaned forward, and spread its wings. With another shriek, it launched itself from the perch. With just three great wing-beats, it rose enough to reach head-height, thrust out its legs and slammed into the wire barrier, locking its talons onto the mesh directly in front of Dhani's face.

"*Hey! Hey!* What goes on here?"

Dhani staggered and nearly fell backwards, away from the eagle's onslaught. "I—I didn't do anything to it," he defended. "I was just looking, and it woke up. But I didn't do anything to it. Really." He turned his head toward the aviary's entrance.

Sahm was striding down the aisle toward him. Claire stood in the doorway, unmoving.

The eagle had let go of the mesh and dropped to the floor. Its feathers were puffed out, and its head snapped back and forth, eyes alternately focusing on Dhani then Sahm.

Sahm stepped up to the wire mesh and knelt to examine the eagle. He held up one hand as if to stop it from flapping around on the floor where it had landed.

"Be calm, my friend. Calm. No harm was done to you. Fortunately, you did no harm to yourself. I see none of your feathers are broken or bent."

At once, the eagle became silent and subdued, ruffling its feathers back into place. That the young bird was not harmed was a huge relief to Dhani. The pounding in his chest slowed.

Sahm slid the panel into place, and Claire stepped up beside Dhani.

"Rondeau noticed you were gone. I volunteered to come find you. I asked Sahm if he'd seen you, and then we heard the noise in here. You need to come back for the rest of the orientation."

Sahm stepped close to Dhani and was looking him carefully in the face. To Dhani, the expression in Sahm's eyes made him seem much older than his twenty-some years. He looked as if he were peering into Dhani's mind, reading and understanding everything.

"How did you make the eagle fly?" Sahm asked.

"It just woke up. When it saw me, it flew right at my face."

"He has not flown for months. What did you say or do?"

"I didn't do anything. I was just standing here, thinking how beautiful it would look if it could fly. How free it would feel. Then it freaked out. I guess I shouldn't have opened the door and looked at it. That thing's crazy."

"The door remains closed because Jo does not want him to get used to humans. She says that would not be good for when he is released back into the wild."

"I just wanted to see it. I'm sorry. I messed up."

"You should go now," Sahm insisted. "Do not come in this area alone again."

They crossed from the small barn to the larger one, Claire walking most of the way beside Dhani in silence. Before they reached the group, she said, "You better have a cover story for Rondeau. Restroom break always works. Now tell me what you did to rile up the eagle."

"Nothing. Really."

"They said it can't or it won't fly. Then you walk in—and suddenly it jumps off its branch and flies right at you for no reason?"

"I told you guys, it just totally freaked at me all on its own."

Claire said nothing, but shot him a side-eye.

8TH

Even before he heard the man coming behind them down the tree-shaded camp road, Dhani had a sense that something felt wrong. When he turned and looked back, a man was moving down the dirt and gravel track toward them. Even his walk looked aggressive.

Dhani felt his stomach tighten. He wished Jo had warned them about this at breakfast when she announced today's first hike, out to the Flow Lands on the western part of the estate.

Tanner, the wilderness survival trainer, was closing in on them.

From the morning they had met Steve Tanner, Dhani had felt uneasy. Tanner had a look on his face that made Dhani's stomach feel sick. It wasn't an angry look, but an edgy expression that said he could get angry at any split-second.

Flashfire temper, was Dhani's snap judgement.

He would stay as far away from this guy as possible, and picked up his pace. He had straggled behind the group, and now did not want Tanner to catch up with him.

Jalil shouted from the road up ahead, where the others had stopped. "Oh man, what happened to this guy? *Crap.* He's busted."

Dhani reached the circle of people around Jalil, and saw he was holding something in both hands. It looked like a small, black helmet with yellow markings. From it, short stumpy legs and a head were hanging limply out of the shell. The top of it was badly broken in a jagged line.

Jo took the limp creature from him carefully and brushed sand off its shell.

"It's spring, and these box turtles are moving from winter hibernation in the woods to the wetlands to lay or fertilize eggs. Most likely, he was crossing the road here and got flipped by a vehicle. Delivery truck maybe. He's dehydrated and probably hasn't eaten in a day or two."

Tanner had caught up, and Dhani could feel his presence and sense him looking over his shoulder. He didn't like or want him this close. The others clustered closely around Jo.

Carter was behind Jalil, who had stepped back to let the others look. She said under her breath, "Smash its brains out."

Jalil took a step away. "Why would you say that?"

"It's disgusting."

"I love turtles—they're like millions of years old," he objected.

Emmalyn, who was closest, said in amazement, "This turtle is millions of years old?"

Garrett choked on a laugh. "Ohmygod."

Jo carefully moved a loose piece of its shell and peered inside. "No inner organ damage. I need someone to run this guy back to the clinic. We'll patch him up."

"He's really busted," said Rocco. "Can you fix him?"

"I'll show you guys how later. You won't believe it."

Ray-Ray volunteered. "I'll take him back for you."

"Ron's there," said Jo. "He knows what to do. Meet us out in the marshes. This path is a loop, so you can't miss us." She pointed across the camp road at a trail head. "You'll see double-blue-blaze markings on the trees."

Carter leaned close to Jalil again. "Should have smashed its brains in."

The trail led west into the woods, following the edge of a twisting brook. Every few yards, someone had daubed two parallel stripes of blue paint on trees and boulders to mark the path. Pouring down at them from upstream, the scent of fresh water and new vegetation flowed on the moving air. It was like a tonic, and they picked up their pace.

"Stay alert," Jo instructed. "Moose sometimes forage in these woods and out in the wetlands where we're headed. It lies at a slightly higher altitude than the estate, but the waters are temporarily trapped there by a natural depression between two mountains. It's a rare eco-system, which is why I want to show it to you."

Dhani had dropped to the back of the line, with Tia Leesha just ahead of him. He watched her swatting at a blackfly that kept landing on her neck and face.

"I never been on a hike in the woods before. It's buggy out here. And I'm already getting a blister on my heel."

"You were issued bug spray and hiking shoes," said a voice behind them.

Dhani turned to see that Tanner was right behind them, followed by Ray-Ray.

"Maybe you should have used them," Tanner said to Tia Leesha, sounding irritated.

"First, they rushed me through breakfast," she complained. "Then I was told to make my bed. All these schedules and rules. I can't do everything."

Tanner strode past them. "Try."

"I am trying."

"Try harder."

Ray-Ray came up beside Dhani. "Well, here's something you're not going to like, Private Snowball."

Dhani stared at him. "Who's Private Snowball?"

"It's a line from *Full Metal Jacket*. You ever see that movie? Tanner reminds me of the crazy drill sergeant, who's always insulting and abusing his own men. Geez, we're not training to fight the Taliban. Mr. Afghanistan War Hero needs to lighten up a little."

Dhani did not reply. His stomach felt uneasy, the way he always felt when he thought a fist was about to slam his gut.

In a half-hour, they had skirted the base of Peregrine Mountain's north side and emerged at the brook's source—an open, marshy area dotted with cattails bent by the winter and by tufts of newly-greening grasses sprouting up from tea-colored water.

Stepping out of the woods on the southern, shady side of the marsh, they saw that the morning's light cloud cover had lifted. Across the expansive, lush green wetlands and above a line of pine trees on the far side, the enormous southern slopes of Lost Mountain rose into a deep-blue, cloudless sky.

Dhani made sure that, whatever side of the group Tanner was on, he would slip to the opposite side. His warning voices told him to stay as far away as possible, and avoid eye-contact. A guy like this would probably see a direct look as a challenge.

"Wetlands like these are carefully protected," Jo began her talk, "because of the fragile plants and animals here. —Tell me what you see."

"It's so beautiful here," Imani answered. "Are those pretty white flowers out in the center water lilies?"

"Yes, and there are some tiny, rare orchids here. I'll point them out."

"That tree line across the water is interesting," said Claire. She wished she'd brought her sketch pad.

"What you see is a nice landscape, these marshes, beautiful mountains. You think the wild creatures that live here—the birds and animals—they all have a beautiful home out here in nature. But there's a war going on. The natural world is under assault."

"I don't see any assault," Garrett shrugged. "If there was, Mr. Tanner here would be on it. Right?"

Steve stared at him with a blank, cold look, and said nothing.

"O-kay then," Garrett muttered.

"Trust me," Jo went on, "a whole bunch of man-made forces are at work threatening the natural world. If we don't step up, we all lose. Besides my work with the animals, I'm collecting data and providing research to government agencies. Maybe some of you will wind up helping me. We'll see if any of you show interest, and how capable you are."

"Why is the water that brown color?" Imani asked, staring at the marsh.

Jo went with the shift in direction. "Good question. Tannins leech out of the leaves that fall in. Think of it as 'forest tea' but do not drink it. It's full of bacteria."

"Gross."

"It's still early in the season," Jo continued, "but I can probably point out a couple of rare, insect-eating plants."

"I'm down for that," said Dugan.

"Laurel Wysocki, one of your climbing instructors, is also a botanist. She'll teach you about wild edible plants during your treks and campouts."

Tia Leesha made a face. "We expected to eat wild stuff?"

"If you're ever lost in the wilderness, it's information you'll need."

"Well, I'm not going anywhere where I can get lost. I'm scared standing right here in this group."

Emmalyn interrupted. "What's that sound? That—*blurp blurp.*"

"Seriously?" Dugan looked at her. "You don't know what that is? That's a bullfrog. They get big here."

"In my neighborhood, we didn't have frogs."

"I thought you were a country girl?" Garrett chided her. "Or is that just an act?"

Dugan's voice dropped to a hush, and he held up one index finger to his lips to silence them. "I see one." He edged closer to the water, crouched, and pointed. *"He's...right...there."*

Imani whispered, "I don't see anything. What color is it?"

Dugan's right hand inched lower toward the surface of the water, through a cluster of arrow-shaped leaves. He mouthed the word—*"green"*.

No one moved.

His arm shot out, water splashed, and his hand came up with a small, dark form that thrashed and flailed its front legs at the air.

The huge frog struggled for a moment. Then stopped, its back legs immobilized in Dugan's grip.

"Whoa—that thing is dope," Jalil said, excited. "I never saw a frog that big."

"Why'd you say it was green," said Imani, folding her arms. "More like a darkish-gray I-don't-know-what-color."

"Let him go," Emmalyn pleaded, wringing her hands.

Dugan held the frog out to Jo.

"Not him," Jo said. "Her."

"How can you tell?" Jalil asked.

Garrett smirked, and grabbed himself. "Probably the same way everyone else does." He looked around to see who would laugh.

Only one person was staring at Garrett—Tanner—and he was not laughing.

Dhani had continued to keep a careful eye on Tanner, keeping as many people as possible between them. Now he looked from Garrett to the hotshot, bossy Marine and caught the quick glance Tanner flashed at Garrett—a look of pure contempt, triggering memories that sent a shock of pain like lightning fire through Dhani. It shook him, and he pulled his hood closer around his face.

Sahm had joined them, and he watched the boy, Dhani, withdrawing, not just into his hoody but into himself, his shoulders curving in. He had been sharp with Dhani when he found him troubling the eagle. Since then, a thought had crossed his mind several times: the portent pointed to an important one who would come.

But certainly not this boy, he dismissed the idea. *He is too weak and full of fear.*

He followed Dhani's gaze to Tanner who appeared to be in an unpleasant mood.

Why does the boy watch him? Why is he so afraid?

An image flashed in Sahm's mind. Of the darkness he had seen in March, up on Thunder Rock with Kate, with a storm coming.

"See here—?" Jo was saying, holding the frog up, her fingers carefully curved under its forelegs, "—in bullfrogs, the male's ear circle is larger than the eye and their throat is a light yellow. In females, the ear circle is the same size or smaller than the eye and the throat is white—like this one's."

Dhani noticed she was glancing occasionally at Tanner, who did not see her watching. From her look, it seemed she had picked up on his mood also, and was keeping an eye on him.

"I gotta tell you guys," she continued, "frogs have developed amazing adaptations."

Dhani said, without thinking, "In the late fall their bodies release a kind of biochemical antifreeze. At the same time, their cells and tissues expel almost all water. That's because, if the water froze inside them it would expand, and their cell walls would burst."

Jo smiled at him. "Very good. How did you know that?"

"I—I'm not sure. The thought just... came to me. I must have heard it somewhere."

"Evolution helped them out with that adaptation," Jo continued.

Emmalyn interrupted. "The Bible says evolution is wrong."

"The Bible doesn't mention evolution at all," Ray-Ray countered.

"How do you know?" she shot back, sounding a little defensive.

"I've read the Bible my whole life. It doesn't talk about evolution. At all."

"We're not here to debate the Bible *versus* evolution," Jo interrupted. "I'm here to tell you a few facts about this frog before we let her go. Listen up.

"In the spring, as the temperature rises, their chemistry changes again, and they come up from hibernation in the mud and look for mates. Look around carefully in this duckweed—see all these plants with the pointed leaves where Dugan just caught her? You might find the egg-mass this female has probably laid."

Carefully, trying not to be noticed, Dhani was still watching Tanner—who this time caught him staring. Dhani cut his eyes away, escaping a look in Tanner's eyes that seemed to carry a message he knew too well. *"What are you looking at? You need a slap?"*

Jalil was crouched now, scanning the marsh's edge.

"What does an egg-mass look like?"

"Put her back in the water, Dugan," Jo directed. "—The mass looks like a ball of clear tapioca pudding with a black dot in each tiny bubble. If you see tiny black commas that are wiggling, that tells you the egg mass has been fertilized by a male."

"A man's gotta do what a man's gotta do," Garrett said loudly, so everyone could hear.

Tanner reacted with a look of disgust.

Dhani's shoulders and neck had become tense, and his left temple ached. He only half-caught Steve's glance his way, and his stomach knotted, remembering. *"Hey, you little puke. Is mama's boy gonna throw up?"*

He reached for the edges of his hood, tugging on it to hide his face from the punishing eyes.

An hour later, they were on the north side of the marsh, exploring where a brook entered it from the southern slope of Lost Mountain.

Makayla called out. "Oh no! Look at this poor thing. Is it dying?"

She had followed the brook a short way up into the woods, and now she returned quickly to the group, her cupped hands held out.

Circling her, they all peered down at the S-curved body of a small, bright-orange lizard with tiny red spots along its back. It lay docile in Makayla's palms. One of its front legs was missing.

"Golden salamander," Jo said. "Show me where you found it."

Fifty feet uphill from the trail, a tree trunk had fallen across the brook, which poured out from beneath a tumble of large stones on the mountainside. Next to the trunk, Makayla pointed at five turned-over stones. "I found him right here."

Jo squatted, then lifted a second salamander, which also lay unmoving in her hand. "This one's missing a back foot. Strange—he should be scrambling to get out of my hand."

"What do think happened to them?" Jalil asked.

"Not sure. Their wounds are closed—see the smooth, clean nubs—so they didn't bleed out. The fact that they're so compliant to handling bothers me. There's plenty of food with mayflies and other insect blooms taking place. Their condition is strange. Let's take them back to the clinic and keep an eye on them."

"Do you think they got into some kind of poison or something?"

"Way out here? Very doubtful. Manufacturers sometimes dump chemicals illegally, and every year chemical dumps kill off more species of amphibians. But we're maybe a hundred miles from any chemical plants I'm aware of."

"People who dump chemicals suck," said Jalil.

"What will you do with them?" Makayla's eyes reddened. She

stroked one salamander's back lightly with one finger. "They're so beautiful."

"Observe them. Feed and care for them. Maybe bring them around and put them back here."

"I'd like to help you," Makayla responded, sounding eager. "I mean if there's something I could do. You said we were going to be divided in teams. Can I be on like, a salamander team?"

"I'm in, too," said Jalil, looking from Makayla to Jo, his face brightening.

Jo nodded. "Here's the thing. I'm taking part in a major study on various types of ground water pollution and animal extinction. Everyone's going to pitch-in with that at some point. But sure, you can focus on reptiles and amphibians."

"My dad says environmental people are Nazis."

Everyone turned to Rocco who had spoken and was staring at Jalil.

"Hey, I didn't say I agreed," Rocco reacted, looking around the group. "I just said he said it."

Jo's voice remained calm. "I hope your dad learns to care about the environment. If all of us don't wise up—soon—we're dead. It's not like we have another planet to escape to if we wreck this one."

A movement out beyond the circle of students caught Jo's eye. Tanner had put his hand over his mouth, hiding a grin.

"Something you'd like to add, Mr. Tanner?"

Busted.

Time to play off what he was really thinking. "Not a thing. Your hike, your lecture, not mine."

Returning along the north side of the trail an hour later, Dhani lagged far behind everyone, his breathing shallow, his mind in turmoil.

He knew all about men like Tanner. They believed they were way superior to everyone. They mocked people they disagreed with, the way

Tanner had smugly laughed at Jo behind his hand. And yet women fell for guys like him because they were hot or had money and put up with whatever abuse they dished out. Steve Tanner was an abuser; he was sure of it. At all cost, he would stay far away.

Emerging from the woods onto the camp road, he found the others had gone back to the lodge for lunch. All except Claire. He was surprised she had waited for him.

She studied his face. "What's wrong?"

"Nothing."

"You're lying."

"Thanks."

"You looked like you were going to be sick back there."

Why did she care? "I don't like that guy."

"Tanner? Why?"

"I just don't like him."

"I never let anybody get to me. Ever. I keep everyone out."

"What about if someone's really bad to you? What if you can't get away from them?"

Claire pivoted and began to walk up the road fast. "Tanner didn't say a word to you. You're making a drama out of nothing. I hate when people do that."

"How do you do what you just said?" he called after her. "How do you keep people out?"

Claire kept walking.

Dhani threw his hands up. *I didn't do anything, and the guy hates me—okay?*

"Why did you wait for me," he called again, "if you were just going to turn your back and walk away?"

She didn't reply.

Staring at her back, he wanted to shout. *Hey, little Miss Independent, I don't need anyone to take care of me, either.*

He felt more confused than irritated, though. Two days before, she'd come looking for him in the aviary. Now she couldn't get away fast enough.

Was she just messing with his head? Or was she the messed up one?

Steve neared the foot bridge leading back to Osprey Island, assessing the situation.

Bunch of real problem kids in this program. He ran through names, faces, behaviors. Garrett—wise ass. Rocco—typical thug. Makayla—fragile, cries. Probably cries a lot. Jalil—goofy, jumpy, probably an addict. No idea about the girl named Carter. Just weird. Tia Leesha—whiner. Expects everyone to wipe her nose. Emmalyn—most likely to drop a puppy at 16. . . .

He reached the cabin as he finished his catalog of challenges and headaches.

Jo. Liberal environmentalist agenda. *Good.* That gave him a reason to keep his distance.

Then there was the evasive kid in the hoody. *Doesn't pay attention for jack.* Like so many new recruits they'd sent him in Afghanistan. Never listened to orders or instructions, and as a result people were wounded or killed. This kid was outright disrespectful, though. Gave him dirty looks. Avoided eye contact. *Seriously hiding something.*

The only place to start with this crew of coddled miscreants, he thought, was with a challenge. A tough one.

15TH

From the first open ledge, halfway up Peregrine Mountain, they could see northeast across the lake to Eagle Rock Mountain. The Arrows were due-east, and Trinity Mountain was south. Below, Lost Lake shone in the sunlight like a great, blue gemstone. Up here, the crystal clear morning air was still cool even under the sun's strong rays.

"It's been an hour. We'll take a break here," Eric Trovert announced. "Sip some water, catch your breath. Keep your sweatshirts and jackets on. You don't want to cool down too much, or your muscles can tighten. In fact, stretch your calves."

Dhani walked to the edge of the broad, rock ledge where they had paused. He felt excited, weightless, a sense of soaring. He looked back at the group as if from a great distance—and liked the feeling that distance gave him.

Claire and Ray-Ray had dropped their packs, and sat back-to-back on a boulder. Claire pulled out a small pad and a pencil, and Ray-Ray rummaged through his pack, searching for granola bars. He pulled out a plastic rain poncho. "Are we going to need these today?"

Eric looked at the sky and shrugged. "Conditions can change quickly here in the mountains, but the weather station guys up here say the Doppler radar is all clear for today. Not a sign of rain."

Makayla was struggling to slip her pack off. "This really hurt my shoulders."

Bay stepped to her side. "Let me adjust the straps before you do that." She snugged the lower strap, then loosened the upper ones a little. "If it rests more on your hips than on your shoulders you won't have a problem. The rest of the trip should be better. Now slip it off."

"Wow. That worked," Makayla responded. "Glad I asked you and not Mr. Tanner. I heard he was pretty harsh with Tia Leesha."

Bay made a mental note and turned to the rest of the group. "I want to remind you that your first treks, like this one, will be short. Don't worry. We'll give you time to build up your stamina. Peregine is the lowest peak around the estate."

Imani had dropped her pack and was bent over, hands on knees, breathing deeply. "Please tell me again why we came all the way up here. This trail is so steep."

"Mr. Tanner's part of the program starts with wilderness survival basics. They connect with life skills for you to work on while you're here."

Garrett stepped up behind Dugan. "There's a couple of ladies here I can teach some skills to."

"Dude—you just like a dog."

Tia Leesha stopped swigging from her water bottle. "Couldn't you just tell us what those life skills are and give us a quiz?"

Eric smiled. "It's not that kind of learning. Life learning happens when you're in tough spots and need to make good choices and know *why* they're good choices." He looked to Steve, who was on his haunches at the edge of the group. "I suppose it's like basic training. Recruits are put into difficult situations to see how they'll react. That way you know where they need more training in order to make them wiser and stronger, right?"

Steve looked around. "Hopefully."

"Well, it makes me nervous being up here," said Tia Leesha. "I can't even look down off this ledge without feeling like I'm gonna faint."

Sahm, who was carrying a large pack with extra provisions and water, sat down on the rock ledge beside her. Since Jo's tongue-lashing and threat of removing him from the animal rehab program, he had felt down. Had it been a mistake coming here after all? He was not a "Sherpa" as Jo had said—they were a special group of mountain people.

Here I am lugging supplies. Is that all I am here to do?—all I am good for?

He shook himself. That was his ego talking, and he stepped back from his own thought-stream, letting the wounded-ego thoughts pass until he was at peace inside again. Dropping his pack, he turned to Tia Leesha.

"I can show you how we breathe in the mountains of Tibet, so that you will feel stronger and not anxious."

Claire looked around for Dhani, who had walked further away from the group and was staring off into the open air. She nudged Ray-Ray. "His head is always somewhere else—like he isn't hearing anyone."

Ray-Ray nodded. "Not quite sure what to think about him yet. Good kid. But sometimes it looks like he's hearing voices."

Jalil was throwing stones off the cliff into the trees below. "So, you're going to make it hard on us on purpose."

"You said 'hard on,'" Garrett busted out, then looked around.

No one laughed.

"In a way, that's true. We'll put you in some stress situations, a little at a time," Eric answered Jalil. "Hopefully, you'll have some fun and learn important things out here. Hopefully, you'll take in the beauty of the wilderness and learn to care about wildlife."

"As long as we don't run into wolves or bears," said Tia Leesha.

"As Jo told you, there are no wolves out here. But speaking of bears, it's a good idea for you to get out your bear bells. They look like big brass sleigh bells. Attach them to your belt or boot laces. We're pretty high up, but you never know."

"So now we all gotta sound like Tinkerbell?" Dugan smirked.

"You'll wish you had magic if a big, male, black bear smells your lunch or we cross paths with a sow and her cubs."

Two hours later, they reached the broad, open summit. Small, bent and twisted evergreens clung to the thin soil between patches of rocky terrain dotted with gray and green lichens.

Laurel Wysocki pointed out several of the trees that were bent in the extreme. "See how these are all leaning to the southwest—they're called 'flag trees'. The way they're tilted tells you the prevailing winds come down out of the northeast. You can tell how severe those winds become by how twisted in one direction they are."

"Is that something we really need to know?" Garrett smirked. "Like is it going to be on a quiz."

"It tells you," said Laurel, "that you don't want to get caught out here in a blizzard. The wind chill can drop to minus forty or lower."

Tia Leesha choked on the water she was guzzling.

Randy Wolfmoon, their climbing instructor, finished swigging from his canteen. "You also don't want to get caught on a cliff face in an electrical storm or windstorm. I've seen the wind blow people off rock faces and scrambles when they didn't take shelter soon enough."

Emmalyn's face was still red with exertion. "Y'all are scarin' me."

"We don't want you to be scared," Bay responded. "Eric and I—and all the instructors—designed this whole Lost Lake program with one main goal in mind. We want you to have a very healthy respect for conditions, and we want you to know how to make the best choices both out here in the wilderness and in life. Your ability to survive and thrive in the world of adulthood is very important to Kate Holman and to us."

Dhani had wandered away from the group and back again. He had a far-off look and his eyes were shining.

"Looks like he's trippin' balls," Tia Leesha said under her breath.

"It's going to storm," Dhani said absently, surprised at his own words.

Eric countered. "Like I said, we checked the forecast and Doppler radar says all-clear. It's highly accurate."

Dhani was staring at Eric's face, as if looking at him from that great distance his mind had retreated to. He felt an energy rising in his body. "Can we eat our lunch now, before it storms?"

By the time they finished eating, the sun was at its peak and the mountain's open rock summit was hot.

"Inside your daypacks you'll find a half-tent," Steve announced. "It's olive green and folded into a neat rectangle. The pieces of pole attached to your packs are the supports. Before you open the half-tent out, study it. It goes back into your pack exactly the way it came out."

"Why *exactly*?" Tia Leesha challenged. "I'm not good at folding stuff."

"It's part of the training," Eric responded quickly, seeing Steve's look of irritation. "Learning to respect everything you're given or work for is a way of respecting yourself and the people who helped you get it."

"Why is it just a half-tent?"

"Today, Mr. Tanner and I are introducing two survival basics. First, the critical importance of a good shelter. Second, the importance of finding and working with good people in life. Ones who have the same good goals you do. Take your time, figure the exercise out together. It's not a competition. It's about cooperation."

Steve stepped in front of him. "Well—since this is my part of the program, I'm going to override that. It *is* a competition. Choose a partner. The two of you will follow the diagram, and make a whole shelter out of your two halves. Let's see who's first and who's dead last. Get moving."

Ray-Ray slapped Dhani on the shoulder. "Let's do this."

In pairs they spread out over the open summit.

Claire had teamed with Emmalyn, who was rambling. ". . .and the time before that I camped at a blue grass festival with my boyfriend and. . . ."

230

Claire looked over at Ray-Ray, who was twenty feet away, and rolled her eyes.

He pointed at Dhani, who was half working and half staring into the air. *"We're gonna lose,"* he mouthed to her.

Steve was still instructing. "Making a good shelter and depending on a buddy can just mean staying dry in a rainstorm. Or it can mean the difference between surviving in a white-out blizzard and not surviving at all.—By the way, you guys should be working while I'm talking to you. Some of you are already slacking."

"I'm not slacking," Makayla said, sounding confused. "I'm reading the instructions. Geez."

Eric was beside him. "We need to talk about some things."

Steve raised his eyebrows in question.

"Not here and now."

"If something's on your mind, say it."

"I said, not here."

It was a simple enough task. The diagram showed the half-tents splice together by sliding a pole through sleeves sewn into the ridge line of each piece. Along with poles there were small metal pegs to stake out the tarps into a pup tent. The problem was getting the stakes into the soil, which was thin with a solid rock layer only two or three inches below the surface.

Ray-Ray was reading ahead in the instructions. "'When you're done with the tent, dig a trench around it. This allows rainwater to run away from it.' Well, I'd say we're on pretty high ground. I mean, we're on top of a mountain. And it's a sunny day anyway."

Dhani had finally focused and was trying to pound one of the metal stakes into the soil with a rock. "Crap. I just bent another one. It's impossible to drive these in."

Looking across the mountain top, he could see the other teams that were ahead of them. Tia Leesha had sat down and given up. The thought of Tanner busting on them for being near last made him grab another peg and begin hammering it in—which made it bend.

"Crap. We need to hurry before it storms."

"Stop saying that," Ray-Ray countered. "It's not going to storm."

He looked at Claire and Emmalyn who were now finishing their shelter ten feet away. Emmalyn had overheard Dhani, and said, in almost a little girl voice, "Look at the sky—it's so blue. See those big fluffy white clouds."

Dhani had turned to look at the open sky, and the rock fell from his hand.

Great currents of charged and stormy air were churning all around him. In him.

"*Done!*" Dugan's shout sounded from fifty yards across the open field. He and Garrett had spliced and staked out their tent.

Garrett raised his arms in a gesture of victory. "In your face, losers!"

"Already?" Imani called over to them. "We just figured out how to put ours together."

Steve inspected Dugan and Garrett's work. "Well, we have our winners," he announced. "But keep going. When you're done with your tents dig a rain trench around them."

Groans and objections erupted.

Rocco had just finished bracing the poles of his and Jalil's tent, and called over to Steve. "But we don't have shovels."

"Figure it out."

Rocco opened his mouth to object—then nodded. "Will do."

"How?" Jalil complained.

"Like he said. *Figure it out.*"

"I was just asking."

"Well don't ask," Rocco jeered at him. "Move your ass."

Dhani had stopped working, and was staring into the blue sky again.

...feeling electricity all over his body... imagining rain driving into his face... stinging....

Claire was watching Dhani now, and waved to catch Ray-Ray's attention.

He looked up from the tarp, which had snagged on his brace pole—then at Dhani. "What are you staring at?"

Dhani did not respond.

Steve also caught sight of him. *Just standing there. Jackass.*

A jolt of lightning, blue and jagged flashed. It struck a cedar tree fifty feet from Dhani, Ray-Ray and the two other teams, blowing it apart and sending pieces of it sizzling in all directions.

Screams and shouts sounded all across the mountain top.

A second lightning strike hit a nearby red pine, igniting a line of fire down its length. The roar of thunder shook the rock beneath their feet.

"What the hell?" Garrett shouted.

The sun was still shining on a mountainous white cloud that had crested over Lost Mountain to their north. The huge billow was laced with flashing, snake-like twists of bright blue and red lightings.

Eric was yelling, *"Don't panic.* Get away from your tents. The poles are metal." He gestured thirty yards down off the peak, toward a large, half-bowl carved into the rock. "Get to lower ground and crouch down on the balls of your feet. Make your body the smallest target possible. *Don't panic."*

"Too late," Tia Leesha screamed, dropping the metal poles and scrambling toward the depression.

Beside and behind her, others were sprinting.

"Don't we have rain ponchos?" Makayla shouted. "We're gonna get soaked."

A blast of thunder like cannon fire roared over the mountains, echoing from the surrounding peaks—followed instantly by a roaring deluge of rain. Gusts of wind poured over Lost Mountain, slamming into them, whipping their clothes and hair around.

As they reached the depression below the peak, Steve shouted over the noise.

"Lightning is more likely to hit one of the trees above us. It strikes the highest places first. Which is why you want to crouch and put your head between your knees. Like this—," he showed them.

Ray-Ray turned to Claire who had sprinted with him to the low spot. "Where's Dhani?"

She turned and pointed up at the summit. "Ohmygod."

"Hey, look at Singe," Garrett shouted. "I guess when you like to play with fire, what's a little lightning storm."

Dhani was walking down the slope toward them slowly. His face was turned up, exultant, blinking as big drops of rain driven by wind pelted his forehead and cheeks. Gusts whipped the hood of his sweatshirt. Lightning flashed all around, and he was soaked.

And smiling.

Sahm muttered something in Tibetan.

When Dhani reached the group, Steve grabbed his sleeve and yanked him. *"Get down."*

"Why? It's over."

And—it was.

In another moment, the wind dropped as quickly as it had risen. The big pellets of rain fell lighter and stopped.

Steve stood and glared at Dhani. "You didn't hear me order everyone to run here and get down?"

"No."

"Yeah, that's hard to believe. You're going to have to listen a whole lot better, buddy."

"It just didn't seem like we needed to flip out."

Steve's face went red.

"When we're out here, I'm totally in charge," he growled. "I don't give a crap what anything seems like to you. What I tell you, *you do.*

No questions asked." He looked around at everyone, eyes flashing. "Is that clear?"

Nods all around.

Makayla was in tears. "Can we go back? Please. We got our tent put up. Can we just go back?"

Steve started to reply—but Eric preempted.

"Yes. We can go back now. Whatever stage your tent was at before the storm—you guys all did great. As I told you, the weather up here is always a factor, and it can be wildly unpredictable. You learned that today, and that's good enough for a first day-trek."

In twenty minutes as they began their descent, the last, distant rumbles of the storm faded into silence. There was little talking, except for Eric and Bay, who were checking-in with everyone one-on-one.

At the end of the line, Claire walked beside Dhani. After the angry reprimand, he looked shaken and miserable.

"How did you know that was going to happen?—the storm, and then the storm going away so fast. It was crazy. Even the weather people didn't predict that."

"I just. . . felt it coming. And then leaving."

Ray-Ray was right behind them. "You got arthritis or something? My grandmother says she can feel a storm coming on."

They had lagged behind the others a little, but caught up, hearing Randy Wolfmoon talking excitedly.

"It's actually called a 'bolt from the blue'. Also called 'anvil lightning'. It happens when cloud-to-ground lightning gets discharged far away from its parent thunderstorm. Apparently, there was a storm going on in the valley beyond Lost Mountain—probably ten miles from where we were—and the lightning hopped the ridge before the storm did."

"That's weird," Jalil said. "But in a cool way."

"Not weird," Randy replied, "but definitely rare."

Jalil began strutting and posturing, as if he were on-stage.

"Just a young gun, with a quick fuse

I was uptight, wanna let loose. . . ."

Randy laughed. "After a whole day climbing, where you getting all this energy?"

"I was lightning, before the thunder. . .thunder. . . thunder. . . ."

"But how did *that* kid know it was coming?" Garrett asked nodding back up the trail at Dhani. This time his voice was without a mocking tone.

At the back of the group, Dhani trudged along, staring at his muddy hiking shoes. He wished everyone would leave him alone. He wanted to be back where his mind had taken him during the brief cloudburst.

. . .Spiraling on an updraft above the storm. Above everything and everyone.

Claire and Ray-Ray remained at the back of the line with him. "How did you know?" she asked again quietly, sounding cautious but also awed.

"I just sometimes know things. That's all."

"Man, if they ever take us into town," Ray-Ray muttered, "you should buy a lottery ticket."

Sahm trailed behind them, carefully watching Dhani. Wondering if what he thought he had heard would be whispered in his mind again.

The packs and their contents were stored in one of the small, equipment barns at the back of Kate's property. Bay had accompanied the two girls to the first aid station in Jo's clinic for blister treatment. Eric turned to Steve as they locked up.

"We need to talk."

"What about?"

"About why you turned a simple survival exercise into a competition."

"Hey, the real world is all about competition."

"We're not here to teach them about winning and losing. Not all of life is about that."

"Really? When they leave here and try to get jobs, do you think they're going to run into your 'every kid gets a ribbon' attitude?"

"You think that's what this program is all about. Just telling these guys everything they do is alright?"

"That kid disobeyed a direct order and could have been flash-fried. A lot of the others whined and complained and couldn't even put together the simplest structure. Even an idiot can put together a half-tent. Believe me, I had a lot of people under me in the military who couldn't find their zipper if they had to piss real bad. And what you told these guys today was, 'Hey, great job kids.' So, yeah. I think you're just patting them on the butt. I think that's both demeaning and, frankly, a bad approach if you want to teach life skills."

He had not finished when Eric spoke over him. "We had a bunch of kids who were tired, soaked, and scared and wanted to get off the mountain. And hell yeah, I gave them a little stroke of positive rein-forcement. You can re-run the half-tent training again. I have to look for chances to build up these guys, because most of them feel like ter-rible people and losers already at fourteen and fifteen. And speaking of losers. . . we are not running this program like they have to compete for approval or to win and lose at your survival exercises."

Steve shook his head. "So it's like I said. 'Every kid gets a blue ribbon.' Gotta tell ya. I'm not on-board."

"Well, there's a solution to that problem."

Bay had returned to finish storing her pack. "Something wrong here?"

"No."

"Yes."

"I hope you guys aren't just butting heads. I hope you're working out your differences. That was quite a performance in front of the students."

Steve squared his shoulders. "In my book, the first thing you need to learn in life is how to do what you're told. There are kids here who were in juvie because they didn't respect authority and broke the rules."

"Interesting statement," Eric interrupted, "since you directly usurped my authority, turning the day into a competition when I had just said it was not about that."

Steve tossed up his hands. "Point goes to your team. But the blue ribbon thing—"

"Stop." Bay intervened. "We're not on different teams here, Steve. But Eric and I were brought on to direct the program and I'm not pulling rank when I say that. We have a dynamic we need to work out here. We just need to clarify who's in charge when we're out in the field and we're working on life skills and you're training them in survival skills."

Eric and Steve both spoke, but she held up one hand.

"*Table this*, guys. We're not going to resolve issues standing here. Steve, your contribution is very important. Eric, we all need to think this through. We need to be united in what we're about and these are big differences to resolve."

Eric stuck out a hand to Steve. "Yeah, sorry for jumping on you. Let's work this out together."

Steve shut down the surge of irritation. "Sure. You guys are in charge."

Who are you lying to? You don't want my opinion.

Jalil closed and locked the door to his room and checked the GPS he had slipped out of his pack before stowing it in the storage barn. Pushing a button, he was happy to see the rain-soaking had done no damage. Big relief. He had gotten a fantastic deal on it last night at the black market price.

Then he buried the GPS down in the back of his closet next to the plastic bottle of pills. Though he was tired, he did not take another hit. It was time to come down.

18TH

Dhani left his cabin and walked the lakefront to the east. He wanted to be far away from everyone, so he avoided the path and shuffled down the beach, around the bay and out the point, staying close to the water.

On the way back to the cabins after the Peregrine hike yesterday, everyone except Ray-Ray and Claire had distanced themselves, staring at him, whispering behind their hands.

Now they really think I'm a freak.

He needed to think. Randy had given his scientific explanation about the storm, but how did he know strange things sometimes? Why couldn't he just be a baseball- or soccer-playing normal kid?

Pushing through a stand of chokecherry bushes at the water's edge, he thought of the times—the many times—he'd felt weird and even terrified meeting some guy his mom brought home and heard her say, "Jerry" or "Len" or "Alex is moving in today." How she had ignored his fears, insisting, "This guy's different", and how he was always so frustrated by that. Those weird feelings had never been wrong.

A crashing sound came at him from the woods ahead, through the undergrowth. Onto the sandy strip of lakefront just ahead of him charged a large, dark gray dog with a coal-black face—but not like any dog he had ever seen.

This animal's shoulders were higher than a dog's, its head was bigger, its eyes more penetrating. It stared, and did not move, not even to wag its tail or growl or sniff the air for his scent. In its dark gold eyes was an intelligence.

He remembered Jo saying someone—Sahm maybe—had a half-wolf. Dhani froze, but strangely was not afraid of the scary-looking creature.

So beautiful.

He *saw* himself—*staring, mouth open, hands hanging* down—as if seeing himself through the creature's eyes.

"*Vajra!*" a voice called.

The animal turned its head and the tip of its tail flicked.

Dhani's mind flipped back, and he was watching it again.

Up on the small rise above the lake, beyond the trees, Sahm called again. "Come. Leave him." To Dhani, he called, "There is a path up here. Much easier to walk."

Probably he was breaking some rule by coming here alone, the way he'd gone without permission into the aviary and, without meaning to, riled up the young eagle. He felt like just a screw-up. When Dhani broke through the undergrowth and joined Sahm on the trail, he expected yet another reprimand.

Instead, Sahm smiled at him. "You are the young man who awakened the eagle. You also knew a storm was coming before anyone else knew."

Dhani tried to reply, but couldn't find words. What would he say?

"Vajra also approves of you very much. Usually, he barks or growls. Tell me how you understand the animals and the weather."

It surprised Dhani that Sahm would ask this, but he went along. "Oh. Well. I don't do anything. Stuff just happens to me. Like the eagle. It just looked at me and... flew."

"He has not flown or responded to us in any way before or after that."

"If he injured himself again, I'm sorry. I didn't mean to hurt him."

"The eagle is fine, though he has gone back to the way he was. Ignoring us."

They had walked the wooded trail further along the eastern side of the lake, Vajra sweeping the woods on either side, scenting, and now it emerged from the trees at a fork. Yards ahead to the right was the footbridge leading to Osprey Island, while the left fork led directly into

The Bow. From here they could see the vertical rise of The Arrow ridges and the sprawling heaps of sharp boulders and rubble in an arc at their base.

Dhani noticed that Sahm was looking at him with a steady, open gaze. That made him uneasy.

"The bridge to the island where the instructor lives," Sahm said, "you should not go any farther than that. One of Kate's boundary markers is there."

No problem. Knowing Tanner was out there, he would not even go near the bridge.

"Why do you look so troubled?" Sahm asked. "I have seen it in your face since you arrived. In Tibet, we learn meditation practices that free the mind from suffering. That would help you."

Dhani's first response was to pull deeper within himself, but at the same time he sensed a kindness about Sahm that began to put him at ease a little.

"I'm trying to figure out why I'm such a. . . a freak, I guess."

"Who told you to think such a terrible thing about yourself?"

Dhani met Sahm's gaze. There was an innocent, concerned look in those eyes. "I did," he replied.

Sahm looked thoughtful. "I think that is not true. Who first told you to believe a wrong thing?"

"This guy my mom lived with," Dhani said, in a flood-release of words that surprised him. "He said I was a freak. And a lot of other bad stuff."

Another poison arrow, left in someone's spirit.

"Why did your mother let someone say bad things about her son? A mother's job is to defend and praise her children."

Dhani became guarded again. Sahm had turned this on his mother, when it was The Monster who had attacked and held him down and hurt him and laughed at his tears. "It wasn't her fault."

"Is your mother still with this man who hurt you?"

"No, we got away from him and she's safe now. I'm pretty sure." He felt himself retreating further from Sahm's probes. "I—I did something really bad because I had to stop him, and the court put me in juvenile detention. And now she's hiding out and I'm here. So we're both safe. Or at least I hope she is."

"I am glad you and your mother are not with someone who was bad to you," Sahm nodded, still studying the boy. There was more; he could sense it.

What else has he done that he is still hiding so deeply in himself?

19TH

A pale, thin moon wavered on the darkening surface of the lake as the sky turned from rose to dark blue behind Peregrine Mountain.

Steve stood at the western edge of Osprey Island. Across the water, a few lights had come on in the lodge and cabins. He felt frustrated with himself.

It's Trovert's program. He's trying to be a good guy. He's naïve, and that'll cost him. But I didn't have to be such a jerk to him.

Still, he wouldn't apologize. And the tension he had felt for days, like he wanted to head-butt something or someone, was still with him.

A faint jingling sound came from behind him in the trees.

Turning, he saw Jo emerge. Trotting ahead in the beam of her flashlight was the black lab.

"Whoa—look at that guy. Walking. All four paws, what the heck? That was a miraculous recovery."

Jo was beside him now. "You could say that."

The lab had dropped to his haunches beside Steve. He dropped to one knee, reached out to stroke the dog's head, and felt its rough tongue lick his hand. "You made it. Proud of ya, buddy."

Standing again, he said to Jo, "Great job, doctor. You sure pulled this guy back from death's door."

While he was speaking, the cool moving air stirred a soft fragrance from her hair.

"Yeah. I guess."

"Come on. Don't be humble. Tom says Kate thinks you're best in the whole North Country. He says the environmental conservation guys all call on you when they have an injured or problem animal."

"Yeah, well, a problem animal is usually only a problem because people have messed with it. Someone invaded its territory. Left food where it shouldn't be. Got too close to take pictures. But about this guy," she said, rubbing the lab's head, "I'm not being humble. There was something unusual about this guy's recovery."

"Like. . .?" He was taking her in—the long, sleek hair falling forward and brushing her high cheekbones, her full lips. He felt a sudden impulse to reach out and touch her.

She hesitated. "I treated him with the best protocols for weeks, but he didn't respond. Or barely did. The infection wouldn't quit. He was fairly comatose. Just hanging between life and death."

"Then."

"Then—well, I'm of two minds about what happened. My logical mind tells me the antibiotics finally did their job. On the other hand. . . ." She searched for words.

"I caught Sahm one day, two weeks ago, praying or chanting or something over him. I was angry, because he was handling the wounded paw, which was still open and draining. I threatened to throw him out of my part of the program if I caught him handling sick animals again.

"Later that same afternoon, Ron and I were taking inventory of meds and supplies, and we heard a low 'woof'. We turned around, and there's this guy—standing up. His legs were shaking, but he was up and his tail was wagging a little. In another hour he was jones-ing for food."

"Must have hurt to be standing on a paw with an open wound."

"That's the thing. It wasn't open any more. It had closed. In just a couple hours, after weeks of being pus-y and nasty, it was closed and the flesh around it was pink—not gray and necrotic. Here, take a look."

She knelt and gently raised the lab's paw into the beam of her flashlight.

Steve squatted, and the lab sniffed his ear and gave his chin a lick.

The paw looked fully healed. When the dog had come out of the frozen lake, the flesh on it had been gray and turning black. Now, though the fur had not fully grown back and there was a scar, it otherwise looked fine.

The lab pulled the paw back, wagged and sidled closer to Steve.

"You think Sahm's chanting did this." He sounded incredulous.

Jo stood again at the same time he did, and the soft skin of one forearm brushed against his. He felt a sudden urge to reach out and brush back the strands of long hair that would not stay behind her ear.

"My money is on the antibiotics. But—it was just strange, that's all. Pretty 'miraculous'. I mean in the medical sense."

He was glad she did not believe in divine interventions. He no longer could.

For a moment, though, he felt off-base, remembering the strange, deep bond he had felt with the dog when they first made eye contact. The connection had felt uncomfortable, as if the dog had been able to see into him. Still, the idea of a spiritual connection with a strange dog was plain stupid. Like Jo, he could not believe in the miraculous.

"Just a week after treatment, he wanted out," Jo was saying. "So Ron and I have started walking him. At first, we had him on a leash, but that didn't seem necessary. He'd limp around the lake almost to the bridge out here, then get tired and turn back. Tonight, he wanted to come all the way out here, so I let him lead the way."

Or did you want to come out here to tell me the news? That would be sweet.

"He seems to be drawn out here."

Or, he considered a less-pleasing alternative, *did you come out here just to bait me into taking on this guy?*

No matter. She was beside him, alone, on a spring evening under the faint light of a crescent moon, and he could not take his eyes off her.

"He's a fighter," Steve deflected. "Probably make someone a great companion."

"So. . . .You said you'd think about it."

That was it then.

"I probably said that, yeah, in the heat of the moment. And anyway, who'd take care of him when I'm out in the wilderness with these kids?"—but even before he'd finished he knew her response.

"Ron and me, of course."

Ron and you. Was it more than a professional relationship? They were always together when he saw her.

"I'm gonna go with *no.* But you can come out here any time."

She looked at him, and said nothing.

"I mean you guys." *No, you don't.* "Both of you, if you happen to be out this way."

"Glad you're willing to share Kate's island with us."

There was emphasis in her words, and the mood he felt—and obviously she hadn't—was now gone.

She attached the lead. "Time to go back, buddy."

"Really. Come by any time."

"Maybe."

Maybe. But probably not.

Crossing the bridge, Jo found herself irritated with men who said empty words "in the heat of the moment." Which was most of the guys she'd ever met. Even, sad to think, this dark blond ex-Marine, with some deep passion—was it for a former lover or a current one?—within his eyes.

Well past midnight, Steve was still sitting by the lake, watching the moon sink lower and more stars come out, listening to the night birds—once in a while, a loon called—and watching bats flutter down, occasionally breaking the thread of silver moonlight that played over the black water.

Her voice, her scent, the softness of her skin remained with him.

The tension he had felt for days was gone but something more painful had replaced it—a feeling like a knife blade twisting in his heart. Worse, he felt like he had stabbed someone else in the heart by betraying her memory and longing for her. Why had he said to Jo, "Come back any time"?

Please, please, please don't come near me again.

5

July

2ND

"The ancient Celts had a saying, 'It is in the shelter of each other that the people live,'" Bay began.

"We were going to talk about this up on Peregrine after you built your shelters, but the storm shredded that plan. So let's talk about it now. What do you think this saying about the human need for 'shelter' means?"

"Oh goody," Garrett muttered to Dugan, "a cute little object lesson."

It was mid-morning, after chores, and they were all gathered on the lakefront, around a fire circle Randy Wolfmoon had built for them, out where the cabins ended and the forest almost came down to the water. Mist off the lake had risen through the cool air into an azure sky, and in the brilliant, early-July morning, small white clouds formed above. It had rained heavily for three days, and more rain was forecast, but in this break the sun was strong.

Sweatshirts began to peel off.

"I guess it means we need to help each other with stuff," Jalil offered.

"Such as?"

"If you can't figure out something, get with someone who can. Like, I didn't know how we were supposed to the dig a trench around our tent when Tanner told us to, but Rocco found a sharp stick and was going to do it. That was going to make our shelter work better.

"Right?" He nodded at Rocco, who totally ignored him. He was staring at Imani.

"Okay, good," said Bay. "'You help me, I help you.' Anything else?"

Carter had been staring blankly out at the lake, and suddenly became animated. "Every one of us—we're all part of a big family. We need to watch out for each other."

Surprised looks passed all around.

"Very good thought, Carter," Bay nodded. "We need to build strong, healthy connections."

Under his breath, Ray-Ray said to Dhani, "Well, look who finally joined the party. Carter's actually smiling."

Claire was sitting with them. "Ever notice how she changes so fast? At any given mealtime, she can be cold and then suddenly she's laughing and doesn't shut up. She's a shape-shifter. A really weird one."

Imani turned to look at Rocco, who was still staring her. "Sometimes you need a room in the house where everyone leaves you alone."

Bay looked thoughtful. "Interesting new take. We all need time to think about our stuff. Giving someone room to do that respects their headspace."

Rocco countered. "What about telling someone what's going on in your head—letting you help them work things out?"

Imani looked away again.

"I don't know about the Celts," said Dugan. "They're part of y'all's White myth-ol-o-gy. I'm thinking about the Black Panther's party platform. Article ten said, 'We want housing.' They didn't mean some poetic, metaphorical shelter. They meant real, good housing, without rats and roaches. There are a lotta slum lords, who won't do jack to clean up low-income housing. Then they hike the rent so poor people can't afford 'em, and turn 'em into high-rent condos."

"That isn't just a problem for Black people," Emmalyn interrupted. "Where I come from, it's a problem for poor White people, too."

Shocked looks passed around. Clearly, no one expected an intelligent sounding comment from her.

"Right," Dugan replied in a heavily sarcastic tone, "and 'All lives matter', not just Black ones. Piss off."

Garrett leaned close to Dugan and said in a low voice, "You know how I know she's trailer trash?"

Dugan growled, "How?"

"Her mama goes to the dump, and comes back with more than what she took."

Dugan snickered.

"Her gramma has 'ammo' on her Christmas list. . . She wonders how gas stations keep their restrooms so clean. . . When all her aunts smile, it makes a full set of teeth."

Dugan punched him on the thigh. "Stop. I'm gonna bust out."

Eric cut in. "Dugan, Emmalyn, I'm glad you're bringing up the issue about poor housing in America. It's a very important discussion to have. I absolutely think you should bring these issues up in your classes, and talk about the minority and poor working-class experience in America."

Bay brought the discussion back around. "I brought this proverb up to talk about offering help and accepting help on a personal level. It's a great life skill. Too many times we go it alone, we don't ask for help when we really need it. You know, for instance, you guys can always come and talk with Eric or me if something's on your mind."

"Can we talk about trust?" Garrett interrupted. He was serious now. "Why did you guys start a check-in time when we have to be in our cabins? Are you gonna start a bed-check, too, like they did in detention? How about trusting us?"

Bay hesitated, and Eric stood, clearing his throat.

"Look, it isn't about trust. It's about you guys needing to stay safe. And be well-rested for all the hiking, work in the clinic, the assigned chores. We want you to feel good and be at your best."

"Why did you inventory all our stuff when we first got here?" Tia Leesha challenged. "I didn't think someone was gonna keep track of my underwear."

"No one went through your clothes. We just listed the electronics you brought," Eric responded, "—iPods, cameras and such. We did it in case someone's stuff gets misplaced. We'll know for sure whose it is."

"Let's get back to the discussion," Bay redirected.

Now Dugan leaned close to Garrett. "You see their faces? I call BS. They're not being honest with us. They don't trust us."

Garrett smiled. "They shouldn't. But let's make them believe they can."

As the circle broke up, Garrett banged into Dhani, with a sharp elbow in his side. "Singe, how's it going? Oh hey, when we're out camping don't burn down my tent, okay?"

Dhani said nothing.

"Come on, Garrett, let up," Dugan chided him.

"How about *shut up*," Ray-Ray intervened, defending Dhani.

Carter was striding quickly up the lakefront toward the cabins, and Garrett tried to catch up. Jogging past Emmalyn who was just behind Carter, he bumped her arm.

"*Watch it.*"

"Yo, Southern Comfort—chillax. It was an accident."

"Stop calling me that."

He caught up with Carter. "Seems like you're in a good mood today all of a sudden. Wanna take a walk after lunch maybe?"

"Sure." She sounded pleasant.

"Really?"

Garrett's eyes met Emmalyn's, and for an instant they were allied. *Who* is *this?*

Jo charged down the beach toward them, looking like she was on a mission. "I've got to run an animal distress call. Perfect time for you three to jump in. Come with me."

"Jump into what?" Emmalyn and Garrett asked at the same time.

"For my part of the program, I'm dividing the twelve of you guys into four teams—each team working to rescue and rehab a certain type of animal. You're my second team. I'm putting Makayla, Jalil, and Dugan on reptiles and amphibians—You three are my small mammals team."

Emmalyn looked unhappily at Garrett then at Jo. "What if—what if some of the people on a team don't even like each other?"

"Work out your differences peacefully. That's one thing you're here to learn."

When Dhani found Claire after the fire circle, she was standing just outside the small, stone cottage beside the Garnet River. She was talking to Grady, who was standing in the open doorway. He was wearing mirrored sunglasses and a green flannel shirt, and he was moving one hand quickly in a circular motion.

"I reeled him *right* up to the edge of the canoe and realized I forgot my net. Just that much hesitation—," his thumb and forefinger were a half-inch apart, "—and he thrashed around enough to cut through the steel leader with his teeth. Like I said, northerns are fighters. Anyway, as long as you guys bring me more intel about game fish you locate, you can borrow my canoe any time."

"Is this where you live?" Claire asked, pointing at the cottage.

He smiled. "All year long."

"It's small."

"Big enough to have a few friends over to play cards and do shots." His voice dropped and his expression changed. "Forget what I said about doing shots. I was kidding."

Claire nodded. *Right.*

Dhani had stood back a few feet the whole time, still wary around Grady after the verbal lashing he had given them weeks before. Though it appeared, since Grady was now relaxed and smiling, that Claire had completely won him over.

"This young lady's got a lot on the ball," Grady said to Dhani.

"So does he," Claire smiled.

Dhani felt a wave of surprise, and stepped closer to them. "I do?"

"You're the magic boy who attracted the great northern, right?"

Dhani shrugged. "I don't really think that's true."

"You did, though," Claire insisted. "Ray-Ray and I both saw it. It swam right up to the surface, looked at you, and splashed water at you. And when you walked into the aviary, the eagle went nuts-o."

"Is that right? I've heard that poor thing has hardly budged for weeks." Clearly, Grady wasn't interested in a response, because he kept right on talking. "When I was a young man, I was taught to hunt by an old Abenaki Indian man—I think they're related to the Mohawks. Wolfmoon would know.

"Anyway, the old guy told me some people are born with a gift. He called 'em 'animal talkers.' Also claimed he met a man living way back in the mountains here who could change into a mountain lion or an eagle. He always talked about the 'old ways' and what people could do before a lot of secret, sacred knowledge was lost. I always thought he was smoking some strong weed, of course. But who knows."

He reached out and slapped Dhani on the shoulder. "Maybe you've got some sort of special vibe thing going on with animals. If anymore big game fish come up to you, report when and where to me. I'll take it from there."

Claire looked like she was thinking, and prompted Grady in a different direction.

"You were telling me you grew up here. That's cool. You must know everything about these mountains."

Grady's shoulders squared. "Yep, I can tell you there's some interesting spots around this estate, especially—," he nodded up at Lost Mountain, "—in certain tucked away places up there. Way up beyond the falls.

"But you sure don't want to take off on your own. It's a big mountain with rough terrain and some very dangerous, deep cuts. You fall, you're gone. People vanish in these mountains and forests all the time. Some of 'em because they want to. But most of 'em just had no business going out alone, because they didn't have a damn clue what they were doing."

"Got it," Claire nodded. "But I bet it's beautiful. And I bet you know every inch of it."

Dhani suspected what she was up to.

"Sure do. I can show you animal trails and markers other people can't spot, and once you know 'em you're way less likely to get lost. I could even show you a couple of hidden bear caves some of my hunter friends would love to know about. Also an underground weasels' nest that's been there for years and years. Those guys are hard to find, because they're little, wily, and fast. Even harder to spot when they turn white in the winter. Then they're called ermines. Guys I know would love to trap 'em because their pelts sell for a lot of money. But I won't tell 'em where to look because I love seeing those beautiful little guys in the wild."

Claire was staring at Lost Mountain and its forested slopes, with the happiest look Dhani had witnessed so far.

"I'm starting to love it here," she breathed. "I'd love to try to sketch some of those wild settings you know."

"You any good?"

"Not really. But I like drawing, and I try."

"Hey, if you can draw you're an artist in my book. Tell you what— you guys wanna see what no one else around here can show you, just say when. If I'm not busy with Kate's list of repairs, I'll take you way back into these mountains. You'd just have to do exactly what I tell you."

Before they could respond, Grady's voice dropped.

"Now Jo—she won't show you those places, because she believes humans and wildlife should have as little contact as possible. I understand that, to a point. You take bears. If you're not careful, it can be very dangerous. When a sow's protecting her cubs, she'll charge you and do serious damage. Rip you up. But as a lifelong outdoorsman, I say there's nothing wrong in having a look at creatures in the wild from a distance. You leave 'em alone, they'll leave you alone. Most of the time.

"So," he finished, "if I take you guys, you do what I tell you *and* keep it between us."

"I guess that means we have another private agreement then," Claire responded.

Grady's eyebrows shot up above his sunglasses. "I guess it does."

He slapped Dhani on the shoulder again. "Like I said, she's a sharp one. Stick with her."

As they walked back toward Kate's lodge, where instructors were waiting with summer reading lists, Dhani said, "You made him think that was all his idea."

"When someone else has all the power, you have to know how to work things."

"I wish I could work people like that."

"Sometimes you have to. But I'm not sure it's a good thing."

Jo pulled her Jeep sharply onto the grass beside the narrow dirt road.

They had blasted into and through the town of Lake Placid until the road bent north, and in three miles she jerked the wheel left, speeding up a road between tall pines, leaving a dust trail. The road zig-zagged several times over a broad stream, rushing and swollen up to the roadsides until finally she had brought them to a sudden, jarring halt at a trailhead.

The sign read, *Long Pond .25 miles.*

"That was cool," Garrett grinned.

Emmalyn looked pale and sweaty. "I thought I was gonna vomit."
Jo jumped out, issuing orders.

"You—," pointing to Garrett, "—grab the three little carriers in the back."

To Carter, "Grab four pairs of gloves. Three thick, leather ones and the soft, blue rubber pair.

"And you—," she focused on Emmalyn, who was still breathing deep and looking paler than normal, "—sorry about the ride. But I need you to do this now. Look in my kit for a bulb syringe. It's a blue rubber ball with a long hollow point at one end. Then all of you follow me."

"What are we doing?"

Jo was already moving fast into the woods.

As they moved quickly down the path where Jo had disappeared ahead of them, the sound of rushing water grew louder through the trees. They emerged onto a flat bed of rock along the swollen stream they had crossed on the road.

Jo was kneeling beside a woman, who sat cross-legged on the rock with a gray sweatshirt in her lap, cradling something. As they neared, Jo lifted a small, brown animal carefully in both hands. In the woman's lap lay two otters, looking like small, dark brown kittens but with sleeker heads and thicker tails.

"Baby otters," Jo said, as the three circled around her. "No cuts, so I won't need the rubber gloves. But this one's struggling to breathe." She reached out to Emmalyn for the bulb syringe. "He aspirated a lot of water."

The woman's eyes were red and brimming. "I missed one. I was able to pull these three out of the flood, but—I missed one." The tears spilled.

"You saved these guys and two look fine.—Let's see if I can keep this one alive."

The brown baby otter in her hands was limp, except for its sudden attempts to breathe. It lay flaccid for a few seconds, then its whole body wrenched and its mouth opened wide. Each time, a little water bubbled out its nostrils and mouth.

Carter touched one of its tiny paws with a finger. "Come on, buddy."

Jo slid the syringe carefully into the otter's small mouth, gently squeezing the bulb, then letting it go. Over and over, she inserted, pulled it out and discharged drops of fluid onto the ground.

Carter had become even more animated than she was earlier, her cool blue eyes almost flashing. "You're going to save him, right? He's not going to die, right? *Right?*"

Garrett was eyeing her—amazed that her cold weirdness was gone—then looked at the baby otter. "Hey, little guy. You can make it."

Emmalyn had regained her color and said with an air of authority, "Otters are related to weasels."

Jo looked up at her. "You're pretty smart. They're in the weasel family, yes. How did you know that?"

Emmalyn's eyes grew wide and innocent. "Oh—I must have heard somebody smart say it."

"I thought otters were like, okay in water," said Garrett.

"Normally, yeah. But I can pretty much tell you what happened here. After the last three days of heavy rains, the ponds and streams flooded with all the run-off from the mountains. These guys' mama built her den a little too close to this stream that comes out of Long Pond. The flood-surge rose fast and washed away her babies. I'm guessing they're about two weeks old. Way too young to swim."

"Poor little guys." Carter's eyes were full of concern. "So terrible they got washed away from their mom."

"That's nature. Here's something I hope your wilderness survival trainer drills into you. Flash-floods come up fast up here in the mountains. If you're hiking in a ravine during a downpour, head quickly to high ground."

The syringing seemed to have worked. "His nose, trachea and lungs are clear," Jo pronounced.

The tiny otter lay curled in her lap. Its sides were no longer convulsing but moving gently and its breathing was smooth.

The woman who had saved him and his litter mates from the stream stood beside them, still cradling the other two in her sweatshirt. "What happens now?"

A man's voice called from the wooded path. "*Carolyn? Did the wildlife lady find you? I called D.E.C. from the gas station.*"

"She's here. It's alright," the woman called back.

"I'll take them back to a facility where they'll be treated and cared for. We have a special tank for aquatic creatures, where they'll learn to swim. When they're mature enough, we'll bring them back here for release into their home territory. And these guys—," she nodded at Emmalyn, Garrett and Carter, "—are going to help raise them until they're ready."

Back in the Jeep, the baby otters lay curled in a soft blanket in Garrett's lap, mewling with hunger. Jo had decided not to put them in carriers. "What are they gonna eat?" he asked.

Emmalyn was looking uncomfortably at Garrett and Carter again.

"You three are going to bottle feed and clean them. I'll make up a special formula with the same nutrients that are in their mother's milk."

Carter stroked the dark, sleek head of the one Jo had saved. "You said they're called pups, right?"

"Yep."

"Sweet."

"Then what happens to them?" Garrett pursued.

"You'll help them learn how to swim."

"Seriously?"

"Seriously."

Emmalyn looked unhappy. "So—the three of us are really a team now?"

"Correct."

She snuck a doubtful look at Carter—who looked back at her, smiling and said, "What? This'll be awesome."

Then Carter turned and looked out the side window, in her own world, an unreadable expression altering her smile.

After clean-up duties in the kitchen that evening, Dhani walked alone back to the empty fire circle. Garrett's elbow-jab and insult came back to him. "*...don't burn down my tent, okay?*"

Almost everyone still ignored him. Would not even make eye-contact. Judge Sewell had told him he had to report that he had made friends. Even just one. That was a condition of his staying in the program. But how was that going to happen?

He thought about Claire. About the nice thing she'd said about him this morning. But she remained aloof. Ray-Ray was a good kid, but he was buddying-up with Claire.

Was it a mistake to come here to Lost Lake—or was it just a mistake to think he could make a friend?

From somewhere up the slope of Eagle Rock Mountain came a sound—a deer, a bear?—crashing through the woods. It echoed out across the lake then faded in the open air. In the tall pine on Osprey Island, a hawk shrieked.

He stuck the toe of one shoe into the fire pit. Eric Trovert had doused the fire when the morning talk ended, leaving only muddy gray and black ashes. Even with a light breeze carrying a strong floral scent from the summer woods, the air here smelled burnt and gritty. Kind of like he felt right now.

The truth was, he really, really liked Lost Lake. Not everyone here, but the place itself. He felt strangely at home, like he had been here before or someplace very much like this. He just could not remember when.

In one small bend of the shoreline, a dozen white water lilies and a hundred green pads dotted the surface of the water. Absently, Dhani kicked off his shoes, rolled up his pant legs above the knee, and waded in a little, feeling the cool lake water climb up his ankles and calves. The floor of the lake was mucky and soft, and his bare feet sank into a pudding-like muck, sending up clouds of black murkiness into the water.

The delicate beauty of the lilies, with their many petals like white feathers, drew him in. He bent down to smell the heavenly scent rising from the vivid yellow center of one blossom. At the same instant, he felt his feet sink a little deeper into the muck, his toes touching hidden roots and lily corms. Something like an electric current wound around his feet.

His eyelids fluttered, his mind flickered and its light seemed to go out as. . .

. . .his body sank, pulled down by a slick, weighty, ooze until he was blanketed in a soft darkness all around. The smell of death and rot surrounded him, and he sank even deeper and deeper into cold muck. If he did not do something, he would die here.

He strained to reach upward, groping through darkness. Instinct would tell him to turn this way or that way and keep reaching up.

Time passed—days, weeks? He continued to strive and reach upward. Why? What good did it do, if he was always struggling in darkness?

Fish flicked by and tore pieces of him, and water bugs climbed with scratchy legs up his body. Still, he kept thrusting his body, which had become long and threadlike, upward through watery clouds and the some-times violent shakings into a growing warmth. Only the faintest, wavering, watery light flickered far, far above.

Now, he started to remember a dream he must have had once, about a wide openness, a great blue brightness. The idea came, like a spark within his mind, that unspeakable beauty and great fulfillment was somewhere just overhead and he could find it if he kept reaching.

And there was a sense of opening out and out and out. . . .

"Hey."

Dhani jumped, and the electric sensation coursing through him let go. He had not heard Ray-Ray coming up from behind. Pulling his feet from the muck, he took his eyes off the lily that had captured his mind and waded back to the shoreline to retrieve his shoes.

Ray-Ray stepped up as Dhani rolled his pant legs back down, and nudged him with an elbow. "Man, did you lose something in the water? I can help you look for it."

"No," Dhani said, rinsing the muck from his feet. He felt confused at what had just happened—the sense that he had entered into the roots of a water lily—no, into the *awareness* of the lily—but how could he explain that? Then there was the wonderful then overwhelming terror of opening himself up.

"I was just. . .thinking about something."

Ray-Ray was studying Dhani's face, smiling. The light of the sinking sun caught the glass stud earring in Ray-Ray's ear and it flashed, like his smile; he almost always had a smile. "Must have been a deep thought. I stood right here and called you three times, and you just kept staring down into the water."

"My bad. I get lost in my head and don't hear a lot of things."

Ray-Ray's smile broadened. "I came to find you because, well, remember how I had your back this morning? Like Bay was talking about. Did you notice?"

"Yeah, that was cool. Thanks."

"I decided I got your back while we're here—so maybe you got my back, too?"

It surprised Dhani that Ray-Ray might want someone to watch out for him. Everyone seemed to like him. He had seen him bantering with Dugan. The girls flirted with him. He was strong looking, and fit in with the other guys when he wanted to.

"I'm not used to having friends. We moved a lot. But yeah. Sure."

"Good. Wanna hang out now?"

Dhani sort of did, and he didn't. What were you supposed to do when you just hung out? "I guess."

Ray-Ray picked up a stone, turned toward the lake, and let it fly—skipping it on the water. Then he skipped another—making it dance-step over the glassy surface. . .two. . .three. . .*four-five-six-seven-eight-nine* times before it sank, leaving only ripples.

"How'd you do that?"

"If I bend low enough and get the angle right, I can skip one way longer than that. Want me to show you?"

"Hell, yeah."

For a long time, as the sky's reflection on the lake went from bright blue to fiery gold, they skipped stones.

On Dhani's fourth throw, he watched the water change where his stone skipped, shimmering in rainbow circles, sending out the faintest hum. He looked at Ray-Ray, who paid no attention. On his fifth and sixth throws the same phenomenon occurred.

"Did you see and hear that?" he asked Ray-Ray.

"I saw the stones skip. You caught on fast."

"But did you hear something?"

"You mean that loon over there?"

Across the lake, a black and white bird with a long black beak bobbed on the water, and made a mournful cry.

"But—did you hear a kind of humming sound?"

"Nope."

"Did you see the water change all those colors when I skipped those last few stones?"

"It's sunset," Ray-Ray said, looking at the red, gold, and purple western sky above Peregrine Mountain. "You musta caught some cool reflections."

Dhani said nothing and went back to skipping stones—and the prismed lights and the sounds did not occur again. Maybe what he had seen was just a trick of sunset light on the water, together with the angle he cocked his head to throw. But secretly he kept looking, listening.

When their shoulders were finally sore, they kicked off their shoes and waded in the warm shallows, picking up freshwater clam shells the seagulls had broken open. The water grew more still and slowly turned to a dark dark blue—and in the center of the lake a pinpoint of light from one star wavered. Then another. . . then dozens more.

"So, why did your dad make you leave?" Dhani asked, when they were back on the beach, putting on their tennis shoes.

Ray-Ray's head snapped around. "Who told you that? I never said that."

"I—I'm not sure why I said it. Maybe someone else said that happened to them, and I got confused. Anyway, I know they don't want us talking about the past. We're supposed to look ahead and think about the future."

Ray-Ray looked a little uneasy, then relaxed. "Yeah. That's right." He added, "My dad's a preacher. He's a man of God."

"Oh," said Dhani. "So he's a good guy. My bad."

Later, before falling asleep, it occurred to Dhani that he hadn't had a friend since he was really little, before all the moves from one place to another began. Maybe Ray-Ray could be one. He hoped he wouldn't say something stupid again and ruin it. At least having someone to hang around with would distract him from the constant fear for his mother that was always nagging at the back of his mind.

What about Claire, though? She could be friendly, then distant.

He had silently studied everything about her. Her smooth, clear skin. The way her deep brown eyes looked almost black when she was angry, and the way they flashed brightly—like stars on dark lake water—those rare moments when she laughed.

He slipped out of bed and padded in bare feet to the cabin's kitchen, where he and Ray-Ray had set their finds on a wooden shelf by the back door. He picked up the prettiest fresh-water clam shell he had found this evening—one whose white interior shone with pink-and-blue opalescence under kitchen's nightlight.

He had an idea.

6TH

The sound of rushing and roaring water filled the valley. Every stream was overflowing, and the Garnet River next to the barns rose up its banks dangerously close Jo's barns.

More days of hard downpour had followed the Trovert's talk around the fire circle and the baby otter rescue. Fireworks in town had been cancelled, delaying their first outing there. Mornings, they met with their fall tutors in the second-floor classrooms at Kate's. Afternoons, Jo showed them the vet supplies and had them clean floors and cages.

During one session, they all watched as Ron handed Emmalyn, Garrett, and Carter each an otter pup to bottle-feed.

"This little guy aspirated so much water he almost drowned," Jo said, pointing to the pup Emmalyn was feeding. "His blood pH level was five when we got him here. Not good. Emmalyn is giving him formula with electrolytes to strengthen his lungs, but the damage may be too extensive to release him. I'll keep monitoring his liver and kidney functions and platelet count."

"He's so amazing," Makayla said, with a tone of awe. "Look at his paws."

The little otter clung to the bottle with both front paws, listlessly drinking, formula running out the corners of its mouth. It turned its head and gave her the clown-of-the-waters look otters possess.

"I call him Otto," said Emmalyn.

"*Stop* naming them," Jo interjected. "The paws are perfectly webbed and also just like hands, for optimal swimming and grasping. Out in the wilds, they would probably be catching minnows and small fish already. Which, by the way, we're introducing to their diet this week."

"What about this other guy," Garrett asked. "His leg is still bent."

"It must have caught on something in the flood—a root maybe—and twisted. The tendons were badly injured."

"What if he can't learn to swim very good?"

"He'll have to live here, too." Jo answered. "I'm not happy about that. They should be in their natural habitat."

Carter stroked the head of the otter Garrett was feeding, and it recoiled.

"Not without gloves," Jo ordered. "I've told you that. They're small but they can draw blood."

"Blood doesn't scare me," Carter said in a low voice.

"You guys should see the box turtle we rescued, the poor guy with the broken shell," Makayla said, stepping away from Carter.

Jalil disappeared, and returned holding it by the edges of its shell. Its head and legs were pulled in, and across the black and yellow dome was a silver colored band.

"You duct taped him back together?" said Ray-Ray.

"Yeah. Jo said when the break isn't catastrophic, we just need to hold it together until the shell grows back together."

The turtle's dark green, almost-black head emerged and turned from side to side, as if it were sizing them up, determining whether they were a threat.

"He's probably ready for his breakfast," said Makayla. "These guys are very docile. Almost like pets."

"I call him Tank," said Jalil. He looked around to see if he had everyone's attention. "Because he looks like a tank. Pretty good, right? Right?"

Makayla rolled her eyes. "About as good as your drum playing."

Jo, who was looking on, said, "Don't get attached. He should be ready to go back to the wetlands in a few months. If a piece of his shell had been missing, it would be a much longer recovery period."

"When do the rest of us get to be on teams?" Rocco asked.

"You'll know soon."

The rain slowed, then stopped, and by 1:30 they were touring the nearby village of Lake Placid on foot, checking out souvenir stores, sports shops, bookstores, and ice cream shops. Through narrow spaces between the buildings along the street, they could see a smaller body of water—Mirror Lake. Across the water from the village and all around the lake, the homes looked like small mansions.

"Dang. There is *muh-nay* in this town," Dugan said to Garrett.

"Dollah dollah bill, y'all," Garrett replied. "Best reason for us to be in this program, in my opinion."

Eric handed them each twenty dollars, and pointed west. "Burgers and pizza on that end of the street."

Bay pointed in the opposite direction. "Great salads and other vegetarian foods that way."

Outside a pizza shop, two kids were hovering beside an older man in a wheelchair whose head was tilted to one side. He was fumbling with a can of Coke.

"Can'cha open it?" one kid giggled. He elbowed the other one. "Ya look thirsty."

Dhani had opened the door to the shop, but paused, watching.

"Hey, we'll seeya later, gramps. Wait here for us and—," he winked at the other, "—drink your Coke."

The two pushed their way through the crowded sidewalk and disappeared down the street.

The old man concentrated on the silver pop-ring, but could not make his shaky fingers catch the edge of it to open the can. He sat, trying again and again, licking his dry lips.

Dhani dropped to one knee beside him.

"Want me to open that for you, sir?"

"Sh-sh-sure," the man stuttered, and stretched out a shaky arm, relinquishing the can.

Dhani noticed the fingers of his hands were curled tight, like claws. Popping the can open, he handed it carefully back into the man's trembling hands.

"Do you want me to hold it up for you, so you can drink?"

The man's head shook just a little more than it had been. "Nope. G-got it." And he gave a bent, thumbs-up.

For a moment their eyes connected—and Dhani wondered what the world would be like if you were in a wheelchair and struggled to do even the littlest things for yourself. He wondered what it would be like to be old and impaired and have a strange kid in a black hoody offer to help you. What would you feel?

When he opened the door to the pizza shop to go in, he noticed his own hand was shaking a little.

When the Troverts stepped inside a deli, Garrett grabbed Dugan's sleeve. "Let's get out of here."

"Where are we going?"

"I'll tell you where when we get there."

Emmalyn, who was ahead of them, alone, looked back, smiled and winked. As she turned away, she casually ran a hand down one hip.

Dugan snorted. "You see that?"

"Not interested."

"You ever notice how that girl looks at you or me or any guy, and then touches her body somewhere, like she's teasing?"

"She doesn't do anything for me."

"I'm telling you, she acts all country-girl innocent, but she got moves that are totally practiced. Professional-like. She ever say why she was in detention?"

"She's just a dumb hick, and she's annoying. Probably in for being criminally stupid."

"Ease up on her, man. I know you got a thing for Carter."

"Yeah, I do. So what? She's starting to come on to me."

"You're nuts. She's the ice princess. No, she's the *ice castle* the ice princess lives in."

"Yeah, well I'm gonna find a way into that castle."

"That door opens, you gonna get a blast from a walk-in freezer."

"You're just saying that, because the chick you're hot for is infatuated with *him*."

Behind them, Makayla and Imani were flanking Rocco, both talking nonstop. Rocco was focusing on Imani, smiling at her—but it was Makayla who touched his arm and laughed, as if everything he said was cute or funny. Imani looked indifferent.

Dugan's mood changed. "He's a flirt. Can't stand that jerk."

"Well, he's a jerk who's got the attention of your lady."

"You tryna start something? She's talking with Makayla, not paying attention to him."

"Dude, she's not paying attention to *you*, because she's with *him*. That's my point. As long as he's around, he's in your way."

"Whadda you suggest—kill him and dump the body?"

"Something like that."

Dugan was wary. "What are you talking about?—and where are you taking me?"

They had passed the last deli on the main street. Immediately, the sidewalk curved away from the blocks of shops and led them in front of the first, lavish houses along the far side of the lake. Beyond tall manicured hedges were homes of log and glass, with Porsches and Ferraris in the driveways.

Dugan whistled. "These people got some dough."

"Exactly right. And so do their kids." Garrett looked around to see if anyone from the group had followed him. The sidewalk was empty. "There's a parking lot across the road at the Lake Placid boat launch. We need to meet a couple guys."

"How do you know people up here? And how'd you set up some hush-hush meeting, when they're monitoring our calls and emails?"

"Don't worry about all that. I got someone who's hooking it up for us."

"*Us*. What you getting me into?"

"Nothing you won't like."

Claire and Ray-Ray had come into the pizza shop minutes after Dhani, and joined him with their slices at a small table that was sticky and needed wiping.

When they stepped out on the sidewalk again, the old man in the wheelchair was still there, alone and waiting for the two kids—grandsons?—to return.

As they passed him, the man reached out and pinched Claire's sleeve between two gnarled fingers. When he had her eye, he pointed another curled finger at Dhani.

"H-h-he. . . ." he stammered.

Claire smiled down at the man and looked at Dhani.

"He—*what*?"

The man shifted his gaze to Dhani's face. "Y- y- you have a gift. I- I can see it."

9TH

Tom rifled through the storage closet in Kate's office suite.

"What are you looking for?" Kate had come through the back hall, and stood in the doorway. Her expression looked strained.

"A can of dust-off spray, to clean my keyboard before I start work.— What's wrong?"

"John Sewell called me late last evening. It wasn't good, and I didn't have a great night. He said that prosecutor has begun to push hard to drag Claire back to Virginia for a deposition—and maybe more. John says it sounds big."

Tom found the can, and turned to her.

"What is the prosecutor looking for?"

The survival curriculum was not coming together. Steve tore another sheet off his yellow pad forcefully and let it flutter to the floor

He kept trying to mesh his training with Eric and Bay Trovert's program for the year, but it was like gears grinding. Sometimes he could focus. Sometimes he couldn't.

He was out on the rear porch of his cabin, drumming his pen on the small table in front of him. Eric had backed off from pushing him for a plan, and that eased the tension between them a little.

"I know you're arriving late to all this, Steve. Take your time. We all want you to feel like you have ownership in the program, too."

Eric was actually a good guy. Pretty much. Then why the irritation with him?

He looked down at the yellow pad in his lap.

His ideas for *Basic Personal Survival* worked with the Troverts' first-year goal for the students: "Know what supports and helps you, and what harms you."

He had already begun to teach them about shelters. What was on the Troverts' suggested list?

Building a fire from scratch.

Easy.

Finding water and food.

Laurel Wysocki knew all about wild edible plants.

He smiled, thinking how grossed out these kids would be when he told them that in extreme circumstances—say, with a severely broken leg from a fall, when you couldn't move—you could survive for a few days by drinking your own urine.

Orienteering.

Winter weather survival.

A big challenge for these kids.

Three-day and ten-day solo trips.

Great way to test their knowledge and know-how.

Something was lacking, though, but his mind would not focus.

From inside the cabin a *click*ing noise got his attention.

When he turned to look inside through the French doors, the black lab was standing halfway across the open living area, sniffing the air.

"What the—"

The dog's tail wagged tentatively when it saw him, and he limped forward.

Steve stepped inside, and stood in the center of the cabin's main room, where the lab stopped and looked up at him, wagging not only his tail but his whole body.

Steve dropped to one knee and rubbed the dog's muzzle and broad head with one hand, petting the smooth fur on his back in long strokes with the other. The lab's coat was healthy looking, shiny black, and thick.

What did you do, fella—escape?

Jo stuck her head inside the front door, which Steve had left half-open to let the fresh lake air circulate.

When he waved her in, she didn't look at Steve but kept her eyes fixed on the lab.

"Come here, buddy. No running away again. Let's go home."

Steve saw that she was avoiding eye-contact.

Well, good morning to you, too.

"He likes this side of the lake for some reason," Jo said. "We were walking along the shore and I thought he was slowing down, so I turned back. He started giving me that squeaky-hinge kind of dog whimper. And then he turned around and took off on me. I kept calling and he wouldn't come. I started jogging, and he started running. *Running.* I couldn't believe it. He must still be in a good bit of pain."

Steve looked into the lab's brown eyes, which were fixed on his face. "A tough guy, huh?"

"I was afraid he'd take off into the woods, reinjure himself and become lunch for the coyotes and vultures. But then he turned onto the foot bridge. And now—here he is. With you."

The lab sat down heavily, one haunch resting on Steve's right foot, tail thumping the wood floor.

"Yeah." That was all Steve could manage.

"So—"

No, no, no. You're not doing a sales job here.

At the same time, he was half-aware that taking care of the dog would probably impress Jo. Immediately, he pushed that idea away.

"I gotta admit, when you were crawling out on the ice to save him I thought that was kind of foolish."

"Oh, really? These creatures are like my family. You're a military guy. No one left behind. Or did I misunderstand that?"

Ouch.

He deserved that. The universe was not going to let him forget.

The lab was doing doe eyes again. Maybe he could make some amends.

"What would I call him?—Buck? Champ?"

"Sahm keeps using a Tibetan word when he speaks to him—*Palden.*
He says it means 'Glorious One'. He fought hard to survive, so I guess
that works."

"Then you didn't ban Sahm from your clinic."

"No."

He let that subject ride and went back to the name, feeling himself
caving-in.

"How about Pal, for short." He looked down. "What do you think,
Pal?"

The lab butted Steve's hand with his nose, tail thumping harder.

Jo looked surprised.

"That's a change of heart. Well, if it's settled I'm going back. There's
a pharmaceutical delivery coming, and I need to sign for it."

That's it? I just got railroaded, and not even a thank you?

"I'll send Ron out with a container of food."

"Whoa. What if he runs away?"

"Don't feed him any junk food."

"I don't eat junk food. What if he runs away?" he repeated.

Jo was heading out the door. "He won't."

"How do you know?"

She called back over her shoulder. "Like I said, dogs are more loyal
than a lot of humans. I guess he chose you for a good reason. Don't
prove him wrong."

Hey, you're welcome.

"Oh, and thank you," she called, heading down the path.

The dog settled on Steve's feet out on the porch where he took up
his yellow pad again.

During the distraction, or maybe because of it, the thing that both-
ered him about the Troverts' program—and the whole Lost Lake set
up—had come clear in his mind.

All their training was about self-care. Soft stuff. And there would be the usual classes taught by tutors. All of it supported by a very generous, kindhearted patron—Kate. Life wasn't soft and kind, though.

Ask me about my "easy" life.

The tip of his pen dug into the paper as he scrawled, for himself if no one else, one word—and drew heavy lines under it.

Discipline.

10TH

Days of wet, cold weather delayed the next, longer trek. To help build stamina, Eric led shorter hikes.

When they could manage a morning fire circle between rains, the girls wore flannel shirts and hooded sweatshirts. Makayla's thin frame was buried inside a coat. "Does it ever really get to be summer up here?"

"It's a short season," Bay told her. "July and August. Maybe a couple weeks on either side of that, if we're lucky. It should get hot any day now. The lakes will warm up, and you guys can swim."

Garrett nudged Dugan. "Girls in little bathing suits, coming soon to a lake near us."

"You're seriously just like a dog. Is that all you think about?" He waved the book he was reading at Garrett—*Our Only World.* "Jo wants us all to read it. This guy Wendell Berry says, '. . .analytic science divides creatures into organs, cells, and ever small parts or particles according to its technological capacities.'"

"So?"

"Let me finish. Berry says, 'I recognize the possibility and existence of this knowledge, even its usefulness, but I also recognize the narrowness of its usefulness and the damage it does.'"

"Why are you boring me with this?"

Man, he's talking about the way we humans overconsume and destroy stuff. He says, 'I am opposed to any claim that such knowledge is adequate to the sustenance of human life or the health of the ecosphere.'"

Garrett rolled his eyes.

"Weren't you listening to Jo the last time she talked to us? She wants us to think about the fact that we are destroying whole ecosystems and a lotta animal species. How we're poisoning ourselves, too, because we don't think about what we're doing to the planet. I never thought about any of that before."

"Ohmygod. You're thinking like them already."

"On this big issue, yeah. And about race relations in this country. Unlike you, I do think about more than getting off."

"Hey, I think about other stuff."

"Really? Like what?"

Garrett flashed a big smile.

"Cash."

20TH

Bay was right in her prediction. After almost two full weeks of cold rain, the sun had come out again full strength, turning the air hot and humid. The sky was hazy by midday now.

All morning, Dhani searched for Claire. First, in Kate's great room, which was now a student lounge area, then out in Jo's clinic and barns.

He needed to find her.

Makayla was sunning in a chair on Kate's back terrace, as he headed inside to Ivy's lunch buffet.

"She's not in there," she responded to Dhani's question. "She's back at the cabin, in her room with the door closed. I knocked to see if she was okay, and she said, 'I'm drawing.' I think that's what she does when she's totally stressed out."

"What's she stressed out about?"

"I don't know. She won't talk to Imani or me. She looks real unhappy."

"Aren't you gonna eat lunch?"

"No. I'm not hungry." Makayla sounded defensive.

His eager smile returned. "Then would you do me a big favor—please? Go tell Claire I have something for her. I'll wait here."

When Makayla returned, her face was clouded. "She said, 'Tell him I know he's looking for me, and I want him to leave me alone.'"

Dhani felt a stitch in his breathing.

"I'm sorry," Makayala said, seeing his expression change. She laid a hand on his arm, and her sympathy sounded genuine. "She's not talking to anyone. I'd stay away if I were you. Something must have happened."

21ST

Past the two rows of cabins, around the bay, across a small bridge, out on a point where pines and hardwoods crowded together, Dhani came to Sahm's isolated cabin, which was tucked in among the trees.

He leaped the two steps, hesitated, and knocked. From inside came the muffled sound of Vajra's bark—a deep-throated, rumbling sound.

Since their encounter along the lake path a month ago, something Sahm had said during the hike on Peregrine stuck in his mind. "Meditation frees the mind from suffering."

He raised his hand to knock, his head an anxious mess.

A week after Claire told Grady she thought he was cool, she now abruptly cut him off. That more than stung.

"Hey man, she's avoiding me, too," Ray-Ray had said, trying to console him. It didn't. He didn't know where his mom was, people were treating him like a freak, and the small buzz he got from thinking Claire might be starting to like him had crashed. Now, the anxiety was making him chew his cuticles till they were raw.

The door opened and Vajra charged out from behind Sahm to sniff at Dhani's hand.

"It is very good to see you."

Dhani balked. "I—I was wondering if you would tell me about meditating. I think it might help me."

Sahm looked at Dhani carefully. "I think so, yes."

Seated up on the boulder next to the cabin, doing what Sahm instructed, Dhani followed his breath in and out and back in. . . again and again.

"I feel a little dizzy. I think I'm breathing too fast."

Sahm was listening to Dhani, and at the same time paying attention to a rapid energy-pulse, like that of a rabbit, which he felt coming from the boy.

"Slow down. Focus your mind on your breath as it goes in and out. Slowly. Don't think about anything else—only your breath."

Dhani was confused. Wasn't meditation supposed to carry you up into some kind of transcendental higher place? Give you a buzz? That's what he had come here hoping for.

After several minutes, Sahm asked, "What is your mind doing?"

"It's kind of like I'm riding on a streetboard on a flat pavement. My mind feels. . . smoother." So that was good at least—but there was something else going on.

"Look around inside your mind," Sahm instructed. "Tell me what is there."

Strange instruction, but he tried it. "Nothing. It's just kind of calm. Well, the streetboard now has this cool, blue alligator-skin paint job."

"In Tibet, we say the mind is riding the windhorse of the breath. So you have a blue streetboard. That is good. But do you have bad feelings or bad thoughts?"

"Actually. . . no. Not right now."

"*Now* is where you should be. In the present moment. You are doing a very good first meditation."

"Really? So, I just keep focusing on the streetboard?"

"Yes. Do that for now. And if your mind tries to jump off your streetboard to make you think about other things, bring it back. Focus on the alligator scales. Or focus on the smoothness of the street. Steadying your mind a little is good enough for now."

Dhani focused again on the cool stream of air moving in and out his nostrils. Or mostly focused. A pebble poked into his left thigh, distracting him. And every few moments his mind jumped to images that flew through his head at random. He imagined. . .

. . .*the box turtle with its silver duct tape bandage, and Jo saying, "Believe it or not, this is the best way to hold his shell together while it grows back together again."*

That the broken turtle would eventually heal made him smile. His pulse slowed a little. Then he saw. . . .

. . .*Makayla's face and heard her say, "She wants you to leave her alone."*

Which made him miserable and anxious.

He tried to focus again on the alligator blue-scaled streetboard, but his mind was jumping all over again.

Sahm had entered into his own meditation, and immediately moved away from bodily sensations into the open space around them. Since the hike up Peregrine Mountain, he had wondered about Dhani and wanted to know more about this boy. His mind reached out.

His body is still, but he is jumpy. Unstable.

Sahm expanded his mind until it was a bright cloud, which he extended around Dhani—the way he would have held and calmed an anxious little child, attempting to steady him. Silently, he chanted,

Awakened Ones, surround and hold this young man in perfect balance and calm.

To Dhani's amazement, he felt a sense slowly rising in and all around him, as if he were beginning to float on a cushion of air or being held up by unseen hands. His breath flowed steadily in and out. Then thoughts of his mom arose, and with them his constant undercurrent of uneasiness.

Beside him, Sahm felt the resurgence of doubt and worry, like an electric sting.

He is suffering in hopelessness and frustration.

He continued chanting steadily, patiently.

Great Awakened Ones, you who act for the benefit of all beings, who bring the natural purity of vision. . . transcendent ones. . . help this boy, who is like a poor, wild creature caught in some kind of trap—like tangled thorns.

Once again, with each deep breath, Dhani felt the anxiety that had gripped his stomach ease a little more. The unseen hands were soothing him and the sense of buoyancy returned.

Awakened Ones who bring natural purity and cleansing. . . from the space of billowing clouds on-high and the sound of rushing wind, elevate his mind.

Dhani fought with his mind to keep from picturing where his mother probably was right now. In some dirty hole of an apartment. He couldn't think of that. It crushed him.

He let those thoughts go, and as he did he also lost track of the rock pressing into his pelvic bones, riding the current of air slowly moving in and out of his lungs.

In a few seconds, it was as if he had slipped from his body out into a vast space. He was floating in an empty pale-blue sky just before sunrise. The vast, clear space spread into distance all around him. . . within him.

Empty of all other thought, he only knew openness and clear light and the deepening blissful sense of buoyancy. He felt as if his body wanted to rise. . .as if he *could* rise, if he would just let himself. A sense of power began to gather in the deep center of his being.

Sahm watched a crack starting to open within Dhani, like a tectonic plate shifting inside the boy, and a pure white light within.

In the next instant, Dhani felt too open, too exposed. In a shock of terror, he fled back into himself.

A thought passed swiftly through Sahm's clear-open mind.

He is recoiling from this.

A flickering image came, of Dhani being pulled back and down by dark cords, unable to free himself.

"Hey, can we go now?" Dhani's voice sounded strained.

Sahm's eyes flew open. Across from him, Dhani's face looked slightly ashen, as if he would be sick.

Dhani arched his back and stretched his legs out. "That was. . . I don't know. It was kinda like I was starting to fly, but. . . ."

"Yes?"

Dhani's eyes darted away from Sahm's. He had closed up entirely.

"Sitting on this rock makes my butt hurt." He slid down off the boulder. "I *think* I got what you wanted me to do. I'm not sure. I kinda liked it, though. At first."

Sahm was caught up in his own thoughts. "Practice all the time. If you do, you will have good results."

"Really?"

What had Sahm almost witnessed in this young man's spirit? Something within him, wanting to be born or reborn.

"Without doubt."

Dhani weighed the two feelings that had arisen inside him. What if he could escape from the bad feelings and have more of the good ones? "Could you help me?"

Sahm nodded. "Possibly. I will try."

Back in his room, Dhani lay on the bed, staring at the square of blue sky he could see through his window, revisiting the strange thought he'd had during the meditation.

For a few seconds, he'd felt a thrill of elation—felt like he was rising up through white clouds, higher than the mountains. A few seconds of transcendence. A pure bliss he could not remember feeling ever before.

He stretched his arms out, imagining they were wings and he was flying.

And then in his mind he heard, *What are you, a little fairy or something?*—and his arms flopped heavily onto the mattress.

When The Monster in his mind turned away, Dhani made hand gestures at the man's receding back.

Sahm prostrated himself before the meditation altar. He focused on the central figure—the lapis blue Great One, now with the fiery, golden symbol on his chest.

Dzes-Sa! My highest Teacher. Who is this boy?

What did it mean that Dhani contained such limitless brilliance and power? Why was it trapped within such thick tangles and darkness?

Words flew swift as birds through his mind, clear and distinct.

"Watch him carefully."

He startled.

"He is not what he appears."

24TH

Claire ignored the wander line marker, and trudged up the path to Thunder Rock. She was angry and her hands were shaking after the meeting with Kate and Tom, her mind replaying the bad news. Kate had told her days before that something was happening legally that involved her—and to be ready. Now she knew what it was.

"Judge Sewell and that woman from Child Protective Services, Monica Saint, are both fighting for you stay here," Tom had told her. "The prosecutor told Sewell he's definitely planning to file papers to force you back to Virginia. You need to know this—and you need to know we're going to go over his head to the District Attorney, to block him from doing that."

"We'll go higher if we have to," Kate said, her voice firm. "I have powerful friends."

"What does he want with me?"

"We have no idea.—Do you?" Tom asked.

"I can't think of a thing I did wrong. But people can lie about you."

"I'm sorry this is happening, Claire," said Kate, with a look of concern. "It must be upsetting. But you have people in your camp now. You have us."

Claire felt herself starting to tear up and her throat tightening. She fought to keep her emotions from showing.

"I'm not upset. I'm a realist. I thought being here was too good to be true."

Now, with her daypack slung over one shoulder, she found the trail on the far side of the Garnet River. If she was going to be wrongly accused, why not really break the rules? She could only guess what lies someone had made up about her this time. Ignoring the yellow wander-line stripes, she charged up the slope of Lost Mountain.

The river's voice fell away quickly below her and, in a little while the sound of Thunder Falls grew louder through the woods as she climbed. Her heels slammed into the path with the force of her rage.

Why can't I get away from the past?

Reaching the ledge above the falls, she dropped down on it, leaning her back against Thunder Rock. The weeks of rain had swollen the higher streams feeding the falls, and the rush of air from the flow sent up a cool mist that brushed her face and arms.

She flipped through her sketchpad, glancing at images she had drawn since arriving here—Sahm's ceremonial dagger, the strange-acting northern pike, moonlight reflected on the lake, the bullfrog Dugan caught, the box turtle found on the camp road with its broken shell. She couldn't decide if she liked or hated her work. If she could just lose herself in sketching today, forget the courts and the system, forget everything. . . .Yes, she would just escape into the scene right in front of her—the falls and mountains behind it—capturing it all in black lines on white pages.

She clipped the lower edge of her sketch pad, to keep the moving air from fluttering the paper, and took out Numbers 4 and 5 and 2B graphite pencils. Quickly, she shaded-in the contours and shadows of the falls and Eagle Rock Mountain in the distance. The shifting sunlight would change the way it all looked in a half-hour, and she wanted to capture the way the landscape looked now, and spend the rest of the afternoon refining.

She wanted to be lost in drawing and left alone. It was time to pull away from everyone, even Ray-Ray who was becoming her friend. And from Dhani, who was puppy-dogging her. She was probably going to be torn away from both of them, so why not just do it and get it over with?

"Poor rich girl wants to be loved. Thinks she can be the great care-giver and get love by hanging around people who are 'less fortunate'."

Claire startled at the voice.

Carter was standing at the end of the path, where it opened out onto the ledge.

"What are you doing here?" Claire demanded. "Are you stalking me?"

"You like to break the rules. So you're not *just* a goody-goody." Carter took several steps closer, looked at the falls, then turned her empty, cold-blue gaze back on Claire.

"Be careful you don't get too close to a killer and find out too late it was a big mistake."

"What are you ranting about?"

"I internet searched everyone here before we came. Most everyone is a big fake."

"You think you can judge everyone because you Googled us? You're a joke with your *I'm the spoooky girl* act."

"You should be afraid of me. And your sick-o friend. You should see pictures from the Washington *Post*. What he did to that drunk guy, with a can of lighter fluid and a match was no joke."

Carter took a few steps closer.

Claire stood up to the challenge and didn't flinch. "You're just so tough, Carter. Big tough girl. You don't intimidate me anymore." That wasn't true—her mouth was dry, and a thrill of terror roared in her stomach—but alone on a mountainside with this unstable girl was no place to show weakness. She grabbed her daypack and started to push past her. "I don't need this.

Carter lunged forward, shoved Claire back against the rock, and grabbed her sketch pad. One of the pencils rolled across the ledge and fell off into the rushing falls.

Claire steeled herself, to keep from shaking and showing fear.

"*Give me my sketch pad,*" she shouted.

Carter was flipping pages and looking at the falls. "You can always buy more, rich girl. Oh look at this. How cute."

She'd pulled out the sketch Claire had begun of Dhani the day she felt guilty for telling him to go away and leave her alone, capturing the eager, innocent look in his eyes. It wasn't quite finished.

"You gonna draw in the can of lighter fluid?"

Claire lunged at her, grabbed the pad back, and pushed Carter away.

Carter's face went blank. She staggered back in an exaggerated, clownish way. "Oh. Oh. She pushed me."

In four backward steps, she was at the edge of the cliff, where she turned with her toes out over the edge.

Claire froze. "What are you doing?"

"You said I don't intimidate you. But see—you and everyone else here are way too scared to do things I can do."

And then without warning, Carter stepped out onto the air and dropped from sight.

All the way down the rugged mountain path, Claire clutched her backpack and tried to breathe through the terror that had seized her.

Her own scream had strangled in her throat, and she'd dropped to her stomach, staring down at the first boulder-strewn pool fifty feet below. Then she craned her neck to see past the lower falls and pool. She expected to see Carter's broken body draped on rocks or tossing in the churning pool or bobbing like a twisted rag doll down the river current.

She was nowhere to be seen.

Half-running the difficult descent, Claire charged to the trail's edge at two different overlooks for any sign of Carter, but the lower she went the more the river disappeared beneath the lower forest's canopy.

When she emerged from the woods onto the river path, tears had begun to spill down her cheeks. The ground was flat, and she started to run faster—glancing at the wooded, rooted and rocky banks as she went along, to see if Carter had washed up anywhere, injured or. . . or worse.

Find Kate or the Troverts or Jo, she kept repeating. *They'll call a rescue squad.*

For half a moment, the thought crossed her mind. What if Carter was still alive, and told them she pushed her?

"*Hey*—are you looking for me?"

The voice from behind jolted Claire to a full stop, and she spun around.

"I win." Carter was sitting in the curve of a tree trunk that hung out over the river. She was soaked and smiling.

Claire was shaking. She wasn't glad that Carter was alive so much as glad she hadn't found her somewhere along the river in a heap of blood and broken bones.

"You're a freak!" Claire shouted, releasing a sob of anger and relief. *"What do you think you won? Why did you do that? How did you do that?—how did you survive that jump?"*

Carter had a satisfied look. "The first time I left home, this guy in Mexico taught me to cliff jump. How to use a gun, too. Do you know how to use one? You never know when you might need to."

Claire turned and began running, then sprinting, fleeing down the path. She wanted Carter gone, erased, nowhere around.

"There's a lot of stuff you should learn," Carter called after her. *"I can show you."*

Sprinting a few turns of the path, Claire left her behind.

"Stupid little rich girl," Carter muttered, sliding off the tree trunk. "I'm stronger than you, and now we both know it."

30TH

In one of the upstairs classrooms in Kate's lodge, he was struggling through Ron Cambric's math tutorial.

The whole time Ron filled the white board with algebra equations, Dhani had fought to keep from staring out the open windows, but not too successfully. Ron's voice had become like a distant drone.

"Dhani, did you take notes in the last tutorial?—you don't seem to know the material." "Anyone have the answer—Dhani—are you with me?" "Hey, come on, guy, I'm trying to prepare you for the math placement exam—Dhani? Dhani. . . ."

It was hardly his fault. Outside, the mid-summer sky was shockingly blue and inviting, and the cool sheaf of mountain air coming through the windows tempted him, much the way discovering a new corner of the estate was now a lure. Maybe he would ask Claire to join him today after this horrendously mind-numbing class.

He looked at her now, leaning over her notebook, scribbling Ron's newest equation. Why had she suddenly changed and become so cold and distant, avoiding him every day—not even speaking?

"Dhani, what is X?"

He startled and sat up, blinking at the blue glom of letters and numbers on the white board.

"X is... a letter."

Garrett and Dugan laughed.

Claire whipped her head around, her look intense, as if to ask, *"Are you trying to make them laugh at you?"*

Ron stared at him blankly, dry marker poised in the air.

"I didn't hear what you were saying," Dhani fumbled. His face was hot with embarrassment.

Ron smiled patiently. "Come on, man. I know this isn't as fun as a video game, but stay with me ten more minutes. And if you need extra help, I'm here for you."

"Speaking of video games," Garrett interrupted. "Are we ever getting any here?"

"With all that's planned for you guys, you won't have much time for that," Ron replied. Then he looked around the room. "Okay, who's got the answer?"

After class—before he could ask if she wanted to take Grady's canoe out, or if not that he could go with her while she sketched something, or if not that maybe they could just hang out—Claire bolted from the room.

She was not in the dining room or out on Kate's terrace or in her cabin.... She was nowhere Dhani looked for her.

The look she had shot him in class, together with her coldness, stuck in his chest like a blade. He had to find her—find out what he had done wrong. He must have done something.

Walking the dirt road behind the cabins and line of woods, Dhani passed the two small storage barns and Kate's greenhouse and garden. A tiller sat between two rows of tomato vines, where someone had left it for the moment and probably gone to the lunch he was missing, and he could smell the freshness of newly-turned earth. He kept walking, scanning the deep grass fields to the north. Maybe Claire had taken her sketch pad, and. . . .

From the corner of his eye, a movement ten feet ahead—something large, coming out of the deep grass—made him draw a sharp breath and stop dead.

A large, dark gray animal stepped from where it had been concealed directly into his path.

Vajra.

Sahm's half-wolf, stood staring at him, his golden eyes bright and piercing.

He was not intimidated by the big creature, though. From the first, he had felt some kind of kinship, though he did not know why or what it meant.

Another movement in the grass drew his attention, and another large dog, not as huge as Vajra, emerged onto the road, limping. The half-wolf turned his head, and licked the black lab on the side of its face.

Dhani let out his breath. "What are you guys doing out here?" He started toward them, hand outstretched, and when he reached them he rubbed their heads. "You guys seen Claire?"

At that moment, both dogs alerted, heads whipping around toward the east end of the field, where two hundred yards distant the first forested slopes of Eagle Rock Mountain began. The dogs' hackles rose, the lab growled and Vajra bared his fangs.

Dhani stared up the rise of the meadow at the far tree line, where he could see the tops of tall, blue spruce mixed in among the green canopy of the hardwoods. For just a second, he had the impression of something moving quickly, darting from behind one gray trunk to another—not a long low figure, like a bear, but—something walking upright? A person? He couldn't be sure. The figure was too far away and had moved swiftly like a passing shadow.

He continued petting Vajra and the lab. "Calm down, you guys."

They scented the air, and the lab relaxed, his body all tail-waggy and happy. The wolf kept staring at the forest.

"*Vajra!*"

Sahm was calling from a strip of forest that separated the fields and camp road from the lake.

Vajra started to fast-walk then run toward Sahm, with the lab limp-running after. Dhani followed, and reached them all beneath a stand of hardwoods. From here he could see down the gentle slope of woods to the back of Sahm's cabin and a bit of the lake beyond.

"Have you seen Claire?" Dhani asked.

"The young woman who has taken your heart?"

Dhani did not respond to that. "I need to talk to her."

"Perhaps you should give her time to be alone and sort out her mind." Sahm stroked the lab's head. "This one is tired and needs water. If you would like a drink, come and join us. Claire will appear when she wants to be found."

Without warning, Vajra turned and bolted away through the deep grass again. The black lab stayed, wagging his tail, allowing Sahm to continue stroking his head.

"Aren't you going to call him back?" Dhani asked.

"He will return when he is ready," Sahm replied, turning back toward his cabin. "Just like human beings, animals have purposes of their own."

"What is this stuff?" Dhani called from the front room.

Sahm was in the kitchen, making tea for himself. The black lab, which had come inside with them, was lapping water from Vajra's bowl next to the stove. Sahm looked out from the kitchen and saw Dhani standing beside the fireplace, hovering over the meditation altar.

Dhani scanned the table carefully. On it were a few natural objects arranged in an outer half-circle—a hawk feather, a snake skin, herbs found in the mountains. He picked up two of objects—first, the ornate dagger, then the small, white stone.

Sahm emerged from the kitchen, carrying a mug from which small plumes of steam were rising, and sat in a chair across the room. The black lab followed.

"Who is this guy?—the one that looks like a blue monster," Dhani said, holding the stone and pointing at the image in the small picture within the ring of objects. "The guy with a blue body, fangs and claws, surrounded by orange and red flames." He snapped his fingers. "Wait. I know this guy somehow. He's not bad, he's very good but he just looks fierce. I'm not sure how I know that."

"Vajrapani is a fierce protector. He represents the impulse that awakens to guard my mind. This thought must be fierce and sudden—," he set down his cup and clapped his hands together sharply, "—to awaken me from wrong thinking."

"What kind of wrong thinking?"

"He says, '*Sahm, stay awake. Do not fall into illusion.*' Vajrapani keeps my mind from straying into the false belief that others are bad people or that they are my enemy."

Dhani put down the stone, and pointed to the small, bright-blue Buddha statue in the middle. "This guy is very cool. I like him. A lot."

Should I speak to him of you yet? Sahm wondered. *Only a certain few must be taught. Only a few know your name.*

"Yes!"—the word was shouted into his mind.

This caught him off-guard.

"Many call him *Nying-re-sa*. To those whose *dharma* it is to do his work, he is dearly called *Dzes- Sa*."

"What does he do?"

"*He must be told.*"

Sahm was hesitant. *Why?—if he is not what he appears?*

"*Tell him. . . and observe.*"

"He is my greatest teacher," Sahm said, "—the Buddha of the Beautiful Earth. The one earth we are given to protect. He awakens me over and over to one of the highest truths."

"What is that?"

"That everything in the whole earth is connected to every other thing—nothing is separate and alone. Earth, air, fire, water, space, everything is needed to make up this living planet. We are all part of each other. Everything and everyone belongs together. With even one piece taken away, everything else is poorer."

Dhani continued staring at the Buddha figure, his brow furrowed as if he were trying hard to recall something.

"I've seen this 'Zesa' guy. Somewhere. I don't know where. That gold squiggly line on his chest is a. . . a one. It means *one*, doesn't it? But that wasn't on there a minute ago. Or was it?"

Sahm nearly spat out his tea, leapt to his feet, and stood beside Dhani, staring.

In the center of the figure's chest, a faint, golden symbol had appeared—the Sanskrit symbol for *one*.

"Do not tell him everything yet. First, there is much clearing to be done within this one, so that his gift is not corrupted and ruined by past injuries. We will awaken him slowly."

But my grandfather said 'Time is running down.' Should we not hurry to awaken him?

There was no reply.

Sahm fumbled for an explanation to Dhani's question. "In a certain light, the symbol becomes visible. And only to some people."

The answer seemed to satisfy, and Dhani looked at the small, white stone in his hand again. He ran a thumb over the faint bumps and gouges, which looked like eyes, a wide flat nose, and the hint of a grinning mouth.

He had the sense that *this* stone had belonged to him, but that was impossible. Maybe he'd had one just like it a long time ago. He had been forced to move so many times, it must have gotten lost. But it *was* this stone—and yet it couldn't be.

When Dhani turned to say something, Sahm was sitting back

in his chair, the cup of tea resting his lap. He was watching Dhani carefully.

"This stone is the coolest thing on the whole table—or altar or whatever you call it," Dhani said, marveling at it. "Where did you find it?"

"It was given to me. A very special stone. Why do you ask about it?"

"It's exactly like one I had. I can't remember when. What makes it special?"

"Hold it in the palm of your hand."

Dhani let the stone rest in his right palm. "Someone is coming up to the door," he said in a moment—then he looked at Sahm, startled. "Why would I say such a weird thing?"

Sahm looked out the front windows, but saw no one walking along the lakefront or in the tree line. He turned to Dhani, and opened his mouth to speak.

A sharp knock at the door surprised them both. Someone had come up unnoticed.

Sahm rose, crossed the room, and opened the door.

Steve Tanner was standing on the porch.

"Have you seen Pal? He wandered off the island and I've been looking for him."

Nails clicked on the cabin floor, the lab rose from beside Sahm's chair and went to Steve's side, wagging his tail.

"Dhani found him wandering and brought him here."

"Buddy," Steve smiled at Pal, "you can't wander off alone like that."

"He was with Vajra. Not alone."

"Looks like you found a friend," Steve said to the lab, stroking his back. "Hope he's better company than me."

Sahm noticed that Dhani had set down the stone and backed away from the door as far as he could. His shoulders were slumped, his head was buried inside his hood, and he was staring at the floor.

Sahm looked back at Steve, who had not looked once at Dhani or even acknowledged the boy at all.

"Time to go, Pal," Steve said, lavishing the dog with petting and with treats from his pocket. "This'll hold you over till we get back home. Thanks, Sahm, for taking care of this guy."

When Steve and the lab were gone, Sahm was aware that Dhani was withdrawn, turned in on himself, and looked unhappy.

"I'm gonna go now," Dhani said.

"I would like you to take the stone you chose. It came to me, but possibly it is yours."

Dhani looked confused. "No it isn't. You said it was a gift from your grandfather. I put it back. Thanks, though."

And he was out the cabin door.

Sahm looked at the small, white stone, lost in thinking of its origins.

It had pushed its way up through the subterranean depths of the earth, gathering ancient knowledge over eons, out onto Himalayan heights, to be passed down from teacher to student for millennia. An oracular stone, known to awaken in those who had the gift, knowledge of that which cannot be seen with the eye.

He had not said the stone had come with him from Tibet or that it had been given by his grandfather. The boy had just known that.

When he looked at the small, blue figure of *Dzes-Sa,* the golden symbol for *one* had remained.

"There is only one beautiful earth, Sahmdup Yangchen. The time to rise and protect all living things is now."

What does this have to do with such a fearful boy, he pondered. *One who is so lacking in boldness?*

Steve scooped kibble for the lab, and stood back watching as the dog buried his face in the bowl. "Hey, at least chew it before you swallow."

He had felt anxiety rising when he realized Pal was gone. He needed this companion. His presence helped to keep the disturbing images and feelings away when they tried to return. And then he had disappeared, and that unsettled him.

Steve noticed that he was gripping the scoop so tightly his knuckles were almost white. Even though Pal was back, the anxiety had not left completely. For a second, he saw himself. . . .

. . .squatting, and tightly gripping the handle of a knife—the Marine Ka-bar he had used to cut away the pant leg of the buddy lying at his feet.

He tried to keep the next brutal image out of his head

. . .of shattered leg bones and torn arteries.

Pal was still noisily chowing down his food, and Steve felt cold beads of sweat on his forehead. He wished his own mind was that clear of everything but basic living needs. When he was not losing himself in ordering or checking gear, hiking or fishing, the unsettledness was always waiting.

The old dream had come back recently, as well.

He would look up from some simple task to see Olivia watching him.

He jumped to his feet, and as soon as he did, she turned away and began to run. . . always looking back to see if he was following.

He ran as fast and hard as he could. Never catching up. Trying to shout to her. To warn her. Nothing came out but strangled sounds.

So she was still here, always at the far edges of his mind. He could feel her with him as he knelt to pat the dog scarfing his food.

What are you trying to tell me, babe? Do you think I'm a bad guy? Is that it? Well, I'm trying to get you. That's why I'm here—I'm not sure but I think.

Stroking the lab's broad back had a steadying effect. He forced himself to stop thinking about his failures and focused on Pal. Maybe he could protect this amiable creature.

His mind jumped. What had Dhani been doing with Pal? The kid had a reputation for lighting things on fire. Like people.

"Don't worry, boy," he said, keeping himself in the present moment as best he could. "I'll keep that kid away from you."

Dhani walked back up through the woods to the dirt road, and focused on the northern fields again. Still no signs of Claire. Sahm's strange statement about the stone played with his mind. *"It came to me, but possibly it is yours."*

He was already the freak-a-zoid, pyro kid who made game fish and birds of prey go ape. Guys who were into magic at his age were mocked as losers and basement dwellers. All he wanted was to be normal. Maybe even some day work out and be a hot kid, like Rocco—a guy girls wanted. The last thing he needed was a goofy "magic" stone.

What he really needed was to talk to Claire. Something brushed his hand and he startled.

Vajra was walking beside him, looking up with those piercing eyes, and he felt himself vanishing. . . .

Immediately after Ron's class this morning, Claire had carried her daypack out through the fields, and laid her sketch pad on a rock beside the lower pool at Thunder Falls. It felt a like protected space here, between a stand of cedar trees and a grove of firs.

She was alone, distinctly refusing to let Carter's bizarre act prevent her from being out on her own. That, and she wanted to see for herself how it was possible to make the jump Carter had made and not smashed her brains out or broken all her bones.

Now, climbing the rocks beside the thundering water that poured down into the lower basin, she struggled her way to the upper pool. Here, she stood close to the base of the high waterfall, wind and spray feathering her hair. This pool was only ten or twelve feet across, maybe half the width of the lower one, and its white, churning water was ringed by big, broken stones sticking up at dangerous angles.

From here, the powerful rushing current plunged down a second falls to the pool below, where she had left her pack—and from there, flowed on as the Garnet River.

She stared higher up, at the ledge where she had been drawing the day Carter went psycho-girl on her. Then looked again at this upper pool at her feet.

You would have to jump just exactly right and keep your body really straight. Then *maybe* you could drop down beside the falling water and land in the center of this pool's circle of broken boulders. If you aimed just right, you might land in the black, swirling pool of water here in the cliff's shadow. Otherwise, it was suicide. But maybe Carter didn't care.

She was about to climb back down to the lower pool, when she had the sense of being watched. Her head swiveled all around—at the ledge above, the expanse of meadow below, and at the two stands of trees. She looked and waited.

There was no one.

You're just spooked, she chided herself. *That's what she wants, for you to be afraid all the time.*

Well, Carter would not win. Claire climbed carefully down and spent the afternoon working.

Over and over, she tried to capture the contours of the falling water, the splash of it striking the boulders of the lower pool, penciling and erasing, with mixed results. She sketched a pair of eyes—Vajra's amazingly beautiful ones came to mind—because she was not going to let the feeling of being watched intimidate her.

Near the dinner hour, she hiked back, the summer wild flowers—yellow-and-black susans and blue chicory—swishing around her legs, with the scent of sweet grass strong in the late-afternoon air. In her daypack, she had five sketches she had scrubbed over with her pencil and only two she half-liked.

Just before entering her cabin, the watched feeling returned strongly, and she whipped her head around quickly to see if someone was behind her. On and off all afternoon, she'd had a very vague, *spider-on-your-neck* sensation that eyes were on her. Once, she thought she heard a low growl, but, looking everywhere, saw nothing.

Carter and the curse of paranoia.

The dirt road and meadow beyond were empty. Then a movement caught her eye.

Coming out of the deep grass along the dirt road she had just crossed, golden eyes focused on her.

Vajra.

Inside, Makayla and Imani were leaving for the dinner hall, and Makayla was saying, "Well I think he's hot, and if you don't want him kick him my way."

Claire guessed they were talking about Rocco. Again.

Makayla added, "But I don't think he wants me, he wants you."

Which confirmed it; she hated "boy talk".

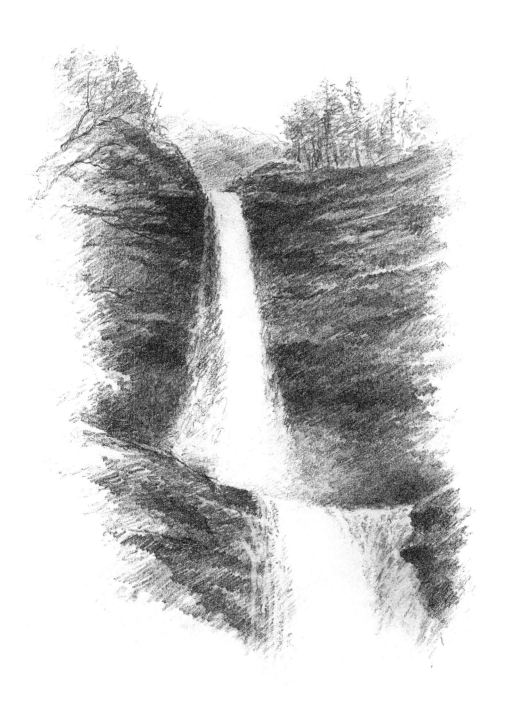

"Can I walk with you to Kate's?" Claire asked.

They both looked at her, surprised.

"I know. I've been keeping to myself a lot lately. Right now, if you guys don't mind, I just don't want to be alone.

Dhani sat still in the deep grass, blinking, trying to get back into his own mind. What had just happened? . . . .

All afternoon, he had moved in a kind of dream, following Claire's movements out to the base of Thunder Falls, watching her climb and sketch—afraid, now that he had finally caught up with her, that she would be angry he had followed. Maybe accuse him of creeping around and stalking her.

But the whole time, it was as if he were watching her from a different body, not his own. One low to the ground. Able to pad quietly, stealthily through the field grass and not be seen or heard. Everything had been more vivid, the tiniest sounds of a field mole, the scents of grass and woodlands almost overpowering. Even at a distance from her, he caught the scent of Claire's body wash and even her laundry soap. Why were his senses so acute?

At one point, he had sensed before he saw or smelled, something—a human?—watching her from the woods near the lower pool where she was sketching. Had growled and driven away whatever it was, wanting only to guard and protect her. Fiercely, if necessary.

Whatever or whoever it was had not approached. . . .

And now he was sitting back here in the deep grass on his haunches, with Vajra licking his hand then walking away from him toward the cabins.

Whatever had happened to his mind—again—he would tell no one.

31ST

The voice at the other end was tinny and hard to hear. "Where are you right now?"

"Walking beside the canal in Georgetown near the drop-off point. Exactly where I always am when we talk."

"I've got some very good news."

"You located the husband?"

"No. His cell phone. I tracked its location to a storage unit in Alexandria, just four miles from you. Apparently, he ditched it. Phone company call records indicate it hasn't been used in well over a year and they stopped billing him."

"You said not to use technology that could be monitored. How did you come up with this?"

"Discrete connection. I said I needed the info because the guy's wife was involved in something that has very high-level, national security implications."

Silence.

"So his phone is dead and in storage. That means he cancelled service or just let it lapse. He really wants to be off-grid. Did you come up with an address for him?"

"Just their old one."

"Can you get someone inside that storage unit?"

"Work on the street is up to you. That's always been the deal."

"So you still trust us?"

"Not completely. Just get someone in there to go through every box and file.—Get on it."

6

AUGUST

3RD

The police officer held up the wristwatch by its broken band, then set it on the wooden desktop.

"Do you know if this belonged to your night security guard?"

The manager of the storage facility on Highway 1 in Alexandria, Virginia, shook his head. "Sir, I have no idea. Never paid that close attention. It could be Jake's. But I can't say."

"We just found it out behind the longest stretch of storage units. The chain-link fence back there was cut. There's some blood on one of the wires, like someone sliced themselves going in or out. It appears there may have been a break-in. Maybe your night watchman heard them and went out back to check. Just speculating here, but there could have been a scuffle and the watchband broke."

"He's my best employee. Absolute best in all my years managing storage facilities in the Washington area."

"Why do you have night watchmen if this property is secure?"

"Because this has become a rough area. And because anyone could slip in when the front gate slides open at night. They'd be caught on the two security cameras pointed at the gate. But that wouldn't protect a customer who came at night to get into their unit. So I employ guards. And around the rest of the lot the fence is topped with heavy razor wire. We can charge more because we're the most secure storage facility in the DC area. Or we were until now."

"Any signs of a break-in at any of the storage units?"

"No, sir. I checked the door of every single unit very carefully after you guys called yesterday morning to ask about Jake. If someone cut their way in here to get into a unit, they had a key or knew how to pick a lock. I'd have to ask every customer to check if anything's missing or broken.—You think Jake may have surprised someone during a break-in?"

The officer frowned and kept making notes.

"I can't say that yet. But his wife reported him missing late in the morning after his last shift on—," he checked his notes, "—the night of the *first*. Two days ago. She said he was always home by eight a.m. He's been missing a little over forty-eight hours now. No one's heard from him or seen him, and his car is still in the parking lot next door."

The manager shook his head. "Yeah, I don't understand that. Sir, he's a good man. Always talked about his wife and kids. Really proud of those kids. Talked about his parents, too. Showed me a lot of family pictures."

"Is there any reason at all why he might have faked his disappearance. Cut the fence himself and slipped away."

The manager looked shocked. "Jake? I guess anything's possible, but my gut says no way."

The officer closed his notebook and picked up the broken watch.

"We'll show this to his wife and see if it was his. This doesn't look good. But for her sake and those kids', let's hope the guy turns up."

4ᵀᴴ

"So you found nothing in storage, and you added to the body count."

"No one will find him."

"Same place as the other two?"

"You don't need to know. Come up with another lead."

5ᵀᴴ

Two weeks after the cold and rain, the skies above Lost Lake were blue-clear again. The early August sun was strong, the air hot and humid. Late afternoon thunderstorms roared through the mountain valleys. At night, mild, damp air poured down the slopes, rustling among the boughs in the dark woods. A few leaves had already turned red during the cooler nights, and the scent of wood smoke from the chimneys at Kate's lodge was often in the air.

Dhani felt inside his pocket, making sure he had brought it with him, careful not to cut himself on the sharp edge.

Claire had dodged him long enough, making him feel terrible. She would not evade him now. She had moved away this morning at breakfast when she saw him coming, and that blow hurt him deeply.

"Since it's steep and rocky, the trail up Trinity will dry fast," Eric announced as they grouped-up at the fire circle for their second day-trek.

This brought on complaints.

"Oh great."

"Steeper than the Peregrine Mountain hike? My thighs were burning the next day."

Ray-Ray elbowed Dhani. "Check this out."

Randy Wolfmoon was looking through daypacks to see if everyone had brought items he had required for the trip. He had finished with Dugan's, and turned toward Garrett.

Dugan said loudly, "Hey, Wolfmoon, I think Makayla needs you— over there."

Randy turned his head to look, and Garrett and Dugan switched packs.

"My bad," Dugan said, when Randy turned back to him. "I guess she was just stretching or something."

Randy checked through the pack in Garrett's hands—Dugan's—and gave him thumbs-up. "Everything on the list. Good man."

Ray-Ray leaned close to Dhani. "Whoa—did you see that? Wonder what's in Garrett's pack that he didn't want Randy to find."

Emmalyn had come up beside them. "Probably an extra pack of *I think I'm so cool.*"

Ray-Ray was about to add, "...*and I'm God's gift to women*", but he noticed Imani shouldering her pack and staring at him.

"What?"

She waved for him to step close.

"It's been driving me crazy, but I finally figured it out. You look so much like someone I've met before."

"Why, because 'all Black guys look alike'?"

"Shut up. Do you have a brother who like—," she looked around to be sure no one was near, "—deals ice?"

"*My* brother?" Ray-Ray sounded shocked. "No way. I have a brother, but trust me he's like a living saint. He leads the praise band at my dad's church. Helps in the soup kitchen. Feeds the homeless. He like, walks on water."

Imani looked uncertain. "It was the middle of the night and this guy was in a van. All I can say is, someone back in DC could be your body-double."

"Yeah, well be careful who you say stuff like that around. People get in trouble when someone mistakes them for someone else."

Single-file they tromped around the north bay, then down along the eastern shoreline. The heavy rain had turned the path here to black mud, and they were forced to walk in the forest beside it, where the stands of silver-green and still-wet ferns brushed against their bare lower legs. If they were not fully awake when they set out, the cold slap of wet vegetation was an unpleasant wake-up call.

Dhani was eager to catch Claire, but she was at the head of the single-file line and he was stuck in the back. She had become so friendly, then made a surprise turn-about, avoiding him for days. That made him feel angry, and guilty for feeling angry, and even angrier at feeling guilty.

Now he had a surprise in store. When he pulled it from his pocket would she look horrified?

Sahm was waiting for them beside the footbridge to Osprey Island. Vajra was with him, trotting up and down the line of hikers, sniffing at hands and daypacks.

Steve Tanner was there, too, standing alongside the Troverts, Randy Wolfmoon, and Laurel Wysocki. He was holding a box filled with what looked like thin metal tubes.

"As we told you guys, each trek is a little more challenging," Eric addressed them. "I hope you've been jogging the camp road or at least hiking the lake trails, as Mr. Tanner recommended after our last hike. You need to build up strength.

"Today—," he nodded at Trinity Mountain, rising above the tree line at the lake's southern shore, "—we're going to have you push yourselves a little harder."

"Our objective," Tanner added, "is to start building out a campsite we can return to. One of a couple outdoor classrooms and campsites where we'll live from time to time."

"*Live?*" Tia Leesha grumbled. "Out in the woods? Ohmygod."

Jalil was beaming, almost dancing with a wild kind of energy. "*Yes.*"

"We told you at orientation a big part of your program is outdoor survival training."

"Yeah," Tia Leesha objected. "You said training, not living."

"How did you think we were going to train for outdoor survival, doofus?" Garrett smirked at her. "By watching Youtube videos? Ever put two and two together?"

Tanner's eyes flashed at Garrett.

"Did someone ask you to speak?—Look, in case anyone else needs clarification, we'll be hiking during all four seasons. Some of the upper-range overlooks and passes will be treacherous in winter. But I'm still going to push you to hike there. You guys are city kids. I'm guessing you wasted a lot of time lying around gaming and partying."

"You don't know us," Imani objected. "You can't say that."

"I've been observing you guys and you all need to toughen up. A lot. Today, though, we're just looking for a lower site to use for cold weather camping."

Emmalyn repeated. "Cold weather camping." She shuddered. "I'm more of a sauna and spa kinda girl."

Garrett opened his mouth. Then shut it.

Tanner reached into the box and produced one of the thin tubes.

"Everyone gets one of these—yours to keep. It's called a LifeStraw™. There's a few million of these in use around the world, where water sources are contaminated. Since we won't be able to carry enough water on longer hikes, you'll have to filter your drinking water through these from streams and mountain springs."

Rocco examined the device Tanner handed him. It was maybe eight inches long and an inch wide. "Can't we just drink out of the streams? The water looks clean."

"But it's not," Randy said. "It's full of contaminants from the ground and also waterborne bacteria and protozoans. These babies have high-end filters that remove *ninety-nine point nine-nine-nine percent* of stuff you really don't want going into your body. Not very pretty or fun to be out in the woods and get the runs and the heaves."

Makayla was chewing a nail, looking extremely uneasy.

"How come Judge Sewell never told us about any of this before we came—especially the winter camping part?"

Others were nodding, looking uncertain or unhappy.

Laurel smiled. "Maybe because some of you would have thought the challenges were too great. Even though I'm a hundred percent sure every one of you can handle everything we're gonna train you to do. What you need most right now is a positive mental attitude about it.

"Right, Tanner?" She clapped Steve's shoulder.

He ignored her, and handed out the last filter to Dugan. Glancing at Eric Trovert, he tried not to sound sarcastic. "Right. Positive mental attitude. That'll do it."

It was a half-mile walk south along the lake, and then another half-mile into the woods before they reached the Trinity trailhead.

Again, Claire had taken off ahead of Dhani as soon as Tanner quit speaking. And again, he was stuck behind slower hikers. He imagined her surprised—or would it be horrified?—look when he pulled out what he'd concealed in his pocket.

"Are you serious?" Garrett said, reading the trail post. "*Five-point-seven miles* to the top?"

"Lots of switchbacks and some nice overlooks," Eric announced, smiling.

"It gets steeper gradually, so you'll have time for your breathing to adjust," said Randy. "There's only one really steep, stair-step section. And then there's a slight scramble up an open rock face just before the summit."

In a half-hour the trail widened and, well beyond irritation now, Dhani pushed his way around the others, determined.

"Hey—you almost knocked me over," Makayla called after him.

"What's wrong with you?" Tia Leesha snapped. "Weirdo."

He passed Ray-Ray, who picked up his pace, too, and they reached the head of the line where Claire was striding up the path.

"What's up?" Dhani said, touching her elbow. "Why are you avoiding me?"

"Yeah, what's the hurry," Ray-Ray smiled. "They giving away a prize at the top?"

She pulled her arm away from Dhani's grip and did not look at them. "What's up? Not a thing. Everything's just wonderful."

That was a lie. Clearly, something was wrong.

"We heard Jo put together another animal rehab team," said Ray-Ray, not wanting to press her. "Rocco, Imani, and Tia Leesha are working with large mammals. Garrett, Carter, and Emmalyn are already working with the small mammals. Jalil, Makayla, and Dugan are amphibians and reptiles. They're calling themselves the Bear, Otter, and Salamander Tribes."

"*And?*" Claire replied.

Dhani realized that grabbing her arm was a mistake, and now he tried to make up for it by backing off and sounding eager. "So that means you, me, and Ray-Ray are on the same team. We'll be taking care of Jo's injured birds. Maybe we'll be able to help that young eagle that won't fly."

"We can be the Eagle Tribe," said Ray-Ray.

Claire kept looking ahead and her reply was terse. "Yeah, well don't count on me. I probably won't be here much longer."

"What do you mean?" Dhani asked, suddenly anxious. He fingered the object in his jeans pocket. She couldn't leave. He wouldn't let that happen. "Where are you going?"

"I told you when I met you that my parents are in prison. They're coming up to an early parole hearing in a few months, and some prosecutor wants to be sure they stay in prison. He wants me to testify about what it was like for me as a little kid, living with two cocaine addicts. Judge Sewell says there's something else the guy is after, but no one knows what that is."

"This is so wrong," Ray-Ray said, sounding angry. "Why can't the guy leave you alone?"

"Judge Sewell thinks he's running for an office, like district attorney, and wants to be seen as very tough on criminals. Especially drug dealers, now that the whole 'war on drugs' is being pushed again."

"Can't someone do something—like Tom or Kate?"

"They said Sewell is pushing back hard to keep me here. But there's no guarantee. He's afraid I may even have to be pulled from the program completely."

This was not the kind of moment Dhani was hoping for when he caught up with Claire again.

Ray-Ray was solemn. "What *was* it like for you being raised by two addicts?"

Claire remained silent for a long time, and they continued climbing.

"It was like—giving myself a bath, putting myself to bed, pretending to read books to myself when I couldn't read yet. Listening to my parents punch it out sometimes. You know. Stuff every little kid deals with."

Dhani was stuck on her statement about leaving. "Isn't there a rule that you can't testify against your own parents?"

"Sewell says there is no parent-child privilege in Virginia. You can be a lawyer or a minister and not have to testify against someone who told you illegal stuff they did. But they can force you to rat-out your own parents. Or try to."

Claire's breathing suddenly became heavier, not from the ascent but because her chest was tightening and she was forcing back tears.

"If you have to go back, how long will you be gone—like, a week?"

"I don't know. It's still just a maybe. But legal proceedings can drag on a long time. Weeks. Months. If the prosecutor has some kind of big agenda and I'm a pawn in it, I might be forced to stay there. Tom thinks he might be using this threat of pulling me from the program to punish and pressure my parents—as if they'd give a crap."

Dhani felt his stomach drop. He couldn't take one more person he cared about abandoning him. It was time to make his move. Fishing in a front pocket of his jeans, he pulled out a small object, and held it up for Claire to see.

It was a small piece of opalescent shell he had found by the lake. On the prettiest side, the one flush with rainbow brilliance in its white luster, he had carefully scratched her name in cursive lettering. He had also punched a small hole at one end, and now it dangled from his fingers on a piece of black cord.

"I made this for you. Do you like it?"

Claire took the necklace and held it out in front of her, staring at it like it was a curiosity or a child's thing. She said nothing for a full minute as they continued to climb, their breath becoming more labored.

Finally, she said, "Thanks"—sounding totally uninterested.

She took off ahead of them up the path. "Sorry, but I'd really like to be alone today."

Ray-Ray started after her, then slowed up. He turned to see Dhani just as he was dropping one hand to his side. "Did you just flick her off?"

"No."

"You did something with your hand. You flicked her off."

"I didn't."

Where the trail switched back the fifth time and became steeper, Eric came alongside Dugan and Garrett. "You guys doing okay?"

Dugan saluted. "Hey, boss. Definitely."

Eric pointed to Dugan's wrist. "Cool sports watch. Looks expensive."

"You like that? It's top of the line. Tells how many steps I take, how many calories I burn. Tells the altitude. Down at the trailhead, we were eighteen-hundred feet above sea level and we're now at almost twenty-three hundred. My legs are burning."

"The thing is, I went through the personal inventory sheets we filled out when you guys arrived. Being a hiker, I think that item would have jumped out at me. I helped you do yours, and I don't recall us listing it."

Garrett jumped in. "Wow. You gotta be the most forgetful person ever, Dugan. You can't remember to replace the t.p. You use *my* towel because you think it's yours. And you didn't even remember to list *that* baby. Forgetful much?"

"When we get back I'll need to review your inventory sheet with you," Eric said. "Remember, it's for everyone's protection, in case something goes missing."

"Yessir. No problem."

When Eric outdistanced them up the trail, Dugan took the watch off and stowed it in his pack.

Garrett punched his shoulder. "A little late for that. You better hope he forgets."

"What are those mountains," Dhani asked when they reached the summit. He pointed at higher peaks to the east and south.

Eric looked puzzled. "Randy just said their names, Dhani. Your head's in the clouds today. That one in the east is Whiteface, the Olympic ski mountain. We pointed that out from Peregrine. And that one to the south is Mount Marcy, the highest peak in New York. Both of them are surrounded by very heavy and challenging wilderness areas. Climbers and hikers are injured or lost there every year."

"Not more than in this area," said Randy. "In fact—," he pivoted and pointed north, "—beyond Lost Mountain is The Solitudes Wilderness area. Hundreds of acres of dense forest."

"A good place for you guys to avoid," said Laurel. "People have totally vanished in there."

"There are some great caves to explore on the far side of Lost Mountain, though," said Randy. "Old Mohawk caves, where the people hid during tribal warfare with the Iroquois. I used to explore 'em when I was a kid, but we never went very far inside. They say that if you know your way, you can crawl the whole distance under the mountain and come out in the Flow Lands. But they're dangerous."

"Really?" Jalil perked up.

"I'd be up for exploring," said Ray-Ray.

Randy changed the subject. "We need to hike back down to the place Sahm located for our first, permanent camping site. Let's go. Tanner has a lot of work for us all to do today."

As the group filed back down the trail, Laurel slapped Randy on the shoulder. "Congratulations for putting that idea out there."

"What do you mean?"

"Caves. Danger.—*Excitement.*"

"Hey, these guys are so wiped out after these treks, they don't remember three-fourths of what we told 'em."

"Right. When you were a teenage boy, what did you do when you heard there were caves somewhere?"

Randy opened his mouth—then shut it. "I think most of the entrances are covered up now due to landslides. Anyway, that area's totally off-limits to these guys."

"Nothing more exciting than something that's off-limits."

"Hey, these boys are more into girls and music and online games than outdoor exploration."

The site Sahm chose, on the western face of Trinity Mountain, was an open expanse of rock protected from wind by a sheer cliff face on one side and a forest on the other. A distant sound of running water said there were streams nearby. Below them to the southwest was more, dense wilderness for miles, leading to a jagged set of peaks.

"Those are the Sawtooth Mountains," Randy said, as they took off their packs.

"Wouldn't that be 'saw*teeth*,' because there's more than one," said Dugan.

"Not if you're from West Virginia," Garrett joked, "where ya don't got more than one tooth—right Emmalyn?"

Tanner's eyes flashed. "Garrett, I'm calling you out on that."

"Aw, come on, man. It was a joke. Lighten up."

Steve felt a surge of anger.

Time to teach these guys respect.

"Front and center, buddy."

Garrett looked around, uncertain, and stepped out on the open rock ledge in front of the whole group.

"We're not just building a campsite today. We're here to build a team. Knocking people all the time doesn't cut it. The rest of you, pick out sites around the perimeter of the open rock, where the soil's deep enough to drive in tent stakes. You'll build your fire circles out on the rock, so they're easy to put out later. Garrett—drop and give me twenty pushups."

"If he can," Dugan smirked.

"You're not serious," said Garrett, smiling, looking nervously at the watching faces. Especially Carter's. She was staring at him with empty eyes. Or was it with a hint of contempt.

"Dead serious. Twenty. Get going. Every five seconds you wait, I add five more."

"Come on."

"Twenty-five. And Dugan, because you busted on him when I just called him out on it, you can drop and give me twenty-five, too."

Eric tried to intervene. "What if instead of making them do that—"

Steve held up one hand. "'Ownership'—remember that word? You guys used it. So let me handle this my way."

Garrett threw his pack down on the ground, and Dugan muttered something.

"Kate paid good money for that pack and everything in it. And bitching under your breath is disrespectful of my authority. Now you both owe me thirty."

Garrett swore and dropped to the dirt. Dugan dropped down beside him and began pumping out pushups.

"Now you can do fifty. Next time you swear, you get fifty more added on for bad language. Now get going, because when you're done, you guys need to pick a site and put up your half-tents together."

"You guys—," Steve pointed at Rocco and Jalil after their tent was set up, "—you're gonna be my fire pit team."

He handed Rocco a smooth stick with a pointed end. Then gave him a small bow made from a second stick and a thin cord.

"You're going to start a fire the genuine survival way. Get your pit dug and surrounded with stones. Then scavenge for bigger limbs."

He looked around. "You two—," he pointed at Dhani and Carter, "—you're gonna collect kindling and branches for the fires."

Carter's eyes were gleaming in a strange way. "Why us? I mean why me and *him*?"

Dhani's head was turned, as if he was purposely ignoring Tanner. Claire's disregard for his special gift had kicked a hole in his spirit.

Steve clenched his jaw. Carter was always half-smiling at him, as if everything he said was just a joke. And once again, Dhani was avoiding eye-contact, as if he was saying, "I don't have to listen to you."

He was tired of the attitudes. It was time for the hammer to come down the way he'd just brought it down on Garrett and Dugan.

"You need to work with him because *I said to*," he responded. "That should be a good enough reason."

"How about a two-*girl* team instead?" Carter pressed, pointing at Claire. "Me and her."

Steve's face flashed anger. More bucking of his authority.

Bay, who saw what was happening, tried to step in.

"I think a girl team is a great idea. Show the guys what woods-women can do. How about it, Steve?" She looked at Carter. "I'll tell Claire to work with you today."

When the teams scattered to collect wood, Bay faced off with Steve, speaking calmly.

"We are working as a team, right?"

The day had started off well for Steve. Then Garrett and Dugan

314

happened, and Eric tried to intervene. Then Bay butted in with Carter.

"The way I see it is, anything with more than one head is a freak," he rebuffed her. He didn't try to hide his impatience. "Out here, I'm the head guy."

"There's more than one way to do things, Steve."

"Whose way is that going to be? Mine or yours? You guys directly challenged me in front of the group. Never do that again."

Bay's eyes remained locked on his. "All right, Tanner, we're not doing this right now. Today, at least, let's show a unified front. All I'm going to say is, this isn't the military. A show of cooperation would actually help these kids learn about compromising in life."

Steve ignored the last part. "Seems like we're not a unified front."

"Then pretend."

Between the group campsite and this stand of trees, Claire watched Carter change. Since the day of the ropes course, she'd been aggressive. Out here, alone with Claire, she was all chatty and high energy, not the intimidating presence she had been up at Thunder Falls. How could she make herself seem so normal around adults, then be a whole bunch of different people when they were not around?

Claire moved away from her into the trees and bent to gather small, wind-sheared branches. The very last thing she needed right now was to deal with Carter.

"Not those," Carter called to her. "We need to build a bonfire. A big one. Get a lot of wood. We need to crush Rocco and Makayla. Rocco's an idiot jock, who thinks he's great. Makayla is a fragile little mouse. A bug. Anyone can crush her. I may do it."

Even at a short distance, Claire could see that the more Carter talked the more her face changed. Her eyes had taken on a wild, dark, glittering look again, and her cheeks turned from pink to red. Then her screed about the others took a turn.

"Must have been nice growing up rich."

Claire felt her skin tingling, and she went on high-alert. She was not going to let Carter get the upper hand, no matter how depressed she herself felt.

"I didn't," she objected, keeping her voice level to prevent a confrontation. "Why does everyone think I was rich? I ate cereal all the time, because my parents were blowing money on drugs and vacations for themselves."

Carter began to sound agitated. "Here's the thing. I told you I checked out you and everyone else here. Your grandparents are loaded and your parents made a ton of money selling cocaine. I just think it must have been cool to grow up with all that money. My father was a handyman and my mother worked in a drugstore. We didn't have crap. I hate people who were given everything."

Claire was fed up. "What part of what I said are you *not hearing*?"

Carter's face was changing again, from high-colored to pale. Mostly, her eyes changed. The excited look dulled to the almost-dead emptiness that had been causing Claire and everyone but Garrett to avoid her.

Carter's voice sounded mechanical now, with a grating edge. "I overheard you talking on the trail. Are you saying your parents didn't stash a bunch of money somewhere for when they get out of prison? That's what big drug dealers do."

Claire felt a cold wave go through her. She hadn't seen Carter anywhere near her, Dhani, and Ray-Ray back on the trail. *Stalking me again.* Her mask of calm began to break apart.

"Well if they did," she snapped, "which I doubt because they were too strung-out on their own product, they didn't tell me. *I was seven.* Why would they tell a little girl anything?"

She was as much answering Carter as yelling at the stupid prosecutor back in Virginia, who was trying to yank her away from Lost Lake. Didn't that idiot know he was destroying her chance at a future that had nothing to do with her past? Couldn't Carter just shut the hell up?

At the thought of being condemned to more time back in the system, Claire's anger surged. She threw down the armload of sticks and branches forcefully, at the same time fighting the tightness in her throat and pressure behind her eyes. Her jaw was trembling, and she willed the rising hot tears not to escape. She clenched her teeth, and would *not* cry.

Her parents were not worth crying over, and anyway no one cared if she cried. No one. Images of little girls whom she had seen on parents' laps, being comforted when they were sad or hurt, flooded her mind—and her fists tightened until her fingernails dug into her palms. Those were the *rich* little girls. The ones somebody wanted and gave a damn about. She was not one of them. Her grandparents were worth millions, and her parents had pulled in more millions illegally. But as a little girl, she had been treated only to poverty of the worst kind, a girlhood without care or love or even consideration.

In a moment, she was able to breathe deep again, let all of it go—*again*—and the tears had been fought back. She felt satisfied with her private win. Crying didn't change anything. It always made things worse. Her foster parents had hated it when she cried, and her foster sisters had seen it as a sign of weakness and preyed upon her even more.

"We need to build this stupid damn fire," she stated forcefully.

She bent down to grab up the firewood, feeling invincible again. The little girl who had been forced to grow up without anyone backing her was not going to crack. Not for anyone or any reason.

Carter was staring at her with the faintest grin. Her look held a predatory joy, as if she were pleased that she had angered and upset Claire.

"Looked like you wanted cry. . .baby girl."

Only Claire's anger returned, with none of the sadness.

"*Shut. Up!* Whatever your creeping around is all about, keep *it* and *yourself* away from me. We go back to the campsite now and pretend we give a crap about building a fire. And then you *leave me the hell alone.*"

"You want to push me off a cliff again, don't you?"

Claire turned her back. "What good would that do? You'd just turn into a vampire bat and flutter off to some dark hole."

Against the tree line, Rocco and Imani were down on their knees on opposite sides of the small fire pit, six feet in front of the half-tent shelter Imani and Makayla had pitched.

Rocco was bent low, fanning the growing flame that Imani was feeding with dried pine branches. He was clowning—blowing on the fire, then high-fiving Imani as it sputtered and leapt into life.

Garrett nudged Dugan, who was frustrated that their kindling pile was just a smoldering lump of damp leaves and green twigs. He nodded at Rocco. "Look at him. He's totally making a move on your territory."

Dugan wiped the smoke-sting from his eyes. "Tell me again why you're so friendly with Rocco when you're around him and behind his back you're so against him? That's two-faced."

"Not two-faced. It's smart. Get close, for the kill. Remember? Anyway, are you gonna turn on me, when all I'm saying is he's stealing your woman?"

Dugan looked over at Rocco, and his lip curled in disgust. "*Hey, La Stidda!*" he called out. "Anyone ever tell you you're a big flirt? Is there any girl here you haven't hit on."

Rocco placed his right hand over his heart, and gestured with the other to Imani. "*Mio fiore nero.*"

Dugan looked at Garrett. "What he just say?"

"Wow. Can't believe he said *that.*"

Dugan bristled. "*What he say?*"

"He said, 'She's mine, negro'."

Dugan's eyes flashed anger. "How do you know that?"

"Hey, I been around the neighborhoods. Lot of Italians where I live. You gotta know a buncha languages."

Dugan jumped to his feet. "*Yo, Gangbang.* You think you're big because you're in the mob?"

Rocco looked at him blankly. "I told you I'm not in a gang. And I said don't call me names."

Dugan tapped his own chest, on the spot where Rocco's five-pointed tattoo was.

"*La Stidda*, man. *Mafioso.*"

Rocco's face went bright red. "You need to be shut up."

"You wanna make me?"

Rocco shook his head in disgust, and turned his attention back to the fire.

"What?—you just gonna ignore me? You embarrassed by the truth?" Dugan called louder.

Imani looked over, glaring at him. "*You* are an embarrassment."

"Right. He's a racist, and *I'm* an embarrassment?"

"A racist? I take it back. You're not an embarrassment. You're crazy. Now blow on your smoky little campfire over there, and leave us alone."

Dugan's face contorted.

Garrett grabbed his arm, and looked around. "Bring it down, man. Bring it down. Don't get into it with him out here."

"I'm not gonna let him—"

"Listen to me. Our top priority is keeping Trovert and everyone else totally out of our business. We got a good thing started, and we don't need any more adult attention right now. Give me some time, and I'll help you take out mob boy. Then you can have a clear shot at your woman."

Dugan took a deep breath, and steadied himself. "You got me all riled, and now you're saying calm down."

"I was just pointing out why we need to stick together, you and me, and remember who our enemies are."

Rocco and Imani were focused totally on building their fire to a small blaze, ignoring them.

Dugan spit, and squared his shoulders. "Okay. *Okay.* Take him out. I'm good with that." Then he dropped to his knees again, and blew on the smoking pile of twigs.

Garrett stood above him. Smiling.

While the teams were working, Sahm had built a stone fire circle in the center of the campsite, much bigger than the others, and started a leaping bonfire. Then he and Randy hiked off to find where the sounds of running water were coming from, to douse all the campfires later. Steve had gone inside the tree line to set up a base headquarters site, hopefully where the radio-phone signal was strong.

Eric announced, "Bay and I are going to check out sites for latrines. We'll build those next time we're up here. We're going to check out some other overlooks, too. When you finish what you're doing, hang out by the fire, and we'll be back shortly."

"Oh great," Makayla said, "we've gotta go to the bathroom in the woods."

Jalil was drumming his hands on one of the logs Sahm had rolled up near the central fire for seating. "You haven't gone on any of the hikes we've done already?"

"I held it."

Emmalyn leaned forward to pick up a stick to throw in the flames. "No big deal. You drop trou, squat, and let go. Just don't wipe with poison ivy. Pine cones work."

"Oh god, thanks for that tip."

"Nice ink on your lower back," Jalil smiled, looking at Emmalyn. "What's it say?"

"It's a black rose—," she stood up, twisted her hips around, and pulled her shorts down a couple inches with her thumbs, "—with the initials of an old boyfriend. L.B.—Lance Beauchamp."

Eyes connected all around the fire.

"He was so hot."

". . .'an old boyfriend'," Jalil repeated. "Didn't it cross your mind when you were getting it done that you guys might break up?"

"Of course it did. I'm not stupid. But when I get my next boyfriend, I'll just get my tattoo guy to fix up the letters somehow. That's what my mama and aunt do."

Everyone had come around, and the circle erupted in laughter.

Ray-Ray leaned close to Dhani. "She's *got* to be making this up."

"Who else has a tramp stamp?" Jalil asked. "Time for show-n-tell."

"I have some body art on my lower back," Imani said. "But I wouldn't call it a tramp stamp."

Rocco smiled. "Who else says, 'Let us be the judge of that?' Show of hands."

She rolled her eyes. "All right, why not. You'll see it when we're swimming anyway." In one quick motion, she stood, looked around for the counselors, and seeing none she unbuttoned and half-unzipped her jean cutoffs—then pulled them down three inches in back, twisting so the group could see.

"That is beautiful," Emmalyn whispered. "It looks eastern or something."

Thin veils of curving, delicate, black lace started at narrow points out at the wide part of her hips. They curved across and down, forming a triangle that dipped until the tip disappeared below the waistband of her shorts.

"Oh man," Dugan whispered.

Rocco stared, mesmerized.

"My boyfriend hired a henna artist to design this. She's Indian, so—*ding, ding*—Emmalyn guessed right."

"Got any piercings?" Dugan smiled.

"*That* is none of your business."

Tia Leesha shuddered. "I could never do piercings. That's just. . . no."

"Some people are into body piercing, grommets, all kinds of stuff," said Garrett, "—even branding and edgy crap like that."

He pulled his stick from the fire and pointed it in the air. A small flame flickered at the end of it, but immediately went out, leaving just a charred end with a thread of gray smoke rising from the red-glowing tip.

"I'll bet old Singe would enjoy branding—wouldn't you? Are you into pain?"

Dhani was still looking at Imani, who had buttoned up and sat down again. He paid no attention to Garrett.

"Hey, I'm talking to you. What do you think? How about a nice 'S' for 'Singe' to warn everyone about you. . . *right on your FACE*."

Garrett lunged and thrust the red-glowing stick point at Dhani's cheek.

Startled, Dhani instinctively thrust his own fire stick at Garrett to fend him off. The end of it struck Garrett's stick, sending red sparks flying, glanced off it, and stabbed Garrett in his right side just below the armpit.

"You *idiot*," Garrett shrieked in pain. "I'm gonna *kill you*." He jumped back, cupping the burn wound with one hand.

Emmalyn said angrily, "You're stupid, Garrett."

"See what you get?" said Jalil. "You need to lay off him."

Rocco shook his head. "Come on, man, it was an accident."

"He burned me. He's psycho," Garrett shot back.

Dugan stepped in. "You brought that on yourself."

"I was kidding around. I didn't even touch him, and he attacked me. You saw it. He's a freakin' pyro."

"We saw *you* provoke him," Imani challenged.

He stomped around, his face enraged, his voice at a low growl. "Go ahead, everyone. Be on his side. Remember he torched a guy in his sleep?" He glared at Imani. "Maybe you'll wake up some night with your pretty face on fire."

"Before we collapse any further into drama, you need the first-aid kit," Makayla said, rising.

"*No.*" Garrett stopped her. "I'll take care of it. If you get the kit, Tanner or Randy will come and ask questions. We don't need them to know what happens between us."

"Who put you in charge?" Makayla challenged. "And you don't think they heard you scream?"

He doubled-down. "Everybody listen—shut up about this stuff. I was just fooling around, and Singe went a little nuts-o. It was just guy stuff. You want to bring *them* into everything we do? I heard them talking about maybe starting cabin checks every night."

Carter looked up from the fire. "How is it you hear so much?"

"Unless you want them going more Nazi on us than they already are," Garrett ignored her, "we keep stuff like this between *us* and no one else."

"I think—," Makayla began.

"You're a girl, and I'll bet you don't want anybody telling you what to do with your body. Well, I don't want them asking questions about *my* body."

"Totally not the same issue, dude," Makayla defended. "That is some twisted logic."

A few moments of uneasy silence followed.

Then Makayla threw her stick in the fire, stood, and went back to her tent, followed by Imani, Rocco, and Emmalyn.

The few left stared into the flames and said nothing.

Dhani had escaped the fire circle, and Ray-Ray had gone after him with Claire right behind. In twenty minutes, they found him on a southern overlook, where they could just barely see the town of Lake Placid miles in the distance.

He was withdrawn and shaking.

"Are you okay?" Ray-Ray asked, laying a hand on Dhani's shoulder. "Garrett is a jerk."

Dhani flinched, and pulled away.

"Dude. It's me. I'm your friend."

Dhani continued pacing, breathing hard, his hands clenching.

Claire stepped around in front, and looked him in the face. Her distance from him and Ray-Ray seemed to have vanished, and her eyes held concern.

"Dhani, it's over. Why are you still so upset? It was Garrett's fault. He got what he deserved. If anyone asks, we'll tell them the truth."

Ray-Ray nodded. "I got your back man, remember?" He glanced at Claire. "She does, too."

Claire insisted, "Everyone will say you didn't do anything wrong."

"Yes, I did. I did something really wrong. That's why I'm here."

Ray-Ray and Claire looked at each other.

"So did a lot of the people who are here," said Ray-Ray, cautiously. "But what exactly are you talking about right now?"

Dhani kept walking in a circle. "He could say I burned him, and that's all it would take. It would look like I tried to set another person on fire. But I *have* to stay in the program. That's all. I just *can't* get thrown out. I can't." He was nearly in tears, and panicking.

"Dhani." Ray-Ray grabbed his shoulder and stopped him from pacing. "We're your friends no matter what. Unless. . . ."

Dhani stopped clenching and unclenching his hands. "Unless what?"

Ray-Ray got a sly look. "Unless you do something ridiculous like get a tramp stamp with someone's initials in it. Then you're on your own. You get a stamp and *'I'm gonna get out of the car and I'm gonna drop you like third period French.'*"

Dhani and Claire stood open-mouthed, staring at him, the tense mood leaving.

"What the hell are you talking about?" said Claire. She was half-smiling.

"*Ocean's Eleven*—the movie—big truck, little truck scene. No?"

She rolled her eyes.

"Humor is the best way to snap someone out of a bad mood. It worked, right?—Just remember at all times, Dhani, it's us three. You, me, and Claire. We stick together."

"You heard what I said, right?" Claire looked at him. "I might get dragged back to DC against my will. I can't say I'll be here for anybody."

"But if you are here, the three of us are tight—right?"

Her smile was a little warmer.

"If I'm here, yeah."

Dhani focused on her. "I just need to know—are you mad at me for what just happened? You looked so pissed."

"Yes I'm mad. A little. Why did you do that to Garrett? You could have just dodged him."

"I don't know. It just happened. Reflex."

"It's a guy thing," Ray-Ray started to say. "Someone comes at us, and we gotta—"

Claire ignored him, her eyes boring into Dhani's. "Things don't just happen. You make them happen."

"But are you still mad at me?"

She made a frustrated sound. "What does that matter? You say you have to be here, but you don't listen, you act like you don't care, and you're making Tanner angry. Keep it up, and you'll get yourself thrown out of this program. It will be nobody's fault but yours."

"Would you care?"

"I don't know yet. Maybe. The only person who has to care is you."

"You sure know how to bust up a good time," Dugan said to Garrett, as they left the somber mood at the fire circle.

Garrett turned on him. "Don't ever call me out in front of people again."

"You were a jerk, and it backfired on you."

"Don't ever call me a jerk. I'm the one who's cutting you in on a good thing. I'm the one teaching you how it's done."

"Oh, you're 'teaching' me. Like I need to be taught something. Is this the White guy parenting the Black guy?"

"Call it what you want. You've got a lot to learn."

At the sound of someone coming up the trail, Steve looked up. In the last hour or so, while the teams were working, he'd cleared and trenched a tent site in a clearing among maple and hickory trees and laid another stone circle for a fire. He had cut two sturdy branches, sliced off the end twigs leaving a crotch in the sticks, and was now paring down the ends into points.

Rocco came through the undergrowth into the clearing, with Jalil trailing behind.

"Who's watching the fires?"

"The Troverts are back."

"You guys ready for me to inspect your campsites?"

"Yessir," Rocco replied. "What are you making?"

Steve showed them the ends of the sticks. "When they're sharpened, they go into the ground two feet from the fire, with the forked ends up. You lay a long, green branch from fork to fork, and you have a drying rod for wet clothes. I'll show you how to make a snare for small game, and then you can use a set-up like this to cook meat next to your fire."

Dugan arrived—along with Garrett, who looked sullen—and focused on Steve's knife.

"That's cool. Is it like, an army knife?"

"Marine issue Ka-bar." Steve held it up so they could see the nine-inch steel blade and the handle of stacked leather washers. Then he went back to sharpening the end of a branch. "All purpose. Butter your bread or stab an enemy combatant in the heart with it," he said, watching their reactions.

Rocco bit his lower lip, and looked doubtfully at the blade. "My dad says I'm not man enough to make it in someplace like the military—when I don't do exactly what he says."

"My grandpa was in Vietnam," said Dugan. "He says I don't have it in me to be a soldier. Stories he tells—when he talks about it at all—they kinda scare the crap out of me to be honest. Do you think that makes me less than a man?"

Steve kept working. "No. I don't. I don't think anyone really knows if they 'have it in them' until you're out there and an I.E.D. blows up a fuel truck right in front of you or a bullet slices the side of your helmet."

"You ever kill anyone?" Dugan asked.

Steve finished paring the second branch to a point. "I'm a Marine. That's what Marines are trained to do."

"You ever get into hand-to-hand with anyone?" Rocco asked.

"Yeah." Steve remained evasive. "What about you?"

"I trained in Muay Thai," said Rocco. "And I've done some street fighting." He added quickly, "Nothing compared to what you've done. You're like a hundred miles above us."

"I've had to do some intense fighting, yeah. A few nighttime raids that were dicey. Lost a guy on one of them. Al Qaeda ambush."

Rocco stared at Steve with a look of adulation.

Jalil was somber. "If you had to kill someone with that knife. How would you do it?"

He took their sudden interest in him as a good sign. The respect they were showing him wasn't bad either. He liked it.

Steve set down the branches. "Okay, I need a volunteer. Never mind—*you.*" He pointed the knife at Rocco.

He stepped away from the fire pit, into the campsite's open area. Sheathing the Ka-bar, he waved Rocco forward. "Come at me."

"Seriously?"

"You guys want a demonstration?" Steve asked, looking at the other three.

"Uh, sure."

"It's up to him."

Rocco twisted and cracked his neck, and got into a stance. "Now what?"

"Come at me, I said."

Rocco stepped forward slowly, his body slightly turned, and raised his hands in a defensive gesture.

Steve crouched slightly, his arms spread out. "Now charge me. Mean it. Get angry. Come at me like a freight train. You hate me, and want to decorate these trees with my guts. Come on, big boy. Let's do this."

Rocco still looked hesitant. "Are we supposed to be doing this?"

"Awww. 'Are we supposed to do this?'" Steve mocked. "Is your dad right—maybe you're not man enough? What's wrong, big boy?"

Rocco's face changed. "Making fun of me? Okay, *big man*. You want me, you got me."

He charged Steve like a bull, with his head down, and struck him in the stomach with a shoulder, plowing him down in the leaves and dirt—where Steve continued to roll backwards, gripping Rocco's body and flipping him over onto his back, slamming the boy hard into the ground.

Fast as a wild animal, Steve leaped around, straddled Rocco, pinning his arms down with his knees and full body weight.

Rocco tried to buck, and kept bucking.

Steve had grabbed a short stick, and held it across Rocco's throat.

Rocco stopped moving. His eyes were wide, his sides heaving. He choked out, "Your face, man. Geez, you look like you *want* to kill me."

Steve's face went blank, and his voice was steady. "If we were still standing, I'd have grabbed one arm and twisted it hard till I turned you around away from me. . . or until your arm snapped."

He sat up straight, still straddling Rocco's pinned torso. "Then I'd do this."

He raised the stick in his right hand to within an inch of the left side of his own throat—"Jugular is *right here*"—and he pulled the fake blade to the right, in a violent slashing motion. "Cuts the artery *and* the windpipe, so there's no screaming and no one comes running to help you. Even if they did, it's too late. You're dead."

He threw the stick aside then, suddenly, as if it were a snake. Jumping off Rocco, Steve stood, shook himself, and stuck out a hand to help the boy up. "Good job, man."

Rocco looked embarrassed, and glanced from Steve to Dugan to Jalil. He ignored Garrett. "I only fight in a ring. You know, exhibition stuff. I—I never got in a real street fight, we just call it that. But if this was real, I woulda come at you in a different way."

"Hey, man. No worries. You were trained for fighting to entertain an audience. I was trained to make people be dead."

Rocco was still rubbing one shoulder. "That was amazing. Respect, man. Respect."

The others nodded. "Yeah."

"Totally."

"Respect for you, too, man, for having the nads to come at me like that. If it makes you feel better," he winced, "you hurt my ribs."

Rocco grinned. "Glad I hurt you."

"Go brush yourself off," Steve smiled, slapping him on the back.

He unsheathed his Ka-bar and retrieved the stick he'd been sharpening. "We don't want the Troverts asking questions. Pretty sure they wouldn't approve of my demonstration."

When they were gone, Steve stood, and walked around the clearing in circles, shaking off the last jolts of the agitated energy that lingered in his body.

On the ground lay the stick he had thrown aside when showing them how to cut a throat felt too real.

The sun was sinking toward the horizon, all the fires were doused, and the air felt cooler the lower they went down through the trees.

Garrett kept shifting his pack. "This thing keeps rubbing against my burn. I want to punch that kid."

Dugan was only half paying attention.

"When I came here, I thought we were going to have more freedom."

"We're hiking and getting ready to camp in the wilderness, man. And classes are starting soon. What made you think 'wilderness program' was a vacation?"

"Yeah, but these people are a little too focused on where we go, when we go, when we're in bed, and what we *own*."

"Come on. So Trovert commented on my sports watch. He'll forget it. Stop worrying."

"Maybe you need to worry a little more. Trovert wants to inventory our tighty-whities."

"You're so worried about that when you've got another problem. Tanner really dislikes you. The year's hardly started and you already got yourself on the wrong side of that drill sergeant. He's looking for weak people to grind down. That's what people like him do. And you gave him a target."

Garrett walked along saying nothing, and shifted his pack again. "Ouch." Then his head whipped around, and he looked at Dugan. "I've got a way to take care of it."

"Which 'it' are we talking about?"

"All of it. Trovert having his big eyes on our stuff. Tanner wanting someone to grind on."

"How?"

"First, get close. Then create a false flag event."

Dhani, Ray-Ray, and Claire were at the end of the line of hikers again. As they approached the trail marker at the bottom of the path, Kate and Tom were waiting. When they saw Claire, they waved her over.

She took a deep breath. "Here it comes," she said to Dhani and Ray-Ray. "One-way ticket home. Nice knowing you guys."

"Can we talk to you alone?" Kate asked.

"It's okay. I already told them the bad news."

"Well then," Kate placed a hand on her shoulder, "they should hear the good news, too."

"Judge Sewell was able to block the prosecutor's request," said Tom.

Kate smiled broadly. "You're staying."

Claire did not return the smile. "For good—or just for now? I know how the legal system works."

"Judge Sewell thinks he's held him off, hopefully, for the whole first year of the program. After that, who knows. Claire, we all want you here, and we're fighting for you. You have a whole group of adults who are really on your side. Why don't you and your friends go back, clean up, and have some fun?"

Kate and Tom went on ahead of them along the lakefront trail.

Claire stood unmoving, watching them go. Dhani and Ray-Ray waited, and still Claire said nothing.

"I don't get it," said Ray-Ray. "You didn't want to go back. Why aren't you happy? You look like you could cry."

She composed herself. "Nobody ever said that to me before."

"Said what?"

"'You have a team on your side.'"

"Seriously? This morning, Dhani asked you to be in the Eagle Tribe with us."

Claire relaxed and smiled. "He did, didn't he? Well, since I'm going to be here, I guess—"

Before she could finish, Dhani lunged at Claire and Ray-Ray, wrapped them in a bear hug and held on.

8TH

When Rocco answered the knock, he found Jo out on the porch. It was early—*6:53*—and he was barely out of bed.

"Did the trek up Trinity yesterday wipe you out?" she asked.

"Nah, not really." He scratched his stomach and stretched.

"Didn't think it would. Get on your hikers, and grab some water. I need you to come with Ron and me."

"Where?"

"Rescue operation. Get going. Meet us at the clinic. I need to fill a couple medical supply packs."

"Why did you pick me?"

"I need someone strong."

"Are we gonna get breakfast first?"

"No. Grab a Pop-Tart and some water."

"We don't have Pop-Tarts," he called after her.

In a half-hour, Jo had driven them down out of the Lost Lake valley, skirted the southwest side of Lake Placid village, and parked on a gravel pull-off several miles down a wooded two-lane road.

"We've got a black bear issue," Jo said. "Day hikers stopped for a swim at Wanika Falls. We may have an injured sow and cubs to deal with. We'll see, when we get there. It's a ways in, so we've gotta move fast."

"How far?" asked Rocco.

"Seven miles."

"Wait—that means it's a fourteen-mile round-trip."

"That's why she tagged you to help us, big guy," Ron replied.

The trail ran within earshot of a river. "That's the Chubb. It runs close to this trail system—called the Northville-Placid. Hundred and thirty-miles from here south. Be glad we're only hiking an easy seven-mile stretch of it."

Ron's idea of an easy stretch wound them in thick woods, around huge glacial erratics, through mucky places, swatting at biting deerflies.

"These guys are killing me," said Rocco, miserably. Twenty minutes into the hike, he had sweated through his tee-shirt in the heavy, humid August air, and was rubbing at the stings and welts rising on his arms and neck.

"Sorry, should have offered you this," Jo said, pulling a bottle of fly dope out of her pack. "Use a lot. These little devils will only get worse as we get deeper into the woods. Bears tend to have a heavy odor, too. Like scat. So there will be a lot of flies around them."

"Make sure she didn't accidentally give you the 'Doe-in-Heat Buck Lure'," Ron laughed—"'cause if you put that on, things'll get weird."

Rocco looked even more miserable, and flipped the bottle around quickly to check the label.

"Hey, don't worry. You're a martial arts guy, right? You can fight off a lusty buck."

Rocco looked from Ron to Jo—who was grinning—back to Ron.

"Dude, I'm kidding," Ron laughed.

Jo shook her head. "Boys. You're killin' me. Pick up the pace."

In just under two hours, they encountered three hikers at the Wanika Falls tent site. One stuck out his hand. "I called from town about the bears. You must have been right on my heels. Are you a sheriff's deputy?"

"You called the sheriff's office, and they called me. I run a rescue and rehab operation."

"Well—you may have two to rescue. Not the mother, though. Looks like some jerk went off-season hunting. She's on the other side of the trail."

They could smell the site and hear the sound of flies before they pushed their way through the windfallen limbs and undergrowth. As they broke through the last branches, there were loud *coo*-ing sounds.

"It's bad."

"How did you find this spot," Ron asked.

The hiker had placed a bandana over his face. "The rotting smell. I knew it was something big.—Why aren't you gagging?"

"He's used to it," Jo responded.

Rocco was not. He pulled his teeshirt up over his face, which didn't help. The sweet-acrid smell of decaying flesh hung heavily in the unmoving, humid air.

Inside a spruce-fir thicket lay a black bear, its back turned to their point of entry. Climbing on the body, which lay unmoving and surrounded in a buzzing cloud of flies, were two small cubs, the source of the distressed *coo*-ing sounds—pawing at her, crying to her, trying to wake her.

"These guys are very little," said Jo, kneeling beside the sow. "Definitely very late season birth. You guys get them off her. I want to check the body."

Ron stooped, and lifted one cub, handed it to Rocco, and then the other. "Whoa, there's some maggots on them. Hopefully just from the sow. See—they look like crawling grains of rice."

Rocco's stomach turned.

Jo was focused on the mother bear, but noticed the exchange of cubs. "You guys both get gloves on. They're cute, but there's feces and god knows what else on their claws."

"What do you mean, these maggots are *hopefully* from the mother?" asked Rocco. He had begun to cold-sweat, and held the cubs out away from him.

"If they've got hotspots, the flies will have laid eggs, and these are emerging from under their skin. If that's the case, we'll have to do a quick, field treatment, and get them back to the clinic as fast as possible."

Jo swore.

"*Look at this.*" She swore again, and with one foot she rolled the sow's body a little, sending the swarm of flies into a loud-buzzing frenzy.

The head and all four paws of the mother bear had been hacked off. Broken white bone ends stuck out at angles from the gory, flesh holes and matted black hair.

The hiker pulled the bandana away from his face, doubled over, and retched into the leaf litter.

"Is that the wound that killed her—right there on her belly?"

"No, it's on her side. Looks like a hunting arrow to the heart or lungs. She didn't get far before collapsing here. And that wound—," she stooped again and, slipping on a rubber glove, used her fingers to pull the flesh aside, "—is where they removed her gall bladder. I can see where the bile ducts were cut."

The hiker wiped his mouth with the back of his hand, and was panting. "Why didn't they haul her away for the meat?"

Jo stood, her face red with anger. "Too much trouble to lug her seven miles out of the woods. Somebody just wanted to make big bucks off this poor creature."

"What do you mean?" said Rocco. One cub was nipping at his hand, the other was docile, almost listless.

"Black bear gall bladder and bile sell for up to three thousand dollars to people who practice eastern and traditional medicine. There are buyers in big cities all over the U.S. You freeze the organ and overnight it—you land a good chunk of cash."

"Somebody did this to her for one tiny part of her body?"

"Well, they took the head and paws for souvenirs, too. I hope what they did haunts their dreams, but it probably won't."

Standing, stepping around the carcass, Jo took a protesting, squirming cub in each hand. "These guys are light—eight and six pounds, I'm guessing. That means they're either really late-season births, or they're both sick or severely dehydrated. And damn."

"What?" said Rocco, leaning in.

"This littlest one has a big hotspot. I can see another maggot crawling out of it—right there."

Rocco felt his stomach churn harder, and he swallowed hard but did not back away. In the brief moment he'd held them, while they grunted and struggled to get to their mother, he had felt a twinge in his chest for the two orphaned cubs. "Poor little guy. How can we help him?"

Ron dropped to one knee and pulled a plastic bottle out of one of the medical packs. "Peroxide. Maggots hate it. Hold him still, while I pour this over the wound."

"Move fast," said Jo, "then we've gotta get these fellas back to the clinic a.s.a.p. I'll need to start a sub-cutaneous flushing to drive the rest of the maggots out from under the skin. Rocco, you come back with me. Ron, you stay here.

"You—," she pointed at the hiker, who was still pale and sweating, "—can you and your friends help him comb the area? These little guys were probably in the den and came out searching when they heard their mother roaring when she was shot. My guess is, if they were with her they'd have been gutted, too. Do a thorough check. There may be a cub or two still in hiding."

Rocco held the weaker, smaller cub gently on the stainless steel table as Jo prepped a syringe. The docile cub had become listless now, unlike its sibling who was alternately lapping at the bowls of water in its cage and bawling for its mother.

Jo looked at Rocco's right hand.

"You took a couple of bad scratches. When I'm done flushing this little guy with more peroxide I'll treat those. Next time I tell you to put on gloves or tell you to do anything, you do it."

He looked at the red marks on the back of his hand. "He barely broke the skin. I'm good."

She stopped working, and raised her voice. "First lesson. The only acceptable answer, Rocco, is 'Yes, Jo.' You're gonna be the student leader of my large mammals team, and when you work closely with me, no questions asked unless it's because you want to learn. Otherwise, you jump when I say jump, and keep going till I say come down."

"Yes, ma'am."

"Just Jo."

"Got it. Yes, Jo."

She nodded. "Fast learner. That's good."

Jo had nearly finished syringing the peroxide flush beneath the cub's skin, driving out the last of the maggots when Ron returned. She looked up. "Any luck?"

"We found the den and a third cub, but she's probably been dead for a day."

"Damn. Well, hopefully the maggot toxins haven't affected this guy's organs yet. Hook up an IV for me."

"What happens now?" Rocco asked. "Is he gonna make it?"

"We'll see. It's watch and wait."

"But I want him to make it."

"Second lesson. Don't get attached. Ever."

His face fell.

"Hey, Rocco. I'm sorry I busted on you a few minutes ago about doing what I say. I'm not that bad. Really. The fact is, I get working with animals, and I get intense. When I get like that, don't take it personally, okay?"

He brightened a little. "Okay."

"You did great out there in the woods."

"Thanks." He petted the now sleeping cub. "I hope you can help these little guys."

"We—your team and I—are going to do everything we can. And Rocco."

He looked up from the bear cub.

"I'll do my best to be more patient with you. But you still have to do *exactly* what I tell you."

When Rocco finished letting Jo disinfect his scratches, he headed back to the cabins to find someone to hang out with. In the back of his mind, he wished his mother could meet Jo, be like her—strong, forceful—not weak and allowing herself to be crushed by his father. Voices from down along the sandy crescent of shoreline caught his attention, and after exchanging his sweaty clothes for swim trunks, he charged down to the beach.

Four people were sprawled on blankets—Bay, Claire, who was drawing on a sketch pad, Emmalyn, and Makayla.

Above, some late-day clouds had piled up over Eagle Rock Mountain and The Arrows, but the sun from the west was still intense and the sky was clear and the air hot. The one he was really looking for had waded out into the lake up to her thighs.

Dropping his towel on the sand, he called out to Imani who was splashing water on her face and arms.

"Guess what? We're on Jo's large mammals team. You, me, and Tia Leesha. I just helped Jo and Ron rescue two baby bears. You gotta go up to the clinic and see 'em later. They're awesome. We're gonna get 'em healthy and let 'em go maybe later this year."

Makayla was lying on a large green blanket beside Imani's beach cover. She got a pained expression and turned her face away.

Wading into the lake, Rocco arched his back and dove in, swam out and down the shoreline a ways. Then he suddenly went butt-up and dove deep.

In a moment, he came up sputtering ten feet away. "Whoa—it's cold when you get down there."

He swam back up the lake until he was a few feet from Imani, where he rolled on his back, kicked his legs and splashed water at her.

She blocked the spray with her hands. "So childish."

He stood up, smiling, with dark streaks of dirt trailing down his torso. "The bottom is really mucky here."

Then he reached back under the water, came up with a handful of black mud—and grinned at her.

"You even think about throwing that at me, I promise you will regret you were born."

He sniffed the muck. "What the heck? Smells like sewage."

"Bay says it's because all the leaves and plants that fall or get blown in sink to the bottom and rot. I'd come back into the non-sewage-smelling swimming area, if I were you. That's why the rest of us aren't swimming where you are. And speaking of smell. You need to wash up. You got that nasty, boys'-locker-room smell going on. There's a bottle of that pure glycerin camping soap Tanner put in our packs back on my blanket. How about you keep your distance, and go use it."

Makayla had waded out, soap bottle in hand. "Oh, hey, I was just going to join you guys and wash my hair. Bay said fresh lake water is good for that. But here—," she splashed over to Rocco, and handed the soap to him, "—you go ahead and use it first."

Then she bent down, stuck her left hand under the water, and came up with a palm full of the black muck.

He stepped back warily, dodging her. "Oh right, an ambush?"

"No, no, no. Let me do something. Claire is on the beach, drawing symbols for the different animal rehab teams."

"She's been really down," Imani said quietly, so her voice wouldn't carry up to the beach. "It's good to see her relaxed and doing something creative. She said what she's drawing are called sigils. She did one that's perfect for the amphibian and reptile guys."

Makayla dipped the index finger of her right hand in the black muck, then painted a long sinewy curve with four short thin legs on one of her forearms. "Salamander sigil. Pretty cool, right?"

"Yeah, very. I like it," said Rocco.

"Claire worked on one for the large mammals team. Here's what she came up with—and since you just rescued baby bears, it's perfect."

Makayla stepped close to Rocco, and with a muddy index finger painted a bear paw on the right side of his chest opposite his tattoo. As an after-thought, she said, "This is your life."

He gave her a strange look. "What does that even mean? Why did you say that?"

"I'm not sure. It just came into my head." She stepped back from him in the water. "It's like, up here with all the quiet around us all the time, you start to think things you never would have thought before. You pick up stuff from out of nowhere, like magic text messages or something."

He flexed his chest and arms and called out. "I am *Bear Tribe.*"

He began to stomp around Makayla, splashing. "You are *Salamander Tribe.*"

He slapped his hands on the water, soaking her and making the mud sigil on her arm run off.

"*Bear Tribe* is greater."

Then he scooped mud, and splashed his way toward Imani. "You are also *Bear Tribe*. You must carry the mark."

She rolled her eyes and turned one shoulder to him, allowing him paint the symbol on her upper arm. "Okay, okay, I'm in your goofy Bear Tribe. Now please take a bath."

He waved the bottle of glycerin soap at her. "With this, I will conquer every bad smell."

He dove in again, and came up sputtering twenty feet away. Uncapping the bottle, he began scrubbing up, covering his head, arms, and upper body in lather.

340

"I am Great White Bear of Bear Tribe."

Imani washed the sigil off her shoulder. "You're overdoing it with the tribe thing."

Makayla had waded up beside Imani, who turned to her and said quietly, "Very clever move."

"I told you. He isn't interested in me. He likes you."

"You don't know he's not interested in you. And him and me? You know exactly why that can never happen."

"Hey, Claire," Rocco called out to her. "I wanna see the other sigils you drew."

In a moment, standing beside her, his eyebrows shot up. "Wow, you sketched me with the bear paw sigil. I look pretty tough, don't I?"

Claire gave him a blank stare. "You look, and still smell, like you need a shower."

8TH

Jo was in the barn beyond the river, when Dhani, Claire, and Ray-Ray found her. She was bent over the side of the huge, aquatic-life tank, wearing thick gloves, and supporting a small, dark-brown creature by its shoulders.

"See how she's trying to swim?" Jo was saying to Garrett, Carter, and Emmalyn. She can't quite get it, but she may be able to come back from the injury."

Dhani balked when he saw Garrett, but Claire took him by the arm and said under her breath. "Just ignore him."

"But—"

"Remember, we got your back," whispered Ray-Ray.

Claire was looking at the animal, then at Emmalyn, who said, "Muskrat. Kind of cute, isn't she—I mean, for a rodent."

"What happened to her?" Claire asked, leaning over the tank beside the others. Dhani went to the far end of the tank, and stood apart. In a moment, Ray-Ray followed and stood by him.

"She was run over by a speedboat that ignored shallow-water warning buoys. Lucky she didn't get chopped to pieces, but she lost a significant portion of her tail and some tendons in one leg were severed."

Jo lifted the muskrat from the water to show them the bandage, which kept one of the animal's legs out straight. The creature looked like a giant version of a guinea pig, but with long sharp claws on all its paws.

"It's very tricky, operating on tendons this small. I re-attached one for sure. Not sure the other will hold, though. Then the other trick is not leaving the bandage on too long so the leg doesn't atrophy. I may not be able to place her back out there if she doesn't recover mobility in that limb. She'd be killed in a day or two by predators."

Dhani sounded sad. "It's crummy to think she might never get to go home again."

Garrett looked across the tank at him, and Claire and Ray-Ray caught the hate-filled look.

Dhani, noticing, dropped his eyes and seemed to shrink into his hoodie.

"If you look here," Jo said, parting the animal's stomach fur, you can see she's lactating. That means she recently had babies. We're going to try to find her burrow, see if they're still alive. If they didn't crawl their way out and become lunch for the hawks, or if minks or coyotes didn't find them, they may still be there."

Ray-Ray had turned his attention back to the muskrat, and reached out to stroke the animal's gleaming fur.

Jo moved her away quickly. "You don't want to do that. See those front teeth? If she bites you, we'll be re-attaching your tendons next. Here's a rule, guys. *Never ever* touch any of these animals unless you've been given careful instruction and clearance by me."

"*We* are going to look for the babies, meaning—*who*?" asked Emmalyn.

"Me, and your team. A nest should be easy to spot. It may look like a smaller version of a beaver's den—made of sticks, mud, and reeds, right at the water line. They're called 'push ups.' There's a wetland area just up a narrow stream from the end of the lake where she was hit. Muskrats follow set trails, so it shouldn't be too hard to find the nest. I just hope it's not inside a bank, though, or I may not be able to reach in deep enough to rescue her young."

"We're going to walk around in a swamp," Emmalyn said, sounding unhappy. "Great."

When Jo finished with the muskrat, she sent Garrett, Carter, and Emmalyn to clean cages.

As Garrett passed Dhani, he patted him on the shoulder. "It's all good. No hard feelings." He picked up a bucket and clean cloths, and followed the girls into the other section of the barn where the injured muskrat would be housed along with the baby otters.

Ray-Ray raised an eyebrow. "Okay, I'm not buying that. Don't ever trust that guy."

Claire asked Jo, "Can we talk to you?"

"What's up?"

"I guess you've assigned the others. So that makes us your bird team. We're calling ourselves the Eagle Tribe."

"Oh, 'tribe' is it?"

"Rocco came up with that," said Claire. "A bunch of us think it's kind of cool."

Jo led them to the other barn and into the aviary. "Birds are more high-strung. I don't like to get them riled, since most of them have wing damage and their bones and tendons are thin and easily re-injured. Never make any fast moves or loud noises in here."

When they slid open the door and stepped inside, there was mostly silence, except for the fluttering sound of a large bird in its enclosure halfway down the aviary. The sliding door that concealed the eagle's enclosure was shut, as usual, but the rest were open. The narrow tree trunks, saplings, and branches used to make the habitats were all quiet and still, with no signs of life.

"Each enclosure opens to another one outside," Jo said, finally stopping next to one cage, where they could see a huge black bird with a heavy black beak huddled on a branch, its head hidden under one wing.

"As these guys get healthier, they want to spend time outdoors.

When they're newly injured, like they all are right now, they tend to stay still. Sometimes we hand-feed. I'll train you how to do that properly after a while. The main rule is minimal hands-on contact."

Dhani had wandered down the center of the aviary, between the rows of enclosures and cages. Jo's voice faded, and he found himself intensely focused on the branchy hideaways inside the enclosures—for no reason, suddenly imagining he knew the ones where birds were in hiding. Like the last one, way down at the far end, where he stopped.

As with other enclosures, there was an upper back corner where leafy branches came together to make a hiding spot. He knew, but didn't know how he knew, a small, injured creature was concealed in this one.

How did you get hurt?

A tiny owl, with a face like a cat set in a large head, stuck its head out of the concealing evergreen branches of its shelter. It stared directly down at Dhani, with bright yellow eyes—then let out a loud, rhythmic *too-too-too-too-too*, fell silent for a few seconds, then began again.

"*Whooo*," Dhani responded.

Ray-Ray called to him. "Wouldn't that be *whom*?"

Claire groaned. "You're funny. In a non-funny kinda way."

"I pride myself."

She looked at Jo. "I've heard that sound at night when I have my bedroom windows open. In fact, it sounds like two birds calling to each other. One is in the woods on the east side of the lake. The other sounds like it's over here. One calls, the other one answers."

The saw-whet owl had rustled out from its leafy shelter, directing all its energy at Dhani, crying—*too-too-too-too-too, too-too-too-too-too.*

Jo whipped her head around. "You didn't mess with her cage, did you?"

"No," Dhani said vehemently. He was not going to be blamed again, and stepped back even further from the wire barrier. "I'm just *standing* here."

Jo turned back to Claire and Ray-Ray. "Saw-whets—they're very pretty little tan-and-cream colored owls. This one got caught in a garden net that was meant to keep the deer out. Severely twisted her wing and broke a tiny bone."

"Is she angry we're in here?"

"No. That's not her angry, *get-out-of-my-territory* call. She's pretty animated right now, though, isn't she? Which is odd because saw-whets are highly nocturnal and rarely alert during the day."

"Why is this one awake?" asked Ray-Ray.

"That's what I'm wondering," Jo murmured.

The saw-whet had not stopped shouting at Dhani. And now the raven in the enclosure midway up the aisle had become highly agitated. It was hopping around, alternately croaking deeply in its throat, then loosing a louder, higher-pitched *crrr-uuuckk*-ing noise.

Likewise, a bluejay in his small enclosure next to the raven began to make a *cheed-lu-lu-lu cheed-lu cheed-lu-lu-lu* call. Which it repeated, until it sounded strangely like a chant.

Ray-Ray looked uneasy. "Should we leave? It sounds like *The Birds*. I feel like Alfred Hitchcock is gonna appear and that we're gonna get our eyes pecked out."

"No—we're safe, and they're not freaking out. But it's very unusual. Something's going on," said Jo, looking mystified. "These are their welcoming calls. Like when they're singing over their hatchlings or a mate shows up. Looks as if they like you guys."

Dhani had stepped a little closer to the wire barrier of the saw-whet's cage again, seeing that Jo was not angry, and without thinking whispered to the small creature.

The saw-whet instantly fell silent, and a moment later so did the raven, followed by the bluejay.

In the sudden stillness, Jo, Claire, and Ray-Ray all stared at Dhani.

"What did you just do?" asked Jo. "They all calmed down."

Dhani moved away from the owl's enclosure again. "Nothing. Really."

"They just—stopped all at once," said Ray-Ray. "That was *weird.*"

Claire looked skeptical. She had not forgotten their chore, and addressed Jo. "Are you just saying these guys really like us, so we'll feel better about cleaning up bird crap?"

"No, it's true," Jo insisted. "They all came alert and were really okay with you being here. Though you're right. 'Hi, how you doing time' is over, whatever that was about. Time to clean up. We don't need the roaches and beetles taking over."

They found the supplies as Jo instructed—mops, a rolling bucket, and a natural cleanser in her clinic's storage closet.

"What did you do in there?" Claire asked Dhani. "And don't say nothing. I saw you whispering to that little owl just before it stopped calling."

"Promise you won't laugh at me."

"*Shut up* and tell us what you did," Ray-Ray pressed.

"I said—'I'm really sorry you guys got injured. I hope I can help you get better.'"

Claire smiled at him—for the first time, a full, genuine, relaxed smile. "That's cool. Why would you think we'd laugh at you?"

"It's just not a very *guy* thing to do—talking to a bird and saying 'sorry you're hurt'."

Ray-Ray had begun to swab the center aisle. "Okay, Bird Man of Alcatraz, can I get some help here? Less yack, more strong back."

Dhani relaxed and grinned.

"You know," Claire observed, "I think this is the first time I've seen you smile. You look a whole lot better when you do."

Later, Dhani went alone beside the Garnet River, stopping at the stand of white pines that marked their wander line. Maybe he could find something else to give Claire, a gift to follow up on the shell, which he'd given her on a bad day and hadn't gotten the response he hoped for.

He kicked off his shoes, rolled up his jeans to the knees, and waded into the broad, shallow, cool flow, slipping a little on flat slate bed before gaining his footing. Hot as it had been, with no rain, the river was down. Jalil, who had been hunting amphibians near here had found a rare fossil, and Jo had identified the beautiful, gold-and-black fanlike ridges in the rock as a stromatolite.

"These fossilized swirls were blue-green algae colonies a billion or more years ago," Jo had said, "before this whole Adirondack area was pushed up from the ocean floor. This is a perfect specimen, and probably needs to be in the State museum in Albany."

If he found a beautiful rock today, it would go to Claire—just like the shell necklace—and not to a museum. He'd tell her to keep it a secret. Their secret.

She said she thought he looked good when he smiled. Or at least better.

He wanted to top off today's small victory with Claire. He was also feeling proud of himself for keeping his mouth shut this morning. *"No one likes sensitive little crybabies. Or brats who make up stories to get attention."* He had been smacked around many times while hearing that shouted in his face.

He began turning over river stones in his search.

It was a good thing, he thought, that he had not told the exact truth about what he'd whispered to the owl. Which was,

"I'm sorry you got hurt. People hurt me real bad, too."

Now if he could just figure out what Claire meant by her comment. Did she like the way he looked? Did she like *him*? A thought crossed his mind—that while he could sense how animals felt, he wasn't too good at understanding girls. Any girls really, but especially Claire.

Turning over three dozen or more big stones, he found the small, fan-shaped fossil he was searching for—a billion-year-old beauty, formed in a perfect arc maybe two inches big. As he lifted the small rock from the water, he realized his feet were tingling, not because of the cold current but as if some energy were rushing up from slate and water in through his heels, shooting up his ankles to his knees, thighs, and the base of his spine. He shuddered. It was like the electric sensation he had felt when Ray-Ray found him standing in the shallows of Lost Lake, feeling pulled into the form and awareness of a water lily.

A voice like the rush of water began to whisper in his head—words just out of hearing—and he had the *déjà vu* sense that he had been here before. If not here at Lost Lake, then to this river. . . or maybe flowing along in a current like this somewhere else in the world.

No, no, no. The sensation that he might leave his body was becoming too strong.

Springing out of the current to the river bank, he gripped the fossil tightly but lost his balance and crashed on his left hip and elbow on a large, flat rock. The painful jolt brought him instantly, solidly back into his body.

These crazy flights of imagination had to stop, he shouted within himself. They *had* to. He would force them to stop.

Claire would never understand if he told her what went on inside his mind. Or if he told her anything about his life. In fact, he felt sure she would think he was a lunatic and abandon him.

17TH

He found Jo in the clinic. She was beaming, and the humidity of the space made her face glisten.

Jalil and Makayla were beside her at the examining table, watching her pull a strip of silver duct tape off the black-and-yellow shell of a small box turtle, revealing a long, zig-zag mark. Down the center of the break was a white, jagged line.

"That's new shell forming, isn't it?" Makayla breathed. "He's healing. He was so smashed up when we found him, I never thought he'd make it."

Steve watched Jo carefully, her graceful movements, her confident work with the small creature.

"You guys have done a great job of keeping him clean and well fed," said Jo, to Jalil and Makayla. "He's going to be fine." She re-taped the shell and handed the turtle to Jalil. "Take him back to the other barn, clean his terrarium and give him fresh greens and carrots. When Dugan shows up, have him see me. There's a wounded rat snake I want him to prep a terrarium for."

"You're in a good mood," Steve said, when they were gone.

"Turtles often don't make it when their shells are as badly broken as that guy's was.—What's up?"

"I ordered a bunch of first-aid kits for the kids' packs, but I'm returning them. They're flimsy and crappy. Trovert suggested I have you place an order for new ones on your account. The ones I want are pricey. He says you order in volume, so they'll be cheaper."

Jo re-taped the turtle's shell, walked to a sink, and soaped-up her hands. "What's better about the kits you want?"

"They've got stuff like 'Quick Clot', a chemical compound used to stop massive bleeding. That's important if someone sustains a serious gash when we're deep in the woods. You rip open a pack and dump it into the wound, and it stops even massive bleeding. Burns and hurts like a mother, but it'll save a life."

Ron was setting up a water circulating pump in a new terrarium. "Hard core."

"In the Marines, we called it a 'blow-out kit', because there's stuff in it you can use to save someone who's had their back, arm, leg, chest or face blown out."

"I'll check with my suppliers," Jo said.

350

Rocco stuck his head in the door. "Excuse me, Jo. What else do you want me to do with the bear cubs' pen?"

"If it's clean and you gave them food and water—nothing else. You didn't pick them up, right? I know you think they're cute and the bigger one is doing fine, but the little guy is still very weak and susceptible."

Steve gave her a questioning look.

"Bears and humans can pass diseases to each other."

"No, Jo," Rocco replied. "I didn't pick them up. I wanted to, but I didn't—like you said."

"That's it, then. Have a nice afternoon."

When he was gone, Steve said, "Good kid. They should all be like him. Some of these guys—." He shook his head.

"Well, they aren't all like him. Looks like it's up to you to figure out how to reach each kid in their own way."

He made a disgusted sound. "More like they need to step up to my standards."

"No flexibility, huh?"

"Someday these kids will need to be worth the time of day to society and to an employer. Right now some of them are examples of misspent human genes."

"*Whoa*—nice attitude, Tanner. What if you have a kid someday who's just like one of these guys?"

"I'd pack them off to military school faster than they could suck their next breath."

Jo stared. "I'd like to think you're kidding, but I suspect you're not. All I have to say is, if that's how you think, it's no wonder there's no Mrs. Tanner."

Steve's knees buckled slightly, but he kept a blank look on his face. He was not going to give her any ground.

For a long moment, the only sound was the noise of the circulating pump bubbling in Ron's new set up. Ron had vanished.

Steve cleared his throat. "But hey, let's not make this all about me. What about the kit?"

"All orders for the clinic go through Tom. I'll tell him where to find what you need."

When he was gone, Ron returned. "Geez, Jo, you were pretty rough on him. He's just airing his head about these kids. That's how I read it."

"Hey, he's a Marine. He can take it."

Outside, Steve took in a deep breath. It had been a long time—seventeen months—since he'd taken that kind of brutal kick to the gut.

25TH

Ray-Ray was in his room, reading, and Dugan was as usual hanging out in Garrett's cabin. At least Garrett didn't come here, Dhani thought, and invade his space.

For several weeks, Dhani had felt more and more uneasy. Constantly, he chewed his cuticles till they were raw and painful.

"Get some lunch if you're hungry," Ray-Ray said, trying to make him laugh, barely getting a faint grin out of him.

Tonight, he felt wired. They had been told to get a good night's sleep, to be prepared for another day-trek tomorrow, but he felt caged and wanted to be outside. His body was like a wound spring, with so many thoughts and feelings circling and circling. His neck and shoulders and chest felt tight. When would his anxieties let up?

First, there had been his uncertainty about Claire. Now, he felt she might be starting to like him, and he'd never had that from a girl. Or not that he'd noticed. He had always been too preoccupied, worrying about what might be happening with his mother. That worry was a constant.

Where was his mother? That's what was troubling him now. It was months since they had last spoken, and if she would just call him once maybe everything would feel okay. *Maybe*, but not for sure. His mind went over and over the painful pattern.

When things were good with a current boyfriend. . . .

. . .she would often stay out all day or all night partying—and then he would put himself to bed and get up early to pace the apartment, turn on the early news, watch for reports of overnight accidents or—please god, no—a fatality. Later, at school he would be exhausted and lay his head on the desk.

When things were bad with a current boyfriend, she would sink into a pit and say, "I don't want to live anymore. I could just. . .end it." She would smoke cigarettes one after another, tears staining her face. "One day you might find me dead on the floor." He hated cigarettes and she knew it, but she would stub out one and light another. And another.

"Mom," he would almost shout, but she was not listening. She was lost in her misery—until the phone rang and it was her boyfriend, and after some shouting she would be settled again. She would put her hand over the mouthpiece and say, "Dhani, get going. You'll be late for school. Why are you still here?"

On those days, his stomach would knot and when someone spoke to him he barely heard them. If a girl had ever liked him—he thought maybe Emily in an English class had—he could not spare the energy to pursue it. Every thought, every minute, was aimed toward getting home and encircling his mother with assurances.

"I'll protect you, Mom. I need you here."

She would stare into distance, smoking, always smoking. "I don't deserve you. I'm such a terrible mother. I should give you up and let someone better than me raise you. Would you like that, if mommy gave you to someone better? If I wasn't even. . . here. . . anymore?" Then she would sob and sob.

Then he would wrap her in a fierce hug. He would try to protect them both from those bad thoughts.

"Stop saying this stuff, Mom, I love you. Look at me, please. Don't leave."

She would shake her head, and go flush the stub of her cigarette down the toilet.

I will always be here for you, Mom. I can save you. . . .

353

He stopped his thoughts about her right there. He would not let himself think any more about his mother or the violent and dark things that had resulted in his being sent away from her. What if because of those things she was now avoiding him? What if Claire kept avoiding him?

His anxious feelings about them meshed, doubling, tripling his frustration. He could not find or check on his mother. Likewise, the wish that he could tell Claire plainly what he really wanted to say, but could not say, drove him to anger.

Muscles tensing, he ripped a picture off his wall—one he had torn from a magazine in Kate's library, of a girl who resembled Claire—balled it, crushed it, threw it. Picked it up, opened, and smoothed it.

I'm sorry, Claire. Remorse for his angry action was painful, and his throat felt tight.

Now, suddenly, the stifling air in his room made his tee-shirt feel like a straitjacket. He had to escape from it—from himself. He thought of one place he could flee to.

Outside, the night sky was a gentle blanket of darkness filled with pinpricks of light. A few night birds were calling. Breathing in the free, fresh air began to calm him, not a lot but a little. Some sweet scent of pine and late season blossoms was on the light breeze. A nearly full moon was rising, lopsided, brilliant, and bright yellow above The Arrows, and the light breeze moving across the lake was like the soft cotton of his hiking bandana slipping over his skin. When his breathing relaxed and his chest expanded, he realized it had been shallow and tight all evening.

Beside Sahm's cabin was the boulder on which Sahm had helped him meditate and find some inner calm. A way to escape from himself. Moonlight threaded its way down through the branches of the towering white pine next to it, spilling onto the great rock, painting thin trails of light over its shadowed surfaces. No lights were on in Sahm's cabin. Likely, he was asleep. Dhani felt comforted a little that he was close by.

He hoisted himself up on top of the boulder and faced the lake. The moonlight was pouring down over the forested flanks of Trinity Mountain across the lake, and Osprey Island looked like a swath of charcoal gray on the lightly rippling surface of the black water.

Little by little as he took in the calm night air, the deep stillness of Lost Lake and its surrounding slopes passed inside of him. He felt the peacefulness of the water and this first relief from agitation was heaven.

Crossing his legs, he recalled the way Sahm had guided him into the simple meditation—letting his hands rest on his thighs and his mind focus on his breath.

Ride the smooth air, he reminded himself, *like I'm riding a streetboard.*

In a moment, he was deeply focused on the current of the night breeze, in and out of his lungs. . . in and out. . . feeling his body relax. . .so pleasantly caught up he did not hear when someone stepped quietly into the shadows behind him, watching.

In and out, Dhani rode the column of air. In. . . and out. . . in. . . and out.

An owl called.

The cry began as a rhythmic *too-too-too-too-too,* coming over and over from the shadowy stand of fir trees to his left along the east side of the lake. In a moment, it sounded again, this time from out over the dark waters maybe fifty yards or so in front of him. Light movements of the night air feathered Dhani's hair and his muscles relaxed even more.

Beneath him suddenly the rock seemed to fall away, leaving him cross-legged on a cushion of air and feeling as if unseen hands were lifting him.

The call came again, welcoming him, stirring within him a longing, and he felt a rising happiness in the center of his chest, as if at the core of his being a locked door was swinging open and he was slipping out through it until. . . .

...he launched out on spread wings, up and over the lake. Catching an updraft of cool air, he rose until he was gliding beside the small saw-whet owl, a young male that was still calling—too-too-too-too-too—and paying no attention to Dhani's presence, as if it were perfectly right for him to be there, gliding on the air. His fingers felt like feathers.

Beneath them, the black lake reflected the sky's irregular spattering of stars and the pale, sprawling band of the Milky Way, as the highways of air carried them on toward the west side of the lake. Here over the water, the air was much cooler, cutting through his clothes, sending a chill along his back, his legs, and out his arms. And at the same time, he also felt hot lightning flashes shooting over his skin. . . just as he had on Peregrine Mountain during the first day-trek.

As the far shore approached, the owl banked to the right and, side by side—or was it wing-tip to wing-tip?—they crossed above the thin strip of beach there. Below, Dhani could see Grady's canoe tipped on its side, the handle of one paddle jutting out from beneath and just visible in the shadow-gray sand. They glided above the broad ribbon of the camp road in front of Kate's lodge, which rose mountainous and crannied in the night, then angled toward the tree line on the far side of the Garnet River. Its dark leafy wall rose right beside the second barn, which housed the aviary. No lights were on, and the big structure was still and dark.

In another moment, the owl buffered the air with wings flared forward, extended his legs and opened his claws. Dhani found himself perching beside the creature on a thin branch of a mountain ash that remained unbending as his weightless body came to rest on it.

How is all this happening? he shouted in his mind.

They were facing the backside of the barn. Here, the big, oblong, outdoor enclosures for the convalescing birds stood half-hidden by the moon shadow cast by the building. Gaping black squares showed where hatches that led out from the indoor cages stood open. These openings allowed the clinic's inmates that were strong enough to hop or flutter outside into the fresher air.

The saw-whet beside him tensed his small form, and released toward the barn a loud cry—too-too-too-too-too.

From inside the barn, muffled but clear, came—too-too-too-too-too. The injured saw-whet female calling back.

It was a shout!—filled with a happiness, and it entered Dhani's heart and made everything inside him leap. Leap higher than it ever had before, with a joy so strong he felt as if it would break out through his skin. He wanted to shout, too, dive from the branch, and circle up into the air. He felt like he had become the moonlight, the two owls, the air that carried their calls, and something even lighter than air. He felt himself expanding, greater and greater, and in another second it seemed his whole being would burst.

Another cry came from the barn, carrying different hues of feeling in its tone.

Dhani knew that cry, and what the changed tone meant. It was a cry of desire.

A stab of longing pierced him. Much like the longing—he realized now—that he had begun to feel for another person. A half-emptiness in the great, open sky of his soul. A flight through the open sky meant to be shared. A yearning ache in the space where he wanted another to be. Pretty, smart, strong. . . Claire.

But the feeling of yearning was painful. In a moment it grew too intense, and became threatening. He had to stop this longing from rising and pouring out from his open soul any further. What if he let it flood out of himself, expressed it in words, and its intensity was not returned? Even worse, what if it was thrown away, as if it were nothing but a stubbed out cigarette end? Suppose he spoke his feelings, and found there were none at all for him?

No, he shouted. NO.

And with that, the explosive expansion of his being reversed. The beautiful wildness that had almost burst the bonds of his body and soul rapidly shrank, collapsed, and he felt himself reeling backwards off the branch of the mountain ash, rushing in reverse over the lake. . . toppling down into the dark. . . .

Strong arms caught him, one under his shoulders, one under his thighs, and set him down carefully in the bed of needles beneath the white pine.

Dhani sucked in air, chest heaving, and opened his eyes to find Sahm standing over him. Even in shadow, with the moon shining from behind, Dhani could tell Sahm was smiling.

"Where did you go?"

Dhani rubbed his eyes, confused and sounding anxious. "I—I was dreaming. I didn't go anywhere. It's okay that I came here, isn't it?"

Sahm continued smiling and did not speak for a moment. He waited till Dhani sat up, then rolled onto this knees and pushed himself upright on unsteady legs.

"A kind of dreaming, yes. Let us call it dreaming for now. That may be best. But tell me, Dhani—how did you enter into this dream state?"

A current of cold night air washed around them, and Dhani's whole body shuddered. It was late. The moon was at the zenith, carving a white swath through the Milky Way.

How did I 'enter into this dream'? He already felt disoriented from being jolted out of sleep. Sahm's question made him feel even stranger.

He had fallen asleep, Dhani told himself, that was how. And then he must have fallen from the rock. Fortunately, Sahm had been there to catch him—but *why* he was there watching in the dark, Dhani was too tired to ask. His thoughts had been so clear and now they were murky, his limbs were lead, and the energy-coil that had wound itself up inside him earlier had let loose and spun itself out.

Now he was faced with the prospect of dragging himself on rubbery legs along the shadowy, branch and rock strewn shoreline all the way back to his bed. Only a half-awareness remained—that whatever had escaped from inside him briefly was back in its cage, the door closed and locked, tucking its awareness safely under the protection of forget-fulness. And then, even that was barred from his mind. Gone.

"What are you even talking about?" He felt empty, vulnerable, sleepy, and unhappy. A thought came out of nowhere. *Wanting someone you really, really care about hurts too much.* "It was just a dream. I want to go now."

Sahm trudged with Dhani all the way back to his cabin to be sure the boy was safely home, then returned to his own to lie wide awake in bed. The lowering moon shone through his bedroom window, the way it had months before when an urgent voice had pulled him up out of a sound sleep and outside into a bitter cold night at *Losar*.

He thought he could feel his grandfather smiling at him, and heard the old man's voice in his head.

"To fly from yourself and the work you must do in this lifetime is not really possible," the old man had schooled him, speaking of other yogis who had abandoned their path in favor of lust or money or fame in the West. *"When you flee, Cetan, you will always meet yourself again, waiting up ahead, along with the work that is still yours to do."*

An hour ago, the same urgency he had felt at *Losar* again awakened and led him out into the night, where the solid world had again shimmered like a mirage. There he had found Dhani sitting in the moonlight, and waited patiently next to the boy's form for him to return from wherever in the wide world his spirit had flown.

Dhani was a young man, who had no idea of the great abilities and purposes that lay potential within him. This he knew for sure.

What he needed to know was what that exact purpose might be.

29TH

Steve pulled his knife from the tree trunk and stepped back. Fifteen paces this time. And made a new mark with his heel in moss and loamy dirt.

Knife practice on the trunk of a dead cedar behind his cabin was his salvation after the conversation with Jo unnerved him.

He fixed his eyes on its center, emptied his mind, coiled his body and hurled the Ka-bar hard as he could. The blade thudded. . . .

...into the body of the man all in black, who had pulled his trigger five times just a foot from Olivia's chest.

"Sir?"

Steve jumped.

Garrett had come up quietly.

"You're lucky I didn't have the knife in my hand." Steve's voice had an angry bite. "I might have reacted. What the hell are you doing here? I thought I made it clear, if anyone needed to see me they could leave a message with Tom."

"I did. Tom said you hadn't been to the office in over a week."

True enough.

Steve walked up to the cedar, and yanked his knife from the trunk.

"So what do you need?" It did not sound welcoming; he didn't want it to. He was not in a great frame of mind and Garrett was not his favorite kind of kid.

"First, I came to apologize. I've got a big mouth. It gets me in trouble. I gotta work on that."

Steve walked back to his mark. He took aim, and hurled the knife into the trunk where it struck dead-center.

"I have an older cousin who was going to enlist in the Marines," said Garrett. "Then he heard about the battle of Keating."

Steve was wiggling the deeply buried blade out of the tree again. "What do you know about Keating?"

"Just what my cousin had me read. How the Marine command left those guys in a remote outpost and forgot to issue the order to leave, and a bunch of guys got killed in an ambush by the Taliban. There was another one. Kadesh or someplace like that."

"Kamdesh."

"My cousin said it was too bad our guys were left to die. He said it was one of the deadliest days for U.S. troops in the history of the war in Afghanistan. He decided no way was he signing up."

"Maybe there was a reason the command left them in place. Who knows."

"My cousin said eight Marines got killed, and the U.S. claimed a huge number of Taliban were killed. He said that part was bull. The Marines were ambushed and totally outgunned. So how did they take out a hundred-and-fifty Taliban? My cousin said it was U.S. military propaganda."

Steve's shoulders tensed. "Your cousin thinks he knows a lot. Me—I don't question authority."

"What if not questioning authority gets you killed? Those guys should have run. They'd still be alive."

Steve was back at the throwing mark he had paced off, and dug in the soil with his heel.

"Not respecting and obeying authority lands you in juvenile detention. And then if you're lucky you land here—with a hardass like me teaching you how to do *what* you're told *when* you're told. No questions asked. No running. No bullshit."

He hurled the knife as hard as he could and embedded it halfway to the hilt. "Life works out better that way."

Garrett slapped his forehead. "Daggone, I did it again. Shot my mouth off. You're right, sir. Sorry if I made you angry, sir."

"Sir, huh?"

"My life hasn't turned out great so far," Garrett said, staring at the ground. "I try to sound like a big man, and I make fun of people. That's what gets me in trouble. Up on Trinity, I realized a guy like you can teach me a lot. The way I was headed, hell, no one was going to trust me enough to give me a job. Sorry about my language. I'll clean that up, too. Anyway, I figure it's time for me to do whatever I have to, to earn your trust."

Steve felt himself relax a little. *In your face, Troverts.*

He was about to throw the Ka-bar again, when Garrett asked, "Can I see your knife. Just hold it for a minute. It's really cool. I can't believe how accurate you are with it."

Steve handed it to Garrett, who took it, turning the blade side to side, staring with awe.

"What are these letters carved on the handle? *TK.* Someone's initials?"

"Something like that." Steve reached out quickly, and took the knife back. "Is that what you came out here to tell me? That you want to play it straight?"

"Pretty much." Garrett sounded hesitant.

"If there's more, go for it."

Garrett shuffled his feet.

"I don't know if I'm being a rat or doing a good thing. That kid, Dhani—," he pulled up his teeshirt, revealing a little, white scar on his side, "—look what he did to me. Tried to set me on fire. You guys don't know what he's like when no adults are around. He's a snap-o, and he could care less about being in this program. Thinks it's just a nice, easy break from juvenile hall."

"Why are you telling me this?"

Garrett stared at the ground again, looking embarrassed. "I shouldn't be—should I? The other kids won't do it, because it's ratting. I should have kept my mouth shut and not ratted on him either."

"That's not what I mean. Why are you telling *me* and not the Troverts?"

Garrett looked up, and his eyes connected with Steve's.

"The Troverts don't want us to say *any*thing negative about *anyone.* They're all positive-positive everything, you know? Just say nice things about each other. Just tell people they're good. Motivational kind of stuff. They wouldn't listen if I told them how Dhani sneaks around, looks in our things, goes out at night after we're supposed to be in our cabins. They just don't want to hear stuff like that. And I know you're not—well, you're not exactly like them. With you, rules are rules."

Steve nodded, but said nothing. He wasn't going to throw the

Troverts under the bus in front of Garrett. But here was proof they were too lenient.

"Tell you what, young man, I don't want you or anyone else coming to me every time someone calls you a name or hurts your little feels. That stuff, you toughen up about. But if Dhani is seriously breaking rules, getting into your stuff or threatening people's safety, you can come to me."

Dugan leaned against the back wall of one of Kate's storage barns, out of sight, where Garrett had told him to wait.

"How'd it go?" he asked, when Garrett met him.

Garrett stuck out an open palm. "Got him eating out of this like a hungry puppy. Some 'yes sir,' 'no sir'. A lot of ego massage. After that, he let me handle his Marine knife."

Dugan shrugged. "Was that some kind of big deal?"

"It's got someone's initials carved in it. I could tell it's like his prized possession.—Anyway, he's my dog now."

"You scare me."

"Nice thing to say to your business partner."

"Just tell me why we're meeting out here."

"I don't want take the chance anyone will overhear what I've got to tell you."

When Garrett was gone, Steve sat on the back porch and chugged most of a beer. He kept staring at the letters Garrett had noticed—the ones he had inscribed on the Ka-bar's leather handle. *TK.*

A week after Kamdesh.

Troy Kirk.

Tough as hell, twenty-year-old jarhead from Tennessee.

Brave to a fault. Best of the best.

He finished the beer and pushed the treasured knife into its scabbard.

Don't let yourself go back there again.

For the first time since arriving five months ago, he actually felt good about his role here at Lost Lake.

Despite stirring up the memory, Garrett's visit did a good thing. On the Trinity hike, he thought he connected with Rocco, Dugan, and Jalil. Now he'd connected with a weasel like Garrett. These guys were *getting* him and his methods, recognizing their need to show respect and earn trust. That's where he would focus his mind and all his efforts. Make it a good year after all.

As for the Jones kid.

Keep it up, weirdo. Keep disrespecting me and getting into people's stuff. I'll see you get bounced out of this program so fast that damn hoody'll fly off.

7

SEPTEMBER

2ND

"What have you learned?"

"Aboud is dead. I warned him not to go into Syria."

"Missile strike?"

"No, he went directly to the radicals to declare his loyalty and offer help. They found out his mother is a Christian. So even though he and his father are Muslim, they considered him tainted. The son of idolaters. When he heard they were coming for him, he tried to escape into Turkey. He called me, saying he was coming back to DC. But he never made it. He was pursued and his head was found on a road northwest of Mosul. Stupid thugs have no idea who they slaughtered. He would have been one of their best assets."

"So now there's no Plan B. We have keep moving forward."

"Yeah, and my money people are getting impatient."

"Remind them you don't have the same access you used to. And now we can't replace Aboud's work."

"They don't want excuses."

"Tell them the husband will surface. He may think he can evade, but as you've told me many times they always slip up. Always."

"They're threatening to hire another group."

"Tell them it will take a lot of time for anyone else to pull off what we've already done—if it's even possible. You know how to manipulate people. Sweet-talk them, then tell them why it's important for them to wait."

There was a disgusted sound. "I'll drop a new phone at one of the other locations. Torch the one you have."

"You like torching things."

"And people when I have to."

6TH

"Tell me, Steve, were you trying to humiliate Garrett and Dugan in front of the others? We're trying to train these young people in self-esteem."

Tom and Steve were in Grady's canoe, fishing just off Osprey Island. It was early morning and the air was cool, but the sun's rays were already penetrating their sweatshirts. A long spell of hot, Indian Summer days had kept the lake's upper waters warm. From the cooler depths, perch and bass would suddenly explode in strikes at the latest spawn of glassy-winged mayflies that flitted too close to the mirrored surface.

"We talking or fishing? Can't do both."

"Talk first—fish later."

Steve cast, and the gossamer line unfurled over the water, the lure hitting the surface in a bloom of ripples. "So, what does that mean to you—*self-esteem*?"

Tom set his pole down against the canoe's gunwale, ignoring the edge of sarcasm in Steve's voice. "You know the four elements of self-esteem, the ones the Troverts talked about in April."

"Help me out here. A lot of new info was thrown at me."

"First, it means helping these guys recognize they have natural gifts and abilities. Second, creating a sense of belonging. That's why Jo placed them in animal care teams. The students call themselves 'tribes'. They're starting to bond with each and feel good about their work. Third, having and imitating positive role models. Hopefully, we all provide that. Remember, one of Kate's main goals is to teach them cooperation, not just competition."

There it was, the *Liberal BS*. Steve kept himself from reacting outwardly, and slowly reeled the line.

"Fourth, giving them a sense of power, which means letting them make choices and not just dictate to them."

"It all *sounds* good."

Tom studied Steve's flat expression. "But. . .?"

"What I do is about wilderness survival. If a bear shows up on one of our treks or a kid falls in freezing water, he won't survive because he feels good about himself. He'll make it because he does exactly what I've told him to do. If he wants to stay warm and dry and alive, he'll build a fire and a shelter the way I've told him to. He's got a voice in his head that's commanding not coddling him. It's that simple."

"These young people have inner needs, too," Tom pushed back. "Most had horrible home lives and ineffective parenting."

"Then they can talk about that in the Troverts' counseling sessions. I won't butt in. But I'm leading the *wilderness survival* program. What I need is to know my program leaders trust that, out there in my territory, I know what I'm doing. That would give me some self-esteem."

The end of Steve's pole bent, the reel made a *buzzing* sound, and the line fed out rapidly. He leaned back slightly, jerking the pole to one side. "Hooked him."

"Steve, this isn't about territories. This whole program is about making them personally strong enough, self-respecting enough, to go back into the world they came out of and be different people. Not sucked back in by influences that got them in trouble, or feeling like pawns of the forces that had control of their lives before. Some of them have already listened to bad authority figures.

"We want them to grow strong *inside*, so that they don't fit in their old world anymore. Some of their personal growth will happen sitting and talking to Eric and Bay. But even more can happen out there, if your part is handled better."

"*Better*?" Steve smirked.

He finished reeling in a large-mouth bass, its salmon-pink gill slits fanning and closing, its body slapping wildly against the sides of the boat. "Hey, open the creel, will you."

When he had pried the lure from its mouth, he dropped the bass in the open basket. "I'm one up on you. You should pick up your pole."

"No. We need to talk."

"Okay. You know the wise-guy kid, Garrett?"

Tom shook his head. "You see, right there. Bad idea to label these young people."

Steve side-stepped that but set his pole down. "He was smart-mouthing on the Trinity trek, and I made him do push-ups. I could tell he hated it. He hated *me*. But when we got back, he came to see me in private and apologized. Asked me to give him a chance."

"Steve, listen—"

"No, listen to me. In the Marines, I led a lot of guys with big egos. I learned that sometimes you gotta break through that ego. Inside, you might find a guy who's willing to learn. But like I said, in a dangerous situation I don't care if someone likes me or hates me, as long as they stay alive to do the job that needs to be done. If that raises their self-esteem—okay, fine. From my perspective, they just need to do what I tell them."

"Some of these young people are here because they were pressured to listen to the wrong adult telling them what to do."

"I can't sort that part out. That's the Troverts' job back here. I need to know if I have the authority out there in these mountains to do what I do to keep them alive."

"Steve, there isn't a *back here* and an *out there*. There's just *here*—the whole Lost Lake program. It has to all work together."

"You're the one who really wanted me to be here, Tom. I'm only here to train the kids who give a crap—for one year. I didn't sign on to play nursemaid to any kid who's playing a game or has something to hide.

"And have you thought about this? Suppose I help you guys weed out the kids who don't deserve to be here? The kids who just wanted a vacation from juvie. Wouldn't that be a valuable contribution?—Remember, Tom, you knew what you were getting when you presented this job to me."

"Don't push that off on me. You're the one who agreed to come. *You* knew what you were getting into, as well."

"I feel like I didn't have much choice."

"Sometimes it's the narrow gate that leads us where we need to go. In fact, it often is."

Steve opened his mouth to object, then stopped. "That sounds like a famous quote. Who said that?"

Tom smiled at him, picked up his pole, and attached a lure to a steel leader at the end of his line. "Someone famous. Look it up. And just remember, you're part of a team, not the head of it. And not a 'detachment'. You should understand chain-of-command.—Now I'm going to see if I can land that huge pike before you or Grady do."

7ᵀᴴ

"Why isn't Dugan here?" Jalil grumbled, wiping down one side of a huge glass terrarium. "He signs-in to work, then he sneaks away. A lot."

"Who cares. He's as big a jerk as Garrett. I wish he wasn't in our tribe."

Makayla glanced at the small bucket that held the golden salamanders while they cleaned their habitat. "I think I'm in love," she said.

Jalil looked across the tank. "Really?" he grinned. "I can totally get into it."

She looked at him without enthusiasm. "Not with you. With these guys."

She set down her paper towel and reached into the bucket, where the two small creatures brought from the flow lands had become very still.

"Oh." Jalil's face went blank. When he spoke again, his voice was flat and challenging. "I don't think you're supposed to be touching them as much as you do."

Gently with two fingers, she lifted one out, and set it on the back of one hand.

"Look how beautiful it is. I love these tiny red spots on its back. They're like jewels."

"You should put it back," he said, with firmness. "They're cool, but we're not supposed to mess around with them. Jo's orders."

She stroked the creature's back—watching it wriggle just slightly. Then it stopped and went limp.

"Oh no.—*Oh no!*" she shouted. *"Jo!"*

"These guys have been a mystery to me since we brought them in," Jo said, then paused, examining the salamanders under a lens. "And. . . ."

Makayla and Jalil waited, staring at the two small, lifeless creatures, whose golden color was fading to gray.

". . .and somehow," she continued in a moment, "I don't think that a predator attack is what started these guys on a downward spiral. It's very weird that after weeks of observation and care, they'd both expire at the same time."

"They're so cool," Jalil said, his expression morose. "I was hoping they'd like, lay eggs and hatch some babies."

Makayla sounded contrite. "Did they die because we handled them?"

Jalil stared at her.

"I mean because *I* handled them. Just a little."

"Not very likely. Even though they've been given proper nutrition, their bodies are slightly emaciated. It's something else. Maybe a water-borne pathogen—but lord, I hope not."

"Why?"

"*Batrachochytrium salamandrivorans* is a fungal pathogen that causes chytridiomycosis in salamanders."

They stared at her.

"It means that a fungus invades the cells of an animal—in this case, amphibians like salamanders and frogs. It's a huge problem in Europe, and we hope like hell it doesn't show up here. It's wiping out whole populations in some areas. That doesn't mean it's what took out these guys, but we're on guard watching for it."

Makayla was wiping her hands on her jeans vigorously.

"Relax," Jo said, "you're safe. It doesn't infect humans. But you should minimize contact with any animal that comes in for study or rehab. They aren't pets.

"Remember, a big part of your program is learning exactly how to care for other living creatures. That means treating them the way they need to be treated, not how you want to treat them. It's a practical way to show respect.—Since you're here to learn life skills, that's a good rule of thumb for life in general."

"Should we bury them?" Jalil asked.

"No. I'm going to send them out for study. I don't have the equipment needed to detect a pathogen like *Batrachochytrium*. And if that's what it is, we're facing big trouble and need to know."

After Laurel Wysocki's morning talk on edible plants and barks, Dugan skipped chores at the barn and went alone again into Kate's library. It was a massive high-ceilinged room with rolling ladders to reach shelves twelve feet up, and he had been sampling books for a half-hour or so when Kate came in.

"I'm glad to see that a few of you are using my collection. Ray-Ray comes in here a lot, and Imani. Sometimes Makayla. What do you like to read?"

"Doubt you have it, but you said you'd order books we want—right?"

"There are ten thousand volumes here. What's the title?"

"The Souls of Black Folk."

Kate motioned for him to follow her. Across the room she pointed to two long shelves with a mix of hardbacks and paperbacks.

"My collection of Black essayists is here. I have all of W.E.B. Du Bois' books. I have admired him as a grandfather of the Civil Rights Movement. Here's the one you want. I'm sure you know, it's a classic of American literature."

Dugan pushed his glasses up on the bridge of his nose and scanned the hundred or so book spines. "You have Zadie Smith's books?"

"She's brilliant.—If you're looking for a particular title that's not here I'll order it."

He whistled. "You already have it—*Black Panthers Speak*. Amazing."

"Why is that? Everyone should know what really happened back then. How the Panthers started out and how the FBI and the media collaborated to turn White Americans against them."

"Why you so interested in what Black writers have to say?"

Kate pulled a thick hardback off one shelf. "When I studied at Georgetown—where Tom Baden was doing campus ministry, by the way—I dated this man." She showed Dugan the title, *God of the*

Black Experience, and the picture of the handsome Black man on the back cover.

"Ephraim Hennepin was a theology student. Exceptionally bright and witty. We dated for a year. He opened my eyes to what Du Bois referred to as the other side of the 'veil'—the world of Black Americans as opposed to the mostly-White world I was raised in."

"You went out with a Black guy."

"I did. And after Ephraim, I met my husband."

"I guess your family wasn't too happy about you being with a Black man?"

"My father liked Ephraim a lot. They talked sports and religion and smoked cigars together. My mother was a little concerned about us being a mixed-race couple, but she loved Ephraim. He showed her how to make a great Beef Wellington. His family worked hard to put an end to us. They lived in the south and were afraid about their son dating a White woman. That's when I first really understood about Jim Crow."

"His family knew the reality your parents didn't."

Kate seemed to withdraw inside herself for a moment. "You know, I believe I would have been a lot happier with Ephraim than the man I married. Jim Holman."

"Seriously?" Dugan looked around the library and spread his arms. "You wouldn't have all this. Mountains. Rivers and waterfalls. Lost Lake. For all this, hell, *I* woulda married him."

She laughed. "I do love it here, don't get me wrong. But it takes more than money and possessions to make a person happy. Seeing you all enjoying yourselves and starting on a new path in life. That's what makes me happy. Anyway, I'm glad to see that you like to read."

He grinned.

But you didn't marry the Black guy. And I hafta cleanse my mind of all the 'everybody be nice and just get along' crap you're feedin' us here. There's a war going on against my race.

The pungent odor inside the smaller bear cub's pen made Rocco pull back. The cub was asleep, the black fur of its sides rising and falling rapidly with its shallow breathing. In the next pen, the larger cub was pacing and bawling, clawing at the wire so vigorously it rattled. Even with the noise, the small cub did not stir.

He was used to the smell of the cubs' feces and urine, even food ignored and gone sour, but the smell from the small cub was something else. A hostile, infected smell.

Reaching into the cage, he nudged the cub awake. It did not move, but opened its eyes and mouth and tried to make a sound. Nothing came out.

"Dude. What's wrong?"

The cub was focused on his face, and for a moment he felt as if the look in its golden eyes was an appeal to him for help. Comfort.

Rocco felt a twinge in his chest, and took off the rubber gloves. "Hang on, buddy. I'm only leaving you for a minute. I'll be right back."

In the clinic, he found Jo at the examining table, carefully lifting one wing of a small blue jay. The creature's yellowish beak was huge compared to its head and turned down at the corners in a froggy kind of frown. It blinked its black-bead eyes, and let out a shrill *cheep*, which made its whole little body jump.

"What's wrong with that guy?" It was hard to tell if the tufts of blue and white fluff sticking out all over were there because it was so young or because it was injured. There was no sign of blood or a bent wing.

Ray-Ray, who was wiping white-and-yellow mess from the stainless steel table, said, "She just found a puncture wound in one wing. It could be broken, which would not be good. Some lady in town just rescued this little guy from her cat."

"The puncture isn't serious," Jo amended. "Jays are feisty, even this young one. He almost pecked the cat's eye out, and really wants to hop and flap."

"Whoa, *respect*," said Rocco.

"Even so, I'm treating him with antibiotics in case of infection and a small dose of Meloxicam for pain. Let's see if he's one of the lucky ones."

Ray-Ray's expression became serious. "What do you mean?"

"Birds that are attacked by cats and sustain bite wounds don't have a great survival rate."

"But he looks tough," said Rocco. "He could make it, right?"

Jo did not answer directly. She slid the jay into a small cage at the end of the table, and it let out another shrill, high-pitched *cheep*. "We'll see. Please take him to the aviary, Ray."

"You should come look at the little cub," Rocco said to her. "He smells weird, and I don't think he's eating. His food is spilled and he didn't eat much of it."

She lifted the cub gently with one hand, and it came up like a black, furry ragdoll, head and legs limp. She lifted his muzzle with the other hand. "You're right. He's weak, and it happened very fast."

In the other cage, the cub's brother gave a loud, strong, bawling sound, and paced. The blaze of blond fur on its shoulder was more visible now.

"Hey, calm down over there, Flash man."

Jo frowned. "I told you guys not to name the animals. They're not pets. That guy's going back to the wild. Soon."

"It's hard not to like them. They're cool. So, what's going on with this little guy?"

"The sharp smell from his feces makes me think his bile acid levels may be too high. I'll run some tests to check his liver function."

"What'll that tell you?"

"Whether or not he has liver disease. If that's present and not treated, he won't last long. Meantime, make sure you wear a surgical mask and wash your hands thoroughly when you have to lift him to clean his pen. His immune system is very weak. Oh, and you're going to be feeding him from a bottle with a puppy milk replacer. It works for bears, too. I'll let everyone know you're going to be in here doing some middle-of-the-night feedings. This guy's on a knife-edge."

9TH

Sahm could hear, down the lake from his cabin, sounds of happy shouts and cheering. A few of the young people—Rocco, Jalil, Imani, Makayla—had tied a rope to the limb of a silver maple. They were using it to swing out over the lake and drop into the water. Each time someone did, they came up yelling. The September nights had chilled the water.

He went on stacking wood in the small shed beneath the white pine near his cabin, until a voice called from behind.

"I never said thanks for catching me when I fell off the rock in front of your cabin that night," Dhani said, approaching. "I probably would've been really hurt if you weren't there."

Vajra came from where he was watching in the tree line, and allowed the boy to stroke one of his ears.

"Why *were* you there that night? I've been wondering. Did I yell in my sleep and wake you up or something?"

Sahm smiled, but he was not ready to say the full truth—"*I was asleep and saw you approaching in my dream.*" He would have to prepare the boy a bit more and be sure he was ready before disclosing what he now knew. Young initiates, even if they were great souls from the past, could do harm to themselves and others if they did not know how to handle extraordinary gifts. Ego was always a tricky adversary to reckon with and had ruined many a gifted yogi.

"You came today because something is on your mind—Steve Tanner."

Dhani's mouth fell open and he stopped petting Vajra. "Yeah. How do you just know stuff like that?"

"When the two of you were here, you both looked as if you had touched something poisonous."

"Yeah, I wish you hadn't let him come inside your cabin. It just felt bad."

"Now I know what the poison was."

"Yeah—him. He's a bad person."

Sahm stacked more oak pieces. "No, no, no. No one is poison. The poison is always in us. We have the wrong view of things when we think that events and people have power over us. Then we experience fear and hatred. We remain unconscious of the forces at work within us. *That* is the poison."

"What are you talking about? I didn't do anything to him. He just doesn't like me. I think he hates me."

"So, you both have the poison. That is one reason why you are both here together."

"He stares at me like he's disgusted or wants to punish me. I've made up my mind. I'm going to do whatever I have to, to stay as far away from Tanner as possible."

Here is a Great One who has returned, Sahm thought. *How can it be that his powerful energies are so blocked in the presence of this man?* "That will be very difficult, since he is your instructor. How will you do that?"

Dhani had become distracted. "I don't know, but I'm going to." He shifted from one foot to the other, and changed the subject. "Hey, I know this is a big favor to ask, but—can we go inside?"

Standing beside Sahm's altar table, Dhani picked up the small, white stone Sahm's grandfather had given him. One side of the quartzite was smooth and gleaming, the other pocked and rough and like a face.

"I really, really like this stone your grandfather gave you. It's cool that his old, meditation teacher gave it to him. You said before

I could take it with me. I've thought about it ever since I was here last time."

Sahm nodded, deep in thought. Again, Dhani knew something he had never been told. In fact, the stone was to be used in a powerful meditation practice, and it had been passed down from Sahm's grandfather's teacher and from many teachers before that.

"You may take it with you, if that is what you came to ask. In fact, you should keep it."

Dhani stared at him open-mouthed. "But your grandfather gave it to you, and you brought it here all the way from Tibet."

"We don't cling to anything in this life, Dhani. Since it speaks to you, I am sure this stone came here to find *you.*—Now let us get back to talking about you and Steve Tanner, because you must learn to live and work together."

"Whoa—did you know these pock marks on the stone look like a face? There's the eyes and nose. This crooked line is the mouth."

Sahm studied him, and shook his head. Clearly, Dhani had slammed shut the door of conversation about Steve Tanner again. Pressing him now would be a waste. Still, he would have to help him deal with his fear of the critical, young Marine or his time here at Lost Lake would only become more difficult. If a simple object like the stone would help to awaken and strengthen him, then it should be in his hands.

In five minutes, Sahm stood out on the porch, Vajra at his side, watching Dhani retreat to his cabin. Why did this boy reach out to him, start to open, then turn away? *He is like the bird that circles and circles, but is too wary to light."*

The sky had clouded over, and he heard voices of the swimmers coming along the lakefront path.

"Carter actually got a higher arc on the rope swing than you did, man." It was the boy named Jalil, at Rocco's heels like a too-eager puppy.

"I said shut up—," and there was swearing from Rocco.

"I don't get why you hate me so much."

He watched them pass, curious. He was sure more was happening here at Lost Lake than met the eye.

Dzes-Sa's voice sounded silently. *"They have all come here for their own lesser reasons. But there is another, higher purpose for each one."*

"What is their purpose?" he whispered back.

There was no reply.

In a moment, his thoughts returned to the last exchange with Dhani just now.

"It's weird," Dhani had remarked, "but this stone kind of makes me think about things. Like right now I'm thinking about the eagle in Jo's clinic—and I really want to help Jo find out why he can't fly. Does this thing have powers, like does it communicate with your mind or something?"

"The power is not in any stone or object," he had replied, "though it is true that even natural objects have their own kind of sentience."

Dhani had stared blankly. "What is *sentience*?"

"Awareness. Everything has its own kind of awareness and its connection to everything else."

"I don't even know what that means."

"I will explain everything to you. A little at a time. When you are ready. But yes, there is something about the stone that will help you open your mind."

Watching Dhani's figure grow smaller in the distance, Sahm thought,

And when you are ready to understand what kind of power is in you, perhaps I will know what I am to do about it.

10TH

"There were violent wind shears with the storm that rolled in last night," Jo told them. "Two campers were killed just south of here. A tree came down on their tent. People shouldn't be out in the wilderness if they don't know what they're doing."

Claire looked at Ray-Ray and mouthed, *That was cold.*

Jo finished her instruction on cleaning the bird bath containers. "Always be sure to wear rubber gloves when you're cleaning up around birds. Their feces carry a lot of bacteria, like *e. coli*. And—," she focused on Claire's irritable look, "—I know it sounds cold, but the wilderness is totally unforgiving. I'm trying to make the point that you guys need to pay close attention to your instructors. Out there, it can make the difference between being safe and being really sorry."

When she left the aviary to check on Dhani, who was hosing off mats outside, the mood was somber.

"Nobody said we would be in danger coming here," Ray-Ray muttered.

"We were in danger where we were," said Claire.

Ray-Ray nodded, and looked grim. "So this is our first official act as the Eagle Tribe—cleaning greasy bird mess. I thought learning to care for rehab animals was going to be, I don't know. . . ."

"Less smelly and disgusting. More fun?"

"I pictured myself feeding little baby birds, like that busted up little bluejay over in that cage. I like that little guy."

"The parents chew up worms and spit them in the babies' mouths. Go for it."

Ray-Ray fake-gagged. "Can I ask you something?"

She didn't answer for a moment, and the only sound was the sudden, heavy drumming of rain on the roof. The noise seemed to drive the aviary inmates into hiding in their leafy shelters.

"I can't promise I'll answer."

"Sometimes you seem to care about Dhani a lot. Like during the wetlands hike and after the crazy thing that happened up on Peregrine. Other times—I know you've got some heavy stuff going on—but you pull away and keep your distance. And I see how much that messes with his head."

"Well, right now some self-promoting prosecutor in Virginia is messing with *my* head."

"I thought that was called off?"

"For now."

"I'm just saying that Dhani's already insecure around you. When you avoid him and hide out, it makes him crazy. The more I hang out with him, the more I know he's a really good guy."

"If he's insecure that's on him. I think he's insecure, period."

"But then you switch back and take his part. I see how that confuses him."

"I stick up for him when he gets bullied. I hate bullies."

"So you don't really like him, *per se*. You just don't like Garrett."

Dhani came slopping in then, his sneakers and the lower part of his jeans soaked, dragging a stack of rubber mats that made a wet, slopping noise.

"It just started pouring again," he said. He hauled one large mat to the far end of the barn, and dropped it in front of the janitor's sink.

"I don't like Garrett or Tanner," Claire finished in a low voice. "They both act like they're superior to everybody. Tanner needs to quit his jerky military act. We're kids, not Marines."

Dhani was walking away from them, back to the stack of mats. Since he'd entered the aviary the air had begun to fill with loud bird calls.

"But what do you think about him?" Ray-Ray asked quietly. "I mean, listen to this. It happens almost every time he's in here."

She considered. "Maybe seeing the black hoody flips them out. But you're right. There's something strange about him."

"Something. . .*bad*?"

"No. Something really unusual, though. He doesn't scare me, but I think we should both keep a close eye on him. I don't think he knows the effect he has on animals."

17TH

Ten days of steady rain and a few late-season thunderstorms finally cleared out. After another two days, the trails were dry enough to hike. Impatient to get her annual hawk migration count underway, Jo had sent Ron and Randy up Eagle Rock Mountain the night before, to prep for the groups' arrival.

Now it was early morning, just after 7:00, the day promising to be clear and cool. Late summer hot spells and windless days were over. Hawks would be on the move, riding the rising fall air currents.

Jo led the sleepy, straggling hikers, who were either sullen or mildly complaining, while Laurel had positioned herself in the middle, and Steve came last. Jo was fine with him keeping a big distance between them. Hopefully, he would not pull his ex-Marine bit on her watch.

"You'll be working in your teams, stationed at four different points on top of the mountain. Something very unusual is going on with the migration this year and I need you guys to be alert and help me get the most accurate count possible."

"On *top*? All the way up there?" Tia Leesha complained, staring at the tall peak.

In two hours, they were nearing the summit. The line had broken up, with slower hikers straggling behind.

"Why does the forest below us have wavy lines in it?" asked Makayla, staring out at the arc of the mountainside.

Laurel smiled. "You have sharp eyes. Those are called 'fir waves'—crescent-shaped bands of dead and dying balsam firs. They're flanked on one side by mature trees that are dying, and on the other by younger firs and other types of trees that are renewing the forest. The waves move over the slopes at about five feet per year. Death and regeneration is a natural process of the forest."

A shift in the wind brought a rush of cool air, and Makayla pulled the collar of her jacket up and shivered. "How does anything grow up here? It's getting so cold, and it's only September."

"Cold?" said Jalil. He'd taken off his sweatshirt. "Climbing made me hot."

"How can you have so much energy?" Imani asked him. "You're like a—a crazy little dog running around. Are you *on* something?"

"We're climbing the western slope," said Jo. "Up ahead, the trail will wrap around to the south, and there'll be more sun."

Laurel replied to Makayla's question. "Alpine tundra plants—you'll see them at the summit—they're very well-adapted to cold. I'll show you different microclimates up there. Black spruce, blue rock lichens, a little waxy white flower called 'mountain bride', pink rosebay, and even tiny azaleas thrive in extreme weather. Whatever takes root up there has to be very hearty because like I said before, the temp can drop to, say, forty- or fifty-below in the winter."

"I tried to ignore that. *Forty below*?"

"Only sometimes. Just for a few days."

"But how does anything survive?"

"Rule of thumb—stay low to the ground and stay tightly packed.

Keeps the heat in. Good rule for plants, animals, and for people if you ever get lost. Keep the wind off you in a shelter, even if it's under a pile of leaves, and curl up in a ball."

The slower hikers had arrived.

Tia Leesha, who had been trudging beside Emmalyn, was wheezing.

Claire, who was with them, Dhani at her heels, turned to her. "You okay?"

"No, I'm not 'okay,'" Tia Leesha gasped. "I think my asthma is startin' up. I'm prolly gonna have a heart attack and die."

"I saw your medicine inhaler-thing on the shelf in the bathroom. I was gonna ask if you needed it, but I forgot." said Emmalyn.

Steve had come up from behind. "Did you make that personal needs survival checklist I told you guys to make?"

Tia Leesha grunted—a noncommittal sound that could have meant *yes* or *no*.

"I told you guys about the Marines' rule of *self*-aid. The first person you prepare yourself to take care of is you, so out in the field no one else has to take care of you." He stared at Tia Leesha. "You need to be more responsible for yourself."

"I have an emergency inhaler in my pack," Laurel said, unzipping a pocket. "The second rule," she said, looking at Steve, "is *buddy*-aid. My brother was a Marine. When someone isn't able or prepared to care for themselves, we step up and help them."

Tia Leesha took the inhaler. "I need something stronger than this. Just that what I need ain't legal."

Further up the slope, the line emerged from the heavier forest onto the southern face of the mountain. Here, there was full sunlight, and its warmth at mid-morning penetrated their jackets and sweaters.

Ahead of Rocco on the trail now, Imani took off her sweatshirt and tied it around her waist. On a steep incline, which involved a scramble over an open rock face on all fours, it came loose.

Rocco came up behind her. "I got you." He put his hand on her hip and gave her a push.

Imani's head whipped around. "Please take your hand off me."

Rocco pulled back, and smiled at her from behind as she kept climbing. "Nice. Very nice."

"You're a big flirt."

"I flirt. You flirt. We all flirt for dee-ssert."

"I am not your dessert. And didn't I tell you to leave me alone I'm not interested? This is starting to become harassment."

Garrett and Dugan had caught up from below. "Come on. Keep moving."

Rocco ignored them and called up to Imani, who was climbing again. "I express my appreciation for the view, and that's harassment?"

Imani's face, which had been ruddy with exertion, flushed red with anger. "Back. Off. I just gave you a clear warning—and, yes, beyond this point it will be harassment."

"I don't get you. You don't mind sitting across from me at almost every meal. And all I said was—"

"Sitting across from you doesn't give you permission to put your hands on my body."

"Girls. I don't get any of you. You flirt, and then you're mad when a guy responds."

"What part of 'don't touch my body' don't you get? Now *shut up*."

Garrett leaned close to Dugan. "Hear that? He won't leave her alone. Step up, man."

Dugan grabbed Rocco's arm. "The lady said to leave her alone. You hard of hearing or just stupid?"

Rocco yanked his arm away. "Never put your hands on me. Never."

"Oh, it's okay you put *your* hands on *her.*"

Rocco smirked. "Notice how she never pays attention to you. Probably because she thinks you're a no-good."

Imani had stopped and was looking down on both of them. "You both need to shut up, go away, and leave me alone. I am not a—a—a hotdog for you two sorry wolves to fight over."

A hundred yards up the slope, Imani was still silent and angry. She turned to locate Makayla, who had suddenly lagged behind and was grinning.

"What's funny?—'cuz see, I'm not laughing."

"'I'm not a *hotdog* for you to fight over'?" Makayla sank sideways against the scored trunk of a hickory tree, and burst into laughter.

Imani's face clouded. Then broke into a grin.

"From now on. . .," Makayla gasped between laughing spasms, "I'm going to call you. . . *Hottie Hotdog.*"

"*Shut up.*" Imani put both hands over her face, her sides starting to shake with laughter.

Makayla doubled over, mocking. "'Hey guys, how do you like my buns?'"

"I will kill you in your sleep."

The summit of Eagle Rock Mountain was bathed in pale gold morning light that fell through high clouds in the southeast. The open face was divided by forests of stunted black spruce and small carpets of alpine meadow.

"All those days of rain brought in an unsettled weather front that created the perfect conditions for the hawk migration," Jo said.

Randy Wolfmoon, Laurel Wysocki, and Mike Yazzie had led three tribes off to other viewing points.

"I told you guys I'm involved in some important studies, and today I'm trying to help solve a mystery," she told Dhani, Claire and Ray-Ray. "So let's get going."

She led them to the western edge of the summit. From here, they could see Lost, Peregrine, and Trinity Mountains. Also part of Lost Lake, the northern shore of which was hidden by Eagle Rock Mountain's heavily-forested slopes.

"We're here," she began, "to count the hawks, falcons, and eagles that are moving southward along mountain ridges and waterways. They catch rising currents of warm air and light winds from the north, and they can travel a hundred miles a day without once flapping their wings."

Dhani set his daypack down beside a tripod with a large, black scope mounted on it. Ron, who had affixed the scope, closed the gray metal case he had taken it from, and moved on to do more setup.

"I want you three to watch specifically for broad-winged hawks. Ray-Ray, you'll be using this spotting scope Ron anchored here on the tripod. And by the way, this case—it's got the scopes the other groups will need. They'll be coming to ask for them."

"What's special about broad-winged hawks?" Ray-Ray asked, squinting into the eyepiece.

"Other kinds of hawks migrate in small groups or alone, and travel closer to the ground. Broad-wings migrate in flocks, but very high up where it's hard to see them."

"How will I know if I see one—or a group of them?"

"They have very distinctive, rounded wings and banded tails. I'm posting you at this station, with the strongest scope. Focus in on any speck you see way up. If you see a group of specks, you've probably picked out a kettle."

"A what?"

"A kettle is what you call a group of hawks. Now listen, you gotta stay on top of it. Look at the eastern sky. With these banks of low clouds blowing through, watch carefully. Sometimes, the broad-wings spiral up to a great height until the warm updrafts cool and they can't go higher. Then they suddenly drop down to catch anothe r big, warm draft on its way up. So you could witness a dramatic rising and falling action. Usually, they drop one by one. Makes it easy to count them."

"Whoa, this scope is amazing. I can see—wait, I see one. Pretty sure it's a hawk. But the wings aren't rounded like you said."

"Not a broad-winged, then. They're white underneath, with distinctive dark bands on the underside of each wing and on the tail. Here's a picture. Look for this." Jo flipped through a dog-eared field guide, and held it open as Ray-Ray, Claire, and Dhani gathered around.

"Where are they going?" asked Claire.

"Central and South America. Then they ride right back here on the thermals of spring as the north country warms up."

"All the way back here? Why?"

"These boreal forests and mountains are their primal breeding grounds. They need to be far from humans when they nest and hatch out their young. And here in the wilderness there are huge numbers of small mammals—mice, chipmunks, squirrels, even rabbits—for them to feed on. In the spring, you'll see their courtship display. Pretty dramatic. They circle really high in the air, then drop like a lightning bolt toward the ground. Usually, the males are the most dramatic, trying to impress the females with their flying and hunting skills."

"Why are they being counted?"

"Other watchers are counting the goshawks. That species flies all the way to Argentina in the winter, and they fill the trees in one particular area. The locals go in every night and shoot them by the hundreds—tens of thousands are killed each winter and others are too wounded to return north."

"Is that what happened to the eagle back in the aviary?" asked Dhani. "Somebody wounded him?"

"No, I've told you, he's a complete puzzle. All these months, and I still have absolutely no idea what's going on. It's like he's broken, but nothing's visibly wrong.

"Anyway," she shifted back to the count, we'll come back in the spring, when these birds migrate back up here to their home territories. Most will return to within the same square mile and even to the exact nests they built the previous year, and they'll fight off new birds that try to take them over."

Claire's eyebrows shot up. "They find their way back to the exact same place they left—all the way from South America? How do they do that?"

"Experiments have shown that some migratory birds, like warblers and buntings, can navigate by the stars. Coming north, they orient themselves by the constellations immediately surrounding Polaris—the north star."

"That's *ridiculous!*" Dhani blurted.

Jo flashed him a severe look.

Claire intervened. "He means incredible, amazing—'ridiculous' means, you know, *wow*."

Jo pointed Dhani to a tripod and camera Ron was now setting up thirty yards away, on the other side of the open summit. "Well, I want you to get some *ridiculous* pictures of birds today. See that huge telescopic lens? Take as many shots of broad wing kettles as you can. That's your job. See—Ron's over there anchoring the second tripod right now in case there are wind gusts. He'll show you how the camera works."

"Why is it over there? Why can't I hang out here with Ray-Ray?"

"I need both of you to focus and concentrate. If you're together, you might distract each other. Claire, I'm giving you this field journal and this anemometer—a wind speed gauge—so you can record your impressions of the day, shifts in the wind and weather, and times when the guys tell you more birds are in view."

"What are the other groups doing?"

"The same thing, but with different species—red-tails, goshawks, kestrels. Like I said, broad-wings can travel in huge clusters, so I want you to concentrate on counting and photographing *just* them."

Ray-Ray had listened carefully. "Wait—you said before that you're trying to solve a mystery."

"I did. The migration patterns are changing radically. I want to find out how much the migration has shifted west from its normal route—then I can work with environmentalists to figure out why. The migration usually follows major waterways miles east of here, where the fishing is great. We're curious as to why we're seeing so many birds this far west this year. Something seems to be happening to the environment on a big scale."

Jo had moved on to instruct the other three teams, and in twenty minutes Dugan arrived.

"Hey, R, Jo sent me to ask you for a scope. She said to get an eighty-millimeter one."

Ray-Ray stepped back from the tripod, and squatted to open the case. "Why are you doing that—listening to Garrett?"

"He's got my back."

"Where is he now—feeding more crap to someone else?"

"He sure ain't like your good friend, *Singe*. Everyone's scared of that mofo."

Ray-Ray looked up at him. "C'mon, Garrett's got your mind. You're acting like his boy."

Dugan's expression hardened. "You just said the wrong thing to the wrong person. Muscle head called me a boy once. That's what started all this bad blood between us. And now you just did it. You wanna be on my enemy list, too?"

"No, I'm trying to be your friend. Look at it. Garrett points to Rocco, blows a dog whistle, and you bark. Think for yourself, that's all I'm saying." He stood, and stuck out his hand.

Dugan slapped it away, and grabbed the scope from Ray-Ray's other hand. "You tell me I'm some White kid's 'boy.' Well, you're the one sniffing around the pretty White girl. I notice you have no interest in ladies of color."

"I'm not doing this with you. I'm saying, for both of us, we need to stay who we are. As individuals. Not be influenced. That's what we're here to learn—how to respect our personal identity. I keep hearing in my head something Ta-Nehisi Coates wrote to all men of color. 'You are all we have, and you come to us endangered.' That's probably true for everyone."

Dugan shook his head. "Here's some more Coates for you.

"'In 2001, a researcher sent out Black and White job applicants in Milwaukee, randomly assigning them a criminal record. The researcher concluded that a White man *with a criminal record* had about the same chance of getting a job as a Black man *without one*.'"

"What does that have to do with what we're talking about right now?"

"I am not giving in to any White boy or man who thinks he's better than me. Not muscle head, not Garrett, not even Trovert or the rich lady. They're all tryin' to 'fix' us. I am my own man. I will fight everything and everyone who tries to keep me from getting what I want in life. I will be on top. And *I* will *be* a danger to Rocco if he keeps playin' his game."

"*That's* what you got out of Coates? *That's* what you get out of being in this program—that we should resist good people who are working hard to help us?"

"Are these 'good people' really tryin' to 'help us'? I don't know. I know for sure I can help myself."

"You know what? Sorry I tried to be a friend. Sorry you got into this program, too. Because you'll probably blow out of here by the end of the year, and meantime you're taking up space some kid who wants a better life could have. Until you wake up, you can just do whatever you want."

"I am awake, and I will do exactly what I want. Without your permission."

Ray-Ray turned back to his scope. "The one who has a game going on is Garrett. And because you just eat up his clever put-downs of everyone else, you don't see that he's got your mind. You gotta watch out for people like him."

Dugan began walking away. "White people turn on you when something bad goes down. Every time. I know that. You just remember who warned you."

"You called Dhani *'Singe'*," Ray-Ray called out, ignoring him. "Where'd that come from? You didn't think of it. A White boy named Garrett stuck that in your head."

At noon, Jalil opened the pack with the Salamander Tribe's lunches. Jo had agreed to let Claire draw the tribe's symbol on it—a salamander, bent in an S-curve—in permanent marker.

"I'm starving," he said.

Makayla sank down on a broad, flat rock next to the scope Dugan was manning.

"You okay?" Jalil called over from his camera stand.

"I'm fine," she snapped.

He tore the wrapper off a turkey sandwich, and took a huge bite. "You don't eat enough," he mumbled through a mouthful.

"Quit stalking me. And you spit out food while you were talking. Gross." Then she dropped her journal, swayed a little and put her hands behind her on the stone as if bracing to keep from falling.

Emmalyn emerged from a narrow path through the black spruce trees, with Steve Tanner immediately behind her.

"You guys got an extra pencil? I'm supposed to journal, but I dropped mine and it rolled right off the cliff."

"Everything okay here?" Tanner asked. "You guys hydrating after that hike?"

"I think Makayla's not okay," Jalil replied, chewing. "She needs food or water."

"I'm fine." She held up her water bottle. "See. I'm drinking. I'm just a little lightheaded." Then her voice cracked. "I wish everyone would leave me alone."

"You're upset about Rocco liking Imani, aren't you?" said Emmalyn.

Steve made eye-contact with Dugan. His look said, *"Oh god, girl drama."*

Dugan didn't smile, and looked irritated.

Makayla's eyes filled with tears, which she fought back. "I just feel so... *off*... here. Like I can't get myself together. Like everything is just wrong. I wish Olivia was here to talk to. I wish she hadn't suddenly just vanished, like every other counselor in the system. Just when you think someone really likes you, they disappear. I mean—what's wrong with me that people don't like me or they just dump me?"

"I like you," Jalil offered.

Emmalyn was staring. "Who's Olivia?"

"My social worker back in DC. Ms. Neri. She was the best. Really kind and patient. She listened to me and I knew she cared."

Steve had frozen in place. At the mention of Olivia, pain wrenched his stomach. And for a moment, there was only silence and the sound of a light, morning wind through the black spruce.

Jalil, who was keeping the tribe's journal for Jo, produced the small stub of pencil from a pants pocket and handed it to Emmalyn. "Here. I have an extra."

Steve had disappeared through the trees.

But he hadn't gone far when Emmalyn caught up to him on the path.

"You probably think it's pretty stupid when a girl has such really strong feelings for a guy, don't you? I mean, being a Marine and all. You guys are just tough. I get it."

Steve said nothing and wished a sinkhole would open up and swallow her. His pulse was pounding in his neck, and he felt sick. Images of Olivia's last morning rose up, not so much from his head but from a well of pain in his guts.

Her wounded look when he insulted her work with kids like Makayla.

Her eyes going blank as she lay on the sidewalk, looking far beyond him.

"Women have very strong feelings. Not like you guys. You must know that, though—right? I mean, don't you have a girlfriend? Were you ever married?"

Steve's mind raced, and his body burned with adrenalin. Why was she babbling—doing this to him? Pressing for personal information? He felt himself losing control, doubling his fists, wanting to turn and punch Emmalyn in the face to shut her up.

Instead, he took a deep breath. Another. And another. Trying to block the vivid images of Olivia.

The evening they met at a beach party, her tan-brown, middle-eastern skin set off by the white cotton blouse and light blue shorts. Her dark brown eyes drawing him to her, opening his heart.

He had stopped dead in his tracks. Now he looked around stunned, at the spruce trees, at the clouds scudding overhead on the light wind. He could not stop the flow of memories flooding into his mind, his body.

He felt her soft arms and legs, her breath against his cheek, her hands.

He shook his head violently and dug his fingernails into his palms.

Emmalyn had stopped, too, and was staring at him. "What just happened? What's wrong?"

"You got what you needed—right? A pencil." Steve's face was blank, his voice numb-sounding. He felt as if he were speaking from a thousand miles away—and as if the girl in front of him was not flesh and blood but a plastic talking doll. The kind that's mouth moves and silly, empty words babble out.

"I'm sorry if I ask too many questions. My mama says—"

"Go back to your team." Steve almost growled at her, pointing down the path ahead of them. "Start writing in that journal. That's your job. Get going."

Sahm had climbed to a slightly higher end of the broad summit where Jo had positioned the four groups. All morning, he had moved between them, helping Tia Leesha when she scraped her ankle on a stone, giving up his own lunch to Jalil, who complained loudly that they hadn't packed enough lunch for him. There was so much complaining—about being tired, about the crisp, fall wind, about having to count hawks—when all around them lay such a rolling, rising expanse of beauty. This annoyed him.

If there is a higher purpose for each one of them, he thought, remembering Dzes-Sa's words, *they will never find it, because their minds are so clouded with petty and negative thinking.*

In the space between two breaths, a halo of blue light engulfed the whole mountain top. In its shimmer, everything took on a dimension he had not seen before—as if each tree, rock and person had depths that lay concealed within them. Some of the students had a faint glow within them. Others looked dull.

A voice in his mind startled him.

"The chance to awaken comes to all, but it is possible that not all will do so. It is your job to watch for those who do, and help them clear the clouds."

Then the halo faded, was gone, and Sahm was left to ponder.

"Jo needs to recheck how many miles west we are from Lake Champlain," said Ron, entering the open rock space where he and Randy had pitched their tent the evening before. "She needs my GPS."

"I'm surprised she didn't bring her own."

"Lugging all the equipment up here was our job. That's why she sent us ahead. And to keep up the count after the kids go back down."

Sahm came into the clearing and stood next to Randy, who had built a fire out in the open, well away from the fragile plants on the nearby alpine tundra.

Ron dove into the small tent pitched on a thick bed of moss next to a wind-bent spruce.

"That one will have something to say soon," Sahm said to Randy, pointing to one rock in the fire circle. "You should move him away from the flames. Or stand back."

"That rock? Um. Okay. Sure."

"He does not want to be so close to the fire. He's starting to tell you now. You can hear him.—*Sssssssss*."

"That could be any one of these logs—"

A loud *bang* and pieces of exploding rock sent Randy leaping and falling backwards away from the fire. One small sharp piece had struck him on the chin, and a tiny red cut appeared.

"*Ow*. What the—?"

Sahm kicked a chunk of shattered rock that lay at his feet, a small thread of steam rising from it. "He tried to warn you. '*Sssssssss*' means 'you are using me in the wrong way'."

Randy examined pieces that lay all around him. "Quartzite."

"That kind of rock looks very hard," Sahm nodded, "but they can hold a lot of water. Then they shout and fly apart when you get them too hot. You can learn their language."

"You talk a lot like my grandfather and the other old ones." Randy shook his head, rubbing his chin. "When I was a kid, they sounded goofy to me—all their talk about natural objects and even places, as if they're alive. But looking back now, they were right about so much. I wish I'd listened more to what they had to say—," he smiled at Sahm. "—and to you just now. They always knew way in advance what kind of weather was coming, where the deer herd was most plentiful. All that natural world stuff."

Swearing from inside the tent distracted them, and the backside of Ron's jeans emerged through the flaps. He stood up, rifling through pockets in his pack.

"I can't find my device. Anyone seen it? Looks like a cellphone. Orange plastic, in a black rubber case. Has my initials—RC—on the front."

"What's it for?"

"It shows me a map of the whole area and pinpoints my location. I uploaded all the trails around Kate's property, so I can find my way to one. I did that in case I have to go off-trail and lose my bearings, and it took a lot of work."

"Maybe it fell out of your pack."

"Could be. One of the pockets was unzipped. I did pack in a hurry. Can you guys watch for it around the site here and on the trail back down? Needle in a haystack, but since it's a bright color it might stand out."

Jo had arrived. "What's all the noise over here?"

"A rock. Too close to the fire," Randy said. "And Ron lost his GPS."

Jo rolled her eyes. "This is the second one of these you've lost in the last three months—but who's counting. Where's your head at, Ron? I can't keep requisitioning replacements from Tom. It's taking money from my budget. If you don't find it, maybe Tanner will get you one from his. In fact—joy of joys—let me go see if Steve has his GPS with him. I need to know the exact distance from here to Champlain."

When she was gone, Randy grinned. "I better not tell her I've misplaced two sports watches since the program began." He held up his left wrist. "This is my third."

"Good. I don't feel so bad," said Ron.

"Yeah, I'm not usually this forgetful. Well, sometimes I can be. I keep thinking I left it on top of the dresser in my room at the cabin. Near where I put my wallet at night. But twice when I went to get it, it wasn't there."

Ron smirked. "I've seen the top of your dresser. Maybe if you tossed all those empty bottles and granola boxes in the recycling, you wouldn't lose things on it."

"Oh right, Mr. I Can't Even Keep Track of My *GPS*." Randy smiled at his own joke.

Sahm had been quiet, listening. "Maybe you should ask your grandfather to help you find your lost things."

"Dude." Randy shook his head. "He's gone." He waved one hand in the air. "He's out there. Crossed over. On the other side."

Sahm's face lit up. "That is good."

Randy and Ron looked at each other with mildly shocked expressions that said—*Seriously?*

"From the other side," said Sahm, "he may be able to help you even more."

He saw her crossing the mountain's crest above him, and winced when she headed to the downhill trail after him.

"Tanner," Jo called.

He kept descending, and thought about continuing as if he hadn't heard. He wanted to find a second bivouac site over here on Eagle Rock Mountain for a higher-altitude trek and campout in a couple of months. That would be his reason for leaving the group and going out on his own. Earlier, before reaching the summit, he'd seen a side trail leading to the south side of the mountain.

"*Tanner*," Jo called louder. "*Stop.*"

He paused and, rather than go to her, made her clamber down the light scree to him.

"What?"

She reached him, said nothing for a moment, and looked at him carefully. "I need to stay focused on the count, and the kids said you checked-in with them. Everyone okay?"

He suspected her words were a probe, meaning, "Are *you* okay?" Why was everyone trying to dig into his head today?

"The blonde girl. Short haircut. Very thin. She's lightheaded. Also emotional about something. Is that all you wanted to know?"

"Her name's Makayla. They've been here almost four months. You should make an effort to learn their names."

He didn't need this right now. "Lotsa things I should do."

Jo wanted to say, *"Yeah, like stop thinking you're better than everyone"*—but said, "Do you have your GPS? Ron lost his again. I just need it for a minute."

He reached under the edge of his jacket, and removed the orange-and-black device hooked to his belt, then held it out.

Jo flicked a switch. "Twenty-two-point-three miles to Lake Champlain from this spot." *And a million miles from Steve Tanner.*

She thrust the device back at him. "Thanks." The word had a cold bite—and the instant she let it fly she wished it didn't.

Just for a second, as their eyes met, Steve looked like a lost boy inside a strong-looking Marine's body.

As his back retreated down the trail, Jo pretended not to watch him. Her harshness had changed his expression instantly to that of a wary and hostile creature. Or a wounded one. The look had stung her heart.

Why are you so unlikable? And why do I want to just hold and take care of you?

Then she felt angry at herself. She rescued wild creatures. Not men. Especially no more self-centered *or* wounded men. Which were the same animal. They let you get close, then drew blood.

She turned back uphill. Whatever the flash of sadness was about, Tanner was on his own. She needed to check on Makayla.

"*Guys!*" Claire called from down the slope. "*You gotta see this!*"

Dhani and Ray-Ray looked across the open rock at each other, then at the huge boulder where Claire had positioned herself earlier to write. They'd seen her sketching, too. Now her coat was there, but not her or her drawing pad.

"You go," said Ray-Ray. "I might miss some broad-wings and throw off Jo's count."

Dhani found her a short way downhill, next to a steep slope. Just below them, a lone yellow birch had grown out from the mountainside over a sheer drop-off. Below, a hundred feet or more, were the cast-offs left after a rockslide.

"*There,*" she said excitedly, pointing twenty yards further down toward the edge of a cliff—at something white and rounded on the top.

It looked as if someone had left, right there on the bare rock, a large, feathered bowling pin. In a second, the rounded top swiveled and a face stared up at them. Great, yellow eyes blinked, then looked away, surveying the green forested slopes below.

"What the heck?"

"Snowy owl. I found it in Jo's field guide."

Dhani could see in Claire's pad that she'd begun sketching it, capturing perfectly the broad face and rondure of its body. "Why is it on the ground? Shouldn't it be hiding in a hollow tree? Isn't that what owls do?"

"The guide says snowy owls hunt right from the ground. They find a high point and watch for prey in the forest below them. Snakes, mice, moles. I think he's watching something right now."

Further down, several stories below, the evergreen forest of the mountain's upper slopes met the hardwood and fir forest mix. Beneath this canopy grew a thick undergrowth. The owl seemed fixated on something there.

"It's so pure white." Dhani's voice was filled with a quiet wonder. "Just like—"

"Snow?"

The owl hunched its wings suddenly, its head shifting side to side, focused and ready to spring. Then it tilted away from the cliff, spread broad wings, and spiraled out on the currents. Down and down over the trees it arced, becoming a smaller and smaller, circling white crescent of wings. Just above the under-canopy of laurels, the owl fanned the air and thrust out its taloned feet. Suddenly, it disappeared inside a thicket of leave and branches.

For a few moments, they heard nothing—then from below there was a small commotion, a rustling, and the white owl emerged from the thicket. Wings flapping hard, its take-off sluggish, it struggled to hoist a medium-sized, brown rabbit that was kicking and thrashing. Pumping harder, gaining altitude a little with every powerful wingbeat, the owl rose slowly higher and higher. It labored its way to tree-top height, wrangling its struggling cargo.

From high above Dhani and Claire's position, a high-pitched shriek pierced the mountain air.

The owl was just above them now, when something like a blue-black bolt fell through the air, struck the white owl, and knocked the rabbit from its talons. The rabbit plummeted, kicking and twisting through the air, struck the rocky slope hard, and slid down to the base of a yellow, quaking aspen, where it lay unmoving.

The owl beat its wings twice—then folded and spiraled, wings bent at strange angles, dropping from the air. Like the rabbit, it was headed for the same deadly crash-landing against the mountainside. But with one powerful, last flap, it sailed toward the yellow birch that was sticking out from the slope just below Dhani and Claire.

"He won't make it," Claire shouted.

"Yes. He will," Dhani replied.

Smeared red with blood, beating the air weakly, the owl reached out, talons wide-open. It grabbed at a birch limb with its beak and claws, pulling itself into the crotch of two small branches.

Down the mountainside where the rabbit had fallen, a dark-colored falcon was tearing with its beak at the carcass.

Claire grabbed for Dhani's shoulder. "What just happened?" He wasn't there.

Catching sight of him, she called out, "Wait. What are you doing?"

He had angled down the slope, and was shinnying out the tilted, yellow birch toward the owl—which kept losing its hold and clutching at leaves, twigs, anything.

"This poor guy's gonna fall and die," he shouted back to her. "I gotta save him."

Under the weight of Dhani's body, the birch bent and tilted, until it was nearly perpendicular to the mountainside. Where the trunk met the cliff face, roots that clutched at narrow crevices in the rock strained and pulled, sending stones falling through the empty stories of air below.

All at once, there was a tearing sound—a *snap*—followed by leaf and rock litter falling away.

Claire screamed, *"Dhani, the roots are pulling out!"*

"Almost. . . got him. . .," Dhani grunted, stretched out full-length and reaching.

His right hand closed on one of the owl's heavily-feathered legs. He pulled the dazed creature to himself as the bird sank the talons of one foot through the web between his thumb and forefinger. The same electric current that had passed into him in the lake and the river raced from his hand up his arm and exploded in a ball of heat between his shoulder blades.

Dhani shouted in pain and surprise, pulled the bird to his chest, where it sank its other talons through his hoody. He let loose a wild yell of pain, nearly lost his left-handed grip on the birch, and squeezed his legs tighter around its trunk.

The snowy owl dangled from his hand, screeching and flapping, spattering blood from its wounds. With each twisting wingbeat, it stretched and tore the skin of Dhani's hand.

"Let him go!" Claire shouted.

"*No*, he'll die," Dhani answered through gritted teeth. The electric current was racing up and down his spine, and it felt as if his skull was going to break open.

Claire edged to the base of the tree, tried to reach for him, slipped on the angled rock face—and pulled herself back to safety. She lay against the mountainside, shaking.

"Dhani, let go of it. Please. *Let go.*"

Stop fighting me. I won't hurt you.

The owl stopped thrashing, turned its head, and stared him in the face.

A large root tore out of its rockhold.

"What the—?" came an angry-sounding voice from behind.

Tanner was charging toward them.

"What were you thinking?" Jo reprimanded. "You could have been seriously injured or killed."

Dhani stared at the ground, holding out his hand for Jo to treat. When she squirted betadine on his puncture wounds, he flinched. "I was rescuing this guy. I thought you'd be all about that."

Sahm had come running at the sounds of shouting, too. He stood holding the owl carefully in the blanket Jo had wrapped it in. Its head twisted wildly as it tried to escape, and it was using its beak to make a *clack*-ing sound when it wasn't emitting a shriek that was half whistle and half angry cry.

Dhani rubbed his stinging hand and spoke to the beautiful, snow white creature. "You're okay now. She won't hurt you. No one will. I promise."

The bird settled into silence—and Sahm looked at Dhani, smiling.

He knows he can talk to them, and they listen.

Jo was not smiling. "Sahm, take the owl back to the clinic. Keep it wrapped so it doesn't do any more damage to itself thrashing around. Let's bundle him carefully, and I'll come behind you in a minute."

When Sahm was gone, she turned her full energies on Dhani.

"What you did was impulsive and foolhardy."

"Didn't you almost die rescuing a dog?"

Steve, who had come and was standing behind her, intervened, his voice nearly a growl. "You put yourself and a teammate in jeopardy. And now you're being insubordinate to an instructor. If this was the Marines, I'd write you up."

Dhani looked down and said something under his breath.

Steve bristled. "Look at me. What did you say?"

Dhani shrugged and did not look up. "Nothing."

"You said, 'This isn't the Marines', didn't you? And did you say, 'dummy'?" This kid was insubordinate, and the whole scenario—the black hoody, the *screw you* attitude—made him grit his teeth. What Garrett had told him came back.

"He's a snap-o, and he could care less about being in this program. Thinks it's just a nice, easy break from juvenile hall."

Dhani's eyes were darting all around, and he shifted from foot to foot. The only route of escape was the path, and Tanner was standing in the middle of it.

All Steve's muscles tensed. "If you're going to talk trash to me, say it to my face."

Dhani's vision blurred and Steve's face disappeared. In its place he saw an angry, liquored-up face. *"Damn whiny kid."*

His legs felt shaky and his eyes teared up.

Steve was irritated. *Oh, lord. Not the whiny little punk thing.* What this kid needed was to man up, and not look for a shoulder to cry on whenever he messed up and got called on it.

Jo dropped Dhani's bandaged hand, and placed one palm on Steve's chest.

"You helped here," she said calmly to Steve. "Good thing you were coming back from your trek. Now it would be more helpful for you to follow Sahm. Tell Ron the owl got nailed out of the air by a peregrine and it has a cracked beak and broken blood feathers. He'll know what to do."

When Steve was gone, Jo knelt to close up her first-aid box.

Claire leaned close to Dhani. "That was risky. You scared me." Then she gave him a faint smile. "There is so much more to you than people think."

His face lit up, and he started to tell her that the owl had understood him. He knew it. But he held back. She was warming up to him again, and he didn't want to risk putting her off.

"Just don't ever make me have to try to rescue you again," she said.

18TH

Out of the corner of her eye, Kate glimpsed a figure in the doorway and startled.

Emmalyn was watching her silently from the office suite's entrance.

"Good lord, why didn't you knock?" Kate breathed out, turning from the email on her computer screen—a carefully-worded progress report to Judge Sewell, who was going to scrutinize every sentence.

She wanted to make it sound like everything was going smoothly without resorting to false spin, and had just typed, "The students and staff are still adjusting to each other." That was both neutral and true. She would leave out the particulars, for now, about all the petty rubs between students and staff, which she had not anticipated.

"I didn't mean to scare you. I was just trying to figure out how to ask."

"Ask what?"

Emmalyn stepped in, looking around wide-eyed. "Your house is so beautiful. This whole estate is so beautiful. You must have a hard time keeping track of everything that has to be done."

"Yes, it's a lot of work, but I have people I rely on. Grady. Ivy. You didn't come to talk to me about the estate, though."

"I was wondering," Emmalyn's shoulders hunched in, making her seem like a timid child, "if you could maybe use one more helper. An office girl."

"I would consider that."

Emmalyn straightened up. "You would? 'Cause I've always told my mama I want to be a secretary someday and work for a big, important executive."

"Instead of being the secretary, why not set your sights on being the executive?"

"Oh." Emmalyn's mouth fell open. "I never woulda thought of that. Is it even possible? My family's always been mine workers and truckers. And my mama and her sister own a place. Like a—," she stammered, looking for a word "—a restaurant back home in the mountains."

Kate felt her heart opening to this simple, hopeful girl. It was unlikely anyone had ever talked to her about possibilities and a vision for her life.

"If you get through the Lost Lake Program with flying colors and do a great job helping here in the office, we could discuss getting you into one of the business schools at the University of Virginia. A woman on the leadership team there was close friends with my husband."

Emmalyn was fast-calculating Kate's words. "Wait. You just said you'll let me work here in the office for you?"

"Tom has more than he can handle, coordinating things with the instructors and scheduling trips for you all back to DC." Kate leaned forward and said in a confidential voice. "He's not very good at ordering supplies and keeping inventory. And lord knows I don't want to do it."

Emmalyn clasped her hands together, like a child who was just given a pony. "Oh! Mama and Aunt Claudine will be so proud of me. I told them I'd do good and make up for—," she balked, "—for what I did."

Judge Sewell's report about Emmalyn went through Kate's mind.

"*. . .exotic dancing in a club to earn 'spending money'; State Police raid. . . .*"

Her mother's "restaurant" was a sleazy, roadside men's club, and there was a very good reason why the girl had been pulled from the woman's custody. In Kate's mind, it wasn't what Emmalyn had done, it was more what the mother had done, using her underage daughter to make money. Though, from Emmalyn's guilt-ridden statement just now, it appeared she looked at it as her own mistake, not her mother's.

"A very wise woman, Marianne Williamson, has said, 'The past is literally all in your head.' Let go of whatever happened before, Emmalyn. Let's help you move on. You can start tomorrow, after classes."

This, Kate thought—after the details were discussed and Emmalyn had gone—*this is why the program has to work. Young people who feel bad about themselves for messing up want a chance to start over.*

23RD

The barley flour in a metal tin on his kitchen shelf had become gritty with September fluctuation from heat and humidity to cold and damp. Fashioning the figure of a small, *soul deer* from the flour would be difficult—but not for this reason alone.

Since the night he had witnessed Dhani's soul journey, and then his effect on the wounded snowy owl, Sahm had sensed he should perform an ancient ritual known as soul retrieval for the boy. There was something much deeper going on in the young man than he had first suspected up on Peregrine Mountain, when Dhani had known of the coming storm.

The problem was, he could not remember the steps of the ritual. There were not many, but his younger self had often been distracted during his grandfather's trainings, and that laxity now left him guessing how to proceed. He imagined the old yogi's voice.

"*First. . . .*"

First *what?* He tried to force himself to remember. Should he chant over the figure as he formed it? Which chant? Did it matter what kind of twigs he used for the antlers and legs? These things needed to be done with order and precision and he had not paid close attention. The *soul deer* had to be made and empowered correctly, if the energy represented by the figure was to be raised and sent to awaken the boy's spirit. But the exact details of the ritual were not coming.

Frustrated, Sahm quit the cabin and stepped outside to quiet his mind and relax his body. Anxious energy would only continue to block the deeper reaches of his memory, where perhaps his grandfather's instruction lay dormant.

He had barely descended his front steps, when a thought flew through his mind, shaking him fully alert.

"Come, Sahmdup!"

His head jerked to the left, in the direction of the voice, and his eyes connected immediately with the boulder beside his cabin. The voice had called from there.

Climbing up on it, he positioned himself cross-legged and faced the lake. Leaning back, he braced himself, the heels of his hands against the coarse-grained stone. Immediately, a small vibration tingled his palms and rose through his hands. The vibration rose through both wrist bones, up through his elbows to his shoulder joints, converging at the center of his spine. From there, the sensation lightninged out to every bone and joint in his body, rocking him gently side to side.

It was the faint hum inside his skull that captured his attention.

"You are coming more fully awake again. Good."

With that, images came flying up at him out of the depths of memory . . . .

He was sitting on the ledge beside his grandfather's yak-skin shelter, feeling this same vibration pouring into him from the very roots of the mountain.

"What do you sense, Cetan?" the old man had asked.

"That I am the mountain and the mountain is me," he had answered. "We are one and the same."

His grandfather smiled. "That is so. This is a very good answer for someone so young. This confirms who you have been in many lifetimes before now."

"Who have I been?" He was only six at the time—and rather than answer in words, his grandfather had prostrated himself before Sahm....

"You were sent into this lifetime to be a great teacher," the voice in his mind told him. *"But because you fled from him, your training will now be harder."*

Before him rose the image of *Dzes-Sa*, the One who was fully awakened to the rare beauty of the earth. He rippled with a blue and clear light, and through his body flowed the ancient powers of creation—Earth, Air, Fire, Water.

"Sakyong!" Dzes-Sa greeted him. *"You yourself have been reawakening. Now it is time to fully re-enter your path again and awaken others."*

At the word *Sakyong*, a shock of energy rippled out from Sahm's heart center through his whole being—a cool and strong tingling that surged into every bone, joint, and muscle. It washed through every inch of his skin and out through every pore, stinging as it passed through him. It felt as if a great lightning from ages past had shot out from him into the air, like the red-yellow-green-blue skyrockets he had seen exploding in night skies over Tibetan villages.

As more surges went through his body, startling him wide awake, memories from many other lifetimes burst open....

He was standing over a young man, who was writhing on a bed of straw, searching inside his body for the arrow head shot by the young man's rival...then withdrawing it by means of healing arts, and cleansing the wound with a strongly-herbed water. "Now," he said to the young man's wife, "give him butter tea. Not too hot. Much butter. He needs to regain strength."

He was the Panchen Lama, oracle to the First Dalai Lama, striding around a group of monks, priests, and village elders assembled in a temple, regaling them about their adulteries, stealing, driving widows from their homes. . . their eyes wide in horror and shame that he knew their secret sins.

He was an old man on mountainside charnel grounds, cutting up his dead wife's body, preparing her for sky burial. Lithe hawks, dark gray vultures, and broad-winged golden lammergeyers circled and circled overhead, waiting to return the body to the elements. . . .

Many other moments from lifetimes past flooded through his mind, images from a long story rolling on and on like a river. With those images, bits of chants came back to him that he had intoned hundreds or thousands of times. . . .

He was huddled in the circle of a dark womb-like shelter. A wood fire was burning at the center, sending silver threads of smoke and yellow sparks up through a small hole in the roof. A small barley-flour soul deer balanced on an angular rock, and he held in two hands the shaft of an arrow made of bamboo, a shale point, and ribbons made of pounded tree bark that were colored green, yellow, and white with herbal dyes. A small, village boy had been stalked by a mountain lion and now was too terrified to gather firewood or haul water or even leave his family's hut. He began a chant. . . .

And then it was all over; the great energy surge ended. The images vanished.

Sahm opened his eyes. He was still seated on the boulder, breathing heavily, his pulse racing. Beads of sweat ran down his temples and inside his shirt. He was holding his hands out in front of him, as if he were still gripping the arrow from the soul retrieval ritual he had performed in some lifetime long past.

"*You concern yourself for no reason,*" said *Dzes-Sa*, the voice dwindling away in the distance. "*When wisdom and insight are needed, you will be told what you must know.*"

Before him were the trees, the lake, the sandy shoreline with the purple-flowered clubs of duck weed bending in a slight breeze. But now there was a faint light within it all.

He slipped down from the boulder and walked back to the cabin. Something his grandfather once said returned.

"There is no power in you, Sahmdup, or in me. The power we need for our work only moves through us. We are the hollow bone flute that greater powers play through. The more empty we become, the greater the power that can move through us."

He would try to remain clear and more fully awake to these things—to a greater reality and to those who had ascended but remained present. Most especially, to this Great One he had known for many lifetimes.

26TH

At 9 p.m., Eric and Bay rose from their seats around the fire circle.

"Jalil and Dhani," Eric said, "you guys are in-charge of dousing this completely before curfew. You've got an hour."

Up the beach in the dark, the closest cabins and woods appeared to pulse with the last reflected flickers of the dying blaze. A chill had slipped into the night air.

When the Troverts were gone Garrett nudged Carter and whispered. "That's funny, leaving Singe to put *out* a fire."

Dhani had kept his distance, and sat between Jalil and Ray-Ray on the far side of the pit.

Carter stared through Garrett as if he were empty air. "Dhani's different. Why does that bother you?" She stood up from the log where he had dropped down beside her, and moved away.

"Hey, pretty woman," he said, trying to grab her sweatshirt sleeve. "Where you going? It's getting chilly. I can keep you warm."

"Not if I fly away from you." She waved her arms.

"What does that even mean?"

Tia Leesha shivered, and picked up his comment. *"Gettin'* chilly? It'sss really colt righ'now. How coldzit git here anyways?"

"Way below zero in the winter," said Makayla, sounding upset. "That's what Laurel keeps saying.—Why are you slurring your words?"

Emmalyn put her arm around Tia Leesha's shoulder. "You poor tired lil' thing. You need to get back to our cabin now before you drop off to sleep right here."

"*You p'or lil' thang,*" Garrett mocked her in a high voice.

Emmalyn's eyes got a fiery look, and she pulled Tia Leesha to her feet. "So now you've turned off *two* girls tonight. *Ding, ding, ding.* You just won the prize as King of the Losers."

Dhani and Jalil had gone ahead, and it was just minutes before the 10:00 p.m. sign-in when Ray-Ray and Imani walked by flashlight up the path.

"SweetbabyJesus, lawdamighty!" said Ray-Ray, stretching. "My legs are still sore from the climb the other day. I need to get to bed."

Imani's head whipped around toward him.

"I *told* you we met before. You kept saying that the night we all partied—'*SweetbabyJesus, lawdamighty.*' It was dark in that limo, and you had a black hat pulled down to your eyebrows, but I *know* it was you. You were gangbangin' with my boyfriend, and came by my place to pick me up."

"I don't party. I never rode in a limo. And I definitely never was gangbangin'."

"Come on—'*Sweetbabyjesus, lawdamighty.*' Two different people in the same city don't say that. It had to be you."

"My grandmother says that all the time. That's where I got it."

"Well, I'm sure it wasn't your grandmother in that limo. You got a brother?"

Ray-Ray opened his mouth—held back—then insisted. "I told you, my brother's like a saint."

Imani said quietly. "If you're keeping your mouth shut about something that happened in the gang, I understand." Then, though no one else was there, she said in a lower voice. "Sometimes I wish I kept mine shut."

He pressed his lips together.

"Anyway, I say it was you that night," Imani finished. "The look, the voice, that thing you say."

Ray-Ray handed her the flashlight and started up the path to his cabin. "You can think whatever you want. But you're wrong."

He woke in a sweat in pitch-darkness, the blanket twisted around his torso. His throat was dry from the shouts for help he had not been able to get out past his lips.

The mental pictures were still fresh, and Ray-Ray made himself breathe. He'd been choking. Instead of pushing the images away, though, now that he was awake, he tried to replay them, thinking he had somehow missed something hidden in them.

His father had thrown his coat out the door after him. Before he could catch it, it landed in the mud beside the single pair of pants and a shirt thrown out first. Behind his father, his brother, Ezra, stood watching.

"Dad, please!"

"You are a disgrace. In my eyes, you bear the mark Cain, and you are an abomination.

"Dad, it's cold. It's raining. I got nowhere to go."

"Like Cain, you are now cursed to be a homeless wanderer."

On a dark side street in Northeast DC, he had heard the footsteps coming up behind him, and could not decide if he should stay cool or run.

He should have run.

The rope dropped around his neck and cinched tight.

"Who gives a crap about 'Black Lives Matter'? We'll treat you Black boys any way we want."

They left him on tip-toe, half-dangling from the street sign, windpipe crushing slowly, painfully, his life choking out. . . before an old man spotted and cut him down with a kitchen knife. If not, he would have been another Black man lynched by angry, white bigots.

Behind the pizza place at 4th and Rhode Island Avenue, he rescued the crusts, half-eaten slices, and burned breadsticks, the ones that rats hadn't gnawed yet. Even those, if he carefully tore away the bitten edges, he could get down, if he didn't think about it.

The metal back door banged open, and three young men his age, all masked, one with a gun, charged out into the back alley.

"Ditch 'em here," one shouted, peeling off gloves and a bandana, as he ran past the dumpster.

The other two running behind him did the same.

In seconds they disappeared around the corner of the building as he stared after them, stunned. And one second later—

"Don't move, you piece of filth." The store owner's Glock was pointed directly in his face. "You even flinch before the police get here and I blow your stinking brains out."...

He tried to straighten the tangled covers, pulling them up to his chin and burrowing into the bed, seeking some kind of comfort. How had this become his life? Lying there, his pulse slowed after the jarring memories, and he was grateful again to the police officer who had tried to defend him against the prosecutor's onslaught.

"No priors. Nothing. Wrong place at the wrong time."

But the jury had bought the shop owner's furious testimony. "Definitely. No doubt at all. He was the Black boy that shoved the gun in my face."

He rolled over and faced the wall, rubbing his throat where the rope had left a slight burn scar.

Dugan's words came back. *"White people turn on you when something bad goes down. Every time. Remember who warned you about that."*

He wrestled with himself, to keep his mind from going down the road Dugan was on.

The Lost Lake program had been a stroke of luck. And here in the center of his painful loss, he was grateful again the police officer, a White guy, who had said, *"I know they're all wrong about you, Aubrey. Hold onto that"*—and then referred him to Judge Sewell.

Still, his chest ached for a different reason. White people were not the ones who had turned on him first.

How could you throw me away, Dad—I'm your son?

Sleep would not come, and the sharp stitch in his breathing would not leave. No one in his church or blood family would take him in after his father forbade them all. And the image of his father in the doorway returned.

"You are no son of mine."

And with it came the image of his brother again, standing behind their father, his face serious or sad or scared or. . .?

He couldn't remember.

He stared up into the darkness, hot tears spilling from the corners of his eyes and down his temples.

Lord Jesus, I'm really trying. Please make me a good person, like Ezra.

8

OCTOBER

3RD

"Smells like snow," Grady said, sniffing the air and momentarily looking past Claire. He scanned the expanse of dense wilderness that stretched for miles north of Lost Mountain, where they had summited hours ago. There was a forlorn, unwelcoming feeling to the woods below that gave it its name, The Solitudes.

The final faint traces of summer had ended in an onslaught of cold and rain from the west. Skies went gray for a week, and in two days the red, orange and deep maroon leaves vanished from the upper mountainsides. Now, when it was not clouded over, the sky was an icy blue dome over the gray forests, and the air was a cold, slow-moving mass crawling over the slopes.

Claire was looking for it again, and said nothing. Twice now, the strange wisp of whatever it was had risen thin and ghostly and then disappeared.

"I guess you know your way around this place?" Ray-Ray said to Grady, sounding uneasy and hopeful.

"Around this area, yeah. Know it like the back of my hand. I can even walk around these trails at night. Sometimes without a flashlight if the moon's full. I love these mountains. Just remember that the Adirondacks is six million acres—that's over nine thousand square miles—of wilderness. That'll remind you to respect this place. Which reminds me, we should get going soon. Don't want to start our descent down the mountain in the dark."

"Do you ever bring women up here with you—like lady friends?" Claire fished, making small-talk to stall him.

It was Saturday, and she had finished chores—cabin scrub-up and vacuuming, then helping to stain the outside of Kate's potting room at her greenhouse. After, she had convinced Grady to bring her all the way up here with her sketch pad, charcoal, and black pencils. On one hand, she thought Jo's high praise for the sketches she had scribbled in the hawk migration journal was exaggerated. She had been a little too ga-ga about the snowy owl sketch.

"This is fantastic," Jo had said.

Claire hated exaggeration. It was manipulative.

But on the other hand, when she had shown her sketch pad to the art instructor, Glynis Candor, who came supplies-in-hand to give lessons, her more measured response and enthusiastic smile seemed genuine.

"You're self-taught—seriously? Well then, you have a natural gift."

Claire did not respond to that.

Today, Grady had jumped at the chance for a hike, but now—just after 3:00—the light was already starting to fade, and Claire's back was getting sore from sitting cross-legged. One more sketch and she would quit—if she could just locate the strange thing that had caught her attention, then quickly vanished.

"See that place wa-a-a-y out there about a mile or so, where there's a little break in the trees?" Grady said, standing behind her but looking out. "One branch of a beautiful trout stream flows into a pond, and the pond is excellent fishing, too. If you can even get back in there," he had added.

Ray-Ray had not forgotten Claire's question to Grady. "So, *do* you ever bring women up here?"

"Nope."

"Do you have a lady," Ray-Ray asked, grinning. "Or maybe more than one?"

"I do alright with women. But I like my life the way it is. No attachments. This is what I love." He swept one arm over the wild, thick tangle of trees below.

"'He had reached the point where all he wanted on earth was to be alone,'" said Ray-Ray, sounding thoughtful.

Claire and Grady both stared at him.

"It's a line from the novel 'Lady Chatterly's Lover'.—D.H. Lawrence."

"The serious books again," Claire said, still working. The failing light frustrated her, but she remained focused, looking for the strange wisp—smoke?—that had appeared somewhere out there in the thick forest groves and trackless bogs. It would add a plume of pale gray at just the right spot in her picture and add a focal point.

Ray-Ray quoted again. "'He cherished his solitude as his only and last freedom in life.'"

"Who are you talking about?"

"Mellors, the gamekeeper in Lawrence's novel. He liked living alone in the woods, but he also had a thing for the ladies. Big time. He just didn't want to live with them."

"I should look that book up."

"It's not an easy read."

Grady looked offended.

"I didn't mean—"

Grady laughed. "I'm bustin' ya. But seriously, can I find the film version online?"

Claire strained to see the white wisp, wondering if it would rise again. She had picked up the faintest scent of wood smoke, thinking maybe someone had built a campfire, but maybe that sweet, distinctive smell had come from Grady's wool vest.

"I'm glad you wanted to climb today," Grady said. "I needed to get up here and look around for signs of hunters sneaking onto the property. It's all posted, but occasionally some doofus blows off the warning signs."

"Jo says there's a lot of struggling people up here, and guys hunt for meat to feed their families," Ray-Ray mused.

Claire gave up searching, and added the plume where she thought she had seen it.

"True, but Kate allows hunting on the other tracts of land she owns. Just not this one. And there's thousands of acres of public land out there where there's plenty of deer and bear and—*Whoa!* Nice work." Grady interrupted himself, looking over Claire's shoulder at the pad spread open across her lap.

Firm charcoal strokes, like a mix of curved and straight quills, rendered the bare trunks of hardwoods covering Lost Mountain's northern slope. Darker, feather-like strokes captured the stands of evergreens and aspen groves.

Claire flexed her fingers. The cold air had begun to stiffen them.

Ray-Ray whistled. "Now that's talent."

Grady nodded. "About all I can draw is money out of my checking account, when there's any in it. What's this?" He pointed to a thin flourish rising above the trees.

She rubbed her hands together. "It's been rising and then going away for a while. A campfire maybe?"

Grady's head jerked up, and he scanned the vast gray forest stretching below them into distance. "Better not be. Fires are prohibited in the back country. Point out where you saw it."

"It was only a tiny thread. It came and went."

He relaxed and sank his hands into his deep, coat pockets. "Could'a been mist rising from a pond or stream then. Dozens of 'em out there. Anyway, there'd be no point in trying to track down someone in that mess. Too tangled and dense to find anything or anyone. There's an old, old logging road at the base of the mountain but that's mostly overgrown now. Really easy to get lost out there."

"You've lived here all your life. Did you ever hike out there?"

"When I was young and stupid. I don't anymore. Hikers go missing in these mountains every year and some are never found."

"This city boy ain't hiking anywhere alone," said Ray-Ray. He pulled his jacket tighter and his knitted hat down over his ear lobes.

Claire closed her sketch pad and put her tools back in the small, travel case Glynis had given her for work out in the field. Sitting unmoving had allowed the cold air to seep inside her coat. And now the thought of missing hikers and hunters lost in the gray desolation of these forests had crept into her soul.

"I'd like to go back now."

4TH

Dhani finished swabbing the eagle's cage. Jo had coaxed it through the small door leading to its enclosure outside. For months now, the young bird had sat on its perch low to the floor, facing the corner, hopping down only to feed on a road-killed rabbit or squirrel, then returned to its isolation.

"Still doesn't make sense," Jo had repeated yesterday for the tenth time. "I can't detect anything wrong with this bird. Labs are normal. He's perfectly fine."

Dhani slid the door to the eagle's cage shut and was rolling the bucket of stinking, gray water toward the utility sink. The smell of it made him gag—and a thought came out of nowhere.

Nothing happens by chance. No one is here by accident.

At the same instant, he saw in his mind's eye, like pieces of an intricate puzzle swirling,

Kate, Tom, Jo and all the animals in her clinic.

Tanner.

All the other students and the instructors.

Grady. . . Sahm. . . the surrounding forests and mountains.

It was fitting together into a pattern in his mind, and the center of the image began to come clear. . . . a blue figure that looked like a man. . . .

Ron called to him from the doorway—"Dump the crap water and come into the treatment room, Jo wants you"—and the image in Dhani's mind dissolved.

Before they reached the clinic, they heard shrieks.

Claire and Ray-Ray were standing next to the stainless steel table where Jo was carefully cradling the snowy owl. She had pinned its wings between her left arm and her side and grasped its legs together with her left hand.

The bird was struggling. Its head pivoted side to side, sharp beak biting at her lab coat, razored claws opening and clenching, trying to attack, shrieking and clacking its beak.

"Ron, get a towel to put over his head. We need to calm this guy down to see how his blood feathers are healing and check his weight. I may want to pull another x-ray to see how the joints in his right wing are doing. The peregrine struck him hard. I want you three to see how all this is done."

Ron walked to a cabinet to get a cloth as Dhani approached the table.

The owl suddenly stopped thrashing and fell silent.

"*Whoa!* What just happened here?" Jo stared at the owl with a curious expression. "The fight went totally out of him."

The owl turned its face toward Dhani, relaxed and perfectly still.

Dhani reached out a hand to stroke its head.

Claire's hand shot out to stop him. "Dhani, don't."

"It's okay, buddy," Dhani said to the snowy, running an index finger down its beak as it blinked at him.

Jo pulled the owl away.

"Don't ever do that again. See that beak? That can tear your hand up again."

But he wouldn't. Not now.

When Jo finished talking them through the examination, she sent Dhani along with Claire and Ray-Ray to inventory seed and other supplies that had arrived.

"Did you see that?" Ron asked, when they were out of earshot.

"Yes. I did."

"I've been in the aviary when he comes in to clean up. It can be really noisy in there but it suddenly gets completely still when he walks in. What do you make of that?"

Jo was silent for a moment. "Nothing. And you shouldn't either."

6TH

"They're promising snow tonight on the higher elevations," said Kate, looking at the local weather site on her computer screen. "The tops of Lost Mountain and Eagle Rock could have a foot of snow by morning."

Tom looked out the rear windows of Kate's office suite. Around the outbuildings, foliage still held its multi-color, red and gold.

"If there's any wind or the snow is wet and heavy, limbs will come down and we could lose power. Would you ask Grady and his crew to check all the generators?"

Tom nodded. "Clayton says it's near seventy back in northern Virginia. Such a short summer and fall up here. Why *are* you up here in the cold, Kate, when you could be anywhere? The coast of Spain, the Caymans. This place is so remote."

"It doesn't feel remote to me. These mountains are home. From the first time I set foot here I felt as if I'd been here for years and years. Lifetimes. I felt that I just knew this place, and—"

Tom raised his eyebrows, questioning.

"—and that this place knew me."

He smiled. "I understand."

"Do you? Because I think I sound like a foolish romantic when I talk about these mountains and lakes. Or when I think about this program."

"Why?"

"Because when I'm with young people, it's like being with all the young people everywhere. Maybe I just imagine some great connection, but I feel their desires and dreams. Knowing that some young people—maybe because of their mistakes or someone else's—will never get to live out their dreams. Or never even find out who or what they are. That leaves an empty feeling in me. And I can't walk away." She paused. "That sounds foolish, doesn't it? Or it did to Jim. Sahm told me that Jim left a 'poison arrow' in my soul with his words."

For a moment, Tom thought how skillful Germaine had become over the years with the dagger-like comments sheathed in a smile. "*My colleagues think it's quaint that I married a 'poor vicar' who has 'such wonderful concern for people' and absolutely no ambition to climb the ranks of the church.*" He refused to indulge his own painful memories just now, though, when he wanted to help Kate.

"Jim was wrong. You're not a romantic. You clearly see the problems these kids bring with them. You don't gloss them over. You're an empath and that's very different. Empathy understands pain and loss and weakness, and moves in to support and help when possible. Which is called compassion—one of the most direct ways to know the heart of God."

"You know I don't have a clue what to think about God, Tom. I wish I did. God is an enigma to me. You seem so sure, but I'm not."

Tom's expression altered. People expected him to know all about God, to speak in certainties. What he had experienced in his forty-some years had led him sometimes toward awe and gratitude, but more often toward mystery. The clergy he knew who traded in certainties, he often found to be tinny and demanding.

"Faith isn't about believing you know exactly what God is up to," he said firmly. "That's presumption. Faith is about doing what you believe is right, even when you can't see why you should or what the outcome will be."

She turned away from the windows. "I want to ask you about Steve. I read his report about rescuing the boy—Dhani. He used some strong, very judgmental language. Recommended some strict discipline. Frankly, it sounded like a personal issue."

"Steve has pulled into himself again since the last trek but I believe he'll come around. He's strong."

"I worry that he's alone too much and that he *is* so strong. Strong men hold too much in, until they don't. Maybe letting him stay out on the island wasn't a good idea. Why do you think he's withdrawn? It can't be just about the boy."

Tom cleared his throat. "One of the girls mentioned his wife. Olivia was Makayla's social worker. She said she really missed having her to talk to. She apparently had no idea that Olivia was gunned down."

"And Steve heard this?—poor man. I can't imagine how he still feels, since he held her in his arms and felt her die. . . ."

Outside the office suite, Emmalyn, who was about to enter, quietly turned and soft-stepped to the back door. Better to keep them from thinking she had been listening and overheard this information. And she didn't want to look like a sneak and ruin her favor with Kate.

That, and her mother's voice was in her head. *"Private information can be very valuable."*

7TH

Bay Trovert hung her coat on one of the pegs just inside Sahm's front door, watching Rocco, who seemed turned-in on himself this morning. Something was clearly troubling him.

Outside, a cold morning wind had risen, blowing the flames in the lakeside fire pit into a wild mess of smoke and flying ashes. Not the place for a relaxed, group discussion. Sahm's cabin was the nearest refuge.

She made a mental note to take Rocco aside later. Now, they were settling all around the open room in the warm glow of Sahm's woodstove.

"You are always welcome here," Sahm said. "I will go boil a pot of water to make hot tea."

Laurel slipped her coat off. "I'll help. Do you still have any of the wintergreen leaves we dried?"

"Yes, they are in a small tin next to the Myrobalan herb I brought from Tibet."

She grinned. "We sure don't want to use that by mistake. Everyone will be wired."

"As I was saying outside," Bay picked up, stepping up next to the woodstove, "some people you meet are coming from an unhealthy place. What you need is to have some standards for checking whether they should even be in your life."

Tia Leesha was staring past Bay, eyeing the small picture on Sahm's meditation altar with wide, suspicious eyes. She elbowed Emmalyn. "What's that a picture of—that monster-looking thing, with fire all around it and fangs and skulls around its neck?"

Emmalyn shuddered. "Some horrible false god. Maybe he sacrifices animals to it. It's all against the Bible."

"For instance," Bay continued, "it's normal to feel attracted to someone who's cute or popular. Or to someone who uses big-talk, or seems to have money, or they're powerful. They may or may not be a good person for you to hang out with. Ask yourself some questions, like these.

"Are they good to people—or do they hurt people physically or with their words? Do they accept you for who you are, or do you have to prove yourself to them in some way—especially a way that breaks the law—in order to be okay in their eyes? Are they honest—or do they steal and lie? Are they cheating on someone else to be with you? If something doesn't go their way, do they have a terrible temper or want to use violence or some other way to punish the person who wronged them?

"Most especially—given where we're all coming from here—do they believe you have to break the law to get ahead in this world and that's just the way it is?"

Makayla leaned close to Carter, who was sitting next to her. "I hate when she says *we*. She doesn't really know where *we* are coming from."

Carter ignored her completely, but turned away from Makayla and whispered to Rocco. "Are you bored? I wish that woman would shut up."

Rocco was leaning forward, listening intently. He held an index finger up to his lips.

"No comments—no questions?" Bay said.

Sahm and Laurel had come from the kitchen, carrying wooden trays laden with steaming mugs of wild mint and wintergreen teas.

"Perfect timing—and perfect follow-up subject," said Bay. "Laurel has already told you how to identify wild edible plants. Now she's going to tell you how to avoid the poisonous ones. So listen carefully."

Dugan raised his hand. "When is Mike Yazzie going to start the martial arts training we heard about?"

"I hear the gym he's setting up in one of the outbuildings will be ready around the end of the year. So, just a few weeks. Some of the equipment that arrived was faulty and has to be replaced."

Bay noticed Rocco, who had stood up and was lingering at the edge of the group. When the others were stirring milk and honey into their drinks, she quietly stepped to his side.

"Something up?"

"No. Why?"

"The way you were looking at me so intently, it seemed like something was on your mind."

He stuffed his hands in his pockets. "Nope. Nothing."

Dhani looked up from his place on the floor next to Claire's seat and saw that her eyes were fixed across the room from where she was sitting. He followed her gaze and realized she had locked eyes with Vajra, who was positioned beside the front door. Neither was blinking.

"You guys having a staring contest?" he whispered, trying to make a joke.

Ray-Ray leaned in. "Maybe that dog is a Trekkie. Looks like he's doing Vulcan mind meld on you."

"I swear, that wolf follows me around," she said, sounding uncomfortable. "I can be down by the lake, or coming out of Kate's, or walking on my own—and I turn around and he's there."

"That's kinda cool," said Ray-Ray. "I'd say he likes you and just wants to hang around with you."

Claire's expression went dark, and she said with vehemence. "Well, I don't want him near me."

"Why?"

"I just don't."

16TH

"Sonofa—" Carter threw the baby otter she was feeding into the water, then shook the fingers of her left hand. "Piece of crap bit me."

Emmalyn looked at her hand. "It's not bleeding."

"If it ever bites me again—"

Emmalyn glanced at Garrett, who was feeding one of the other two otter pups. His face was clouded. "You guys are so bitchy today—what's up with *you?*"

"Ron Cambric's algebra class sucks," said Carter. "It's boring."

Jo had come into the small mammals area along with Ron. "How's my Otter Tribe doing?"

Shrugs all around.

"Seriously, are you guys getting along?"

"It's all good," said Garrett.

"You guys all say that even when everything's bad. Look—when we brought these pups back here, I was focused on getting them checked out and fed. As I recall, I barked at you guys and told you to work out your drama. What I should have said was talk with the Troverts. Resolve your differences. You need to be relaxed when you're in here with the animals. They pick up on human stress signals. I also need you to be team-focused."

"Animals pick up human stress?" Garrett smirked. "That sounds bogus."

"When you're stressed, your body is juiced with cortisol, the stress hormone. Animals may be able to smell it. So you need to be relaxed and non-aggressive with them."

"Tell Carter that," said Emmalyn. "She can't handle a baby otter without making it bite her."

From behind Jo's back, Carter mouthed, *I'll cut you.*

Emmalyn smirked.

Jo turned. "Are you having a problem with the otters?"

Carter had a blank look. "They're just sweet little furry babies. I think they're great."

"Good. And since you're done giving yours his bottle, come with me. You can help Ron inventory the medical supplies we just got in. Emmalyn and Garrett, here's a couple boxes of gauze. Cut these big rolls into bandages."

"So—," Ron said, when he left Carter working and found Jo writing out medical charts in her office, "—if animals can pick up the stress signals from people, isn't it possible they can pick up peaceful signals?"

"What are you talking about?"

"When we're stressed we produce cortisol, like you said. And when we're really happy we produce the hormone oxytocin. Isn't it possible animals can pick up the scent of both from our skin?"

Jo put down the charts. "What are we *really* talking about here?"

"You just told your Otter Tribe guys they needed to not be stressed when they work with the animals. That animals can pick up stress signals. But you totally dismissed the fact that when Dhani walked into the treatment room the owl calmed down instantly. When I asked what you thought of that you blew it off."

She was quiet.

"So, I'm asking you again," Ron pushed. "What do you think about this kid, Dhani, and the effect he has on the birds? Maybe he's got super-oxytocin dump going on and they can scent it."

"I think you have a lot of work to do," she responded, picking up her pad. "And I think you need to stop wasting your time trying to catch me in a contradiction. It's annoying."

When he was sure Jo and Carter had gone to the other barn, Garrett shoved the gauze away, slipped his arms around Emmalyn's waist and pressed his face close to hers.

"Stop it."

"Come on, you'll like it. You should come out to Kate's gardening shed behind the greenhouse after curfew. We can get something goin'."

She pushed him back. "I thought you were totally into psycho-girl Carter?"

"She's not exactly available. Yet."

"Oh, so any girl will do."

"I hope so."

"Pig."

"If you're not going to play nice, I'll roll these bandages and you can go get the stinking bucket of fish to feed the muskrat."

Emmalyn made a pouty face. "You're bossy and mean."

"Hey, Southern Comfort, you can cut the sweet little dumb girl crap when you're around me. I see right through your ridiculous act."

She was still for a moment. Then her look and tone changed. "Dude, you're the one who's clear as glass. I see how you play people against each other. You play everybody."

"At least I'm not obvious."

She smiled broadly. "Yeah? Well, for a wise guy you're pretty stupid. This is a great gig. You want to get kicked out, just keep being a smartass. Jo doesn't like you. I see it on her face every time you open your mouth. If she gives you a bad evaluation, you might catch a fast bus straight back to juvenile detention. You need to play it a whole lot smarter."

Garrett smiled. "You're good."

"That's what they tell me."

"So, Miss Fake-Out Everyone, what should I do different?"

"Try a lot more charm. 'Yessir, no sir.' 'Yes ma'am, no ma'am.'"

"That's it—brown nosing? Already used it on Tanner and he went for it. He's my tool now. What else you got?"

"That's just the smokescreen. You do everything exactly the way they tell you. And act grateful for everything they do."

"You're *really* good. I could use you to help me out."

"The key phrase was 'use you.' Like you said, one thing I'm not is dumb."

"I mean use you as a partner."

"Here's the thing. I need to be here, as far away from home as possible, chilling in this program. No mess ups. I gotta walk out of here with my record expunged. All of it."

"Sounds serious."

"It is. Very."

"Tell me what else I should do besides butt-kissing."

Emmalyn stared at him, and her expression changed again. She looked devious.

"Okay. Here it is. First you get close to the opponent. That's the charm and butt-kissing part. Then you get them focused on a scape-goat, or someone who's weaker and vulnerable. That distracts them from what you're doing. Then you can get away with whatever you want."

"That's awesome. Who did you learn that from?"

She had a self-satisfied look. "A police investigator who's in business with my mother."

"Doing what?"

"Running a bunch of meth labs out in West Virginia."

"How were you involved?"

She twisted a strand of hair with one index finger. "Pretty country girl. 'Let's party.' You smoke up, and when you're messed up I take pics of you sucking on rock. *And* I lift your credit cards. If you're a cop and you report that, you're in way more trouble than me, because I'm a minor."

"*Whoa.* Serious." A big grin spread over his face. "And really, really valuable information. The police would like to know what you just told me. Ticket to a deal. Unless you decide—," he shrugged, "—to give me anything I want, any time I want."

Emmalyn's face flushed suddenly and she looked scared. "You tricked me. *Oh crap oh crap oh crap.*"

"Hey, I'm no friend of the cops. I need to stay as far away from them as I can. But way out here in the backwoods, I got needs."

Her voice sounded close to breaking. "Now you know our secret. I already slipped up a little once and got sent to juvie. But if the cops knew the rest of it, I could maybe get tried as an adult and my mom would go to prison. *Please, please,* just leave me out of whatever you're doing, and forget what I told you. See, I'm not as smart as you. I'm dumb, and I'd just mess up again."

He smiled triumphantly. "Nah, I'd teach you how it works. I got connections downstate. Meantime we can have a lot of fun."

She teared up. "That sports watch Dugan had—that's hot, isn't it? And that iPod Jalil sneaks around with. You got that for him. How are you getting stuff in here?"

"From the distribution centers, up the interstate in the night, straight into your hands. We only purvey the finest. Cheap. Sure you're not interested?"

Her eyes cleared and she smiled. "Only in the fact that I know your gig now. And that you're breaking curfew to party in Kate's greenhouse."

His face fell. "Hey, I know your secret, too."

She threw her head back and laughed.

"First you suck them in, then you punch them in the throat. There's no cop blackmailing my mother, *idiot*, and we don't run meth labs. You fell for the 'terrified, helpless, oh please don't tell on me you big powerful man' crap. Like my mother says, *all* men are stupid—even little boys."

His face was red. With one arm, he swiped all the bandages off the counter. "I hate your guts."

"What were the chances?" she said, her eyes bright with satisfaction.

"Of what?"

"Of you trying to play me and get me down on my back, but I flip you over instead. Was it good for you? Get it in your head, child. I only play to win. And I always win. Ev-ry-time."

She turned to walk away. "Better pick up all that gauze and start rolling again."

He called after her, angry. "What if I make you a full partner? *Hey*— you're not going to ruin this by ratting me out, are you?"

"You so much as touch me. You make me the butt of one more stupid joke. You do anything I don't like, and I kick you under the bus and dance on your crushed, dead body. That's how this works."

He swore. "Okay, okay. I got it."

"That's good because Jo *needs us to work as a team*," she mimicked. "So keep your dirty-little-boy mind off me. Loser."

17TH

"You guys are going to build more endurance," Steve announced. "Mr. Yazzie and I have a whole program of winter workouts planned. Today, we're going to summit on Lost Mountain—our longest hike so far. Highest point on the property."

"Cold up there," said Yazzie. "Possibly at freezing, with the wind chill."

The group was gathered, sleepy-eyed and sullen, on the bridge over the Garnet River. A month before, the river had rushed by with a relaxing rush and the water was sunlit and inviting. Now, thin bibs of ice surrounded the rocks, and cold poured down at them above the current of dark water.

"Oh, goodie." Tia Leesha yawned. "We get up at the crack of dawn, in the cold, and now we gotta climb up the highest mountain."

"It gets dark at five," said Eric Trovert.

Bay pulled up the collar of her jacket. "We need to be back down and out of the woods by then."

"You're wearin' me out already with these hikes," Tia Leesha resisted.

In a half-hour, they left behind the northbound trail along the river, and in another few minutes the current's roar faded away behind lower ridges of Lost Mountain. Steve picked up his pace until he was twenty yards ahead, leaving them to Sahm and his cheerful attitude—which he himself could not drum up.

"Focus your mind on your breathing," Sahm instructed. "Ignore every thought that comes into your mind, that way—no negativity."

Sahm was great for everyone's morale, Steve thought, and could even jolly Tia Leesha out of complaint mode. Personally, Sahm's always-happy manner grated on him. He would deal with them all from a distance today, and continued at a brisk pace.

Garrett was quickly at his elbow. "Cool headgear, sir," he said, looking at Steve's khaki knit cap. "Marine issue?"

"Yep."

"You get that in Afghanistan?"

"Yep."

"Looks warm."

"Polar fleece."

"Looks like it's been through some action."

"It has. Lotta memories. Not all good."

"Why do you wear it then?"

"It's special to me. A way of honoring some very good people."

"Any stories you can tell me?"

Steve's face remained placid, but his voice had an edge. "No. And I'm not in the mood for twenty questions."

"Sorry, sir." Garrett had blown his bid to buddy-up. "What's our objective today, sir?"

"I already told you. Endurance.—Pay attention."

Garrett was thrown off. "Yessir. Nothing like a good workout." He nodded back at the others spread out behind them on the trail. "I don't know about all of them, though."

"Just keep your head in your own program. What they do is none of your business."

"You're right, sir. Sorry."

"I thought you said Tanner was wrapped around your little finger," Dugan laughed, when Garrett fell back in stride next to him.

"That guy is so freakin' moody."

"You should stay away from him. Why do you need him anyway?"

"I need his trust, because I may need to cause a distraction."

Behind them, Sahm settled into pace beside Dhani whose face was beaming.

"You have wings today."

"What?—Sorry, I didn't hear you."

"You are flying up the mountain." Sahm was used to Dhani's habitual distance, his inattention.

"Why so happy?"

"I think Claire likes me. She's hanging out with Makayla and Imani today. But I still think she likes me."

"Ah, a girl. Very good, and dangerous."

"Why?"

"*Good*, because love and kindness are always good. *Dangerous*, because you are so young. You can easily lose yourself in someone else. Many people do, and they never progress spiritually for whole lifetimes."

Dhani was confused by that, and ignored it. "I wish I knew for sure."

"Maybe you should tell her that you like her," Sahm nudged him with an elbow, smiling. "See what happens."

Dhani looked uncomfortable and ignored that, too. He pushed one hand in a pocket of his jeans, and pulled out the white stone Sahm had given him.

"You said this is a stone used by seers, right? Would you teach me how use it?"

"*An Old One has returned.*" The voice echoed in Sahm's mind. "*But his soul must be clearer before you begin instructing him.*"

"Would you?"

Sahm shook his head. "I think not yet."

Dhani let out an exasperated breath and stomped in a circle, sending small stones skittering down the trail. "Then why did you even tell me about it?"

Why indeed? Sahm wondered. *What is the obstacle within him that needs to be moved?*

There was no clear answer, but a vague impression came.

In the hands of a fearful soul, a stone can become a weapon.

Eric hitched the daypack around on his shoulders. Bay was with the girls or he would have asked for her help adjusting it. In fifty yards, he rounded a bend in the trail and came up behind Jalil, who was alone and singing loud and off-key.

"All the other kids with their pumped up kicks better run better run. . . faster than my bullet. . . ."

Eric reached out and placed a hand on his shoulder. "Hey, can you help me adjust these shoulder straps?"

Jalil startled and pulled the buds out of his ears. *"Holy crap.* I thought I was alone on the trail for a while." His face had suddenly flushed a little.

"Hey, don't worry. Bay says I shouldn't even sing when I'm in the shower. It's that bad. More important, you're supposed to be with trail partners. Where's your tribe?"

Jalil had reached up and was rubbing his neck.

Eric realized he was trying to cover something—a white cord, running out from under his knitted cap and down under his collar.

"First of all, it's a bad idea to listen to music on the trail. You can miss someone calling you or miss the sound of a bear approaching. But—where did you get the iPod? No one had one when we did the intake inventory. And if you pick up something like that with your spending money you're supposed to tell us."

Jalil dropped his hand, pulling an earbud from his left ear. His face was now bright red. "I picked it up in town the last time we were there. Sorry about breaking the rules and not telling you. I just—I really like music is all."

"There are no electronics stores in town."

Jalil looked at his shoes, then at Eric. "Someone was selling them on the street. Like—a street market kind of thing."

Eric studied Jalil's face, detecting a deep uneasiness there. "I'll have to look for it next time I'm in town. Usually, they sell vegetables and handmade stuff at street markets. But hey, I could use a new iPod."

Jalil pulled the other bud from his ear and stuffed both of them in a jacket pocket. "They said it was the end of the season. So they're probably gone."

Eric shook his head. "My bad luck. I'll ask in town, and see if anyone knows when they open again in the spring."

Sahm and Dhani reached the spot where the trail skirted around Thunder Falls. To their immediate right was Thunder Rock, and as they continued beyond it, they saw where four streams flowed down steep cuts in the mountain into one current, fifteen feet across, then roaring around boulders before plunging over the sheer drop-off into the pools far below.

"As I showed you before, hold the seer stone in the center of your hand," Sahm said, as they continued climbing. "What do you think about?"

Dhani let the stone rest in his right palm as he climbed.

"I think about flying. Like in the dream I had of flying beside an owl. Remember that night I fell off the rock and you caught me? I think about flying south with the hawk migration. I feel like I could step right off this mountain—"

"But you will not try to do that."

"I said I *feel* like I could. But I know I'd fall and die. I'm not crazy, Sahm."

"Wrap your fingers tightly around the stone. Feel how solid it is, just like the rock at Thunder Falls and the one beside my cabin."

"Then what?"

"That's all."

"That's all?"

"To start with, yes. Any object is only a stepping stone deeper into your own mind. Once you feel how solid it is, you can move your mind beyond the stone. You will realize that what you are feeling—steady, solid, strong—is not in the object itself. Like every other sensation—happiness and peace, anger and sadness—the sense of strength already exists within you. Always. Find it."

"This is where I did the sketches," Claire told Bay, as Eric caught up with them. They had reached the overlook just below the highest summit, the same place where Grady had led her and Ray-Ray two weeks before.

"Your artwork is excellent," Bay said. "When Glynis Candor showed me the one you gave her, I was stunned. You really captured this view of The Solitudes. Not only the look, but the feel of it. Sort of strange and foreboding."

Claire pressed her lips together.

"Really, it's very good, Claire."

She turned her face away.

Garrett, Dugan, Tia Leesha, and Carter emerged from woods below the overlook.

Claire reached for the picture. "Can I have it back now—please?" She took it from Bay's hand, quickly rolling and slipping it into her daypack.

Eric had waited to speak. "Bay, can I talk with you—alone?"

After him came Jalil, who looked anxious. He made a small, quick hand signal to Garrett.

"A 'street market'? Dude, you're an idiot." Garrett clenched his jaw.

"I didn't know he was right behind me. And I had to think of something fast."

"You should have left it in the cabin. You screw this up for everyone and you're dog meat."

"You mean if I screw it up for *you*."

"You gotta fix this."

At the summit, Steve was down on one knee beside a small rivulet of water that ran in a stone groove between thick blue-green tufts of reindeer moss. He refilled his water bottle with a LifeStraw™.

"I'm empty, too," Eric said, stepping up beside him, "but I forgot my straw. Can I borrow yours?" Squatting beside Steve, he said casually, "Seems like you want to be alone today. Everything okay?"

Steve handed his straw to Eric. He hated Eric's way of probing for personal information. They could be climbing or rappelling buddies again. Maybe. But shrink and shrink-ee?—No.

"Good as I can be," he said, dodging.

"How good is that?"

He gritted his teeth and suppressed the urge to punch Eric in the head. "You done with my straw?"

Two hours later on the descent, Jalil came up beside Eric.

"Sir, there's something I need to tell you."

"I'm listening."

"When you're in juvenile detention, they confiscate everything from you. Whatever they don't take, other kids steal. I lied about just buying the iPod. I hid it when we got here, when I should have reported it to you. I'm really sorry."

Eric said nothing, and for long minutes the only sound in the gray woods was the crunch of their feet on the trail. Then he turned to Jalil.

"Maybe you want to think about it a little more, and tell me later where it really came from."

Dhani had been absorbed most of the day in flipping the seer stone over and over in his hand.

"I sorta get what you mean," he said to Sahm. "It's smooth and that makes me feel, I don't know, kinda *slick*. I guess you'd say 'slick' is a feeling that's already inside me. The stone just helped me find it."

Sahm beamed. "Yes, you are starting to understand. I want you to practice doing this whenever you become anxious. Like you were this morning."

Dhani balked. "How did you know that's how I felt? I never told you. Are you like, a mind reader?"

Sahm skipped over the full truth about the way he had begun to pick up vibrations from people at odd moments. "Listen. You are a young man, thinking about a young woman you like. But you do not know how she feels. She is with her other friends and not with you. That means you can't reassure yourself constantly that she likes to be around you. So—you are *anxious*."

Dhani smiled. "You're really wise, Sahm."

Sahm brushed that aside. "If you follow the path I teach you, it will make the uneasy feeling go away. Then one day you will realize you are really a very powerful being."

"I don't feel powerful."

"That is because you are so used to feeling weak and small."

"If you want me to feel more powerful, I think I need a bigger stone."

For a split-second, Sahm saw within Dhani an image much like a volcanic chamber miles beneath the earth's crust and seething magma lakes. . . a place inside Dhani filled with terror and anger. . . and felt shaken by what he'd seen.

The line of hikers had reached the lower slopes again, when Bay stepped up beside Claire, who had separated herself from Imani and Makayla. Now, near the end of the hike, most everyone had fallen into a tired silence.

441

"I'd like to ask you something. Is it okay if we talk a little?"

Claire shrugged.

"When someone compliments your work, why do you withdraw into yourself?"

They came to a rock scramble, and carefully picked their way down it before Claire answered.

"I hate compliments. You can't trust people who use them."

"Because—?"

"Because they always want something from you."

"Does Glynis Candor want something from you? Does Ray-Ray? Do I?"

Claire was silent and looked away. "Ray-Ray doesn't."

"Dhani's in your tribe. What about him?"

"He definitely does."

At the bottom of the trail, as the group made its way back along the river, Garrett caught up with Eric.

"I snuck a couple things in here. That sports watch you asked Dugan about and the iPod Jalil was listening to. They were covering for me, so I'm the one who needs to step forward."

Eric was expressionless. "From the very beginning, you broke the rules."

Garrett hung his head. "Yes, sir. I probably don't deserve to be here, I know. But please don't send me away." He looked like he might cry.

"Why would the other guys lie for you?"

"They're good guys, I guess. I loaned them stuff that they knew I snuck in. They didn't want to get me in trouble."

"But why sneak it, when all you had to do is report it?"

"Because—well, what Jalil told you is partly true. In juvenile detention your stuff disappears and it isn't always the other kids who take it. The guards and counselors confiscate stuff. Even stuff your parents were allowed to give you. And you never see it again. If you complain, it just makes things worse. So you hide stuff."

"You don't trust us, your counselors and instructors. You think we'll rip you off. Is that it?"

Garrett's shoulders slumped, and he looked dejected. "So now I get punished—right?"

"I'll take into account what you just told me when the other program leaders and I decide what to do."

"I'm sorry I didn't trust you."

"We'll get back to you."

21ST

"Remember, midterm exams are in two days," Mike Yazzie said at the end of the language tutorials. "Ask me if you need extra help in Spanish or French."

"How many languages do you speak?" Imani asked.

"Four. French, Spanish, German, and Creole."

"Creole? Isn't that just pidgin English?" Garrett laughed. The verdict had come in that morning: some light restrictions, no note to Judge Sewell—this time, and he would be staying. His swagger was back.

"No. Creole is a language. And it's tough to learn. So I'm going to teach it to *you* next semester."

"I didn't know there was going to be so much school work," Emmalyn said, sounding overwhelmed.

"We went light on you this term. Next semester we add in history and introduce pre-calculus."

Ron Cambric had stepped into the room. "I'm available if you need help in math or health."

"The line of girls forms behind Ron," Garrett snickered.

Carter stared at him. "What's that supposed to mean."

"Everyone knows girls are bad at math and science."

"That's just wrong—," Ron started to intervene, and stopped short.

Carter had shoved her chair back, stood, and walked to the white board behind Mike Yazzie. Picking up a dry marker, she drew a dotted, horizontal line across the center of the board and a dotted vertical line intersecting it in the middle, forming a cross.

Yazzie's brow furrowed. "What are you doing?"

"Math is beautiful," she said, ignoring him, her voice flat. "It's the language that perfectly describes the intricate way the universe is made."

Every eye was on her now, as she quickly wrote numbers along the two axes she had drawn.

"The mathematics of this theory represents the geometry of a three-dimensional physical process. It's written like this." She wrote a short formula above the crossed lines.

$$e^{i\pi} + 1 = 0$$

"Euler's formula?" Ron said, his jaw dropping. "You *know* Euler's formula?"

She continued scrawling numbers and letters, then drew a circle, a wave, and a radius. She sounded almost feverishly driven. "Euler's formula states that for any real number, represented by x, where e is the base of the natural logarithm, i is the imaginary unit, and *cos* and *sin* are the trigonometric functions *cosine* and *sine* respectively, with the argument x given in the radians. . . ."

For ten minutes, Carter rapidly recited in a deadpan voice, until the board was filled and every eye was wide, staring at her.

"Done." She tossed the blue marker in the tray, and returned to her seat.

Mike Yazzie looked at Ron, who looked stunned. "What did we just see?"

"A perfect explanation of what's been called the most remarkable formula in mathematics. Also known as 'the God equation' because it tells us in words and numbers how everything came into being."

Garrett made a derisive sound. "*Pfft.* Okay, so one girl isn't bad at math."

Carter looked straight ahead. "There's also a formula for making idiots shut up."

"Oh really," Garrett smirked. "What's that?"

"I think she means a combo punch," Dugan laughed.

"Keep opening your face," she said in a low voice, distantly, as if she were talking to no one, "and you'll find out."

After class, Makayla caught up with Rocco in the hallway. "My god, she's scarier than I thought."

Rocco did not respond.

She touched his arm. "Do you want to go see how the workout building is coming along?"

"Nah."

"I heard there's going to be weight machines and benches and a kickboxing ring," Makayla persisted. "The ring is almost done."

"They. . .need me down in Kate's office."

She stared at his face. "Right. That's a nice lie."

Silent, Rocco watched until she had descended the stairs and the great, carved front door of Kate's lodge closed behind her. He didn't dislike Makayla, but the fact that she could see through him—that was uncomfortable.

"What's up?" Bay asked, smiling as Rocco sank into a leather armchair in Kate's office suite. It was empty except for the two of them.

"What if the people you're around all the time are all just like what you said at Sahm's cabin a couple weeks ago? I mean, what if they're the bad way, not the good way—even people in your family? What are you supposed to do about that? You can't just walk away from every single person in your life."

Bay nodded. "You're right. It's not easy. Right now you can't maybe, because you're young and your family has a lot of power. They pay for you to live, basically. And it takes a lot to go against the way you were brought up.

"So—," she hoped to get to the core of his issue, "—who's the strongest person in your family? Who does everyone think they have to listen to?"

"My dad. After him, his brother—my uncle Carl."

"What makes them so powerful in your family?"

"If you don't do what they say, they get mad. Really mad. And you get punished."

"Did you ever go against your dad."

"Not since I was little."

"What happened when you did?"

"He slapped me around. Kicked me. Threw me into a wall. Sometimes he'd put me down and call me 'baby' or 'girl'."

Bay was quiet for a moment. "Do you like your dad?"

"I respect him."

"You respect him—but do you like him? Think about it for a minute before you answer."

Rocco sat silent a long time, staring out the window. "That hike up Lost Mountain was killer. But I kind of like that Mr. Tanner is pushing us to get in better shape."

Bay side-stepped that. "You said he called you 'girl' as a put-down."

"Yeah."

"Can I ask, how does he treat your mom?—I mean if she's still around."

"My mom hates my dad, I think. Or—I don't know. Maybe she loves him."

"You're not sure."

"No. I think they hate each other maybe. Shit, I don't—oh sorry, I'm not supposed to swear here. I mean I don't know. I can't tell. It's confusing."

"Just for the sake of discussion today, let's say your mom doesn't love your dad. If she didn't—why would that be?"

"He treats her bad sometimes. If she doesn't do what he wants right away he gets sarcastic and mean with her. He calls her names and puts her down. One time he said to her, 'There's a lot of younger women who really want to be with me if you don't. A lot of 'em. Women who aren't old and fat like a pig.'"

"What happened?"

"They were fighting and screaming at each other. But when he said that, her face just. . . she just. . . she walked away and went outside our house. My dad shouted at her. 'Don't forget I own you. You do what I say, or I can toss you away like yesterday's trash.'"

"You heard all this."

"Stuff like that and worse. All the time. He tells my mom she's useless and terrible in bed."

"He says these things in front of you?"

"He says whatever he wants in front of anyone when he's mad."

"So on the day she walked out on your dad, where did she go and what did you do?"

"I wanted to go after her, but my dad shouted at me and told me to stay out of their f-ing business. But in a little while he left and I went outside to find my mom. I knew she didn't leave, because her car was there. She was sitting on the back deck of our house crying. Really hard."

"How did you feel?"

"I wanted to kill my dad."

"But of course you didn't, so what did you do?"

"I put my arms around my mom and told her she was beautiful, and not to listen to him. That I love her. That my dad is a jerk sometimes and I wish he didn't hurt her."

"What did she say?"

Rocco started to speak, then got a startled or confused look. He tried again, putting one hand over his eyes, rubbing them. Then he shook his head, as if fighting back an inner force.

"She said one day she was going to go out in the garage and get in her car and start the engine and just. . . ." His voice trailed off and his jaw tightened.

"Rocco, I'm so sorry. That had to be so painful to hear."

He took a deep breath and spoke in a rush. "She said, 'I hope you're not the one who finds me.' And she said, 'Don't turn out to be like your dad.'"

Bay studied him carefully. "Do you want to take a break?"

He sat up and his expression changed. "No. I'm good."

"You're good?" Bay repeated.

He nodded.

"So—," she was looking through a file she had picked up off the small table next to her, "—does everyone in your family do exactly what your dad says? It says you had a brother and you have a sister."

"My sister argues with my dad a lot. She wants to be a psychologist and help people. Like you, kinda. She moved out into an apartment when she was eighteen. My dad said, 'Good riddance to bad rubbish,' but he pays for her apartment and her college. And he tells his friends his daughter wants to be. . . a stupid shrink. Hey, that's what he said. I don't think that way."

"I take it your brother is deceased."

Rocco shifted. "You know, I think I want to stop talking now."

"Understandable. You told me a lot, Rocco. Can I tell you what I see, as an adult and as a trained professional?"

He shrugged and looked noncommittal. "Yeah, sure."

"You are not like your father. That's first. You care about people's feelings and you don't like bullies. You are a very good son to your mother. And your father isn't as powerful as you think he is. He just gets loud and mean and hurts people and that makes everyone afraid of him. Isn't that right?"

"But I also love my dad."

"Of course. And that's what's so confusing for you, I'm guessing. You love him, but you don't like the way he is a lot of the time. Is that fair to say?"

"Yeah. That's right."

"Do you want to know why I think your dad isn't as powerful as you may think he is?—Because your sister defied him and he didn't 'throw her away like rubbish.' He kowtowed and he's paying for what she wants to do with her life. She's winning her power struggle with him, even if it's at a distance. Good for her."

She paused and let that sink in. "One more question, why did you come to talk to me. I'm glad you did. But why me and not Eric?"

"I don't know."

"I can always be wrong, of course, but maybe there's a reason. Just think about it a bit, and see if anything comes to mind. You can tell me next time."

"What do you mean?"

"I hope you'll feel free to talk with me again—or with Eric—any time you want to."

He considered. "You won't tell anyone what I said, will you? Like, if you're talking to other kids."

"That would violate professional ethics. And I wouldn't anyway, just as a human being."

"I didn't think so. But I probably won't want to come back."

"That's fine, too, of course. No pressure. But *if* you do, just know we're here for you. I'm here. And whatever you say is strictly between us."

26TH

"We have some serious trust issues going on with these guys," Eric began.

He and Bay were meeting with Tom and Kate in her office suite.

"I have to file another report with Judge Sewell," said Kate. "He doesn't know where things stand with the prosecutor, but he thinks the issue with Claire is not over. He's also got Child Protective Services pressuring him. That woman named Saint, who's a stickler for detail, has become anxious about something. And frankly, I need some good news."

"The good news is that big life issues are coming to the surface," Bay said. "You can't deal with an issue unless the client is aware of it. Rocco's reaching out. Claire is slowly starting to trust us. She's starting to show artwork she's kept hidden."

"What about Dhani Jones?" Tom asked. "You said he'd been bullied a bit by Garrett."

"Garrett seems to have laid off. And Dhani appears to be very close with Sahm."

"Seems to be a good friendhip," Bay added. "When they're hiking together, Dhani is all smiles."

Eric cleared his throat.

"What is it?" Tom asked.

"I'm becoming more concerned about one of the instructors—Steve. He does know his stuff skill-wise, but he also goes through some big mood swings and the kids seem to have picked up on it. I also think some of them might be playing up to him and others are avoiding him. Dhani in particular seems intimidated—though that's hard to say for sure. He generally keeps to himself or hangs with his two Eagle Tribe buddies. But no one else."

Kate glanced at Tom, with a questioning look.

"Steve will warm up, I believe. I trust that he will. You all know where he's coming from. He lived on my farm for a year and I know this man. I'll talk to him, too. Give me a little time."

When the Troverts were gone, Kate swiveled in her chair to face Tom directly.

"How much is 'a little time', Tom?—It's been five months. I trusted you that Steve was the right man for the job. He seems to be a polarizing force. Twelve adolescents from difficult backgrounds is enough to deal with. Are you still willing to stand by him?"

Tom pressed his palms together and raised his hands to his lips. Did his faith reach that far—when not only Steve's future but that of twelve young people and Kate's program were involved? He was thrown back to the crossroads moment when both Kate's need and Steve's had intersected.

"Yes. I do stand by him."

"I'm trusting you, Tom," Kate replied.

"Thank you."

"I mean I'm trusting you to straighten Steve out. Back in March, you believed it was more than a coincidence that I showed up needing a wilderness survival expert, just when he needed an open door. But now I'm watching him very closely. I'm not as convinced as I was in the beginning. You know a lot is at stake here."

29TH

"I don't get girls."

Dhani was pacing the open room in Sahm's cabin.

Sahm stared at him. Why did he have the sense that Dhani was caught up in something greater than anyone knew?

"He is caught in a trap within himself," Dzes-Sa's voice said, as if from a great distance.

"You don't mean girls," Sahm said, shaking off the distraction. "You mean Claire. Please stop pacing like an anxious snow leopard."

"Yeah, *Claire*." Dhani's voice became louder, and he waved his arms. "First, she kind of acts like I'm a hero for saving an owl. Then I compliment her artwork, and she doesn't say a word. She acted like I'd insulted her, and she's hardly looked at me for a *whole week*," he almost shouted.

"Now you are howling like a yeti. Please sit down."

"There are yetis? For real?"

Sahm did not reply to that. "Tell me why you are in such distress."

For twenty minutes Dhani talked and Sahm listened. As best he could. He'd lived alone with his grandfather on the side of a mountain most of his life, venturing into villages with the old man—one girl smiling at him here, another timidly offering him a meal of *dal* there. He'd heard of a possible arranged marriage, but it never came off. What did he know of girls, except all the questions he, too, had about them? He did much more listening than talking.

Which seemed to be the right thing.

"You say she has a big concern. She does not know if she will be able to stay here, so she is very unsettled. She pulls into herself because she is anxious. She cannot think about you and your feelings at this time."

Dhani relaxed, the confused look leaving his face. "Thanks. You really help me a lot."

Mystified, Sahm replied. "You are welcome any time."

When Dhani had walked away down the lakeshore, the earlier mystery surfaced in Sahm's mind.

For days, he had experienced—behind him, around him, in him—a sort of shadowy feeling. It was far different from the other energies he had felt, and it came over him at odd moments, like right now. A kind of uneasy awareness.—Was it a trace of the anxious energy Dhani often carried with him and left behind? No, something new was trying to circle and engulf him.

Sitting cross-legged before his altar, he opened his mind in meditation, finding himself

. . .beneath a blue clear sky, approaching a precipice, until his feet were at the edge.

On the far distant horizon, a slight shadow was beginning to stain the sky, a hint of darkness he noticed only if he looked carefully. The faintest sense of dread passed through him and was gone.

He came out of the reverie, feeling a mild sense concern. Why, he did not know.

9

November

2ND

Steve kept pace with Sahm even on the steepest parts of the trail up Eagle Rock Mountain, at least when they set out. As they rose above the valley, Sahm began to out-distance him.

He kept an eye on Sahm, who was unusually focused for some reason. He had his own distraction. At first it was only a vague sense, but the more they climbed the more uneasy he felt. It was a wariness, as if he felt the weather pattern changing and a storm moving in. There was no sign of that, though; the cold updrafts swaying the trees and roving over the mountains rushed up the slopes into cloudless blue. Still, he felt on high-alert.

"Did anyone sweep this trail for mines?"

He was on a trail in Kamdesh.

Half-concealed behind doors and shutters, mountain villagers were watching him and his men pass by.

No. He clenched his eyes shut. *I'm here in America.*

Hundreds of feet above them was the eagle silhouette, left on the cliff's face when ice or a tectonic shift in the earth broke away part of the mountain's southern slope. They were past the second switchback, sidestepping rain ruts, rising through the lower forest toward the upper slopes. Up here, the November winds carried the sharp scent of pine and balsam.

Steve flipped up his coat collar. What was up with Sahm? He was staring off into the woods when he was supposed to be scanning the upper slopes for a viable campsite.

He wished he had postponed this search for a second bivouac site, a task he had failed to accomplish during the hawk migration count two months ago. The night had been difficult. He had twisted the sheets around him into the early morning hours, avoiding sleep and dreams. He would have called off the climb, if Sahm had not banged on his door at 8 A.M. Pal's half-hearted woofs killed the possibility of ignoring the summons.

His breathing became labored, and a heavy bead of sweat ran down his neck.

"You will have a better time if you breathe with your belly, not just your chest."

Sahm had stopped and was facing him, not at all sweating or red faced. He pulled in a deep breath with his lower diaphragm, making his belly pooch out. "See. If you breathe from the belly, it fills the whole lungs."

Steve's response was stiff. "Got it."

Sahm watched him with an curious look. "I made you angry?"

"No."

"Your mouth is smiling, but your eyes look like Mahakala's eyes."

"I have no idea what that is."

"He is a fierce aspect of the Buddha."

"You'll have to explain that," Steve said—but as soon as Sahm began, he held up one hand. "Not now, please. I've got a little headache is all."

In fifty yards, as Steve adjusted his breathing, he was no longer sweating heavily and his thighs had stopped burning.

Maybe drinking a six-pack last night wasn't the best idea. A slight dehydration headache, he told himself. That was why he had reacted poorly. Sahm was a good guy. Easygoing and happy. A hard worker on hikes and campouts.

Sahm was scanning the woods on both sides of the trail. He stopped, peering into a thicket of bare shrubs beside the trail. Along its twisted branches, moving with the wind, were dozens of small flowers that looked like withered, yellow spiders.

Steve caught up. "You studying the plant life or waiting for me?"

Sahm pushed his way through the leafless undergrowth to the upper edge of the thicket, scanning the ground as he went. Stopping, he pointed down at the yellow and brown leaf litter. "I am wondering why someone climbs here but walks next to the trail. Not on it. It is much more difficult to hike."

Steve stared into the low, scrub brush to where Sahm was pointing. "I don't see what you're looking at."

Sahm bent down and carefully pulled back some twigs. "Behind these bushes. See—the wet leaves are pushed back downhill. A man walked here beside the trail moving *uphill*." He pointed up the slope a couple of feet. "There is his next step, where the leaves are pushed downhill again."

"You think a human made these tracks, not a bear. And that it was a man?"

"Yes. Look. The top part, where his toe dug into the dirt made a deep impression. That means a heavier person. Also, the toes are pointed *out*. Most often, a woman walks with her toes pointed *in*. So—a man was climbing here."

Steve shook his head, relaxed and smiled. "How did you even spot these tracks in this thick underbrush?"

"In the Himalayas, if someone is lost you must know how to read every sign to find them. Also, you must be aware if you are in the area of bears or wild dogs or leopards. I was taught to watch for signs as a young boy."

The cold updraft of air had picked up, and a crow called.

Steve pictured Sahm as a boy, living, learning how to survive in the remote fastness of the Tibetan mountains. Something shifted.

The way Steve had viewed Sahm up to this moment—as a simple hauler of gear, probably not very bright, *chop-chopping* along in animal dumbness—had dissolved. Before him stood a keen-eyed, knowledge-able tracker. Also a guy who could instruct you how to regulate your breathing on a tough hike. Which, he had to admit, worked. Also some-one who could read trail signs and find people lost in wild places. What else did Sahm know that he would never have given him credit for? It was as if, to this moment, Steve had not seen the real Sahm at all.

"To my thinking, the man who walks here does not want anyone to know he is here, so he stays off the trail. Or it may be—," he fingered one of the shrub's yellow flowers, "—that he comes to harvest this."

"What is it? What's it for?"

"Laurel Wysocki told me it is called Witch Hazel and it is for clean-ing wounds and healing blisters." He touched the seat of his pants. "Also for the painful things. . .inside here."

"Hemorrhoids?"

"Yes. Those. She says it is very effective."

Steve nodded. "I learned in Afghanistan not to be skeptical of folk medicines. Sometimes it's the only medicine people in remote villages have. And Laurel's the expert here." He was, again, impressed that Sahm had sought out this kind of knowledge.

"As an ointment, good to rub on your temples for your headache, too," Sahm grinned.

"How do you know I have a headache?"

"You rub here." Sahm touched his temples. "So—headache."

"I've got something for it in my daypack. Guess I should take it."

He slapped Sahm on the shoulder. "You're amazing. A real asset to my survival program."

"Thank you."

Steve fished in a pocket of his pack for a small plastic container with headache capsules. "So, do you think some guy—or a woman—strolled up the mountain here on Kate's property, harvesting this shrub to make a natural medicine?"

"Not a woman. Most definitely a man. But I have not seen any branches cut or broken off. He was not gathering medicines. I can't say why he was here."

Steve was ready to move on. "Well, Grady likes to hike. And there's Randy. Probably one of them."

In a hundred yards, Sahm reported, "Look. His tracks cut across the trail." He turned his head to the left. "He moved across the slope and went. . . there." He pointed northwest toward Lost Mountain.

Steve had lost interest. "Let's focus on our main objective. We need a great spot near the top, maybe near that Eagle face, for a permanent bivouac."

Sahm stared at him uncomprehending.

"A campsite?"

Sahm had learned the word *bivouac*. He was looking past Steve, seeing in his mind's eye a halo of gray emptiness around him, like a vacuum. And far out on the horizon, the thin stain of shadow he had seen before had grown. Now it was the purple-black color of a bruise. In his spirit, he felt a creeping cold.

5ᵀᴴ

"Hey, you guys," Jo said, stepping into the janitor's storage room behind Dhani, Claire, and Ray-Ray. "Forget the buckets and mops right now. We're turning the saw-whet loose this evening."

Dhani felt an unhappy twist in his gut. Jo had made it clear that any animal brought into the clinic was only here to recover, unless there was a reason to keep it longer for study. He had hoped the little female saw-whet would be a keeper.

"It's almost supper time," said Ray-Ray, "and then we've got homework."

"Saw-whets are most alert at night, and this girl is ready to go. We're not driving very far."

Ron called from the doorway. "She's caged and in the Jeep."

"You guys go with Ron. I'll be out in a minute."

Climbing into the back of the vehicle, Claire could see Dhani had retreated into himself. He leaned against the back door, arms wrapped around his torso, staring out the window into the fading gold light of oncoming dusk.

"What's wrong?"

"I don't want her to go."

"You can't hold onto things. People. Pets. It doesn't help."

"I'm not like you."

"Maybe you should be."

Ray-Ray intervened. "Maybe we should just let each other be who we are."

"When you're finished cleaning the bear cubs' pen you can go," Jo told Rocco. "Remember to secure their door or they'll get out and get into trouble. Bears can cause a lot of damage. Even small ones."

Rocco had on gloves and was holding the smaller of the two cubs, rubbing the ruddy-gold fur that had come in behind its ears. The damage done by the maggot infestation under its skin had left bare or thin patches in its soft black coat, and in almost three months it had not grown much. Pacing in the cubs' pen, biting at the wire and bawling for attention, its sibling was half again as big, and sturdier.

"Do you think the little guy is going to be okay? He isn't eating his dinner. Why isn't he gaining weight like his brother? Sometimes he doesn't play at all. He just lays in my arms."

"He isn't thriving the way I'd like him to, and I'm concerned about his muscle tone. But we'll keep an eye on him. Rocco, you're spending too much time with this little guy. *Don't get attached.* Now put him back and finish up."

When Jo was gone, Rocco watched through the window until he saw her vehicle pass by outside. Then he took off his rubber gloves and rubbed the cub under its chin. The cub responded by grabbing his hand with both paws and gnawing at it. Rocco rubbed his head against the cub's.

"Looks like you're a little stronger. Yeah, you're a tough guy."

Walking in a circle, he announced, "In this corner, weighing twenty-four pounds four ounces, underweight for his age but a real tough guy, covered in black fur with a blond shoulder blaze—*Blackie Blackmeister, a.k.a. Ursus Americanus.*"

He made a crowd-cheering sound, and raised the cub's right paw in a victory salute.

"And in the opposite corner, weighing one-hundred seventy-six pounds, solid muscle—our middle-weight champion—you know him, all the girls love him—*Rocco, the Dream Lover.*"

Still holding the cub's paw, he smacked himself lightly in the jaw with it.

"*Ohmygod,* ladies and gentlemen!" he announced, with a shout. "Blackie punched Rocco before the bell! An illegal move, and the ref's not even calling it!"

He staggered back against a wall, pretending the cub was knocking him around, shouting, "Now Blackie slammed him with the steel chair!"

He heard a half-suppressed laugh and, wheeling around, saw Imani watching him from the doorway.

"The *Dream Lover*?" She grinned, then burst out laughing.

He squared his shoulders and grinned back. "Yeah. That's right."

Gently, he set the cub in its pen, and crossed the room. Reaching out, he touched her arm, expecting her to pull away.

She didn't move or flinch, but stared him in the eye with no expression. "Does that mean you love to dream?"

"No. It means this." He leaned forward and pressed his lips to hers, holding the kiss for a long moment.

When he pulled back, she was still staring at him, expressionless.

He grinned. "If you're so devoted to your boyfriend, why'd you let me do that?"

"Just seeing what it's like."

"And?"

"Not as bad as okra. Not as good as champagne."

"I can do a lot better."

"I hope so. I've kissed girls who kiss better."

His grin vanished. "That's cool, I guess. You're into girls *and* guys?"

"No. But my girlfriend—my best friend who is a girl—she taught me how to kiss."

He looked deflated. "And you think I'm not as good as a girl."

"I don't know. Maybe. Maybe not."

"I was just getting started. I said I can do better."

"Thanks. But I know all I need to know now."

Turning, she walked out.

"What does that mean?" he called after her. "What is it you think you know?"

Behind him, a stainless steel cart crashed to the floor, scattering broken tubes of vaccine and a bottle of orange disinfectant on the floor.

He had forgotten to lock the door of the cubs' pen.

He wanted to be angry, but he couldn't be. The bigger cub bawled, and the little one looked at him with an impish look, like a misbehaving child.

Makayla's words when she had drawn the muddy Bear Tribe sigil on his chest came back. *"This is your life."* She had just blurted them out not knowing why then. Why were they in his head now? His life was back at home in DC, where he would step into his father's business

460

not many years from now, and not running around the woods here to deal with dead, rotting mother bears or play nursemaid and clean up stinking, bear cub mess.

That's for damn sure.

Jo stopped a half-mile past Kate's greenhouse and two big out-buildings, out where the estate's dirt road ended. To the left, the fields stopped and the forested slopes of Eagle Rock Mountain began. To the right was the narrow strip of woods and the path that led down to Sahm's cabin by the lakefront. The sun's late light was fading fast, washing the mountains, trees, and field with golden-red hues. A beautiful spot, but this evening it had a lonesome feel.

They stepped from the Jeep and now could see that a nearly full moon was rising in the deepening eastern sky above The Arrows' deep-cut cliffs.

The air was cold, and Dhani stuffed his bare hands in his pockets.

"We'll turn her loose here," said Jo. "She's strong. She's got the forest nearby. She's got this field full of mice, moles, maybe a few snakes on the warmer days."

Ron lifted the saw-whet carefully from the cage. He walked twenty steps out into the field, set her down, and returned to stand with them on the road.

Out in the tall grasses, the female saw-whet looked so small. Vulnerable.

Dhani felt the twinge again. "She'll be alone."

"She's a wild creature," Jo said. "Instinct is already kicking-in. She'll be fine."

"Lots of people and animals live alone," said Claire.

Ray-Ray squeezed Dhani's shoulder.

"Is it alright," Dhani asked Jo, "if I walk back?" He looked at Ray-Ray and Claire. "By myself."

"Yes. But don't go near the owl. Leave her."

When they were gone, he stood alone on the dirt road, watching the small, living form out among the gray, dying stalks of grass. He knew she had to go. He felt stupid for feeling the way he did. Claire probably thought he was a jerk.

But he wanted to watch over the owl. Be sure nothing came out of the forest and got her. A fox. A coyote.

For a long time, he stood there, with the moon rising higher and the sky changing from gold to deepening blue. The cold air made his eyes water. So he told himself.

The owl preened her feathers, and called. Twice. Three times. Then again.

From the treetops to his right, another owl suddenly called back.

The female turned her head, fluffed her wings, and took off from the ground. With a dozen strong wing-beats, she lifted herself into the air, and landed on a gangly, lower branch of a jack pine at the edge of the woods. In a moment, the male saw-whet launched from the upper branch of a tall ash tree nearby, swooped down, and lighted three feet from her. He was larger, but not by much. They looked like a pair of small, brown, hand-puppets huddled together.

Dhani stood stock-still, enthralled, remembering a night back in the summer not far from this spot. Wishing that dream had been real. Wishing he was able to tell Claire of his feelings for her, the way this male saw-whet had called out his need for his mate.

The smaller owl leaned forward, dove into the air again, and winged its way up the slope of Eagle Rock Mountain to the higher, deeper forests there. The male stayed where he was, watching after her. Why didn't he follow?

Then it turned its head toward Dhani, and called.

Too-too, too-too-too-too-too.

Again and again it called, as if shouting at him. Or to him.

A warning—stay out of our territory?

A word came to Dhani's mind. *Friend.*

In another minute, the male saw-whet dove from the branch into the air, circled once over Dhani, and followed after the female.

As he walked back along the dirt road in the falling darkness, Dhani realized the sadness he had felt was gone. In its place he felt something he had never felt before. That maybe he belonged somewhere.

Here.

7TH

"What did you want to talk about today?"

Rocco and Bay crossed the bridge by Grady's gatehouse and headed down the camp road.

"I kissed someone I really like."

Bay raised her eyebrows. "You seem troubled. Did you force it on her? Is that why we're here?"

"No. I just stepped up to her and leaned in—didn't put a hand on her—and she let me."

"So, she didn't act like there was a problem. What did she do when you kissed her?"

"*Nothing.* But she said some girls kiss better, and that it told her everything about me that she needed to know just from one kiss."

"That could mean a lot of things. Probably, it told her she doesn't have feelings for you. That's normal. Have you ever kissed a girl and not felt anything for her?"

"Yeah. I acted like it did. But it didn't always. Not every time. Does that mean anything about me?"

"It means you're a human male and you're not attracted to every other human female."

"Shouldn't kissing a girl turn me on, though? Shouldn't I be able to like, heat up any girl?"

"Uh—no. That's not how it works. Where did that idea come from?"

He walked along beside her, silent, scuffing his shoes on the dirt road.

463

Bay waited several minutes before prompting. "Are you worried about something else besides that kiss?"

"I asked to talk to you the first time because of what you said about keeping bad people out of your life."

"Yes."

"I never back down from a fight. My dad taught me that."

His thoughts were disjointed, and she walked along quietly, waiting, but he couldn't seem to continue. "Do you always think the way your dad thinks?" she prompted.

"Well, I did. Until you made me think about some things."

"What did I make you think about?"

"How my dad would hate the stuff you're telling us."

"Ah.—But what do *you* think?"

"I don't think you can keep bad people out of your life. At least not in the world I come from."

"Rocco, we all have the power of choice."

Absently, he bent down, picked up a stone from the road and hurled it hard into the trees. "Like I said, not in the world I come from."

9TH

Watching in the sideview mirror, Dhani saw Steve come out of the convenience store. He loaded a bag into the back of the Range Rover along with two twelve-packs of beer. He looked away just as Steve raised his head to see if any of the guys in the vehicle were watching. A guilty move.

When Steve slid in behind the wheel, Dugan asked, from the passenger's seat beside him, "Why'd you bring us into town with you today?"

"I thought we could use a break from Lost Lake," Steve replied. "And I thought I should get to know each one of you guys a little better." Those were Tom's words, during a meeting yesterday. Along with these: "Kate and I both want you to work on your rapport with Dhani Jones." Those he kept to himself.

"Thank you, sir. Much appreciated," said Garrett from the backseat, next to Jalil who was squashed in between him and Dhani. "Very nice of Mrs. Holman to loan you her Range Rover. Thank her for us."

Dugan shot a quick look of disgust over his shoulder.

"Gratitude is a good thing," Steve said, nodding. "Make sure you thank her yourself."

"Will do, sir."

As Steve shifted into gear, he caught site of Dhani in the rearview mirror. His right leg was jumping. *People are antsy when they're hiding something.* "You nervous, Jones?"

"No," Dhani said. He sounded defensive. His neck and shoulders felt tight, and he quickly turned to look out the window.

As Steve pulled out of the parking lot, Dhani caught sight of two men talking on the far side of a dumpster. One had his back to them.

"Isn't that Ron?" Garrett asked.

Jalil leaned forward and peered out. "Could be."

"He's wearing bright blue running shoes like Ron wears."

"Wait—that's his truck. It's got marathon stickers all over the tailgate," Jalil said. "Why's he hanging out by a dumpster?"

Dugan laughed. "Man, you ever seen inside his truck? Maybe he's finally tossing out all the coffee cups, protein bar wrappers, and other crap."

He doesn't want to be seen, Dhani thought.

Inside the coffee shop at the west end of Main Street, Steve looked across the table at Dhani, who stared out the window beside them. The others were still waiting in a long line for breakfast sandwiches.

"If you take your hood down, it'll be easier for us to talk."

Dhani took a huge bite of his bear claw, and kept staring outside.

Steve tried to keep his voice level, and stay open. "You're a quiet guy."

Dhani shrugged.

"What kind of stuff do you like to do—online gaming? read books? write stuff? draw? skateboard, surf, ski?"

Why do you want to know? "I like video games," Dhani murmured, his mouth full of chewed pastry.

You need to have your butt tossed into the military. "You any good at them?"

"I can beat every level on most games."

Right. That'll get you a job. "Any kind of sports. Outdoor stuff?" Steve already knew the answer.

"Not really."

"So—*no.*"

Dhani could feel the irritation coming from behind the smiling mask across the table. He felt his stomach grip, and dropped the bear claw on the table. His head was starting to swim, and in his mind he heard a different voice—one that always set him up, trapping him with loaded questions.

"So, how *do* you spend your time?" Steve pressed.

Dhani heard it as, "How did you spend your time today?" Which meant he was supposed to list all the chores he had completed. And there would be trouble if he hadn't done *exactly* the most important one *exactly* the right way. It was always a guess what the right thing was, and he was usually wrong.

"I don't feel good. I think I ate too fast."

Steve felt his jaw tighten. Before he could speak, someone knocked hard on the window and got his attention.

Two women, one in a leather jacket, one in a parka, both in tight jeans, were smiling at Steve. They charged inside through the shop's glass door and dashed up to him.

"Hey, we haven't seen you at the pub lately."

"Where you been hiding?"

Before he could answer, the small-talk and fawning was interrupted by Jalil, Dugan, and Garrett's arrival.

Back in the Rover an hour later, Garrett laid it on. "Thank you again, sir."

Jalil was chowing down a third breakfast sandwich, and Dugan looked at him disgusted. "Dude, you got a tapeworm."

"You're welcome," Steve said to Garrett, but his mind was focused on Dhani. *This kid's a waste of space.* He would keep that to himself or it would bring on another of Tom's sermons.

Dhani stared out the rear window as they flashed by the grocery store again—Ron's truck was gone—and the pharmacy and a bike shop. He wished he'd had the guts to tell Steve's little groupies how he spent his time. Garrett had quietly spread the word about seeing empty beer bottles out on the island.

He hides out from everyone on his island, breaking the no-drinking rule. Because I guess it's okay to be a hypocrite. Just like every other bullying male he had ever known.

When Steve dropped them off at the path to the cabins, before Garrett walked away, he made a small gesture and summoned him back to the driver's side window.

"I want to talk with you."

"Yessir?"

"In private sometime."

"Today?"

"I've gotta get an equipment order in to Kate by tomorrow and then plan a challenge event. But I'll get with you—soon. And by the way don't mention it to anyone."

The field right behind the outbuildings was perfect for having a smoke. Not a long walk from the cabins and anyone approaching could be seen at a distance.

"What do you think that's all about?" Dugan asked.

Garrett tapped a cigarette out of the pack, then slid it into his jacket pocket. "Pretty sure it means you were wrong about me pushing it too far with Tanner. The good old Ober charm is working."

12TH

Jo stared at Mike Yazzie. "Flag football. Guys against girls, and you all want me to play? You're kidding, right?"

She straightened up from the examining table where she'd been checking the progress of the box turtle's broken shell with Ron.

Yazzie smiled. "Nope. Serious. The girls said they want you for team captain."

"Whose idea was this?"

"Dugan's. He talked a few of the girls into playing *touch* football, but I said, '*No*. Nice try. I'll organize a *flag* football game, though. You do not put your hands on these young women."

Ron lifted the turtle from the table, and its stumpy legs flailed in the air. "This guy's doing great, don't you think, Jo?"

"He needs another six or seven months here before that crack in his shell has bonded together enough. Mark his chart for a May or June release." She turned to Yazzie. "Okay."

He looked surprised. "Great—well, everyone's gathering on the lawn behind Kate's in about thirty minutes. We can use you, too, Ron. I'm ref-ing."

"Warn the guys I played a lot of flag football during college and vet school," Jo smirked. "We'll crush them. Who's their captain?"

"Tanner."

The world's most stuck-on-himself man, she thought.—"Perfect."

Steve pulled off his sweatshirt. In the strong, afternoon sun, jeans and a tee-shirt were enough.

"Sun's out, guns out, sir?" Garrett said. "Looks like you've been lifting."

Steve grinned. Then he knelt down and drew some patterns on the grass for Dugan and Jalil. "You guys are my running backs. Here's a couple passing plays. . . ."

"What do I do?" Garrett badgered.

"You're gonna be my secret weapon. I've got a couple of trick plays in mind."

Garrett flashed a grin at Dugan, who shook his head.

In another minute, movement to his right caught Steve's attention.

Jo emerged from the clinic, crossed the road, and joined her team—Imani, Makayla, Carter and Laurel Wysocki—on the grass. She had pulled her hair up into a loose ponytail and was wearing a tank top and running shorts—and Steve's mind flew back to the day she'd stepped out of Kate's rescue helicopter. She had been soaked to the skin, with a blanket falling open to reveal her athletic body. And there was the summer evening she had first brought Pal out to the island, when she stood so close to him he could feel her warmth.

"Hey, Tanner, we're gonna kick butt," she called out. Looking at Yazzie, who had the football, she held up her hands. "Toss me that baby."

Steve turned his head away. Why hadn't Mike told him *she* was playing? "We'll see who kicks butt."

Yazzie lateral passed the ball to Jo. "Let's go over the rules. This is for fun. No hard hits. Grabbing *flags only.*"

A half-hour into the game, Imani lunged at Jalil, who had just caught a pass, but stepped sideways and rolled her ankle. She fell to the ground, shouting and wincing.

Steve knelt beside her. "Did you feel anything pop or pull?"

Imani looked more annoyed than injured. "I'm fine. Just a dumb move. Inner-city girls don't play much football."

"Let's take a look. Can you get your shoe and sock off?"

Jo was kneeling on Imani's other side now, helping her sit up, and looking around. "Ron—?" she began.

He was already jogging across to the clinic. "Be back with an ice pack," he called over his shoulder.

Jo turned back to Imani—but found herself focusing on Steve, whose face was now close to hers.

Imani's shoe and sock were off, and Steve carefully lifted her foot—then looked at her. "Does that hurt?"

What caught Jo's attention most was his expression and the tone of his voice.

His deep set, brown eyes had always seemed hard to her, but now there was a softness, a gentleness. Likewise, his voice, which usually had a sharp edge, now held a note of care. She let her eyes roam over his muscular upper body. . . but quickly refocused on his face. His lips, nicely shaped, were now pursed in an expression of real concern.

Who was *this* guy? It would be nice if he showed up more often. She could almost wish she had not insulted him about having no woman in his life.

Ron tapped her on the shoulder. "Jo? I said here's an ice pack."

Grabbing it from his hand, she said, "Relax. I heard you."

Really, she hadn't.

20TH

"Are you seriously going to do this?" Makayla asked Rocco. She was shivering.

They were hiking out through the open fields behind Kate's outbuildings. The sky was clear and cold, and after last night's heavy frost, the tall grass was now bent, dry and sere. The stalks of summer wildflowers bent at sharp angles, gray and broken.

A river of icy air flowed over them, pouring down in two great currents from Lost Mountain to their left and Eagle Rock Mountain on the right.

Makayla's breath came in puffs. "The thermometer outside our cabin says it's twenty-seven degrees."

Rocco smirked. He swung his towel up over his shoulders and tied it around his neck like a cape. "Hey, I can handle it. I'm Superman."

Makayla pulled her scarf around up over her chin. "No. You're super crazy."

Imani laughed. "And here I thought you called yourself The Dream Lover."

They reached the lower pool at the base of Thunder Falls, where the others were gathering. Tanner was already there and had built a bonfire thirty yards back from the falls, next to a grove of cedars and away from the splash and spray that coated the rocks and boulders with glittering slashes of ice. Around the fire stood Garrett and Dugan, also Jalil, and Emmalyn, warming their hands, stamping their feet on the ice-gray grass.

Garrett called to Carter, who was standing alone, leaning against a rock wall on the far side of the pool. She was without a hat or gloves, her cheeks and hands bright red. "Hey, come get warm by the fire."

No reply.

"Water temp is right at freezing," Steve announced. "Who thinks they can take the plunge?"

"Polar bear challenge!" Jalil yelled, flexing his biceps.

"I'm in," said Rocco and Dugan simultaneously. And Rocco added, "At least I hope I can handle it."

Garrett grinned and shrugged. "Piece of cake, sir."

Emmalyn cough-laughed.

"Let's see what you say," Steve challenged, "when the ice cold water makes your skin feel like it's on-fire."

Jo and Laurel were coming across the field. Behind them was Ray-Ray, who was carrying a towel—also Claire, Dhani and Tia Leesha, who were not. Sahm was behind all of them with Vajra loping at his side.

"Why we out here today?" Tia Leesha asked. It's so friggin' cold."

"We've all gotta toughen up for the winter campout," Laurel smiled. "Keep moving. You'll get used to it."

"*Winter campout*?" Tia Leesha balked, stamping her feet to warm them. "You mean *sleep out in the snow*? Judge Sewell never told me about that. I don't like all these surprises."

Ray-Ray tried to lighten her mood. "Guess you should have read the travel brochure better before you left juvenile detention."

"Guess you should forget about a career in stand-up," she shot back, "because you're not funny. My eyeballs are freezing in my head." Tia Leesha sounded miserable. She stepped up to the bonfire and turned her butt toward the leaping flames. "I'm staying *right here.*—Why you having people jump in ice cold water anyway?" she called out to Tanner.

"Survival training. Those of you who aren't trying it can watch, listen, and learn."

She looked skeptical. "You ever try this before?"

"Sure have. During my training evolutions with the Royal British Marines in Norway. Only we did it in January weather. We cut a hole in an ice-covered lake, and built a small igloo next to it. Then we'd jump in the water for two minutes or we'd push it to three, which is about the limit anyone can handle. You know because your feet and hands start to not work. They feel like clubs. Then you have to haul yourself out and crawl in the igloo to revive."

Jalil looked impressed. "You went through that in training? I just don't think I can do it."

"Yeah. Also S.E.R.E.—which means, Survival Evasion Resistance Escape training. That's for when you're assigned to missions with a high risk of capture and torture."

"How do you train for that?"

"They torture you."

The only response was a circle of breath-plumes on the icy air.

"After the plunge," said Laurel, "you can slip into dry things inside that stand of cedars next to the falls. No one wants to see what you got."

"Says you." Garrett elbowed Dugan.

"Then we're going to cook out over this bonfire, and I'm going to talk about recognizing and treating hypothermia. You'll want to listen very carefully."

Steve pulled off his gloves and coat. "Let's do this. Lay all your clothes out by the fire, so they're warm when you come out."

He peeled off clothes down to gym shorts, then hung his shirt and pants, his polar fleece hat and gloves on sticks propped next to the fire. Then he stood up, bare chested in shorts and old running shoes.

"Last call for volunteers. Who's got the guts?"

"I already took a plunge in a frozen pond back in March—remember?" said Jo. "I'll stand by the pool and hand out the blankets as you guys come out."

Rocco and Dugan were peeling down to gym shorts and sneakers, with Garrett less quickly following their lead. Carter had come back to the fire, and was already stripped down to a tee-shirt, gym shorts and bare feet.

Once he stripped down to gym shorts, Garrett followed after Carter, who had moved away from the fire. He fought to keep from shivering and kept his muscles flexed.

"Tonight, me and couple others are gonna party. You wanna come?"

She glanced at him for a moment, as if she were trying to figure out what species he was, then looked past him. "Where do you guys party?"

"I'll tell you if you say you'll come. I only give out info on a need-to-know basis."

"First, tell me why you hate Rocco."

That surprised him, but he answered. "He's a jerk."

"Not more than any other boy in this program. Not more than you."

"Did I do something to you?"

"No. And I don't want you to."

"You'd like it."

He followed her gaze. She seemed to be staring at Imani, Makayla, or maybe Claire.

Carter laughed. "Has anyone ever liked you or liked what you did to them—*ever*? I can't even imagine that."

He was angry now. "Wait. I get it. You wanna hook up with one of them. Who is it—Claire, but she's not interested? Is that why you do the cold, vampire-girl thing all the time?"

She moved passed him toward the falls and drove a fist into his stomach.

"Yeah, and I haven't sent anyone to hell in a while."

"Can I go first?" Rocco volunteered.

Steve slapped his shoulder. "Brave man."

Garrett had followed them to the base of the falls, still holding one hand to his stomach. "Isn't there a saying—'fools rush in'?" Garrett jabbed.

"Yeah, and there's one about cowards hanging back," Steve threw at him.

Rocco let out a whoop and sprinted into the pool, splashing in the icy water until he was waist-deep. "OH. MY. GOD," he shouted. "MY NADS."

He dove under the surface and came up seconds later, shouting. "IT'S FREEZING."

From around the fire came cheers, whoops, and loud clapping.

Rocco was hopping up and down, his lips blue, his jaw shaking. "MY FEET ARE GETTING NUMB."

"Dude," Ray-Ray called to him, "it's not your feet you should be worrying about if your nads are freezing."

"*REALLY?*"

Steve was looking at his watch. "You're fine. See if you can stay in for at least two minutes."

Dugan was staring at Garrett.

"What?"

"You think you're 'in' with Tanner. Kissing up to him that day we went to coffee made me wanna puke. It's been two weeks, and he didn't ask you to come talk with him yet, did he?"

"He said he was busy for a while. He'll send for me."

"Uh-huh. Did you hear how he just dissed you when you tried to insult Tats? If you really want to get tight with him your next move better be good."

"Or bad."

Dugan shook his head. "That doesn't make any sense."

Sahm had been stoking the bonfire to a roaring blaze, and now stepped up beside them.

"May I join your counsel of war?"

"Why'd you say that?" Garrett looked wary.

Vajra sniffed at his hand and backed away.

Sahm was looking at his face with a placid, clear-eyed expression. "You have a spiteful look. So—inside you, I think there must be war."

Rocco was jumping up and down, slapping his chest, stomach, and arms. At the edge of the pool, Jalil walked back and forth unsteadily, his tennis shoes slipping on the icy rock scree. He was already shivering, his pale skin already mottled blue with cold.

"I'm next but—oh man, I don't know about this."

Tom keeps telling me to reach out to him, Steve thought, catching sight of Dhani, who had wandered away from the group. Thirty yards downriver, there was Dhani staring at a stand of fir trees—just gawking—hoody pulled close around his face. Why did he never take that stupid thing off?

Steve handed his watch to Jo. "Time Jalil for me. See if they can do one minute minimum."

"Unless they can't handle it," Jo rebuffed him.

He forced a grin. "They need to handle it."

He turned, and started to move over the strewn rocks and broken branches beside the river toward Dhani.

"Shouldn't you put some clothes back on?" Jo called after him. "At least a shirt?"

Steve ignored her.

When he was away from them, Laurel looked at Jo with raised eyebrows. "That body could melt ice."

"Not interested."

"Not even a little?"

"Walking around with his shirt off in this cold. Who's he trying to impress?"

"Maybe. . .you?"

"Lord, I hope not."

Dhani studied the flock of small, brown-gray birds flitting all around him. They looked like sparrows with bright red caps and chests. They had alighted in this stand of firs, pecking at the small cones, flitting from one tree to another. A few were hopping around on the snow beneath, snatching at the tiny brown seeds the others shook loose. With their feathers puffed out for warmth, they looked like round little Christmas ornaments that had come to life.

It surprised Dhani that he could get close to them, and they were not scared. At least they didn't fly off. More than that strange fact, he was drawn to their energy and animation. And by their movement as a group, which seemed to be choreographed.

All at once, they would shift suddenly from one tree to another, as if moved by a silent command. Maybe it was a special chirp or a certain flutter of a wing that one of them, a sort of flock leader, used as a signal.

Quietly, step by careful step, he approached one of the firs. Were these just small clicks, chirpings, electric-buzz-sounding trills, or some kind of bird whispers? He had the strange idea that there was a language here, and he had the even stranger idea that if he listened closely enough he could pick it up.

He was so near to one of the trees, the one where they were all lighting, that he could have touched it. What were the birds saying?

Hrrrrrrrrrrr—

"*Fly!*"—a warning shout resounded in his mind.

There was an explosion of wings. Small, feathered bodies burst from the green depths of the trees and scattered in all directions, wings flapping in Dhani's face, startling him—at the exact moment strong fingers dug into his shoulder and spun him around.

Tanner's face was two feet from his. Too close.

"Hey—I'm talking to you."

"I didn't hear you."

Steve forced himself to keep his cool, again, as he had at the coffee shop and too many other times.

"Seriously? I'm standing right behind you. You ignored me."

"I'm not lying."

Steve took hold of one sleeve of Dhani's hoody and tugged. "Why don't you take this off, and come do the challenge? Like the other guys. You need to participate."

"Don't *do* that." Dhani jerked his arm away, and looked anxiously past Steve. He was suddenly sweaty. "You said this was voluntary."

Steve's jaw clenched. "Maybe you should do it even if you don't want to." He reached out suddenly to grab Dhani's arm.

Dhani stepped back, avoiding his grip, and felt himself start to shake.

"No," he resisted. "Stop trying to force me. You're not allowed to touch me. That's a rule."

Everyone had gathered around the pool as Rocco stumbled out, shaking, teeth chattering. He accepted the towel, dry clothes, and a blanket from Jo, and stepped inside the cedar grove to change.

"Come on, Sahm," Garrett challenged him, lips pressed into a thin smile. "Why don't you jump in? You Tibetan guys know how to do that *sumo* thing. You should be able to stay in for—what?—maybe an hour or two."

"I believe you mean *tummo*," Sahm replied. "Fire meditation. Like all other practices, *tummo* is not for showing off. It is for thinning the ego, not for making it stronger."

The sound of splashing interrupted.

Carter had marched past Jalil into the icy pool, slowly and without flinching. Spray from the falls fanned over her. When she was up to her waist, she dove into the dark water, and came up—all without making a sound and ignoring the cheers.

"This one has very strong ego," Sahm declared. "Very strong."

Watching from beside him, Imani turned to Emmalyn and Makayla. "What planet did this girl come from?"

"Be nice," Emmalyn said, wide-eyed. "The Bible says—"

"If you say that one more time, I will *beat* you with a Bible."

Garrett stepped up behind Emmalyn, and put his lips close to her ear. "So the fake country girl is back."

"Just under three minutes," Jo announced, as Carter emerged from the pool, stumbled, and regained her footing, to shouts and clapping. Which she continued to ignore.

During Carter's ordeal—which is how Claire thought of this whole day—she approached Jo.

"Can I go do some sketching? I brought my pad."

"Sure," said Jo, distracted by timing Carter. "But make sure you're back when the challenge is done and everyone's warmed up again. Laurel's going to talk about hypothermia and winter survival practices."

No worries. I don't do stupid, polar bear challenges, Claire thought—but said, "I won't go far."

Though that was exactly what she planned to do. Get as far away as possible from the shouting and noise. She craved the spare emptiness of the late-fall forest.

Where the rock ridge came down from Thunder Falls, it met the edge of The Solitudes, all those miles of tangled wilderness that guarded the northern perimeter of Kate's land. Claire saw how the hardwoods grew close together here—a mix of stark silver maples, oaks clinging to last leather-brown leaves, and bare ash trees. A stand of massive blue spruce, their tops thrusting up like spires through the canopy, caught her eye and she headed toward them.

The sounds of shouting and laughter had faded away behind her, and when she slipped inside the wood line, the only sounds were the wind in the bare trees and the crunch of her footsteps in the fallen leaves.

She had come for what this part of the forest promised—solitude—but something about this particular spot was uninviting. Grady had said no one liked to hike here, and now she could see why. There was a threatening closeness in the solemn trees, and the twisted undergrowth crowded together creating heavy shadows all around. It did not help that this November gray-sky day made it look gloomy in under the trees.

Grady had said no hunters were allowed anywhere on the property, and she could not imagine why anyone would want to go much deeper into these woods.

A little further into the shadowed woods and she found what she'd come looking for. A sense of stark, bleak reality, which matched her mood.

Isolation. Emptiness.

A little further in, by a stand of blue spruce trees, there was a small, moss-covered boulder. She pulled herself up on it. Taking out pencils and her sketch pad, she laid them in her lap. In the lonesome forest all around her, a low, mournful sounding wind moved through the bare branches.

Perfect, she thought—ignoring the snap of a branch not far away in the deep woods.

Dugan slapped Rocco on the back. "Good job."

They'd stepped away from the pool, where Steve was now coaxing Jalil to do the challenge. Jalil had taken off his hat and handed it to Sahm. "Would you put this near the fire for me, next to Steve's stuff? I want it to be real warm when I need it."

Even through Rocco's sweatshirt, Dugan's slap stung. "Dude. Keep your hands off me," he growled.

"Did I hurt the widdle boy?"

"Smack me again, I'm gonna hurt you."

"You can try."

"I can do more than try."

Dugan looked around.

"DO IT. DO IT." Everyone was focused on Jalil, who had just emerged from the group of cedars wearing the pair of green gym shorts Steve had handed him.

"You think you can take me?—come on," Dugan challenged.

"Nah."

"Little girl can't stand up for herself. Just what I thought."

Rocco clenched his fists. "If you insist."

Dhani had taken off running in the direction of the bonfire, propelled by fear of Steve's anger. He didn't stop, and rounded the circle of clothing hung on sticks before the flames. Sprinting, he reached the

480

east side of the field, where the wooded slope of Eagle Rock Mountain began to rise.

Out of breath and gasping for air, he sought the shelter of the woods. Just inside the treeline, he sank down among tall ferns, next to spent raspberry bushes, against a weathered stump. The spongey rot of the wood cushioned his back, and he felt safe here in hiding. He would wait till his heart stopped beating in his neck before going back.

As his breathing slowed, a stirring among the ferns beside him drew his attention.

A small rust-brown creature with eyes like black beads and tiny twitching whiskers sniffed at the air for his scent. It sat up on its haunches, paws folded in front, looking like the world's smallest worried person.

Woodland jumping mouse. Jo had talked about these small creatures during one of her talks about endangered species. He recognized it by her detailed description—the longer back legs, its distinctive coloring, and very long tail.

The mouse's worried look made Dhani relax and smile. "Hey, buddy. You're not in any danger from me. I'm not going to try to grab you or anything."

Steve flashed in mind. He had almost grabbed Dhani's arm. He would never let Tanner get close enough to do that again.

He stared at the small frightened creature, started to say, "I feel ya, buddy"—but it was as if a camera had turned on in his mind. . . .

A big creature in a black hoody towered over him, saying, "If anyone comes, I'll protect you."

Heart beating, he dove into a hole beneath the raspberry bushes where he had feasted in the summer. Into the damp, dark earth he ran, but only a foot or two before turning to see if the predator was coming in after him.

A shadow passed over the small entrance to his underground hiding place. Then he turned and dove deeper into the passageway, and into blackness. . . .

He rubbed his hand over his eyes, wishing all these mind tricks would go away. *No wonder they call you the psycho kid who burned his mother's boyfriend. You* are *psycho.*

Blinking, he watched the woods stop spinning, and he stared down at the hole in which the mouse had disappeared.

These events had to stop. He did not want them to keep happening.

There was no rush of energy into his body this time, as there was with the lake, the river, and the snowy owl, but the vision was much stronger. A rush of *déjà vu* experiences came at him, but they could not be anything he had experienced before. . . .

He was hiding in a field of tall wet grasses, scenting the misty air, nosing the frozen ground for seeds.

The shriek of an owl startled him, and he dove for a different hole he had tunneled into the earth. The moist warmth and scent of loam was strong all around him as he plunged into safety. . . .

Then he was firmly in his own mind again, with the sense that he *was* safe. At least for the moment.

"You must become stronger," said a small voice in his mind. *"You were not brought here to hide."*

"Brought here?" he said out loud. "By who?"

A cold breeze in the field grasses was the only reply.

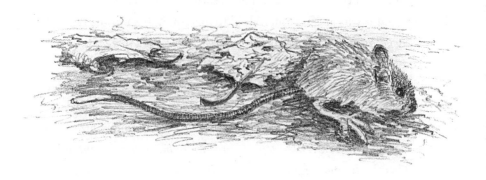

"*Fight!*" someone near the pool shouted.

Before Rocco could return many punches, Steve was beside them, wrapping his arms around Dugan's waist and hauling him off, while Sahm dragged Rocco up from the ground by the collar.

"My win," Dugan sneered.

"*Quiet,*" Steve shouted.

Rocco spat blood from his mouth, and started to lunge. Sahm stepped in the way, blocking him.

"*I can take you any day!*" Rocco shouted, veins standing out on his neck. "I'll bust your face."

"Maybe with your whole, mafia crime family behind you."

Rocco swore, and tried to pull away from Sahm. "*You bigoted—*"

"Both of you—*shut up!*" Steve shouted again. "Get yourselves together, and go sit by the fire. Opposite sides. And don't make eye-contact. This training day isn't over. When it is, you're going to report to me for nice, hard work detail."

When Rocco and Dugan were gone, Jo challenged. "Report to you?—or report to the Troverts?"

"They're just guys blowing off steam."

"Fist fighting is a pretty big infraction of the rules."

"A hundred-fifty pushups will do a lot more good than talking out their feelings."

"Tanner, there's a protocol here."

"I'll take that into consideration."

Laurel had arrived, and she looked at Sahm. "Where's your wolf?"

"He is right here—," Sahm began, then stopped.

Vajra had shadowed him all morning, but was now gone.

A few snowflakes were drifting down, now landing on the forest's carpet of dry leaves amid the skeletons of wildflowers, weeds, and shocks of brittle, dead grasses. Claire's attention had first been drawn to the tree next to her, a pin cherry with reddish bark and tiny orange spots along the branches.

The air had gotten colder, and she breathed on her bare fingers to warm them.

"Those spots on branches are called *stomata*," Laurel had told them. "They're how a tree breathes. Just like us, trees and plants have to exchange gases with the atmosphere. They're more like us than you'd think. They have a kind of awareness, and can sense danger and put out toxins to protect themselves."

". . .a kind of awareness." That sounded weird—but could it be true?

Her focus settled, not on the pin cherry, but on the steel-gray beech beside it. Each branch ended in tiny twigs that zig-zagged with no clear direction. Behind and all around these jutting lines was the looming emptiness of the gray sky. The tree's strange angularity against bleak air spoke to her mood. She bit the end of her pencil, then began.

In the back of her mind something troubled her, an awareness of. . .something. Like a presence.

She ignored it.

Engrossed in sketching, she quickly lost track of the sounds of the surrounding woods—the soughing of the wind, the occasional faint crack of a stick nearby. She shut out everything that was not beech branch, twig, and gray sky. Above all, she wanted to forget about the prosecutor who could force her to go to court where she might have to see her parents again.

A familiar sound caught her attention—a cough?—but the very instant she was aware of it the woods was already silent again except for the low wind still moving among the branches.

Nearby, maybe thirty feet to her right, another twig snapped.

She put down her pencil and stared at the grove of blue spruce. The sound had come from in there.

She waited, pencil resting on her pad. A dry, yellow leaf spiraled down from the beech tree, landing on the boulder beside her. Otherwise nothing moved.

Just a squirrel, she decided.

Focusing back on the point of her pencil, she spooled out more of the thin black line that was capturing the next beech twig on paper.

Another snap. This one a little louder and nearer.

A tingle shot up Claire's spine this time, and her hand froze.

It's nothing. Stop freaking out. She was fine out here alone, just as she'd always been fine on her own her whole life.

She forced the pencil's black line to keep moving, but in a moment another sound came. This time from her left.

From twenty feet away, Sahm's wolf stood watching her.

She let out a long, relaxed breath. "Vajra. You scared me."

The creature's ears perked, and its penetrating eyes were fixed on her.

She felt a small shock of anxiety. All alone with this creature, she realized how huge it was—its shoulders higher than her waist, its head and jaws massive.

Vajra growled, lips curling back to reveal curved, white fangs. Lowering his head, he began to move toward Claire.

Those snapping sounds she had heard in the trees. *He's been following me. What is he—*

Vajra went into a low crouch and moved closer, snarling.

"Vajra—good boy."

Teeth bared, he slowly crept through the crunching leaves until he was close enough to leap at her.

Claire wanted to scream but this far from the group who would hear her, much less reach her in time to stop him from tearing her apart?

With a snarl, Vajra lunged.

Claire wildly threw her pad and pencil at him and wrapped her arms over her head—small defense against the crushing, tearing jaws of a wolf.

But he charged past her, barking and snarling, dashing into the wall of blue spruce, snapping branches with the force of his strong body.

Immediately, there was a loud *thump*, followed by sharp yelps of pain—and whatever was concealed by the thick trees went crashing away from Claire deeper into the woods, breaking branches as it ran. By the sound, whatever was fleeing was large. A bear?

Claire dropped her arms. *"Vajra!"* she shouted. *"Where are you? Come back."*

Vajra emerged from the thicket, limping, and letting out small whimpers of pain. He kept turning to bark and snarl, though, as the sounds of escape grew more distant and finally ceased. Then he turned and hobbled through the leaf litter back toward the boulder where Claire sat, arms now wrapped around her knees, forcing herself to stop shaking.

Vajra was heavily favoring his right front leg, but Claire could see no sign of a wound caused by whatever had struck him. He stopped beside her, as if on-guard, turned his head to watch the deep woods and growl again—but no more sounds came.

Slipping down from her seat, steadying herself, Claire retrieved the pad and pencil.

Vajra circled Claire once, then leaned against her, sides heaving. Up close, she now saw a trickle of blood in the fur on his right shoulder. Something had struck or bitten him there with enough force to cut him.

He had been with Sahm an hour ago, and it occurred to her to wonder *why* he had come looking for her. To protect her?

An unexpected rush of warmth came, and she stretched out a hand to pet him. She stroked the broad crown of his head once—then quickly withdrew the hand.

No.

She was sorry he was hurt. But she would not let herself connect with anything or anyone. No person or animal. There was a stark security in believing she was all alone in this world with no one to count on. Wishing someone would be there for you was stupid. Alone was best. Alone was reality.

The wall inside her was quickly rising again. And with it came another thought. Were Kate and Tom really working to keep her here in the Lost Lake program for her own sake—or was it for the sake of the program and Kate's success?

When she made her way out of the woods, heading back to Thunder Falls, Vajra remained with her, quietly limping two steps behind.

The group was gathered around the bonfire again and Tanner held up a khaki hat that was partly charred black and smoldering. The air stunk of burnt wool.

"Anyone see who did this?" Steve's voice shook with anger.

Claire stepped up beside Ray-Ray. "What happened? Where's Dhani?"

"Tanner thinks someone threw his hat in the fire. And I don't know."

"Maybe a gust of wind blew it in," Jo said calmly.

"What about Singe?—I mean that Dhani kid," Garrett suggested. "I saw him running by here a while ago during your polar bear thing."

"What about Carter?" Imani interjected, as if she sensed what Garrett was up to. "She disappeared, too. And by the way, Garrett, after you changed your clothes behind those cedar trees, I didn't see you at the falls."

"It took me a while to get dressed."

"In this cold weather, it took you *a while* to get out of wet, freezing cold shorts and put clothes on?"

Jo intervened. "Steve, you're making a big assumption that someone threw your hat in the fire. The more important thing right now is we've got two not accounted for. We need to locate Dhani and Carter."

"They shouldn't have wandered off. We're not here to babysit." He was red faced, and on the verge of rage.

Jalil pointed to the north side of the field. A figure was emerging from the thick woods. "There's Carter."

When she finally stepped up to the group, every eye was on her. She ignored them all and stared into the fire. "I had to pee," she said, as if she knew the question.

Jo challenged Steve again. "Now there's a legitimate reason to go off on your own."

Ray-Ray whispered to Claire. "I wonder where she really went. She left a while ago. It doesn't take that long to pee."

"If you're looking for that Dhani kid," said Carter, "I saw him running away maybe an hour ago. It was like he was running from something."

Claire made a disgusted sound, and Ray-Ray whispered to her. "Geez, if your eyes were lasers that girl would vaporize."

She was glaring at Carter. "That's the idea. Why would she say that, unless she's trying to shift the blame?"

Steve ignored Jo and Carter, and held up his charred hat again. "If anyone knows who did this come and see me in private. Now finish getting dried off and dressed."

Jo stepped beside him and said in a low voice, "Let it go, Tanner."

He pulled on his shirt, and his eyes locked on hers with a look of hostility. "I want to know who did this."

"The wind could have blown it in, and you can get another hat. It's not a big deal."

"It's a big deal *to me*. I got this when I was serving in Afghanistan. Something none of these hand-fed adolescents can even remotely understand."

"Excuse me?" Jo bristled. "Hand-fed? Did you ever read the files on some of these kids?"

Steve stared back at her, his eyes flashing anger, and held up the scorched hat.

"No one here, including you, has been in a war zone. *This* reminds me of men and women who served and gave their lives—for you, by the way. Some of them didn't come back alive. If some little smartass who has no respect for that kind of sacrificial service did this, I want to find out who it is. Now you can help me or not. Simple as that."

"I choose 'or not'," she replied. "Now you did your thing, and Laurel needs to do her thing."

"And I choose—"

She cut him off with a sharp whisper. "You're *part* of this program, Tanner. Not the *center* of it. You see enemies where they don't exist. Accidents happen. *Refocus*."

He felt the urge to hit her. And then felt ashamed and sick in the pit of his stomach.

In the next hour, a heavy blanket of darker gray clouds moved in, adding to the dark mood. The air became even colder, and an occasional snowflake drifted in the air. Next to the bonfire, Laurel was finishing up, when Dhani returned.

He was careful to notice where Tanner was standing, and walked around to the far side of the fire, where Claire was rubbing her arms and Ray-Ray warmed his hands.

"When you're outdoors in the winter," Laurel was saying, "especially when the temperature drops fast like today, here are some signs that hypothermia is setting in. We call them the 'umbles'."

"Where did you go?" Claire hissed to Dhani. She was shivering, moving her legs to stay warm.

"Nowhere."

"You were somewhere."

"I was with this cool, little mouse."

Claire ignored the weird answer. "Tanner thinks someone threw his hat in the fire. Did you do it?"

"*No.*" He sounded fierce. "Why would I? I want to be as far away from that jerk as possible. Why would I want to piss him off at me? I hid out for a while in the woods." He reached up and pulled the strings of his hood tighter, so only a small circle of his eyes, nose, and lips was showing.

"You *look* like you're hiding something."

Her accusation stung. "I'm *not.*"

Laurel rubbed her hands, warming them, and ran through the list. "The 'umbles' are—stumbling, mumbling, and grumbling. If you see someone's personality changes and they get physically weaker or can't focus, then you're dealing with hypothermia. Sometimes it's hardest to catch it in ourselves. Our mind can keep telling us we're okay, we're doing fine, and all the while the cold is taking us over. It can happen pretty quickly."

"If it was Tia Leesha, how would we know?" Jalil laughed. "She always mumbles and grumbles."

"If it's a mild case, you can walk fast or run a little, eat food, sip something hot. That will raise your body temperature fast. If it's moderate, you just stop caring or answering or your responses don't make sense. Then you have to curl up in a ball or wrap yourself tightly in a blanket or coats. Do the hot drink thing, too. Severe hypothermia is very hard to reverse without medical assistance. Go for help."

Tia Leesha had ignored Jalil, and looked solemn. "You can die from the cold, right?"

"Yes, but here's the thing. Severely hypothermic people who only appear to be dead have been revived. There's a saying. A person is never dead from the cold until you warm their body and they're still dead."

Rushing water and snapping flames were the only sounds. Tia Leesha and Emmalyn both stepped closer to the bonfire.

"If I ever look like I'm dead," said Tia Leesha, "don't stop trying to revive me. I don't wanna die."

Dhani looked across the fire.

Tanner was staring at him, looking like a predator ready for a kill.

Imani broke the brief silence. "Why are we talking about dying?"

"Because," said Laurel, "so far we've been doing safe hikes. We're gonna push it pretty soon, and whenever you push the edge things can go south. Fast. You need this information."

Carter stared into the fire. "I'm bored here. I like the edge. I like pushing it."

Dhani fled as soon as things broke up, moving quickly back to the cabins to stay ahead of everyone.

A strong hand clamped down on his upper arm.

"Why're you trying to escape so fast, dude?" Tanner had caught up from behind. "Second time in one day you ignored me when I called to you."

He held up the charred, khaki fleece hat, shoving it close to Dhani's face so he could smell the stink of burned fiber. "Did you do this?"

Dhani tried to pull away, but Tanner's fingers dug harder into his bicep.

"*Ow.*" Dhani squirmed in pain. "Take your hand off me. Why are you blaming me?"

Tanner's face was so close to Dhani's he could feel the breath.

"You're the guy who likes burning things. You torched your mother's boyfriend. You stuck Garrett with a burning stick. People saw you running past the fire, when everyone else was watching the challenge."

"If they were watching the challenge how did someone see me?"

Tanner's face went bright red. "My commanding officer always said, you can trust a thief sometimes but you can never trust a liar."

"I'm not lying," Dhani objected.

He twisted hard, pulling painfully out of Tanner's grip, and bolted.

Crossing the field behind them, Claire saw Dhani running away from Tanner.

"Something's wrong," she said to Ray-Ray, who was at her side. "Maybe you should get back to your cabin fast and see if Dhani's okay."

She could not focus on Dhani now. As soon as Ray-Ray was gone, her thoughts flipped back to what had happened inside The Solitudes. She had thought the sounds from the deep woods were made by a wild animal. What she had heard after returning to the group changed her mind. Not some*thing* but some*one* had been stalking her. Again.

Ahead of her, Carter was walking alone. As always.

Picking up her pace, Claire passed Carter. Then stepped in front of her, and stopped.

Carter did not stop, and slammed into her full force, knocking Claire backwards.

Claire grabbed her by the arm. "Why did you follow me today? You didn't leave the group to take a pee. You're always stalking or watching me. What did you do to hurt Vajra?" She felt herself losing it and her voice rose. "*Why can't you leave me alone?*"

Imani and Makayla came up on them.

"Whatever's going on here, you guys should stop now," said Imani.

In place of her usual blank mask, Carter had a strange look.

"I'm not stalking you. But I'll bet you wish I was. That would give your pathetic, little rich-girl life some drama and meaning."

"You stalked me that day at Thunder Falls. You were watching me back in the summer when I was outdoors sketching. And today I saw you come out of the woods, right near where I was when Vajra charged at someone hiding in the trees."

"How did your drawing go today?"

"So you admit it. You were following me again."

Carter rolled her eyes. "You're holding your little sketch pad and pencils, jerk."

"What did you hit Vajra with? He's hurt."

"If that wolf-thing came at me, trust me, it would be dead."

"What would you do—freeze it with your icy stare?"

492

"You're accusing the wrong person. Other people in this program are a lot more wily than me."

Without warning, Carter slammed her hands into Claire's shoulders, a blow that knocked Claire backwards. "Get out of my way. Maybe I should get a restraining order against you. That would look bad in Holman's reports to the judge about you—wouldn't it, rich girl?"

Claire doubled one fist, and slammed Carter in the shoulder as she passed. "You're trying to provoke me."

"*Stop*," Imani raised her voice—and Makayla shouted, "You're both out of control."

"You're the one who just got all up in my face," Carter gloated at Claire. "Now you hit me. Go ahead. Do it again. I'll even give you the first three or four punches. Better make 'em good ones."

"LEAVE ME ALONE," Claire roared in Carter's face.

Carter pushed past, knocking her in the shoulder as she went.

"*I'm going to Kate right now*," Claire shouted after her. "I'm going to tell her what you're doing."

Carter glanced back over her shoulder, first at Imani and Makayla, then at Claire. "Who hit who first? I have witnesses."

21ST

Ray-Ray pounded on Dhani's bedroom door, and tried the handle.

There was no answer and it was still locked, as it had been all last evening.

"It's Sunday morning, dude. You know Ivy serves waffles with real maple syrup on Sundays. You like that."

Still no answer.

"Want me to bring you some?"

Ray-Ray waited another minute. "You missed dinner last night. You gotta come out sometime. You gotta talk to me and tell me what's going on," he said—though obviously the run-in with Tanner had shaken Dhani badly.

"Okay, I'll be back after breakfast. We can hang out."

Curled in a ball on his bed, Dhani had not taken off his clothes or shoes from the day before. He had slept only a little.

When he did sleep, the Monster came at him out of the dark. Cornering him. Grabbing his arm, digging in his fingers, pinching, twisting—telling him what he was about to do to him. Painful, tormenting things.

Each time the image came, his body trembled and shook, and he felt the heat of shame on his face.

The Monster had always followed through on his threats, even the most terrible ones, and didn't stop until Dhani screamed and peed himself. He let his mind return. . . .

. . .to the darkness and safety of a small tunnel in the earth, and to the softness of a fur-packed nest.

Even if his vision in the woods was childish imagination, or some trick of his mind, it helped.

But he would have to remember not to mention these things to Claire. She had clearly thought he was weird when he mentioned yesterday's encounter with the wary little animal.

I don't want to be psycho boy.

Steve walked in a circle around his cabin's open room. He would not make eye-contact with Tom.

"What else do you want from me? I reached out. I took him for coffee, and he totally blew me off. I tried to encourage him to hang out with the group, and he tossed my favorite hat in the fire."

"You don't know that for sure. That's point one."

"You and Kate and everyone else are watching and evaluating me all the time. What about these kids? Do I get to evaluate them? I'm doing everything I can to reach the Jones kid. *Just like you asked.* And he doesn't give half a crap."

"He's come from a very rough place."

Steve stopped and turned on him, raising his voice. "*So does half the planet, Tom.*"

"What if this kid's not the little victim of a bad home, like you guys think he is? He's just fine when he's hanging around with his two buddies. But if I go anywhere near him, ask him a question, he turns away like he's got something to hide. Every time. Oh, and tell him to do something?—he goes into retrograde. If you ask me, this kid is here for a free ride in a place where he only has to put out minimal effort."

Tom kept his voice even but firm. "I want you to promise me you'll stay away from Dhani Jones. Clearly, he's triggering something in you. Focus on the students you think you're reaching."

Steve stopped pacing, and tossed up his hands.

"Stay away from him? Fine. Focus on the kids who're responding. That I can do. Gladly."

Tom had been gone for hours when someone knocked at Steve's cabin door.

Garrett was leaning against the boulder next to the steps. "I got your message. Why did you want to see me, sir?"

Steve held up the burned hat. "I need eyes and ears on the ground, to keep a better watch on things. I'm sure some of these people put on a good show for the Troverts and the other instructors."

Garrett's mind was quickly recalibrating. During the cold water challenge, he had thought Tanner's attitude toward him had soured. He did not expect this—exactly what he wanted. He tried to look innocent, uncomprehending. "Not sure what you're asking, sir."

"What really happened yesterday? Who started the fight—Dugan or Rocco?"

"Why are you asking *me*?"

"I'm asking because you've got sharp eyes and you notice things. You were the one who saw Dhani near my hat right before it got tossed in the fire. And you were near those guys when the fight broke out. You seem to have respect for authority, and you get the way I'm trying help you guys shape up. So I'm asking—will you be my intel guy?"

Garrett saw his opening but, to be safe, faked a look of concern.

"I'm not gonna lie. That puts me in a tough spot, sir, reporting on my peeps."

"I'm not interested in adolescent drama and angst," Steve said, abruptly. "I think you know as well as I do, some of your 'peeps' are here for all the wrong reasons. Some of them have agendas. So, are you my man or not? If not, you need to keep your mouth shut about this conversation and I'll find someone else."

"I'd be honored, sir."

"Good. I need someone I can count on."

Garrett met Steve's gaze with a wide-eyed, innocent look. "Since you asked—it was Rocco, sir. He's respectful to your face, but it's a front. When no adults are around, he starts stuff. He's a bully, and he's all over the girls all the time. I think they're afraid no one will believe them, so they don't speak up."

Charging back across the bridge from the island to the shore, Garrett's mind was wild with possibilities. Suddenly, unexpectedly, things were about to become so much easier than he could have hoped.

Steve sat out on the cabin's back porch for a long time, hands clasped, satisfied.

The Troverts might be all heads-up-their-butts about "understanding" these kids. Tom and Kate might be blinded by their own compassion. He was not going to let anyone gaslight him into believing the real problem here was him.

He would prove that certain kids needed serious discipline—or they needed to go back to detention. He had at least one in mind.

26TH

"This little lady is a female Indiana bat. Not the same as a small brown bat, though they look a lot alike at first. Randy found three of them."

The little brown creature in Jo's gloved hand emitted tiny, high-pitched squeaks, and tried to flap its charcoal gray wings.

"See—you can tell by the color of the snout, the way her fur shines, and by this small bit of cartilage where her wing meets her leg just above the foot. They're important to me. To all of us, really."

Jo had gathered all four tribes in the small mammal wing of the barns. In the corner, near the otter pool, Ron was building a large enclosure made of fine mesh and had stacked rocks to form a small cave.

"What's wrong with them?" asked Ray-Ray. "Why do you have her here?"

"Sharp-eyes over there spotted them." She nodded at Randy Wolfmoon, who had slipped into the room behind them all. "He was laying out some climbing and rappelling routes over at The Arrows and he saw this one's head peeking out from a crack in the bark of a tree. They find little hiding places like that. The other two were tucked into small fissures in the rock face."

"It's too late in the year for them to be out on their own," Randy added. "And they were severely lethargic. I knew they'd be dead soon."

"Why?" Makayla asked.

Randy picked up on her question. "Why would he be dead soon? Because it's only okay for these guys to nest out on their own in the warm months. In the fall and winter they need to pile up in big heaps in caves to conserve body heat.

"Over in the Mohawk caves on Lost Mountain, I used to see hundreds of them piled on each other in one square yard. There used to be tens of thousands east of here around Lake Champlain. Now they're declining really fast there, along with other bat species. Even faster than anywhere else."

"Weren't you afraid she was going to bite you?" Imani asked. She appeared interested in Jo's talk—but Ray-Ray had noticed she was also eyeing him from across the room.

"I had thick climbing gloves on, and I could tell she was lethargic. With the rapid metabolism these guys have, she was burning up her small amount of fat stores fast. Pretty much, she was going to die."

"Lots of animals die from the cold, though—right?" said Garrett. "What's the big deal about saving a couple little bats? Don't they carry diseases, like rabies? Shouldn't we just snuff them out?"

"That brings us to why Randy saved her," said Jo, "and why Ron is building an enclosure for her. Yes, Garrett, any wild animal can carry rabies. But Indiana bats are highly endangered. In fact, all bats are in trouble, because of what's called white-nose disease—caused by a fungus that infects their muzzle, ears, and wings during hibernation when they're most vulnerable. Indiana bats, in particular, have been on the Federal Endangered Species list since 1967, and their numbers are dropping rapidly."

"But why do we *need* them?" Tia Leesha jumped in. "They scare me. I think they're going to get in my hair and bite my head."

"You're watching too many horror movies," Jo responded. "Among other things, bats keep the mosquito population down. Each one eats hundreds of mosquitoes every night. The point is, we can't afford to lose any bat species, and apart from loss of habitat we don't know all the factors that add up to why these guys are dying out. We need to learn what's killing them off."

Ray-Ray looked thoughtful. "You told us during the hawk migration count that bird species are dying off, too. Why do I feel like something really bad is happening all around us?"

"Because it is. Some call it the 'sixth extinction'. Lots of species are in rapid decline, and we're losing *two hundred* species a year."

"What about humans?"

"We could be next if we don't get our act together."

Ray-Ray was still watching Imani, who was still watching him. She was nodding and smiling now.

"*What?*" he mouthed.

"Here's the thing—because these three guys are from an endangered species, we're going to keep them over the winter for study. This one's healthy, as far as I can tell—but why was she staying away from the main group over at Champlain, where she would have been safer and not gotten cold and lethargic? The other two have very early signs of white-nose, and I've got a new bio-agent—called chitosan—being overnighted so we can start her on it."

Jo looked at Emmalyn. "You called the order in yesterday, right?"

Emmalyn nodded vigorously. "Kate had me order a bunch of supplies yesterday and I called your order in first. They said it would be here today."

When the group broke up, Ray-Ray stopped Imani.

"Why were you staring at me again?"

499

"I figured out why you look familiar. It was your *brother* in that limo that night. Had to be."

"Not possible."

"Man, your brother's in a gang or he's hangin' out with bangers, and you don't even know."

"I told you that's not possible. I told you, he feeds the homeless and stuff."

"What's his name?"

"Ezra."

"Right. And they kept calling him 'EZ'. Guess that's what he goes by on the street."

"'EZ' could be anyone." He deflected. "Is that why you're here— because of something you did in a gang?"

She got quiet. "No. Not what I did. What someone else did."

"You got blamed for a crime someone else pulled off? I know all about that. So what did they do?"

It was her turn to dodge. "Next time you talk to your brother, tell him he has no idea what the people he's with are capable of doing. Gangbangers let wannabes hang out with them. They test them to see what they're willing to do before they let them come inside. Get them to run drugs. Assault a rival gang member. Lotta people think it's cool to hang with the bad dudes, but pretty soon they're in and can't get out. He should get away from them now. Very. Far. Away."

Ray-Ray rolled his eyes. "Whatever. My brother's not try'na be in a gang."

"I guess he's safe then, and I just wasted my breath."

"Dude, your bucket's overflowing."

Claire was behind Ray-Ray in the janitor's room. "What's up? You look like you're a million miles away."

Just five hundred, he thought, his mind back in DC.

He was wishing Imani would shut up about Ezra. He also wished he knew why his mind kept replaying the day his father threw him out. There was something he needed to recall about it.

An image was stuck in his head, somehow incomplete—of his father standing in the open front door, his face harsh and forbidding, with Ezra half in shadow in the hallway behind him.

10

CHRISTMAS

The van Claire had climbed into was full. Disappointed, Dhani had to stuff himself into the backseat of Mike Yazzie's car with Garrett and Dugan for the drive to the Troverts' party on Christmas Eve day. The holiday lights and greenery of Lake Placid village did nothing for his mood.

He would, he had to, stop thinking about home and his mother. She had not reached out to him with a phone call, an email, or a card. He held onto her offhanded remark that, in a small way, made her silence make sense. "It'll be easier if you forget all about me and all our troubles while you're away."

He guessed that she was only trying to make it bearable. It almost was.

"Singe-o," Garrett snarked, breaking Dhani's reverie. "Maybe you can light the Troverts' holiday candles."

Dugan punched his leg. "Shut up, man. It's Christmas Eve. Lay off him."

"You got some kind of mouth on you, don'cha Garrett," said Mike Yazzie, staring at him in the rearview mirror. "Maybe you could use it to answer questions better in my class. A 'D' is nothing to be proud of."

Garrett kept his cool. "You supposed to be telling everyone my grades? Isn't that a violation of teacher ethics or something?"

"You got that confused with medical or legal ethics. *I* can say what I want."

That shut Garrett down, and the rest of the ride through Lake Placid and up the narrow pass between mountains east of the town was silent.

"Christmas can be tough, I know, but who has a good Christmas memory?" Eric prompted them. "Like—when I was seven I got the bike or computer game I really wanted."

Those who had stayed at Lost Lake, which was most of them, arrived at the Troverts' at two, when the sun was already behind Whiteface, the Olympic ski mountain scarred by avalanches, which lay to the west. The cabin lay in shadow already. Candles shone from the windows, a fire roared in the family room fireplace next to the Christmas fir tree, and the scent of cinnamon and ginger met them in the kitchen, where the table was crowded with platters of meat and vegan sandwiches, frosted Santa and snowman cookies, a pot of fondue cheese with cut vegetables for dipping.

"So, who's got a really nice memory?" Eric repeated.

Bay leaned close. "I don't think it's a good idea to be mining for good memories right now."

He winked at her.

Mike Yazzie spoke up, to break the silence. "My mother got me Muay Thai lessons when I was a kid. Where I grew up, that probably saved my life a few times."

Rocco, who had been quiet all day, looked over at him. "Cool."

"My boyfriend bought me a twenty-two pistol one year," Carter said.

"Of course he did," Imani whispered to Dugan, who was standing close to her on the other side of the room. "What else would you buy for the girl who has everything, including 'scary disorder'?"

He had just taken a bite of roast beef sandwich and he cough-spit the glob into his hand. "Don't do that. I almost choked."

"My brother and I built a snowman on Christmas Eve one year," said Ray-Ray. "That was rare for DC. We don't get much snow."

Garrett rolled his eyes—and Dugan elbowed him in the ribs and whispered. "What's your best memory—the year your dad gave you something that *wasn't* hot?"

"I remember one Christmas Eve I didn't get hit or sent to my room," said Dhani.

Except for the sound of Eric pouring cups of hot cider, the room was silent.

"Rocco—anything?" Bay asked quickly.

He shifted uneasily. "I'd really like to see High Falls Gorge? It's like, a half-mile up the road, right?"

Bay nodded. "Be careful on the footbridges. Really icy. Mike, would you go with him?"

There was foot shuffling around the buffet table and plates were filled, followed by the scattering of ones and twos throughout the cabin.

Bay sipped her cider, and said to Eric, "So that went well."

Monica Saint, the woman from D.C. Child Protective Services, asked a lot of questions—and judging by her scowl and voice, she was in a bad mood.

"I drove all the way out here from Washington to this farm at Judge Sewell's insistence," she said, when she closed the French doors and parked herself on the sofa in Tom Baden's parlor. "It was very difficult to find my way on all these winding, dirt roads."

Emmalyn felt trapped in here with this gray-haired old woman, who seemed to have an axe to grind today. She grilled her about studies, cabin cleanliness, whether her encounters with the instructors and chaperones were appropriate. It felt as if she were looking for flaws.

After each of Emmalyn's replies, Monica Saint wrote a long note on her legal pad.

"I must tell you, I was not in favor of sending twelve young people hundreds of miles away. Sewell likes to pull strings and use his government connections. But I can tell you, my standards are not going to be ignored.

"Now, is there anything you'd like to tell me about the program—you can speak freely—anything that's troubling you?"

"No."

The old woman's eyes bore into her, and Emmalyn felt she had to serve up something.

"Well, one thing sorta bothers me. There's this guy who's into this weird religion. His name is Sahm. He helps with the outdoor stuff and in the animal clinic, and he's a Tibetan witch doctor or something. It's his false religion. That's what my mama would say. It's against the Bible. He's nice, but he's got a weird altar that creeps me out."

Monica's pen stopped and her eyes were steely. "Why is that?"

"It's got statues of his gods on it. I think he prays to them. And rocks and pictures of demons he uses to do—I don't know—voodoo, I guess."

"Does he teach you about his religion?"

"Not me. But I heard he's teaching one kid how to pray to his gods or something."

Monica's pen began to move quickly. "Thank you. Will you send in Jalil Malik?"

Claire had wandered away from the group into the Troverts' family room. Makayla was already there, alone on the sofa, and Claire sat at the far end of it. Neither one spoke for a long time, lost in their own heads.

"I hate Christmas," Claire said finally, wishing her words could drive away the whole tableau in front of them—the silver and gold ornaments shining on Eric and Bay's perfectly trimmed fir tree, the flaming logs singing in the fireplace.

At the far end of the sofa, Makayla wrapped her arms tightly around her torso, as if protecting a hurt child or blocking a blow. "I hate it, too."

"Everything. My whole life. It was all wrecked on Christmas," said Claire, her voice grim.

They looked away from the fire, each staring out a different window at light snowflakes drifting down outside, recalling different pasts. . . .

Every cereal box in the pantry held only crumbs. The top two shelves in the refrigerator were packed with beer and the freezer was empty except for two bottles of vodka.

Claire closed the refrigerator and stepped back into a cold puddle. Annie, the white fur ball that was her Great Pyrenees puppy, had piddled on the kitchen floor. Knowing her father might kick her pet, she wiped up the puddle with paper towels while the dog kept wagging her tail and stepping in it, pawing at her for food—though there was none for her either.

She walked on bare, cold feet from the kitchen through the family room toward the stairs, Annie at her heels yipping. Her parents had forgotten and left the Christmas tree lights on all night. They had forgotten and left the flue open, as well, and an icy draft was scattering ashes on the brick red oriental carpet. Under the tree were toys in their factory boxes, each with just a bow stuck on it so she could see exactly what the toy was before even opening it. She could see a French porcelain doll, brown hair done up in a twist, dressed in forest green, a frilly white umbrella dangling from one wrist—identical to the one they'd given her last year.

"Why aren't they wrapped in nice-colored Christmas paper?" she had said to her mother, who was placing the packages under the tree the evening before.

"Why are you making it a big deal, Claire? It's all stuff for you. That's good enough—right? Go put on your nighty and get in bed."

Her mother had slurred her words, and Claire knew she and her dad had been partying. That's what they called it. They had sent her to bed, then sat up by the fire and drunk alcohol and sniffed white powder—she'd watched them do it, peeking around the doorframe into the family room. Her mother laughed at her dad. "You're wasted."

"Here's to a record-breaking year," he grinned, swigging from a vodka bottle.

They both laughed.

Now it was Christmas morning, and there was no cereal, and she would go and try to wake them, but they would not get up until noon, and she was hungry and the house was cold.

She had just begun to climb the stairs in the foyer, Annie stumbling after her, when a crash at the front door made her scream. A second crash, and the door splintered wide open and a dozen men in helmets and uniforms poured in with a wave of frigid air, pointing guns at her.

She had clutched the bannister and kept screaming—hearing from upstairs her mother shout something and her father swear.

The men had charged upstairs past her, while one of them took her by the arm, not roughly, peeled her fingers from the bannister and led her from the foyer back to the family room, where he sat beside her on the sofa and kept saying, "It's alright. Trust me, no one's going to hurt you."

But the men's loud voices and her mother's shouting back at them went on and on, along with Annie's yipping from wherever they'd taken her. Shaking, terrified to look up, she had stared down at the boots of the man who sat beside her on the sofa, now holding her wrist too tightly. He had on black boots. Like Santa's.

From a corner of her eye, she caught a movement outside. Through a side window, she saw her father, running. He must have fled down the back stairs and out the mudroom door.

Over his shoulder was a large, khaki duffel bag. He dodged around *his Mercedes sports coupe and her mother's Porsche, leapt the low fence next to the drive, and headed out the path through gray trunks of the apple orchard, sprinting towards the stream and her grandparents' property.*

He was escaping.

Claire felt a shock of pain in her chest—a surge of sadness and rage—and could hardly breathe.

Her father was abandoning them, leaving them here with these men. From upstairs came the sound of smashing and breaking and her mother's tearful shouts.

The man's fingers came off her wrist and she looked up to see him staring out the window, too. He unclipped a small radio from a silver loop on his vest. "Male suspect is running through the apple orchard. Repeat—"

"We've got him in sight," a voice interrupted. "He's not going anywhere. The whole perimeter is surrounded."

The men would tear apart the house, seize everything—even her clothes—and her mother would be taken away in handcuffs and she would be driven away in her nighty and a blanket by a strange woman with a pale pale face who said over and over, "Trust me, you're going to be alright, honey," until behind them her home, the dog she loved, and her childhood vanished.

Why did everyone keep saying, "Trust me?" Whenever someone said that, she knew things would get worse. "You're going to be alright" meant seven years of being bullied by foster sisters and withdrawing into her own world....

"I hate Christmas," Claire said again.

No response from Makayla. Her seat was empty.

Only two cars passed them as Rocco and Mike Yazzie slid their way up the winding, north-country road to High Falls Gorge. They reached the parking lot, then picked up the trail across the first glazed-over footbridges. The gorge was already disappearing in deep, late-afternoon shade, but high clouds reflected light from the setting sun down around them. It tinted the snowdrifts in gold in contrast with the crevasses in the steep, rock walls, which looked dark blue. The roar of falling and rushing water echoed on the icy air. This place was a great escape from any reminders of Christmas.

"The spray is making my face freeze," said Yazzie, turning up his collar, "but it sure is beautiful, isn't it?"

Rocco stared at the water, solemn and silent as they moved carefully along the trail.

"What's on your mind, man?" Yazzie said, over the roar of the water.

"Nothing."

"Bull. Talk to me."

Rocco had never been alone with Mike Yazzie or talked to him very much before. Maybe it was the moment or maybe it was the need. "Okay.—I'm sad about my mom."

"She sick?"

"No. My dad has a girlfriend."

"And I guess your mom just found out?"

"Nah. She knew about her for a long time, she said. But last month my dad told her business was down and so he couldn't take her on the holiday cruise he promised. Then he said he had to go away on business, but last week she found out he's going on the cruise with his girlfriend. That's why I didn't go home for Christmas—my mom is staying at her mom's, and she's on some drug to keep from totally losing it. I couldn't understand half of what she said, but she told me not to come home. She doesn't want me to see her the way she is."

"Poor woman. She going to leave him?"

Rocco went silent again, listening to the rushing water before answering. "She's way too afraid."

"What's she afraid of?"

They reached the point closest to the falls. Icy air poured over them and Rocco turned up his collar, too, as much to retreat from Mike as to defend against the cold.

Yazzie looked at him, waiting.

Under the roaring sound of the waterfall, Rocco said, "You don't want to know."

In a half-hour, on the road back to the Troverts', Yazzie jabbed him in the shoulder. "Hey, the workout building at Kate's is almost ready—finally—and I could use a sparring partner. You interested?"

"You'll kick my butt."

"Probably a few times. But I'll train you right."

Rocco nodded. "Yeah. That's cool."

Makayla was standing out on the Troverts' back deck, staring into the now-dark woods, when Rocco found her. The woods were covered in a heavy blanket of snow and even the still air had a muffled feel. She had stepped away from the light streaming out the back windows and was smoking a cigarette and shivering.

"What are you doing out here alone?"

"Does it ever occur to you that we're all caught up in meaningless little conflicts, when there's a whole planet with problems we need to deal with? What if we all get free from our past, wake up from our petty dramas, and do something important with our lives? I mean that's what we're here for—right?"

"Wow. You're going deep."

She flicked the ash off her cigarette, shaking. "Getting free enough to do something greater is the issue, though, isn't it?"

"You look cold."

"I want to be alone. I'm fine."

"You don't look fine—and I didn't know you smoke."

"Well, there's a lot you don't know about me." A wave of shivering seized her thin frame, and her whole body shook.

"We're not allowed to smoke, remember? Where'd you get the butt?"

She looked at the windows, to see if anyone was watching. Then took a long drag and blew plumes of white into the freezing night air. "Did they send you out to check on me?"

"No. I wondered where you were is all." Rocco stepped up, wrapped her in a bear hug, and she tensed.

"Hey, don't freak," he said. "I'm not trying anything. I just want to warm you up, you're freezing. Come on. Let's go back inside."

She clenched her eyes shut, and her lips trembled. "You thought of me. How nice. But I don't want to go in." She shook violently. "It depresses me."

"Hey, I miss my family, too. My mom and sister anyway."

"What about your brother. I heard you have one."

"He cut out a couple years ago. No one knows where he is."

Makayla stubbed out the cigarette and, by some huge effort, regained control of her body. Rocco was saying something else, but she was far away. . . .

"I'm so sorry, honey. I have to be with grandma tonight. Probably tomorrow, too. Grandpa's cancer is taking him away from us maybe tonight, maybe tomorrow."

"Can't I go with you? Tomorrow's Christmas."

"We'll do Christmas when I get home."

She hadn't wanted to stay alone with her father. He spent too much time hanging around her when she wanted to be alone. Or he was moody.

"Honey, grandpa's unconscious and I'll be busy with grandma. It's better if you stay here with Dad."

No, it's not, *she wanted to shout.*

Christmas Eve late, she had turned off all the holiday tree and house lights. Outside, the moon shone silver, and other houses in their gated community were still glowing in white twinkling lights. She walked quietly down the hallway toward her room, the house dark and silent. Thankfully, her father had disappeared a little while before, and was probably asleep.

Before her, the entrance to her bedroom was a black oblong. She was sure she had closed the door but it was open. . . .

The curtain that sometimes opened and closed before her mind's eye... closed.

"*Makayla—,*" Rocco gently shook her arm. "We need to go in. You're shaking and your lips are blue."

She felt her stomach flip, the dark forest receded, and the curtain opened again. . . .

"*She's a pathological liar," her father had told the judge, his eyes sad. "She rarely tells the truth about where she's been or who she's with. She's run away a half-dozen times, we believe she's stealing, probably on drugs, totally out of control. We don't know what to do with her. Frankly, she would be much better off in juvenile detention. Maybe they can straighten her out.*"

Before she was led away, the judge had allowed her father to give her one last, long embrace from which she'd fought and pulled away. "Be good, baby," he said, gently rubbing her back. "Come back to us when you're ready to stop resisting us."

For days, she had showered under water so hot it burned her, trying to cleanse away the feeling she could not scrub off her skin. She could not get her mother's questions out of her mind.

"*He was in your room, wasn't he?*". . . .

Inside, laughter spilled from the kitchen—they could hear it from the family room, where Rocco had led her. Someone had stoked the fire again, so the room was cozy and bright with leaping firelight.

Makayla could not stop shivering and her eyes were dark with misery. Yesterday, she had gotten a Christmas card from her mother— elegant, gold-engraved, with trumpeting angels on the outside and a short, handwritten message inside.

"*If you come home,*" her mother had written, "*I'll keep him away from you. We can celebrate at the club, just the two of us. Some of our investors will be there.*"

Rocco watched her carefully, wary and confused. "I wish you'd tell me what's going on. Or tell someone."

She wanted her parents to not be in her head, making her crazy right now. "How's that littlest bear cub?"

He stared at his shoes. "It's kinda up and down. Jo and I think he's getting better, then he gets worse. He's got some kind of lung thing going on."

"Sorry. You're really attached to that little guy, aren't you?"

"No. Jo told me not to be."

"But you are. Why deny it?"

"Men don't get attached to baby animals. That's a girl thing."

"What a crock."

"Speaking of lung problems, you shouldn't smoke."

"Why do you *care*? Isn't that a 'girl thing'?"

She could try to push him away, but he felt confused and bad for her and would not leave her in her misery. "When we were outside—where did you *go*? I was trying to talk to you, but you weren't even there."

She wished he still had his strong arm around her shoulders. And at the same time, the thought of being touched left a hole in the pit of her stomach.

"I wish I wasn't anywhere."

The dining room table in Tom's farm house was set with Germaine's best Belgian lace table cloth, imported blue china, and Italian silver. Clayton's wife, Lissa, held a lighted match to the white tapers sticking up from the antique candlestick holders Germaine had brought back from Italy. A bright yellow feather of flame rose from each wick.

"I'll go back and help Clayton finish cooking," she said. "Dinner's in an hour."

Tom nodded, feeling grateful to her for buying and wrapping gifts from him for the three students he had brought back to the D.C. area—Jalil, Emmalyn, and Tia Leesha—for brief, family visits.

So many reports to write, so many appointments to make. He hadn't had time.

Right now, he wished he had pressed harder for Steve to come, knowing he would just be holed up all alone over the holiday. That weighed on him.

And there was the woman from Child Protective Services. On the phone earlier, Monica Saint had struck him as officious, the kind of person for whom the rules and filling-in forms were very important. "Yes, I know it's Christmas Eve day, but I'll be out at noon and I'll see them in forty-five minute appointments. I need information for my reports."

Also, there were old memories. He looked over the table set with Germaine's lovely things and heard her voice.

"In 1870, Italy developed a unique system of hallmarking silver. The dealer who sold these pieces to me pointed out that they're unmarked, meaning they pre-date 1870."

Italian antique silver marks interested him not at all, and Germaine knew it.

With the next thought, the sting came back.

"Why did I marry a man who cares so little about everything that's important to me? A man with so little culture."

"Lissa said you're looking for me?" Emmalyn had slipped into the dining room. "We walked out through the fields to the pond."

"Your mother called. Three times. The phone is in my office."

When she was gone, Clayton burst through the swinging door from the kitchen, wiping his hands. "Hey, Tom, I meant to tell you yesterday when you arrived about something strange that happened."

Tom raised an eyebrow.

"I was at the feed store, and Wayne said some guy came in looking for Steve. Said he only had a P.O. box number and the post office wouldn't give him a physical location. You know how suspicious and close-mouthed Charlene can be. Well, there was something about this guy he didn't like. When the guy told Wayne he'd gone through boot camp with Steve, Wayne asked him how he liked Camp LeJeune."

Tom stared.

"Steve trained at Camp Pendleton in California. I thought you knew that. Then he did his mountain warfare training up in northern Cal near Bridgeport."

"So then, who was the guy?"

"Since he'd lied about training with Steve at LeJeune, Wayne just wanted him gone. He gave him totally bogus directions that would take him on so many back dirt roads he'd get really lost, end up in the next county, and give up."

"That's one reason I love this county," Tom chuckled. "Not easy to find anyone out here. I'll have to remember to tell Steve about this."

"Tell him Wayne's sorry if this was somebody Steve wanted to see. But he said he knew that Steve is trying to *not* be found by anyone for a while."

"Poor man, whoever he was," Tom muttered. "Probably still lost on some of these twisting, dirt roads."

"No, Amber," Emmalyn snapped at her mother, speaking in a low voice into the phone. "I do all the work, take all the risks—and you get *half*? No. Besides, I just don't want to do this for you anymore. They all want to do weirder and weirder things."

"This is the assistant district attorney," her mother hissed at her. "His wife's away till tomorrow and he's paying a lot for this. Don't get all high and mighty. You never had a problem with it before."

"I did have a problem with it. Always. You just don't listen."

"Do this, and I won't ever ask you again."

"You said that before. A lot of times. If this goes bad, if this is a sting, I'll be pulled from the program and get thrown back into detention."

"You got something goin' on up there, don't you? You always got somethin' goin' on."

She didn't respond. From out in the other room, she could hear the clink of silverware being set out on the dining room table.

"Tell your chaperone guy that you have to see your grandma this evening because she's having emergency open heart surgery tomorrow, *right on Christmas day.*"

"What if I just say *no,* Amber, and hang up?"

"We need this money. I got serious bills, Emmalyn. You don't have a single clue about the pressure on me. And trust me. You don't say *no* to the assistant D.A. He can shut down my club. I'm stuck and you gotta help me."

Emmalyn made an exasperated sound but said nothing. She felt sick and like a butterfly struggling in a web with a dark thing creeping toward her.

"I'll be there in thirty minutes—I'm already in the car—and have you back by ten. It's just a few hours, so get your mind in the right place."

When Emmalyn hung up, she thought of the way she had twisted Garrett's mind, telling him she partied with older men then saying she'd lied about it. It messed with his head and put him right where she wanted him, confused and vulnerable. Right now, she hated the way her mother messed with her head.

At 9:30 p.m., the Troverts' party was over. They returned to Kate's lodge, where Jo's gift was the first one awaiting them—tee-shirts with the four tribe symbols on them.

"I want you to come up with a word that best describes your animal symbol and tribe."

Ron added, "Something you want to be known for, like 'hard work' or 'honesty'."

Kate handed each of them a small gift wrapped in dark blue paper and white ribbon—knitted hats and fur-lined gloves.

"This is to thank you all for being part of this program. Lost Lake is so much better with all of you here—but," she smiled, "it's going to get very cold soon. Beautiful but cold."

Dhani brought Claire a small, red plate with homemade gingerbread and whipped cream. She had retreated to the balcony above the great room. Below them was a huge, lighted wreath hanging above the blazing fireplace, where everyone else was gathered.

"Why didn't you go back?" he asked. "Don't they ever let you see your parents in prison—like now, on Christmas?"

"Thanks for bringing that up. They might let me, but I don't want to see them."

Dhani hesitated. "Is—is that prosecutor guy still trying to make you go back to Virginia?"

"Thanks for bringing that up, too."

He felt stupid.

Claire kept talking, though, as if she wanted to talk and let things out.

"Judge Sewell has heard that the prosecutor is still looking into my parents' drug business—all their connections, how they spent their money. The drug enforcement agents found cocaine and cash when they raided our property. It was all hidden in crates at the bottom of an old, abandoned well on our farm. A couple million dollars in hundreds."

Dhani whistled. "Millions?—are you kidding me?"

"Nope. It was the biggest cocaine bust on the whole east coast at the time. The prosecutor wants to see if I remember details about my parents' illegal activities."

"Weren't you little?"

"I was seven."

"So, he's being a jerk. Using you to punish them."

Below them by the roaring fireplace, Laurel Wysocki was trying to start up a holiday song—

"Dashing through the snow. . . ."

—and one by one, others were joining in, half-hearted and in different keys.

"Yep. That's my life. Where the fun never stops."

"What about your grandparents. Still no contact with them?"

She turned on him. "What about yours?" she said, sounding defensive. "Why aren't you back in D.C., eating grandma's Christmas sugar cookies?"

"My grandmother says I'm not her responsibility." He did not look sad or angry, just matter-of-fact.

"I told you before. Mine said the same thing." She looked at his calm expression. "I wish I could be like you—just accepting the way things are."

"I guess you had kind of a nice life and they it took away from you. I didn't really have one, so I don't miss it. Did you have a good life before your parents got arrested?"

"O! jingle bells, jingle bells. . . ."

"Since you want to know so badly—it wasn't a nice life. My parents sure didn't spend any of their drug money or their time on me. And when the federal agents swat-teamed us, it got a lot worse. The Drug Enforcement Agency took everything. My clothes, my toys and books— even my puppy. I never saw her again. They put my parents in prison and gave me to Child Protective Services. When my grandparents wouldn't step up, I got shoved into foster care."

"That's crappy."

Claire straightened herself and her face remained stoic. "It doesn't matter. They didn't want me, so I don't want them."

"Don't you feel bad sometimes, though?"

"I told you, I never let myself feel bad."

"You said that, but it's bull. Except when you're drawing, you're sad *a lot*. Or else you're angry.—Do you ever think about your dog?"

Her eyes narrowed and her voice had a sharp edge. "Why are you prying into my past right now? Christmas is bad enough—." She broke off, her voice sounding choked.

"The horse was lean and lank, misfortune seemed his lot. . . ."

Challenging her, he knew, might break the fragile connection he felt with Claire, but he gathered courage and pushed ahead. After all, she had said back in the fall they were friends. Were they?

"No. I just—I'm *concerned* about you is all." He'd stopped himself at the last split-second from using the word *care*. "You're my friend, I think."

She sidestepped. "What about you? I guess they haven't found your mom. Why is she hiding? I told you about my crappy family. Tell me about yours."

"He got into a drift and then. . . ."

"It's just my mom and me, and she's real cool."

"But why's she hiding from you?" she pressed.

She had turned the tables on him, and her question made him feel a sudden stab of irritation, which he swallowed.

"The last time my mom and I talked, she told me her boyfriend was threatening her."

"What did he tell her?"

"She said he told her, 'If I ever find you, no one's gonna want you after what I do to your face. Same for your whiny brat kid.' He'll do what he says, too. He's sick and evil. She needs to stay in hiding. Maybe for a long time."

"So you don't even have a phone number and you're not going to be able to contact her—what, the whole time you're in this program? It doesn't make sense, Dhani."

Now she was bringing up things he had not considered, and he started to feel confused and angry. "I don't know." He put his hands over his face. "I don't want to talk about this anymore."

"Sure. You want to give me trinket-y gifts, but you don't want to be honest. Some friendship."

That stung. And he was trying to fight off memories of his last Christmas at home, before the terrible thing happened. . . .

"I know you're upset about him being here," his mother said. "Make up some of your animal stories—the ones where you pretend they're talking to you. That always helped before. You were cute when you were little."

Did she even remember he wasn't little anymore? Did she remember that his talk about hearing animals was one thing that enraged the Monster?. . . .

Claire set down the gingerbread, which sat untouched, the whipped cream melting. "Great way to spend Christmas, isn't it? Hundreds of miles away from families we don't even want to think or talk about."

Dhani blinked, but still had a far-off look. "It's snowing."

Claire glanced out the huge wall of windows on either side of the chimney. Outside, the moonlit sky was clear of clouds or flakes. "No, it's not."

"It is. Really."

"Dhani, it isn't. Look."

"On the other side of Lost Mountain it is. And it'll be falling here in a little while."

"Oh lord, the weather thing again. Just tell me you're not hearing voices and seeing things."

That snapped him to attention. "*No,*" he said, with ferocity. "That was all just my goofy imagination. It was. . . a game I used to play when I was a little kid."

At eleven, under a black moonless sky, they walked by flashlight down the small slope from Kate's and along the lake back to their cabins. The air was still and smelled fresh, and a few, slow heavy snowflakes were falling. Kate had said there was a new prediction and there would be another half-foot or more on the ground by morning.

"Fresh snow," she beamed, waving goodnight from the front door. "Tobogganing tomorrow. I'll have Grady build a bonfire out in the field at the foot of the sledding hill."

Makayla caught up to Rocco, who had left ahead of everyone else, and touched his arm. "Sorry I was terrible company earlier. Actually, I was a wreck. It helped a lot when you came out to talk to me."

He did not look at her or speak, and seemed to withdraw from her deeper into his parka.

"I guess I brought you down," she tried again, feeling guilty.

"You didn't."

"What's wrong then?"

"Nothing."

"Yeah, well your eyes look really sad tonight. *Really* sad."

For several yards, there was only the crunch of their footsteps on frozen ground.

When he reached the short pathway to his cabin, he turned up it, saying nothing. He left her standing by the lake front, and in a few steps he placed his hand on the front door knob, then heard footsteps hurrying up the path behind him.

"Rocco, stop. Don't go inside."

"Why not? I'm tired."

"Let's go back down by the lake and watch the snow fall."

She turned the beam of her flashlight up toward the sky, which was filled with more and more feathery flakes. "Look—it's beautiful. The clouds just broke a little and you can see the Milky Way. It's like the sky is on fire."

In the black heavens above them, white stars spread like a broad roadway of lights.

He held back.

"Hey, I'm not trying to start anything either," she insisted. "I just—I want to pretend my whole life before tonight never happened. I do that sometimes. Bay told me I'm 'blocking out reality,' but I don't care. When I'm feeling really terrible it helps. I make myself go back to a time before it was all bad."

He was listening now. "How do you do that?"

"Well, tonight I want to catch snowflakes on my tongue, like when I was little. Didn't you ever do that? I pretended they were different flavors. I want this night to end in a good way. I don't want to go to bed feeling the way I've felt all day."

"What will playing a little kid's game change?"

"The next hour."

He nodded and relaxed. "I don't want to keep feeling bad either."

In response, she tilted her head back, stuck out her tongue and caught a flake. "Mmmm, *peppermint.*"

Rocco tipped his head back, mimicking her. "Mmmm, *beer.*"

"We're not allowed to drink."

"We're not allowed to smoke either."

She laughed—"Right"—and stuck out her tongue again. "Marsh-mallows."

Tilting his head back, Rocco saw she was right. Above them, the sky was on fire. He stuck out his tongue. "Cuban cigars."

Claire had slipped out of Kate's by herself. Being alone in the dark suited the mood she had sunk into as she made her way back to her cabin. Snow was starting, and she wanted to slide under warm covers and into dark forgetfulness.

Sahm, in his red and yellow wool coat, came up alongside. She hoped he would pass by, but he fell in stride with her.

"You are unhappy."

She almost said, "Duh," but that was rude. Sahm was always kind to her, the way he was always nice to everyone. She settled for, "Yes, I am."

"What is troubling you?"

"I may have to see my parents again soon. Some prosecutor wants me to tell a lot of bad things I saw my parents do."

"They want you to *testify*."

She had forgotten Sahm was not dumb, he just had a heavy Tibetan accent.

"Yeah, testify."

Dhani and Ray-Ray were talking not far behind them on the path, and she really wanted to get away before they caught up.

"You would testify against your own parents?"

"Well, if I was in a court of law I'd have to, I think. And why shouldn't I? I'd tell every detail. They ruined my whole life."

"Only your life before now perhaps."

"Isn't that bad enough?"

"It is. But what are you going to do with the rest of your life?—the much bigger part that is still ahead of you that no one has touched yet?"

She opened her mouth, but nothing came out. For a split-second she felt irritated with Sahm. "I have a right to be angry."

Sahm had a mystified look.

"Every new moment is like this—a fresh snow fall," he responded, spreading his arms wide, gesturing at the freshly blanketed landscape all around them. "You can walk in any direction you choose. Make a new path. That is also your right."

Dhani and Ray-Ray joined them, and at the same time Claire heard laughter coming from down along the dark lakeshore.

"I drank way too much cola today," said Dhani, talking fast. True to form, he seemed to be back to his sweet, simple self. "No way I'm gonna be able to sleep for a while."

"I'm wide awake, too," said Ray-Ray. "I wish we didn't have to go to our cabins."

Sahm was listening, as well, to the happy sounds coming to them in the dark.

"Maybe tonight, fun is most needed. I think it will not be a problem for you to stay out for a little while longer."

Fun.

Claire unexpectedly found herself at a crossroad, one she hadn't realized it was possible to encounter—a moment where her past and her present intersected.

She was not ready to offer a blanket forgiveness to her parents, and certainly their gross negligence and felonies had cost them the right to parent her. But tonight, just for this moment, she did not want to feel the way she had felt for the past seven years, mired in heaviness and depression. Vaguely, she became aware that she shielded herself from accepting the kindness that any person—or even any creature, like Vajra—tried to show her.

Off in the dark distance, Makayla was laughing loudly—and Rocco shouted, laughing, too. "*Ohmygod,* you hit me in the face with a snow-ball? I'm gonna bombard you!"

She thought of Dhani's sweet and buoyant spirit. What if she allowed herself to step away from the past just for *now*? What could that hurt?

". . .*any direction you choose.*"

Dhani was looking at her, so hopeful. She had hurt him earlier, dismissing the clam-shell necklace he had made for her as a silly trinket.

"I'm sorry, Dhani. You gave me a really sweet gift a while ago—that necklace you made. Then you gave me that beautiful fossil you found in the river. And I didn't get you anything for Christmas. I wish I had."

He shrugged and mumbled, "It's okay. Really."

It also occurred to her, as a snowflake brushed her cheek, that Dhani had known this snow was on its way. Who was this sweet, strange boy, who seemed to hear and see and know things no one else did?

She bent down, pressed loose snow into a ball—then stood and threw it at Dhani. It hit him in the chest and the cold powder sprayed up into his face.

"Hey, why'd you do that?"

"Snowball fight!" she yelled.

After Emmalyn's return at eleven, an hour past her due-back time, Tom sat falling asleep in his office chair. He was avoiding going upstairs to an empty bed, when something said in the thick of dinner conversation came back to him.

"Man, that Saint lady was really interested in Sahm," Jalil had remarked. "She asked a million questions about him."

"I know, right?" Tia Leesha volunteered, her mouth full of buttered roll. "I kept trying to tell her about my sinuses, but she didn't even care."

Why on earth would Monica Saint press for information about Sahm? He was in the country legally, everyone liked him, and he was a big asset to Kate's program.

Maybe, he thought, she was impressed with the program's cultural diversity.

Just as drowsiness began to take him, he also recalled what Clayton had told him—about the supposed Marine friend trying to find Steve. For some reason, the last thing Clayton said came back now.

"Wayne said the guy had a slight accent. Kinda middle-eastern."

And how could anyone forget where they'd gone to boot camp? Well. No matter now. He was tired and pushed these small confusing details aside.

His last thought of the night as he forced himself upstairs was of Steve, and his last prayer was for him.

He had slept most of the day out here on the island—thankfully, without dreaming—and filled the rest of his emptiness with sports radio and throwing his knife, hard, into the frozen trunk of the target tree. Alone out in this winter solitude except for the black lab, he was glad he had fended off everyone's invitations.

Until now.

Pacing the cabin, nothing left to distract him, memory became a prison. Then a torture chamber.

He had fought all day to keep from thinking about "the event", as he called it. But it was trying to press itself into his mind more now than it had during the whole year of solitude on Tom's farm.

He kept seeing Olivia's hand in the hand of her friend, the reporter who was there that day, though he didn't know why his mind latched onto that frame of memory. Maybe it was just to distract himself from remembering her face.

But it was Olivia's face that rushed before his mind's eye now. Suddenly. Her deep brown eyes penetrating his. Loving him. He could feel waves of that love, and more images flooded in.

Laughter. Firelight. Champagne. Touching. A different Christmas Eve at a ski lodge. He could see, hear, taste, feel all of it.

No. No, no, no, no, no.

White flakes tapping at the windows stirred the old images without mercy. He tried to slam shut a mental door, block the mounting memories that were starting to choke his soul.

As if that avalanche of memories was not bad enough—the Ka-bar lying on a small table by the back door flooded his mind with another set of images. Months—years—of effort to block them were weakening, and his breathing became shallow.

Winter in Afghanistan. So close and vivid again. He could see the hundreds of remote mountain valleys. Hear the raw, relentless wind rising. Feel the snow chafing his face till it stung and burned. See the white wall blowing in around him and his men, dropping visibility to nothing. He was there again, surrounded by ghosts. . . .

The pounding mortar fire blew apart shelter after shelter.

After the surprise attack he scrambled to dig the young Marine out of the red spattered snow and slice open his pant leg, revealing shattered bone, torn arteries and veins.

Gore and pieces of muscle covered his hands, his Ka-bar. He fought to tear open his blow-out kit, fingers slippery with blood. . . .

Panic rose and beneath his shirt sweat ran down his ribs. He pulled on his down jacket and leather boots, couldn't find his gloves, and fled outside. To where, though?

Anywhere but inside this damn head.

Outside, he sucked in deep breaths of cold, damp air. He didn't need a flashlight. Even in the pitch of night, he now knew the island's short, twisting trails by rote. Across the lake, the lights of Kate's lodge and the crescent of cabins shone—tiny flecks of warmth in such vast cold—and he moved away from them further into the freezing darkness, both the world's and his own.

The images and the voice followed him.

"Don't let me die."

He gripped the young Marine's hand to give him the confidence all his men drew from him, and answered with bravado. "I won't. We're sending you home with your head held high."

Now, exhausted, it would be so easy just to find a place out here in the cold and lie down, let forgetfulness and the dark take him.

On the south side of the island, he came to the end of the small dock, where a little snow was building up. Before him, the faint white outlines of snowdrifts and ice upheavals revealed a lake that had become a trackless waste; there was no further to go.

Large, slow flakes stroked his hair, brushed his forehead and cheeks like the gentle fingers that had once touched him. A wrenching loneliness seized his gut, and he felt overwhelmed by the bright memory of laughter and love now gone. . . and also by the pleading voice that he could not shut out—the voice of a young man choking on his own terror.

He put his hands over his ears. *Stop, please stop.*

For all his military training in evasion and escape, he could not get away from himself. He dug his fingers into his temples, wanting to cry out for help—to yell, curse, or pray—but who would hear him lost in this wilderness of pain? And how could anyone help what nothing would help?

Lowering his hands, he forced himself to breathe deep. Fought to push it all back, feeling weak.

Something cold bumped the fingers of his left hand and he startled.

The black figure of Pal was beside him on the dock—probably he had scratched at the door till it opened—now wagging his whole body. He nudged Steve's hand again with his soft, wet nose.

Sahm had named him *Glorious One*, and so he was. Sweet, faithful Pal, happy just to be with Steve, offering good company when he was horrible company for himself. He had come now as if in response to Steve's cry of helplessness.

Steve's throat constricted, his eyes burned, and his gut began to heave. Dropping to one knee in the wet snow, he buried his face in the lab's coarse fur and suddenly let out all the months of anguish he had been shoving down inside.

Patient, unmoving, Pal sat on his haunches and waited until the wrenching sobs tapered down, snow alighting on the crown of his head.

The dark, snowy path along the lake crunched beneath Sahm's boots. He had felt a sudden urgency to say a healing prayer for Steve Tanner, and wondered why.

As he crossed the ice-covered stream next to his cabin, though, he was more in mind of what *Dzes-Sa* had told him months before, that each of the young people had a higher purpose they could awaken to. Tonight he had witnessed lightness and fun in a few of them— but awakening? Did he see glimmers of it in some of them? He was not sure.

"Listen, Sahm—what do you hear?" said Dzes-Sa.

He stopped, listening to the stream murmuring, its lithe spirit concealed beneath the wintry covering.

"That is how it is with some. Their true spirit is concealed—even from themselves. You must help clear their minds of useless distractions. Only then will they realize the true course of their lives. The world needs them for the great work that lies before us!"

Sometime after midnight, the snowfall over the Adirondack High Peaks region grew heavier. At intervals, the clouds broke momentarily, and in the fleeting moonlight the evergreen stands on the mountains around Lost Lake now looked like so many clusters of white feathers.

Kate could not sleep and, wrapped in a bright red comforter, she went out to the front porch to stand in falling snow and recall the earlier sounds of laughter and happy shouting. She had purposely stayed mostly in the background this semester, giving the students space and time to settle in. Yet, she had read their files and, more importantly, read their struggles on their faces. She felt deeply for them, squeezed hard for them to succeed, willing them to grow toward a better life.

Would they—all of them? Any of them?

The outcome of all these efforts lay ahead, in the future. She thought of a piece of wisdom Sahm had passed on from his grandfather months ago up at Thunder Falls. *"To be enlightened is to understand that our whole karma can be lived in a single moment. If that moment is filled with compassion, we will see miracles."*

At this moment, she was thankful for whatever miracle had caused some of the students to drop the guilty and painful weights they carried and just have fun tonight. Their exuberance coursed in her blood and she felt more alive than she had in years. The world could be such a dark and difficult place. That, she knew for sure. But maybe it was also shining at times with small miracles like the pinpoints of stars above her in the blackness, if you had eyes to see them.

She smiled at one now.

By morning, the blanketing flakes would probably half-bury the lumpy little snowman Rocco and Makayla had left in front of her lodge as a gift.

She thought about all the young people and instructors and counselors, thought about all the wild creatures in the barns—every one of them wounded in some greater or lesser way. Despite their foibles and flaws, all of them were gifts to her.

. . .and I share them with you tonight, Jim Holman, if you can hear me. You said the money you made was yours and not mine. But I saw a lot of good in you when we were young. Before all your success. I only wish you'd lived to see this moment. To see what good that money is doing now. It may have healed whatever damaged your soul.

Months ago, she'd had terrible doubts about the program and herself, mostly because of the poison arrow Jim had left in her soul. Her last gift to Jim tonight was to remove it; all of her *karma* lived out in this single moment.

I forgive you.

A heaviness she had felt for years, caged within her. . .lifted.

Sahm stared at the wire racks on his kitchen table, the ones he had filled this morning with ten Tibetan flat breads needing to cool after baking. The racks were empty.

His cabin's back door was open a little when he had returned just now, and a few good-sized puddles of snowmelt on the kitchen floor told the tale that something large had wandered in from the snowy night woods. Bears were known to lumber out of hibernation sometimes. They were clever enough to break into cabins, he knew, and even into cars. They were observed turning doorknobs, pulling at car door handles to steal goodies and food.

He was too tired at this late hour and also too happy to be upset about the lost loaves. In the morning, if the overnight snowfall did not cover whatever tracks there were outside, he might try to follow and see which way the bear went....More likely, he would just bake more bread after his morning chores at the clinic, and offer prayers and blessings for all the hungry creatures of winter.

Dhani entered the quiet aviary, lightly stomping snow off his boots. Outside, a breeze had sprung up, and he heard the brush of blown snow on the night-black window panes.

He had pushed aside sad thoughts about his mother and could only hope she was safe and happy. Momentarily, he thought of Judge Sewell, and wanted him to know he made two friends, one more than the goal Sewell had set for him. Now, he even pushed aside thoughts of Claire. One day soon, he would kiss her and maybe she would kiss him back. One thing was sure, he would never tell her when strange things happened in his mind. In fact, he was determined that nothing weird was ever going to happen to him again.

But why had he felt compelled to come here now?

He walked to the snowy owl's enclosure, and stood with

snow-melt dripping from the gloves Ray-Ray had loaned him earlier for the snowball fight; he'd forgotten his new pair at Kate's. He was strangely not tired—it was more than the Cokes and Dr. Peppers he had chugged this evening—a wild energy was running high within him, and he had felt lifted and carried here as if by invisible currents of air.

The aviary felt silent and still as the deep night outside and everything—the walls, the enclosures, the floor and roof—had begun to flicker like flames.

Up on its perch of evergreen boughs, the creature was like a beautiful little drift of snow the wind had blown into the shape of a bird.

"Whoo-whoo," he said softly, his voice sounding distant, solid things growing fainter by the minute.

The huge black pupils of the snowy owl's yellow eyes flared then narrowed, focusing on him sharply. . . .

He felt a jolt of pain, as if he had been struck by a fist, and felt himself falling. . . landing in a tangle of branches. He saw a boy in a black hoody and jeans, crawling out a tilted tree and reaching for him. The boy's hand closed on one of his legs and, terrified, he sank his claws into the boy's palm. . . .

"I wasn't trying to hurt you," he heard himself explain. Seeing himself through the owl's eyes just now seemed more like a memory than a trick of imagination. "I was just trying to save your life."

The owl ducked its head and responded—*huuhuu huu.*

He felt a wave of gratitude pass through him, as if some energy were coming into him from the owl. How was that possible? He also felt as if he were expanding somehow, the way he had felt the night he imagined flying across the moonlit lake with the saw-whet owl.

From the eagle's enclosure came a shriek, the strangest cry he had ever heard. It had the power of a summons, a command, and made the hair on his neck stand up.

When he went and looked in, this time the eagle was not facing the corner. It was staring up at the one-way glass, and there was a look in the creature's eyes—one of utter joy—that made Dhani's soul leap and he felt his mind fly open. . . .

. . .*He was looking up through the window's mirrored side.*

Seeing himself. Welcoming himself. . . .

Surprise propelled him back into his own head, and he staggered away from the window.

What's happening to me?

As the image faded, he felt a strange and wonderful new sense arise—a deep, strong wave of connection. He had never felt so connected to anyone in this lifetime. Not his mother nor Claire nor Ray-Ray. No one.

A bright blue light filled the aviary and a voice spoke close to Dhani's ear.

"It is time to let yourself arise."

Before Dhani could turn to see who had spoken, the eagle shrieked again, and a bright, strong cry flew through the opening sky of his mind.

"We are trying to awaken you.—You are the one we have waited for."

ACKNOWLEDGEMENTS

Early readers and advisors contributed so much to helping finalize this work. Heart-felt thanks to Dan Sheehan, Linda Sittig, Cristina Windover, David Hubbard, Bonnie Leonard, Aaron and Elena Hazard, Joel and Carly Hazard, Sarah Hazard, Jeanne Selander Miller, Cindy Deugo Johnson, Amanda Bailey, Maria Dampman, Tom Sweitzer, Jessamyn Ayers, Debra Havas, Marcia Keene, and Joe Straka.

Many thanks also to Susan Rimato Hazard for generously allowing me a gracious place to write at your beautiful hide away in the Adirondacks, giving me time to advance the story and capture details of those ancient mountains and pristine lakes. Thanks, as well, to Dean and Mary Gordon for the days I spent writing on your lovely, secluded point.

Very special thanks to Mark Ivan Cole for guiding Claire's pencil to create the brilliant graphic renderings—far beyond what I had hoped for—that help bring these pages to life. To Peter Gloege, as always, for eye catching cover art, meticulous page design work, and brilliant website—LostLakeSeries.com—which far, far exceeded my hopes. And to Jan Blacka for designing my Facebook page, David Hazard Author. No one could ask for a better design team. And great thanks to Robin Pennington for extraordinary proofreading skills.

Finally, a great deal of thanks goes to my coaching clients all around the world for allowing me to continually learn about the art of narrative writing as we develop your novels and memoirs together for publication. Pursuing our mutual passion for storytelling, we lift each other up.

Much love and gratitude to each and all of you.

ABOUT THE AUTHOR

The natural world is my first home.

 I spent my early years with stream water and black muck overflowing into my rubber boots, witnessing frog's eggs hatch into tadpoles, and listening to the croaking call of redwing blackbirds perched on bent-broken cattails of the nearby marshes. Later, hiking and backpacking in the Adirondack Mountains of upstate New York, where my ancestors had settled in the 1740s, the boreal forests of that great wilderness became my sanctuary. Any time I witness an eagle circling, whenever a snowstorm or thunder storm rages through the peaks and river valleys, if I catch sight of otters playing on a muddy river bank—that's when I'm fully alive.

The natural world is my concern and my calling.

Serious concerns for the living wilderness arose in the 1970s. Acid rain created by belching smokestacks west of the mountains decimated fish populations in Adirondack lakes. Suddenly, the once pristine lakes where I fished, swam, and canoed became toxic to aquatic life. Blue mountain waters where trout, northern pike, bass, and muskies spawned now brought about their death. DDT use had decimated the bald eagle population. Waterways were further damaged as manufacturers dumped tons of toxins into lifeline waterways, like the great Hudson River.

How had we, as a culture, allowed this to happen? Could we reverse the damage?

The answer was, and is, yes. We have been able reverse some of the damaging footprints of our manufacturing, farming, and consumption. Some, but not all, and our vigilance is needed if we are to protect this one earth.

Speaking of the need for help and protection, through youth organizations I helped to found in my adopted state, Virginia, I became acutely aware of the needs of young adults—especially those who come from severely troubled homes or who make critical mistakes so early in their lives. Too many were labeled as "lost causes," to be tossed aside.

How could we, as a culture, ignore these valuable human beings, who needed help to start over? Could lives be redirected, and "troubled kids" rise to do great things?

Again, the answer was and is, yes—if we invest ourselves, not just in financial capital but in human capital.

As for what I do now, my professional career has been spent coaching and launching more than four hundred authors into successful publishing careers, first, through my decades as associate publisher with several publishing companies, and now through ASCENT, an international coaching program for authors. I have published more than thirty books of my own, one of which—Blood Brothers, the true-life story of Palestinian peacemaker Elias Chacour—is an international bestseller published in twenty-nine languages.

My true heart is in the wilderness, though, and my true calling is its protection and preservation. My heart is also with people, and with every effort that helps us work for a safe, clean, healthy world. I deeply hope that our children's children's children, mine and yours, will learn to protect the earth and value all life. I hope that we will be the ones to show them how.

The *Lost Lake* series and the small but vibrant movement that is rising up around it is one way I hope to inspire people—maybe *you*—to invest in the future of our one world and in the lives of people. By every one of us, doing whatever small or great things we can, we will protect this one beautiful earth.

Please visit *LostLakeSeries.com* to see what you can do.

—David Hazard
January 2021

DHANI SINGH JONES encounters a startling scene from a past life—or is it just another flight of imagination? If the experience is real, who was he before he arrived in this lifetime? And why is he being drawn into the minds of wild creatures?

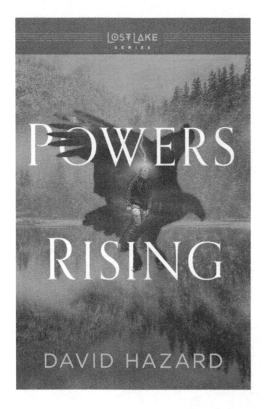

More woodland animals are in dire need of treatment at Lost Lake's wildlife clinic. More golden salamanders, a female mountain lion thought to be extinct in the Adirondack Mountains. These creatures and others show up with strange afflictions. Josephe Rondeau, the wildlife vet begins sending bodies to the New York State lab, trying to determine if some environmental factor is causing the deformities and deaths of these beautiful, vulnerable animals.

For months, tension builds all around, and everyone backs away from Dhani, eventually leaving him in a panic about his future at Lost Lake.

In this strained atmosphere, Steve Tanner's dislike of Dhani, ramped up by lies, builds toward an explosive confrontation.

Then, in a final, startling twist, Steve is rocked by a shocking truth about his wife Olivia's tragic death.

In *Powers Rising*, as conflict around Dhani intensifies, a few at Lost Lake start to feel a deeper connection with the wilderness and its beautiful creatures. Will it go deep enough to redirect the course of their troubled lives?

Made in United States
Orlando, FL
19 October 2023

38015375R00300